MYSTERY ATK

Atkins, Ace.

Dark end of the street

Please check all items for damages
before leaving the Library.
Thereafter you will be held
responsible for all injuries
to items beyond reasonable wear.

NOV   2002

ALSO BY ACE ATKINS

Crossroad Blues
Leavin' Trunk Blues

Dark End of the Street

Dark End
of the Street

ACE ATKINS

wm

WILLIAM MORROW • *An Imprint of* HarperCollins*Publishers*

M.

ATK

Grateful acknowledgment is made for permission to reprint from the following:

"The Dark End of the Street." Words and music by Dan Penn and Chips Moman © 1967 (Renewed 1995) SCREEN GEMS-EMI MUSIC INC. All rights reserved. International copyright secured. Used by permission.

"Still Here" from *The Collected Poems of Langston Hughes* by Langston Hughes, copyright © 1994 by the estate of Langston Hughes. Used by permission of Alfred A. Knopf, a division of Random House, Inc.

"Polk Salad Annie." Words and music by Tony Joe White © 1968 (Renewed 1996) TEMI COMBINE INC. All rights controlled by COMBINE MUSIC CORP. and administered by EMI BLACKWOOD MUSIC INC. All rights reserved. International copyright secured. Used by permission.

FIRST EDITION

Printed on acid-free paper

Library of Congress Cataloging-in-Publication Data
Atkins, Ace.
    Dark end of the street / Ace Atkins.—1st ed.
    323 p. cm.
        ISBN 0-06-000460-6 (alk. paper)
        1. Travers, Nick (Fictitious character)—Fiction. 2. Private investigators—Tennessee—Memphis—Fiction. 3. African American singers—Fiction. 4. Missing persons—Fiction. 5. Memphis (Tenn.)—Fiction. 6 Soul musicians—Fiction. I. Title.
PS3551.T49D37 2002
813'.54—dc21   2001058332

02 03 04 05 06 WBC/RRD 10 9 8 7 6 5 4 3 2 1

for Angela

At the dark end of the street,

that's where we always meet.

Hiding in shadows where we don't belong.

Livin' in darkness to hide our wrong.

—DAN PENN AND CHIPS MOMAN,
"The Dark End of the Street"

I've been scarred and battered.

My hopes the wind done scattered.

Snow has friz me, sun has baked me.

Looks like between 'em

They done tried to make me

Stop laughin', stop lovin', stop livin'—

But I don't care!

I'm still here!

—LANGSTON HUGHES, "Still Here"

Acknowledgments

TO MEMPHIS AND BACK, the following provided needed help, inspiration, or some top-notch grub: my family, Michael Baker, B. F. Vandervoort, Gayle Dean Wardlow, Jim Kennedy, Harry Smith, Debbi Eisenstadt, Bogie "Raven" Miller, Joe Durkin, Darryl Wimberley, Burnis Morris, Elvis (my canine companion), the gang at Square Books, and the staff at Ajax Diner, Taylor Grocery, and the Bottletree.

Much thanks to Richard and Carolyn for their continued direction, support, and for being great friends to Loretta. I'm looking forward to many more adventures.

Without a doubt, Peter Guralnick's *Sweet Soul Music* transported me to Memphis 1968, and Edward Humes's *Mississippi Mud* took me into the core of the Dixie Mafia. Shangri-La Records's *Lowlife Guide to Memphis* and Tad Pierson provided invaluable information and true "grit" away from Beale.

Special thanks to Robert Gordon, whose article, "Way Out on a Voyage," gave voice to Clyde James and Paul Bergin, who heard of an evil woman that I had to meet.

While writing this book, the world lost three soul legends: Johnnie Taylor, James Carr, and Rufus Thomas. Without them and their inspiration, this book wouldn't be in your hands.

Dark End of the Street

Prologue

December 17, 1968
Memphis, Tennessee

THE DREAM OF SOUTHERN soul music was dead. It died last year when Otis Redding's twin-engine plane crashed into an icy Wisconsin lake, killing him and the Bar-Kays, a bunch of kid musicians from the old neighborhood. It died a few months later, too, back in April, when some peckerwood sighted a rifle from a run-down rooming house near the Lorraine Motel, taking out a man who only wanted to see some garbage workers get their due. It died again every night that summer, when hate filled the neighborhoods of south Memphis. But for Eddie Porter, it died most when black musicians raised on gospel and white musicians weaned on country and blues quit working on a style of music that was the sweetest he'd ever known.

Porter could still remember that day in June when he was helping the bass player in his band carry milk crates full of guitar cords and microphones from the Bluff City studio. A cop car filled with two white men had stopped, the doors popped open, and the men aimed their pistols at Porter. Tate, shaking like an ole woman, spoke to them in this tone that kind of broke Porter's heart. Kind of like he was embarrassed for his race. Tate, that bucktoothed country boy, had stared at the cops as they slid their guns back into their leather holsters, as if in some way he was responsible for all the shit that was happenin'.

For Otis and Dr. King. For the burning buildings. And maybe he even took the blame for the white politicians Porter watched on television in the apartment he shared with his mutt dogs and wife he didn't love.

For a few weeks after the cops came, Porter tried to fill the silences between Tate and Cleve, his rhythm guitar man, with all the soul he could stand from his battered Hammond B-3 organ. The music soaked into red shag carpet walls of the old movie theater that served as their studio and out through the newly barred windows and into an emerging ghetto. He played as if somehow dance music could solve Memphis's problems.

But Memphis kept boiling. Soul kept dying. Their horn section broke up. Porter's drummer quit. His organ broke. And he knew he couldn't stop any of it.

Wasn't till June that the idea came to him.

When it did, he was at the Holiday Inn by the airport, caressing the soft face of a woman who was carrying another man's baby. He remembered the stiff mustard-colored curtains were slightly drawn and the room smelled of chlorine, gin breath, and cigarettes.

He sat there smoothing the curly black hair away from her brown eyes and feeling the child kicking in her stomach and thought about the future for the first time in his life. He knew he didn't have anything more for Memphis. And Memphis owed him something.

The owner of Bluff City Records—that sold nothing but black music— was a potbellied white man who spent his time sweet-talking teenaged girls in his second-floor office decorated in cheetah print and velvet paintings of naked Mexican women.

Porter never could figure out what the man did. He had Porter run the sessions, deposit the checks from distributors, and pay out the other musicians. Most of the profits came from one man. Their holy God almighty, soul sensation Clyde James.

That night at the Holiday Inn, Porter found the answers with James's wife in his lap as he watched the swirl of blues, reds, and yellows play on the stones and plastic flowers near the swimming pool. He knew he couldn't see anything beyond tonight and that scared him like nothin' ever could.

He could hold back a little cash with each deposit and by December he'd be free. So that's what he did. And man, he was so cool about the whole thing. For every five checks, he'd only deposit one in his account down at the First National. It worked so good that he had more than he needed by September. And by Thanksgiving, shit, he had more than he could ever spend. Two hundred and seventy-one thousand dollars and some change. He tried like hell to get Mary to leave with him. But by that time she was fixing to have Clyde's baby and the whole thing had turned to shit.

So, tonight, he'd packed his alligator briefcase with bundles of hundreds and covered them with paperback Westerns.

As Porter packed, he watched himself in a mirror spotted with rust. He tucked a ticket for a midnight flight to Buffalo into his corduroy jacket and smoothed his goatee.

He felt light and hard in his yellow turtleneck and brown bellbottoms. He had a Smith and Wesson tucked into a wide leather belt at his spine and almost shook with its power. Felt like the first time he'd ever been moved by a woman.

Porter was a goddamned man who was about to take what he deserved. Besides, who was going to miss that cash but fat boy Bobby Lee Cook and those hoodlums he hung around?

It was night. The moon looked like the cut edge of a fingernail and a brittle cold wind made his skin feel like paper.

He slid into his white Toranado with gray interior, cranked up WDIA, and listened to his competitors at Stax, Booker T. & the MGs, play out some soulful take on the Beatles. He could do anything. He could go anywhere and be anybody.

Porter knew he should wait it out at the airport. But he guessed he wanted to shove his deceit in Cook's face. He circled his car to downtown and on to Germantown, where rich white people played golf and held parties under candy-striped awnings, and where the only blacks held silver trays of chilled pink shrimp.

Porter parked on Bobby Lee Cook's lawn, nearly tripping over one of those little iron black men holding a lantern, and strutted out of the bright, cold night and into a Christmas party filled with politicians and pimps, musicians and wannabes of every kind. Some were black. Most were white. He even saw a Chinese girl wrestling with another woman in a dark room filled with a pile of mink coats.

People were drinking martinis and whiskey on ice. There were trays of liver wrapped in bacon and fat olives and candies and little sandwiches dyed red and green for Christmas. The light was dim as hell and lamps burned out green and yellow and red bulbs. Almost made you drunk to walk inside and feel the pulse of the music and see the couples rolling on the green shag or hear loud laughing in huddled circles.

Porter just wanted to see Cook, look him in the eye again, and be gone. Cook had made a point of calling him five times that day to make sure he came. At first he thought Cook was onto the scam, but then Porter figured he'd be on his doorstep if he knew.

Porter first saw Cook out of the corner of his eye in one of those silly Nehru jackets with slim black pants and Italian boots. He looked ridiculous. A fat white boy trying to be hip.

Cook ushered him into a closed office by the dining room where the muted sounds of Eddie Floyd singing "Blood Is Thicker than Water" played low on his Fisher Hi-Fi. That upbeat song really gave Porter a headache as Cook walked over to the little bar covered in zebra print.

He made a big deal out of feeling the skin on the bar, pulling out a gin bottle, and examining the damned thing like it was a newborn child. He poured himself another drink over crushed ice.

"Eddie," he began, "I want you to quit messin' with Clyde's wife. You know more 'an anyone his head ain't right. I need that boy. If he falls again, we all do. Comprende, podna?"

"Ah, fuck you, Cook. Ain't none of your concern what goes on in my world."

Porter caught a glimpse of his reflection in the mirror behind the bar and he somehow looked smaller than he felt.

"Just stay away from there tonight," Cook said, feeling for one of his silly cheetah-print chairs like a blind man. He sat down with a sigh and closed his eyes. "Just stay away from there tonight."

"I'm quitting," Porter said, walking away. "Find someone else to shovel your shit."

"Eddie?"

He turned back.

"How long we knowed each other?"

Porter shrugged.

"I consider you a friend."

"You're drunk."

"Do what you need to do. But do it tonight. Stay away from Clyde's wife."

Porter gave a short laugh with his exhaling breath.

"You ain't listenin'," Cook said again. "Do what you need to do. But keep away from there tonight."

"Sweet Jesus," Porter said. "You motherfucker."

He picked up a fat gold statue of Buddha and threw it into the glasses and whiskey and flickering red cocktail candles. The mirror broke into jagged knives knocking over the candles and liquor bottles. The glass sounded like tiny bells in the wind.

"You motherfucker," he said again. It wasn't a yell. Porter said it more to himself than anything as he headed back to his car.

Twenty minutes later, he sped across Lamar Avenue as slatted light played over his face and prized fingers. Somehow he knew they'd catch up. It just happened a whole mess sooner than he thought.

He mashed the pedal of his Toranado and the cold wind howled through the ripped holes in its canvas top.

Mary lived down in south Memphis, in a house built from her husband's million-seller, "Dark End of the Street." A song about a cheating man who can't face his lover in the light of day. Clyde didn't write it, two white boys did, but he sang it like it was his damned life story. Porter had heard it so many times he wanted to throw up, he thought, while pulling into the circular drive.

The house was one of those places designed in weird geometrical patterns and shapes. Huge plate glass windows, doors made out of circles of brass, and sharp triangle edges at every corner. He could see a white-frosted artificial tree in the window decorated with red balls and green blinking lights.

Clyde would be in there somewhere passed out. A ghost in his own home wearing that mind sickness like a cape.

Sometimes Porter didn't know why he and Mary even bothered.

As Porter rounded the corner, he could see someone sunk down into the seat of Clyde's old Lincoln Continental. The black one he drove into a lake in Mississippi about three years ago. Man had it pulled from the scum and mud of the lake, fish flopping off his seats, to have it rot in his front yard.

Porter glanced down in the car and saw Clyde huddled on the floor-board like a child, a bottle of cheap rum in the driver's seat. His face was wet and his eyes red and he was making sounds like that time he had to be pulled off stage at the Apollo. Sounded like he was going to choke on his own tongue.

Porter reached through the window of the tarnished car for his hand but Clyde crawled deeper in the floorboard and closed his eyes. It was almost as if he was willing Porter to disappear. Porter could feel him slipping through the small space and into the cloudy lake bottom where they'd found the car.

He walked away.

The door to the house was open. Yellow light spilled out onto the gray steps and dead lawn. As Porter approached the door, he kept hearing Clyde. That perfect voice singing the song like his whole life depended on the story he was going to tell.

If we should meet, just walk on by.
Oh, darlin', please don't cry.

A gentle smile crossed his lips as his mind exploded in black light flickering with violent white swirls.

Someone had hit him across the back of his head as soon as he stepped over the landing. He fell into a macramé rug and rolled onto the brown tile floor and felt boots kicking at him. Blood rushed through his ears and he covered his head with his hands. He saw there were two of them in leather and black, ski masks covering their faces.

One jerked Porter to his feet, his head still reeling with Clyde's song.

Tonight we meet
At the dark end of the street.

The kitchen was bright and obscenely yellow and covered with thick smears of maroon blood. Porter tried as hard as hell to get loose, but the man just shoved his face into a Formica breakfast table and laughed. He felt his teeth in the back of his throat.

And then he saw her.

Mary, clutching her fat stomach in her hands, blood across her thin yellow top. Blousy sleeves, daisy edges.

Goddamn.

They're gonna to find us.
They're gonna find us, Lord, someday.

A man, smelling of onions and cigarette butts, tied Porter to the chair facing her. He felt the cold cylinder sink into the soft spot at the base of his skull.

"Where is it?" the man asked.

Porter leaned forward and vomited onto his shoes. The ticket to Buffalo twirled down to the floor catching into the sticky mess. Through blurred eyes he stared into Mary's face. She bit her lip, and her eyes went soft, and he heard her praying like a child, like a twelve year old. It was something simple and quiet and for a moment Porter felt more like her father than her lover.

But tonight we'll meet
At the dark end of the street.

He mouthed the words that he loved her.

She smiled. Weakly.

Then he heard the click.

"My trunk," Porter said. Praying, too.

You and me, he heard Clyde sing in his mind.

And with the blast, came silence.

Chapter 1

WHEN I WAS A KID I used to keep one eye open while I prayed. It wasn't that I lacked faith in God or wanted to show any disrespect to the folks in church, it was just that I was curious about human nature. In that one silent moment, when everyone's power was turned to their deepest wishes and desires, I tried to imagine what everyone around me wanted. The more I watched and later learned about death, the more I believed all those desires were fleeting. And really kind of sad. In the end, everyone just wants some kind of miracle. His own private resurrection.

I kept thinking about those weird life patterns as I walked behind the old scarred mahogany bar of JoJo's place in the French Quarter, and reached deep into the brittle frost of a dented Coca-Cola cooler. I searched for my fourth Dixie.

JoJo's Blues Bar had closed about thirty minutes ago. It was late. Or early. Dark as hell. Tables had been cleared and stacked with inverted chairs. Stage lights cast red beams on microphones and a lone upright piano. Over by the twin Creole doors, beaten and weathered with time, only the faintest orange glow came from the old jukebox pumping out Otis Redding's "Cigarettes and Coffee."

All that remained were four of my closest buddies in a back corner booth, underneath a poster of the American Folk and Blues Festival 1965, celebrating with one of my *former* friends.

Well, I guess Rolande was still a friend. But he was dead. So did that mean we weren't friends anymore?

Didn't seem to matter to JoJo. We guessed Rolande had died about an hour ago, collapsed into his Jack and Coke with a thin smile on his lips. He was a wiry scruffy man who'd worn a scrunched Jack Daniels baseball cap for at least the last decade I'd known him. Rolande still wore it in death, just drooped a little farther down in his eyes.

"Bring the bottle, Nick," JoJo said. "Shit, son. Don't you learn nothin'?"

I swung back behind the bar, a Marlboro drooping lazily from my lips, and grabbed a half-empty bottle of Jack. I plunked it before JoJo and settled into the booth crossing my worn Tony Lamas at the ankles.

Joseph Jose Jackson—a.k.a. JoJo—had to be in his late sixties by now. Black man with white hair and neatly trimmed mustache. Black creased trousers, white button-down shirt rolled to his elbows. Hard to explain the completeness of my relationship with JoJo. To begin with, he was a surrogate father, harmonica teacher, and all-around Zen master on life.

I asked, "On the house?"

JoJo pulled out a well-worn wallet from Rolande's coat pocket and said, "Ain't no such thing."

The men laughed like tomorrow held more promise than today, all was right in the world, and God was watching down from heaven with a smile on His bearded face.

On JoJo's left sat Randy Sexton, my colleague and head of the Tulane University Jazz and Blues Archives. I'd known Randy since my early retirement from the Saints when I returned to Tulane for a Masters in music history.

Randy was usually physically out of step with his subjects—a white man with a big head of curly brown hair—but always spiritually in tune. He was the author of about a million books on early New Orleans jazz players and had been featured in Ken Burns's *Jazz* documentary series.

Always cracked me up when Randy got drunk. This man was one of the most respected music historians in the country, but sometimes I swear he acted about thirteen.

"Fuck, man," Randy said. "I'm wasted."

I was sandwiched by a three-hundred-pound black man named Sun on the one side, and a transsexual tattoo artist named Oz on the other. Sun was crying for his lost friend, his straw hat shredded to bits in his almost-ham-sized hands. Eyes red, damn near sobbing.

"Rolande always love you, Nick," he said, kind of blubbering. "Remember that night when you dumped that Gatorade on your coach's head?"

"Yep."

"Well, he love you for that. Love you for tellin' the man to go fuck hisself."

I smiled and said, "Oh, I try."

Oz didn't seem to be listening. He was just singing along to Otis's ballad to a late-night love. He had on his standard black lingerie with thigh-high stockings. On his face he wore white pancake makeup and black lipstick.

He'd strolled into the bar just minutes after a midnight showing of *The Rocky Horror Picture Show*. The movie was his obsession. His life. Based every decision on what Dr. Frank-N-Furter would do.

"Good Lord, pour the man another drink," Oz said in a recently acquired British accent. "Death is so hard for some people to get over. Isn't that right . . . What was his name again?"

"*Ro*lande," JoJo said with a slight edge. "Rolande *Good*ine. You sure remembered it when you need him to rewire that piece-of-shit tattoo parlor."

"It is, first off, a house of medicinal cures and potions."

JoJo raised his eyebrows and looked over at me.

"Goddamn, Nick, I don't mess around with none of them hoodoo fuckers. I don't care about the way he dresses, 'cause whatever gets you through the night and all that, but I *will not* mess with any of that hoodoo shit. You hear me?"

"It's cool," I said. "It's cool. Let's just drink. This is Rolande's last party. He wouldn't want us fighting."

I reached across the table and filled everyone's glass to the rim. JoJo looked away from Oz, over at Randy still grinning like a fool, and then over at sobbing Sun.

JoJo shook his head. "Goddamn, no wonder he wanted to leave this world. Look at y'all. Like a fuckin' freak show in here."

"I know a man who can drive a railroad spike through his nose," I announced. "You want me to call him?"

"I know a man in Algiers who'll bring back your friend for fifty bucks," Oz said with pursed lips. "But then Rolando would be a zombie and kind of a grumpy pain in the ass. You know how zombies get."

"Nick!" JoJo yelled.

Rolande's head rolled over to JoJo's shoulder, mouth agape.

The music stopped. And no one said a word as a brittle wind blew down Conti Street. I could only hear Sun's heavy breathing and a rock band jamming at the new Irish pub a few doors down.

Suddenly, the back door burst open and Randy dropped his glass on the hardwood floor. The glass scattered in shards dripping with amber whiskey.

And even my heart skipped for a second until I saw it was Loretta, JoJo's wife. Her flat face was full of frustration and exhaustion. She wore a long camel hair coat and her hair had been pulled back into a net.

A hard wind shot inside.

"What you want, woman?" JoJo asked like a man who wasn't afraid of shit.

Loretta—a two-hundred-pound-plus woman whose voice could make the bar jump when she sang—didn't even glance at the men. "Not you, you ole fool," she said. "I need Nick."

I crawled over Sun and followed her out to a loading dock facing a crushed shell lot where she crossed her arms and stared at JoJo's 1963 Cadillac. Withered leaves from a dying palm tree brushed against the stucco outside the bar.

"I'm sorry, Loretta," I said. "I was the one who asked JoJo if we could . . . you know, like the old days when . . . you know."

She shook her head.

"It's not that," she said. "Nick, I need some help. In the worse kind of way, baby."

Chapter 2

LORETTA JACKSON DIDN'T ask for favors. She sang deep, soulful blues from the pit of her big, curvy frame, she cooked jambalaya so sweet and spicy that all other food tasted hollow, and she took care of the ones she loved with such intensity that it even patched over that old familiar hole in my heart. A favor from Loretta wasn't a favor at all. It was an opportunity to do something for someone who'd given me everything she had.

We walked down Conti to Decatur and then continued upriver north under wooden signs swinging in the fall wind and beneath wrought-iron balconies heavy laden with palms, banana trees, and stunted magnolias. Twisted Christmas lights shaped like chili peppers and little skulls burned from the rusted ironwork. We passed the new, tourist-friendly Tipitina's, dozens of gift shops selling lewd T-shirts and cheap posters, and tired old restaurants serving reanimated crawfish, dead since spring, and watery gumbo.

We turned down the flagstone walkway running along Jackson Square—closed since dusk—and toward St. Louis Cathedral. The air smelled of the Mississippi's fetid brown water and cigarette smoke from a loose gathering of skinheads playing with a mangy puppy by the front doors of the church.

Loretta ignored them and took a seat on a nearby green bench. I didn't figure for wandering about tonight and had only worn a thin suede jacket over my black Johnny Cash T-shirt. It was the pose Cash did for Def Jam records when he wanted to thank the country music industry by saluting them with his middle finger.

I was pretty proud of it.

"If you don't want to do this, you tell me," Loretta said. "Right, baby? You don't owe me nothin."

"Nothin' but the world," I said, grabbing her hand. "What's on your mind?"

"I just been thinkin' while we were walking 'bout all the things you do for folks. Like when you kicked the butt of that man who dress like Jesus. You know the one who took Fats's money? And what you did for sweet Ruby Walker in Chicago last year? Nick, you 'bout got yourself killed to get that ole woman out of jail. I don't want to be no burden."

I squeezed Loretta's plump fingers and smiled. "You remember you and JoJo taking me in when I lost everything? You remember cooking for me and taking me to church and sewing my ratty Levis? Loretta, you're my family. I helped those people 'cause I wanted to. Because it's what I do. But with you, it's not even something I'd think about."

Loretta peered up at the three spires of the cathedral. She seemed to concentrate a long time on the middle spire topped with a hollow cross. On the cathedral's clock, the long hand swept forward and bells chimed for 3:00 A.M.

I rubbed my unshaven face and asked, "Loretta, tell me what's bothering you."

"You remember me telling you about my brother?"

"Hell yeah, I know all about your brother. He's a legend. You kidding me?"

Clyde James started his career singing in a gospel trio back in the 'fifties with Loretta and their sister, whose name I couldn't remember after a few Dixies. Clyde went on to be a big crossover star in the 'sixties with a small soul label called Bluff City. He was kind of a mix of Otis Redding and Percy Sledge.

Even though Loretta rarely spoke of him, I had most of his records. Mainly scratchy 45s with their dusty grooves filled with songs about longing, heartache, and all-around woman pain. Many a night they'd exorcised the latest shit I'd been going through with a woman I'd known for the last decade, Kate Archer.

I watched Loretta's face fill with light from the street lamps and over at the skinheads playing tag with the puppy. The puppy licked their faces and rolled over on his back. He barked a couple times and the skinheads hooted with laughter.

"Well, yesterday two men come to see me at the bar about Clyde.

Scared me so bad I ain't been back down there since tonight. I didn't even tell JoJo about it. 'Cause JoJo and I don't discuss my brother. Not after he'd tried so many times to help. You know?"

I nodded. I had an uncle who'd been a moonshine runner turned preacher and used to ask my dad for donations for his "church" every Christmas.

"They were asking me all about Clyde," Loretta said, reaching into her small jeweled pocketbook for a change purse. It killed me the way she could sing such nasty blues and then be such a proper old Southern woman. "They wanted to know when I seen him last and where they could find him. I tole them I ain't seen him for fifteen years, but they didn't believe me. They started breaking bottles and turning over tables. One of them even put his hand over my face and said he'd kill me if I didn't help 'em find Clyde. JoJo'd gone down to the A&P on Royal to get me some milk and coffee."

I could feel my cheeks flush with anger. "Did you tell them Clyde was dead?"

"They called me a liar. Said they seen him in Memphis two weeks back. Why would a man say something like that to me?"

I pulled out a Marlboro from a hard pack and lit it. I took a deep breath of smoke and settled back into the bench reaching my arm around Loretta.

"First off, I think you need to tell JoJo. And I can walk you guys home after the shows. That's no problem."

She looked back up at the slow-moving clock and then down at her hands. She unfolded them and reached into her change purse pulling out a wad of hundred-dollar bills. She crushed the money into my palm.

"When you headed up to Mississippi?" she asked.

"Monday."

"I want you to ride up to Memphis and find out what you can about Clyde."

"Clyde's dead."

She looked at me and patted my face as if I were a child with only a child's understanding. "We always thought he was dead. In the end he turned us all away. His family. His friends. Only thing he wanted was that hurt he carried 'round with him. When we lost track of him, I had to say good-bye. I had to pray for his soul."

I placed the money back in her purse and shook my head when she opened her mouth to speak. Her eyes closed and a single tear ran in a twisted pattern down her powdered face.

"You never told me what happened to him," I said, finishing the cigarette and tossing it to the flagstone pavement. A young couple walked past, drunk and kissing madly. They tripped over a curb as they turned into Pirate's Alley.

A gas lamp burned at the end of the alley by a house once rented by Faulkner. It was one of the loneliest sights I'd ever known but wasn't sure why.

"Somebody killed a man in his band," Loretta said. "And Clyde's wife. She was pregnant, Nick. Woman was six-months pregnant."

Chapter 3

PERFECT LEIGH DIDN'T like cartoons with talking animals, men who wore aftershave or Italian suits, self-appointed faith healers, peanut butter and jelly sandwiches, songs on the Waffle House jukebox, soap opera divas, collard greens, or sex of any type. She liked herself and that was enough for her. She liked the way she smelled like butterscotch candy. She liked the way she looked, with a mane of platinum blond hair and thirty-six, twenty-four, thirty-six measurements. She liked the way she appreciated the way Nancy Sinatra used to dance, the smell of new leather in her Mustang convertible, cheese sauce served in bad Mexican restaurants, and the way her Herb Alpert and the Tijuana Brass album skipped because it warped during a hot day at the beach in Panama City, Florida.

She especially didn't like good-ole-boy gatherings where men played poker in cigar-infested rooms and laughed with false self-knowledge and fears of their own inadequacies. She hated the smell of Scotch on their breath and of their crooked yellowed teeth. But they were gone now except for some poor old bastard named Fisher and his wheelchair-bound wife who screamed every time he plunked down a silly hand.

This was Tunica. From catfish farming to casinos in a few simple years. You could still smell the cowshit caked to the gamblers' work boots.

She sat with the Fishers in this little glassed-in room on the second floor of the Magnolia Grand Casino, just a spit away from Highway 61. The old man ate the remainder of a tired wrinkled hotdog and his wife slobbered on herself while laughing at the ketchup that dropped on his horrible tie.

For days, Perfect had been watching and listening to them from closed-circuit cameras. In the main casino, in the restaurant, and even in their bedroom. She read their profiles down in Humes's office about how they'd lost their daughter in a car accident about fifteen years ago and how they had some kind of benefit every year for her at a lake house with tons of deep-fried catfish and bream.

They had just given the money to some Tunica preacher who had a cable-access show in Memphis where he pretended to heal people. Said he gained the gift when he was a child and fell beneath a frozen lake only to re-emerge two-and-a-half minutes later with a vision.

What a crock of shit. Now he just passed out silly little flyers on Beale Street and casino bathrooms speaking out against men humping other men or drinking whiskey like idiots.

The Fishers were blind. But Perfect saw everything. By watching, listening, and waiting, she'd learned just how much they wanted their daughter back.

So in the last twenty-four hours that's what she'd become. She studied pictures of their dead little girl. She combed her platinum hair over one eye like the girl did, bought a wooly, early 'eighties sweater, and even found some of those Madonna rubber bracelets at a vintage clothing shop in midtown Memphis.

Last night, she just sat there in the casino bar and studied that poor old child trapped in a real silly time.

Girl's name was Gina.

Gina. Gina. Bobeeena. Mofanna-fanna. Momeena.

"Can I get you another hotdog, Mr. Fisher?" Perfect asked.

"No, Miss Leigh," he said, rearranging the cards like an idiot. She saw everything he had. But she'd let him win. Again. "I appreciate it though. My Lord, look how much I got. Must be two hundred dollars here."

"Be a lot more if you take the offer," she said. Real sweet. Not hard or hustly. But the way she imagined Gina would say it. *Please,* her words whispered, *please* accept your future.

"Ma'am," he spoke, real indignant as if he'd just had a cattle prod inserted into his rectum. "We bought that land in 'sixty-two and don't see no good reason for leavin' now."

Perfect—in full Gina mode now—smiled. Real tight smile with her eyes crinkled up but not showing a bit of teeth. Maybe even showed a bit of broken heart in her failed mission.

"Well, if you folks ever reconsider," she said, "we'd appreciate it."

Her smile dipped into her glass of wine tasting their souls and their fears and desires. By morning's end, she'd own them. They'd already opened too much. And they were hers.

She didn't have them bent until 7:00 A.M. the next day over a breakfast in the casino's Mardis Gras Time! restaurant. Some dummy in a red-and-white-striped vest played some New Orleans music on a Casio keyboard while a bunch of tired old people mashed soupy grits and butterless eggs into their dry mouths.

She'd stayed up with them all night, until a white sun washed through their curtains and over their soulless faces. Both full of whiskey, packs of cigarettes, totally spent from telling a volume worth of Gina stories.

Gina once adopted a stray cat that had a cyst the size of an orange in its throat. She cried and cried until her daddy took it to a country vet who cut it out for five hundred dollars. That old cat lived for another fifteen years and ate grits with honey and sugar.

And then there was the time Gina thought she'd created the world's best chocolate chip cookies. She called the folks at Nestlé and asked them if they'd pay her a million dollars for the recipe. That's when she was fifteen and, to be honest, to Perfect, Gina sounded kind of stupid.

But Perfect nodded and nodded.

Why were they telling her all of this after all these years? the Fishers asked. They'd barely spoken about dear Gina since the accident.

Yeah, Perfect wondered, as she combed the platinum hair back over the left eye and adjusted the rubber bracelets on her wrists.

When they got to the point about Luke, the tractor, and the wedding ring, she knew she had them. She just watched their faces fall, their hearts empty like a broken water main, and their bodies convulse with memories buried for far too long.

She didn't even have to ask. She simply walked to the phone and called for the Cobra—her little pet name for the casino's oily attorney.

Within fifteen minutes of the contract signing at breakfast, she was washing that really god-awful Vidal Sassoon mousse from her hair in a room Humes had gotten for her. For some reason, Duran Duran songs kept playing in her head like a bad insult to a horrible night.

Soon they'd be kissing her ass before she headed back to her small apartment in Memphis where she lived with her 'sixties picture books and her antique mirrors.

The money would come Western Union.

She'd live for months without the virus of the outside world to taint her.

But as she was letting down the top on her 'sixty-five Mustang convertible, Humes stopped her. She lifted her travel bag into the backseat and stared at his face framed by the purple and green lights of the Magnolia Grand floating in a fake river.

An agriplane buzzed overhead and a stray cloud on a cloudless day shielded the sun.

"What?"

"He has something for you," Humes said, his gray hair looking like silver against his black skin.

"Not interested."

"It's more money than you've ever known."

"Keep talkin'," Perfect said, checking out her reflection in the glass of an SUV parked behind him. "I'm always open to new ideas."

Chapter 4

FORTY MILES OUTSIDE MEMPHIS, I blew a tire, almost ran over a skin-and-bones mongrel dog, and nearly barreled off Highway 61 and headlong into a fundamentalist Baptist church. But luckily I missed the dog by a snout and came careening to a stop a few feet from the church's cemetery. It was about noon and dry and hot as I climbed out of my dusty 1970 Bronco; a friend of mine dubbed it the Gray Ghost for its color and phantomlike ability to perform. I quickly began searching in the flatbed among milk crates full of cassettes of field interviews and juke house music for the jack and frequently patched spare. I could only find my Army duffel bag full of T-shirts and jeans and work boots, my case of Hohner harmonicas, and a box set of interviews conducted by Alan Lomax for the Library of Congress. The tire. No jack.

I took off my blue jean jacket, wiped my now-sweating face, and threw the jacket into the passenger seat. I wore a white T-shit, already smeared with sauce from a barbecue breakfast at Abe's in Clarksdale, and rolled up my sleeves as I hunted for a greasy jack in the backseat. Finally, I found it and began to work.

I'd been out of New Orleans for the past three days and had only left Greenwood with about two hours of tape from a childhood friend of Eddie Jones, a.k.a. Guitar Slim, one of the greatest blues guitarists I'd ever heard and the subject of my often-delayed book. A book I'd delayed so much since joining the faculty at Tulane that they gave me until the fall to wrap up the project. I agreed. It was October and I was reworking chapter two.

As I cranked the jack, I looked at the countryside surrounding the highway. Besides the church, there wasn't much. A rotted barn with a rusted roof, a defunct convenience store among a row of three other storefronts. Even the church looked abandoned in this Delta ghost town. About the only thing around here was cotton, and being that it was mid-October, the fields were brown and bursting with white bolls. A complete sea of those little white dots blowing under a cloudless blue sky in a wind that quickly dried my sweat from working the jack. My biceps swelled and heated with exhaustion.

I grunted and clenched my teeth when I finally got the truck up and began concentrating on the tire. As I worked, I thought about where I'd start looking for Loretta's brother in Memphis.

Taking a break from Slim would be a welcome distraction. Of course, I'd become kind of an expert on these distractions. When I finished up playing defensive end for the New Orleans Saints about ten years ago, I found myself kind of lost for a trade. Hitting people really hard wasn't something that you used on your résumé. So, I went back to Tulane, which I attended as an undergrad, got a masters, and then kept rolling on to the University of Mississippi for my doctorate in Southern Studies.

My specialty was recording oral histories or hunting information on long-lost or dead musicians. That meant crisscrossing the Delta or Chicago or parts of Texas searching for hundred-year-old birth certificates or trying to find folks who'd rather stay hidden. Among music historians, I was what you'd call a blues tracker.

And my limited trade often got muddled with helping musicians out: from royalty recovery to getting criminal cases re-examined.

But hunting down Loretta's brother didn't have a damn thing to do with my job teaching blues history at Tulane, or even with the small-time music articles I sometimes published.

I'd known Loretta and JoJo since I'd come to New Orleans as a skinny teenager from Alabama. After my parents died, the Jacksons kind of adopted me. Their apartment on Royal and the blues bar on Conti became my homes. JoJo taught me how to play nasty licks on my harp and Loretta taught me how to cook some mighty fine soul food. She also gave me a place to do my laundry and hang out while other kids were going home during Christmas and summer vacation. They attended every home game that I played at Tulane and with the Saints, and my graduation ceremonies with even more satisfaction.

JoJo also introduced me into the network of old players and gave me an access into the blues that I would've never known. And during a few instances where I'd stumbled a little too far into the life of a blues player, they'd yanked my ass out of self-pity and Jack Daniels and made sure they set me straight.

I'm a curious person, I thought, loosening the last nut off the tire and sliding off the flat, and I believed I'd found out everything about the Jacksons. After all, I was an oral historian and prided myself as a listener. But although I knew the connection, Loretta seldom spoke about her brother Clyde.

A few times, especially some research I was doing into the connection between Civil Rights and 'sixties soul, I asked a few questions about her days in Memphis and her brother being one of Southern soul's headliners, among Otis Redding, Percy Sledge, and Wilson Pickett.

But she always found a way to change the subject. And I didn't want to push. After what I'd read about Clyde going crazy and taking to the street, I knew it only caused her pain.

Before I left New Orleans, I'd spent almost all night in the archives searching for articles about Clyde. I found a lot about the music—with a cursory mention of him—about how soul began to find roots after Ray Charles matched gospel structure with secular lyrics. Basically how *oh, baby* replaced *oh, Lord*. This was the time of Sam Cooke and Solomon Burke, an exciting period in black music that replaced blues in popular culture. But *Southern* soul was something else entirely. This was not Motown. Motown was black music for white teens. Southern soul, Memphis soul, was black music for blacks. This was grit. Funky, marinated, and deep-fried in gospel roots with the intensity of a church revival. Although he sang mainly about love, Otis Redding wasn't far removed from a preacher. Wilson Pickett was a shouter who could've been telling the world about Jesus, but instead chose "Mustang Sally."

I loved the music. It was Memphis.

But most people, even feverish fans, didn't know Clyde. Still he managed to be a cult figure in Britain and some critics believed he was the best soul singer who ever lived. Desperate. Almost operatic. One critic said, "Clyde sang sad songs not like his life depended on them, but like what his life depended on was gone and these songs were what was left."

It was pretty close to the truth. Just as James was getting national attention, his haunting version of "Dark End of the Street" topping the charts,

James started suffering from some deep mental problems. His wife and a member of his band had been killed in south Memphis, and in the time that followed, articles said James had suffered more emotional problems. Sometimes he even climbed onto the roof of the old movie theater that served as a recording studio and dared anyone to pull him down.

I read that there were rumors James ended up in a mental institution and that his new record company tried to keep it quiet. He reappeared briefly in the early 'seventies and did an unreleased album for Willie Mitchell at Hi. Then he was gone again. Some say a prison in Florida. Others say they saw him singing in the early 'eighties in Germany.

About the best thing ever written on James was in a four-year-old issue of a British music magazine called *Mojo*. The writer threw out a lot of theories from James's contemporaries about what happened. The accepted story was that he killed himself about a decade ago. *Broke. Forgotten.* The man who could've been the next Otis, still a shadow.

I replaced the tire and tossed the dirty flat and oily jack into the back of the truck. No cars passed. The cotton stretched all around me in silence.

I started the truck and headed north to Memphis.

I could do this quickly. No bars this time. No jukes were needed to find the answers. I would treat this like an academic exercise and return back to NOLA.

That's what I told myself as I saw the loose outline of Memphis just over the Tennessee border, already tasting a sandwich from Payne's and a cold forty on Beale. My heart began to pound in my chest like a child first seeing the rides of an amusement park form in the distance.

Chapter 5

BY 2:15 A.M., I was dancing with the largest woman I'd ever seen in my life. She had double-wide hips, ham-sized arms, and breasts the size of watermelons. Right in the middle of Wild Bill's Lounge, she held me close to her chest, shakin' her big ass as the band tore into a nasty, up-tempo version of the Johnnie Taylor classic, "Who's Makin' Love." The singer was about as large as my dance partner, in a tailored pin-striped suit and Jheri Curl hair, preachin' the gospel of Memphis soul. Driving drum beat, that spooky 'sixties organ, almost country and western guitar, and a small horn section punctuating every emotion. The singer stopped in the middle of the song, drum and guitar carrying on the rhythm, bragging to a woman in a plastic snakeskin coat, "Ain't nothin' short on me but my mustache."

Wild Bill's was a straight shot of a bar with long tables where everyone smashed together commune-style, a place where three dollars and fifty cents would get you a forty ounce and a clean glass. The room was narrow, painted orange, and decorated with Christmas lights, Polaroids of drunken patrons, and posters of black women in bikinis.

A juke house usually meant an old clapboard shack or storefront in some tired Mississippi town. But Wild Bill's lived in a strip mall occupied by a dry cleaner, a deli, and three beauty shops. One offered no-lye relaxers and body weaves.

I seriously didn't come to party or dance or act like a complete fool. Actually, I had just been sipping on the last of my forty and working on a plate of spicy chicken wings when she'd pulled me out onto the floor. Soon I was bumping, shaking, and strutting at her side. Didn't want to offend anyone.

I even tried to move with her, but she kept on bumping me with her butt and about knocking me out on the street. So I planted my boots hard to the floor and tried to hold my ground, even smiling a bit when the band finished out the tune.

Felt like Travolta when he stayed on the bull in *Urban Cowboy*.

But as I began to walk away to my beer and wings, the band took it down a notch with a slow ballad. The woman grabbed my hands, locked them around her waist, and took me for a slow ride around the small dance floor.

She twirled me all around—my boots barely skimming the floor—and I felt like something stuffed with sawdust that you'd win at a county fair. I finally returned to my seat, chewed the remainder of meat off the last wing, and drank in the whole scene.

She watched me from the other side of the room and sent me another beer. I nodded at her, careful not to get too close. She looked like she wanted to keep me as a pet.

All around me, people were passing about bottles of Canadian whiskey, screw-topped bottles of champagne, and more quarts of beer. They sweated into plastic hotel ice buckets, hooted with laughter, and unwound from the hard week.

Besides the rhythm guitar player, I was the only white boy in the house.

I took a sip of warm beer and watched the man work his guitar. He was skinny and kept the kind of beard you'd expect to find on a character from the New Testament. Wore a T-shirt advertising Atlanta blues mecca Blind Willie's, Wranglers faded almost white, and Birkenstocks.

Man's name was Cleve Mack and thirty years ago he'd created the nerve center for some of the greatest soul music ever recorded. Always worked that way. Didn't matter if it was Stax, Fame Studios in Muscle Shoals, or Bluff City. The greatest soul music was a blend of white and black artists, a pure Memphis melting pot of country, gospel, and blues.

I pushed away the skeletal remains of the wings and the last of the amber beer in my glass. My thin notebook was in my back pocket and I was ready to get some leads. That big woman had worn my ass out. No more hip shakin' tonight.

I found Cleve out back behind the strip mall smoking a joint beside a rusting Dumpster that smelled of sulfur and shit. His face wrinkled like old parchment around his blue eyes. His body so thin, he looked as if he were sick or on a hunger strike.

I walked over, introduced myself, and told him about Loretta and her desire to find her brother. Cleve sucked on the joint and kicked at a paper basket of wings. He toed at it for a few moments but wouldn't knock the messy bones on the asphalt.

"Man, ole Clyde James, best there ever was," Cleve said in a drawl crossed between a black from south Memphis and a white Delta farmer. "Too bad that poor motherfucker is deader than a choked chicken."

Cleve took another hit off the joint. He offered it to me, but I shook my head, pulling out a pack of Marlboro Lights. The smell of Cleve gave me a sudden rush of growing up in lower Alabama, blaring Led Zeppelin and the Stones, and eating handfuls of M&Ms under blacklit posters.

"How'd you know he's dead?"

"Bobby Lee Cook told me a while back. Said Clyde finally done and shot hisself."

"How'd he know?"

"Bobby Lee Cook, man. He ran Clyde's label, Bluff City."

I remembered Loretta mentioning his name.

Everything was wet in the back alley. Trash. Chicken bones. Somewhere in the distance a child screamed, and then starting laughing.

"Goddamn! What the fuck was that?"

I peered beyond a high fence, but could only see endless rows of dilapidated houses occasionally shining with yellow bug lights.

"Man, that scared the cat shit out of me," Cleve said, with a touch of anger in his voice. He laughed and held on to his chest in a Fred G. Sanford move. "Dude, you said you write about music?"

"Yeah."

"How'd you find me?"

"You know Tad Pierson?"

"Yep."

"He's the one."

"Well, listen," Cleve said. "Me and the fellas in there are puttin' out a CD in a few months. You got a card or somethin'?"

I handed him one embossed with the Tulane logo, not bothering to tell him I was a researcher and did little reviewing. "What was he like?"

"Oh, that was like another lifetime ago," Cleve said and sighed, playing with the loose ends of his long, greasy hair. "I don't know. Man kept to himself. For most of the time I knew him, he wouldn't say shit. He'd play cards alone in the back of his tour bus or make these weird little drawings of heaven and hell. Real strange. The devil he drew was always a good-lookin' woman. . . . I guess the only time I saw him come alive was when his manager or handler or whatever would put a suit on him and push him out on that stage. He never had that holy rollin' kind of thing like Otis or Sam and Dave, and that's probably why he wasn't a big star. But just for pure singin', man could sing clear as a church bell. Makes the hair raise on the back of my neck to think about it."

I finished the cigarette and ground it under my boot. The front of my T-shirt was soaked in sweat and the cold wind began to make me shiver. Cleve kept on sucking on the joint until it burned his fingers and he dropped it to the wet ground.

"So what happened to him?"

"Everything got crazy for us when Eddie died," he said. "We were changin', the music was gettin' rougher. No one wanted to hear "When a Man Loves a Woman." People wanted to hear "I'm Black and I'm Proud." About that time, Clyde gone and got this new manager, just a kid, really, who didn't know how to handle his problems. I mean Clyde had always been crazy, but after his wife and Eddie died and all those rumors started . . ."

"What rumors?"

"That the baby was Eddie's. You know she was pregnant when she got killed?"

"Yeah."

"Well, Clyde just kind of split. You know in these slivers. You had happy Clyde, sad Clyde, mean Clyde, all in about five minutes. We couldn't deal with it anymore and he was gettin' freaky on stage, too."

"How?"

"Forgettin' words. Talkin' to himself. You name it, brother."

"Did you know his wife?"

"Lord, I was never too much into black women. But if you talk to Tate, that country ass will tell you another story. But me, not that I was preju-diced or nothin', it just didn't appeal to me. But Mary—wow. She had this beautiful dark skin and these wide almond-shaped eyes and these legs never did end. I still don't know how Clyde got her. When he wasn't on stage he was just plain weird. She treated him like he was a little boy or somethin'. Like this one time we were playin' this hotel in Montgomery. Clyde just started cryin'. We were all havin' a good time listening to this football game on the radio and drinkin' vodka martinis, 'cause we thought we were pretty hip in our mohair suits and all. But Clyde all of sudden has these tears fallin'. His face wasn't messed up and he wasn't makin' a sound. It was just the eyes. Man was carryin' some dark things."

Cleve shook his head, used a guitar pick to scratch his bearded chin. You could tell he was back in 1968. He was in his twenties, the women were dancing with loose hips, and he was living in the center of a cultural explosion.

"You see him much after you guys split?"

"I haven't seen Clyde James since 'seventy-three," he said, staring down the long stretch of alley. His eyes closed for a moment and then opened as if waking from a lengthy nap. "But you know what? Whatever I do, I'll always just be Clyde James's guitar player. Only played with him for a couple years. Be on my tombstone, though." He nodded to the back door of Wild Bill's. "You hear those cymbals?" he asked.

I nodded.

"Bill doesn't go for long breaks."

I asked him for his number in case I had more questions. I was already thinking about my nice, warm bed at the Peabody and maybe getting up early enough to have breakfast at the Arcade. "Go talk to Cook," Cleve said.

"You know where to find him?"

"Hope you like eggrolls and pussy."

I looked at him.

"Find the Golden Lotus down by the airport and you'll understand just fine, my brother."

Chapter 6

OFF HIGHWAY 7 near Oxford, Mississippi, Abby MacDonald stared at the house that once held her entire world. Seemed like another lifetime ago when she lived there with her parents. The old house was one-story, broad and white, with a tin roof and wraparound porch. On the corner by the driveway, a wooden swing hung from metal chains. Her mother's plants and flowers—that had withered and died since late summer—lay by the front door.

Behind the house stood the stables, but the horses had already been taken away. She guessed that her cousin Maggie had picked them up. Their dogs Hank and Merle, too. She remembered what the cop had said about Merle finding them. How he stayed at their side. *Whimpering.*

From the shoulder of the two-lane, she could just make out the crumbling plywood of her old playhouse in the magnolia tree. A knotted rope hung loose below.

She wished she could climb through its twisted branches, through the white, fragrant flowers, and into the safety of a world she'd created for herself. Up there, she never had any worries. True evil never existed. Only the sweet voice of her mother calling her to dinner, making her leave tins full of mud pies and discarded toys.

Her scarred knees and broad grins were all gone now.

She pulled the keys from the old F150's ignition and took a deep breath. It was about 5:00 A.M. Loose traffic blew past her on the way to Holly Springs and Memphis as she looked at herself in the rearview mirror. A weak, predawn light crept around her.

Dark circles rimmed her brown eyes. Her curly blond hair was limp and dirty and her face flat—washed of any color. Any life. Twenty-two years old and already tired of living.

Maybe it was that she was tired of being on the run. For the past two months, she'd existed in a hazy fog in roadside motels and truck stops. No one knew where she'd disappeared. She only wanted to be left alone and for the pain to stop. The days had passed with bottles of cheap wine and a blur of blacktop and scattered yellow median lines.

Being anonymous could be reassuring.

Abby gritted her teeth and got out of her car, a black duffel bag in her hand. The silence was almost too much. Each step she took on her lawn, as she looped to the back of the huge house, was pain.

She remembered how proud her father had been when he'd bought the place back in the late 'eighties. Always told people he'd renovated it. But, really, he'd just paid the contractor to make some adjustments. There was a large skylight in the kitchen where he cooked his spicy Cajun food, and a sunken room he'd added that he called his theater where he made her watch John Wayne movies on a big-screen television. Big bowl of popcorn, Cokes in those small green bottles.

Never let her just watch the film, always talked about patriotism and true grit.

Seemed like she always wanted to be out with her friends, cruising the Square, or trying to sneak into frat parties. But now she'd give her life just to watch one of those faded, hokey movies with him. The smell of his cheap aftershave. His silly laugh.

On the side of the house, she took the brick steps onto the creaking porch. Yellow crime-scene tape sealed off the landing but she ducked beneath it. The sky was starting to turn a swirl of yellow and purple like a halo that surrounds a healing wound. A few small clouds were black and thin.

She went to the back door and dropped the bag, pulling out a crowbar and a flashlight. More crime-scene tape sealed the back door. She ignored it and sank the crowbar behind the metal wedge that held a new Master lock in place.

She pulled the wedge until her muscles screamed and the lock broke free. She inserted her own key into the door's lock and pushed it open with her foot.

This was the first time she'd been inside since it happened. She'd been living just a few miles away at her sorority house on campus when she got a call from her cousin. She remembered speeding along the highway and seeing the ambulance and squad cars lined up outside. All of them parked haphazardly on the lawn.

Today, she felt like she was walking through a mausoleum. The kitchen was hot as an old attic. It smelled of stale bread and rotten oranges. The sun was rising over the barn in the backyard, its rays filtering through an oak tree. Beams shot into an antique stained-glass window mounted over the kitchen sink.

Abby turned on the flashlight and walked through a narrow hallway, passing pictures of her family on horseback and on ski trips, and into the den. More tape blocked her path and she ripped it aside as she felt her face break and her throat crack.

Her legs buckled and she dropped to her knees when she saw his old chair. Brown leather, a history of the Civil War lying in its well-worn seat. She pulled herself up and slid into the chair still smelling his presence.

She imagined her mother cooking now. Maybe shelling peas or chatting with their maid, Lucy.

She closed her eyes and felt the tears bleed down her face.

She clasped her hands over the heat of the flashlight, pushed herself to her feet, and walked back to the study where he died. She rolled back the twin doors and saw the fat, mahogany desk and chair that creaked when he would lean back and study cases.

She placed her hand on the desk, sitting flush next to the far wall, and reached to its corner, pulling as hard as she could. The desk barely budged and she tried harder. Finally, it squeaked on the wooden floor and she could see the square pattern he'd cut into the wall. She pulled back the desk a little more and used the crowbar to pop out the square.

Inside, she saw the face of the safe. The combination was easy, her parents' anniversary. She wheeled through the numbers and cracked it open. Without even looking at the headings on the dozens of manila folders or the contents of the velvet-covered boxes, she slid them into the duffel bag.

She closed the safe, reinserted the square, and pushed the desk back flush with the wall.

She didn't need the flashlight anymore. Dawn had arrived. A gray light burned through the curtains. A stale heat pulsed in the room.

She walked to the front hall and looked at the door to her parents' bedroom. She knew that her mother had been there when the men—the police said it was more than one—had entered and emptied their guns into her father.

She'd almost made it to the door—maybe running to her husband—when a slug ripped into her shoulder and another into her temple. She'd been wearing that goddamned housecoat Abby hated so much. The ratty terry-cloth thing with ripped pockets.

Abby stared at the door and dropped her head. Her fine hair fell into her eyes and matted to her damp face.

The answers were in her bag now. She knew it. The local cops were idiots. They said it was a robbery. But he'd still had a ten-thousand-dollar Rolex on his wrist when they found him.

Abby shook her head at the thought, gripped the black bag tight to her chest, and sprinted to her car. *The ghosts were too close.*

From a clearing along the back highway, Perfect studied the girl's face through a pair of small binoculars. She'd followed the girl all the way from Meridian where she'd stayed for the last couple of days in a run-down trucker's motel. The girl, whose name was Abby, didn't see Perfect, though.

Perfect had kept close to the shadows watching the girl's movements, listening in on her phone conversations with her cousin—amazing what the manager of the motel could do—and sifting through the girl's old truck while she was asleep. She found a photo album, a duffel bag of used clothes, and receipts from the last couple of months.

Abby. Hmm. Liked to spend daddy's money. Banana Republic T-shirts. J. Crew underwear. A pair of Nike running shoes that probably cost a hundred and fifty bucks. Caswell-Massey lotion mixed in with tiny bottles of motel shampoo.

Perfect would have to straighten her hair, shear it at the jawline, maybe even lose the platinum. Girls like Abby didn't know how to be sexy. They liked blending in. They liked wearing boys' jeans and tattered baseball hats.

She watched Abby run to the truck with the same black bag in her hand. Was it weightier now? Sure it was, Perfect thought, reaching into her Navajo-print purse and pulling out a pack of Capris. She lit a match and sucked in some smoke as Abby's truck disappeared from her rearview mirror.

There was time.

Perfect fussed with her hair, trying to imagine how it would look with a few inches trimmed away and a wash of brown color. She'd have to stop by one of the shops on Oxford Square and buy a roll-neck sweater, preferably gray, and a pair of jeans. Only slightly faded, of course. And was there a sporting goods store that sold really good shoes? She couldn't remember.

Makeup? Almost none. Maybe a dull gloss on her lips, and, yeah, she'd have to remove the color from her nails and then cut them down a bit.

The sunlight bled over the far grassy hill and stretched its weight across the old farmhouse, a dilapidated barn with a tin roof, making the light shine hard in her eyes, and over the bumping green hills close to the highway.

What else did she have? What else did she know? Oh, yes, the cousin.

She remembered from the phone the way Abby's cousin had this smoky confident voice that kept on asking her to come back to Oxford. At one point, she almost thought the cousin had her convinced, but Abby would start crying and say she didn't want to talk to the police again or any of their family. Especially some pussy uncle. What did Abby say? She hated them all, or something like that.

There was something else she spotted in that old photo album about both the cousin and the mother. They had the damned most intense eyes Perfect had seen. Almost like they saw everything. Three hundred and sixty degrees. Kind of grabbed you right through the photo.

Kind of a weight or maybe a heft to what they saw. Sort of sleepy. Sort of intelligent. *The eye thing.* Yeah, she could do the eye thing.

The thick yellow light stretched its way across the pavement and onto Perfect's face as she buttoned the top three buttons of her tight red angora sweater and practiced the husky voice.

"You've been out too long, Abby," she said, feeling her eyes grow heavier. "Darlin', it's time to bring you on in from the cold."

Chapter 7

AFTER DRIVING ALL morning and night, a big truck stop was exactly what Abby needed. One of those places that sold mesh hats with redneck sayings and beef jerky by the truckload. She wanted to grab a couple of buttery biscuits, a cup of hot black coffee, and find a clean bathroom to wash herself off. Maybe they had showers, too, she hoped, spotting a billboard made out of neon and chrome near the Tennessee border and pulling off the highway. Besides, her engine light had been on red since Holly Springs and she was pretty damned sure her whole motor was about to blow unless she got to a mechanic.

But sometimes you just had to keep riding things out and see where fate would take you.

She parked underneath a huge portico and listened to fat drops splatter the roof. Her radio blared some bad country while her windshield wipers flapped a steady beat. On the other side of a long plate glass window, hardened truckers shoveled country-fried steak and mashed potatoes with gravy into their mouths. She licked her dry lips, counted out a few crumpled dollar bills and four quarters in her hand and wondered if she could go a little farther without a meal.

She wanted one more day alone, without calling her cousin or without answering questions about her parents. *Was she all right? Did she need anything? They were fine people, weren't they?* Goddamn it. She didn't need another fucking person telling her how fine her parents were. She knew her mother once bought a mess of socks for a deaf boy named Pooky, and that her father once donated the five hundred dollars he won for killing the largest buck in the county to Oxford First Baptist. Everyone was trying to make saints or Mother Teresa out of them now. But all Abby could remember was how her mother bought that good Minute-Maid pink lemonade and hugged the crap out of her when she heard that Abby's boyfriend had split for a Tri-Delt from McComb. Or that the last time she saw him, her daddy wore his reading glasses upside down to make her laugh like when she was five.

The memory burned away in a truck stop window dripping with water and steam, pink from the neon. The neon read: SHOWERS, ATM, CHECKS CASHED, CHEAP CIGARETTES. After she pumped out five bucks, Abby bolted for the front entrance as the hard gray rain soaked her face and stung her eyes.

Perfect Leigh watched Abby make a run for it, the girl's feet splashing through the oily puddles. Inside her car, Perfect crushed a thin cigarette into a dirty ashtray and turned down the *Best of Nancy Sinatra* CD. Perfect looked at her reflection in the rearview mirror and decided she'd done a great job with the makeup. Dull gloss on her lips. A little mascara. These college girls liked their simplicity for some reason.

Hair wasn't bad either. Only took a handful of brown-tinted mousse and some bobbing shears she kept in a little overnight case. Hell, the whole transformation was done a few hours ago at Lake Puskis when Abby was walking around feeding the squirrels and communing with nature. The clothes were in the car and the rearview worked as her canvas.

Perfect closed her eyes, took a deep breath, and ran her hands down over her shoulders, breasts, and stomach. She kept her hands on her stomach for a few moments, just feeling her breath. She started inhaling a little faster.

She was quick, she was perky, and brimming with energy and kind of a motor mouth.

Abby knew women like this. Never give Abby a second to doubt you or your intentions. *You are Ellie.* You were born in Houston, Texas. Your father owned a wicker furniture company and your mother was a former Miss Texas runner-up. When you were a child, you moved to Memphis and grew up in the wealthy suburb of Germantown. You like Chinese food but not Italian. You like Pop Tarts and Tootsie Rolls and anything sweet. And, one time, you rescued a puppy from drowning when the levee broke near your aunt's mink farm in Louisiana.

Perfect smelled her new perfume and she liked it. She liked this body.

She liked the way Ellie smelled and spoke with this clarity and cleanness. *Ellie*. Ellie was special.

The truck stop was loaded with bad food. A Dairy Queen, Subway, Taco Bell, and a big restaurant called Grandma's Country Cookin'. Grandma's was a place where a bunch of scruffy guys wearing flannel shirts took their coffee and talked about their latest loads. Auto supplies to her right and Western wear along the back wall. Who needed all this stuff on the road? Abby thought as she shook the water from her head and strolled through the bright, fluorescent coldness.

Felt good to stretch her legs and be among people again. Didn't matter if they were toothless or a little haggard. She smiled at a little Asian woman who passed her carrying a crate of Yoo-Hoo.

Abby could barely afford one. All she had was two dollars. There had to be something in the cooler for that. She wasn't thirsty anyway. Maybe one of those horrible egg salad sandwiches or a microwavable roast beef sandwich. She grabbed the egg salad.

"Abby?" someone asked. "Is that you?"

She turned and faced a young woman, who was maybe in her late twenties, with brown hair cut all one length. She wore a gray sweater, dark jeans, and running shoes. Abby studied her face and smiled. She was too old to know from class.

"I'm sorry," Abby said, shrugging.

"Ellie," the woman said. "The Grove? Met you and your cousin last year?"

It was a voice she recognized from every bourbon-drinking, cigarette-smoking Southern woman she'd ever known. The woman's thick lips curved into a welcoming smile. Her big blue eyes dropped into hers with a familiar look Abby knew but couldn't recognize. The woman's skin was tanned and her eyebrows thin and arched.

"Sure," Abby said, lying.

The woman suddenly reached around Abby's neck and squeezed her close. She smelled like Calvin Klein perfume and Abby felt the woman's weighty breasts smash against her like two balloons filled with concrete. "God, I'm so sorry about your parents. My God. What you've been through. I spoke to Maggie just the other day and she said she was just worried to death. Cain't believe I just ran into you like this. On my way to Memphis, you know, and stopped off for gas. You look so tired. Are you all right? Abby, I'm so sorry."

For some reason, she didn't know why, maybe because she was so tired and maybe she wanted to be held, but Abby hugged this woman back, who she didn't know shit about. It felt good to be with someone familiar.

"My car. I think the engine is about to burn up," Abby said.

"Oh, Lord," Ellie said. "Sit down and let's have a cup of coffee and figure it all out. I know this place is absolutely awful, but would you like lunch? I mean, a hamburger? No one can screw up a hamburger or breakfast, or at least that's what my daddy always told me."

Abby opened the freezer and replaced the egg salad sandwich.

"Sure," she said.

As Perfect rambled, she watched Abby's eyes follow the water sluicing down the foggy window like it was worms racing. Perfect loved to ramble like Ellie. It was like letting loose and peeing outdoors in the rain. She talked about when her father died from cancer and how she'd lost twenty pounds in two months. She spoke of recently finding comfort in God after a ski trip to Aspen where she saw sun fall across the snow like a halo. And of course, she offered to drive Abby back to Oxford and maybe find Maggie and go out to dinner at City Grocery.

She could tell Abby was barely listening. The girl just sat there at the Grandma's counter as eighteen-wheelers rolled by outside. Perfect decided to try the human-contact move. Basic shit. She reached over, spread her fingers wide, and covered Abby's hand noticing overgrown cuticles. *No manicure?*

The trick was not to grasp the hand, but just to give a warm reassurance. Levi taught her that. Levi had taught her everything.

"How 'bout it?" Perfect asked, keeping her hand in place. "Leave that old truck here and come with me. Let's just circle back, I don't need to shop anyway. We'll find Maggie. She's so worried about you, Abby. She really is."

Abby had barely spoken. Strange little bitch. She was petite and loose-limbed and had the same sleepy eyes Perfect had noticed from the family photographs. The girl didn't wear makeup and kept an Ole Miss hat scrunched down in her eyes. Greasy hair. White T-shirt stained with old coffee.

A little stubble under her arms. *Good Lord.* The girl needed to be hosed off and shaved.

"How do you know my cousin again?" Abby asked. Still not looking Perfect in the eyes.

"One of her friends is big buddies with my boyfriend, and Jamie—that's my boyfriend—throws these massive parties after football games. Last year he had this crawfish boil where we all just got sloshed and ended up fighting with those little buggers. Shells in my hair and in my ears. Maggie was there. Funny, I haven't seen you at one of those parties, too."

"Doesn't sound like something Maggie would do," Abby said. "She'd rather spend the night at Square Books reading Eudora Welty and drinking coffee than vomiting with a bunch of ex-frat boys."

"C'mon, Abby," Perfect said. *Never give them the time to follow your eyes or reverse your flow.* She gripped Abby's hand in hers. "Follow me on back to Oxford. You need a decent meal and a warm bath. I've got buckets of bath beads and this big old copper tub with claw feet. You can soak away everything. Please. If I left you and saw Maggie later I'd just die."

Abby pulled away and looked down at her hand as if it had been infected. Her fingernails were cut close and her hands dry and chapped. *Moisturizer.*

"Well," Abby began, staring at the purse that Perfect had by her side, a Navajo-print bag slightly open. At the top edge, a handgun's muzzle poked out. Son of a bitch.

Perfect covered up the edge of the gun, politely smiled, and said, "Woman has to watch out for herself."

Perfect then rolled her eyes like it was the silliest thing she'd ever done in her life and again cupped Abby's hand in hers. "C'mon, let's go."

Abby excused herself and walked back to the bathroom where she brushed her teeth with a portable toothbrush and twice had to push away the urge to vomit. Just the thought of having to face the fucking town again made her sick.

Since she left the house that morning, she couldn't even bring herself to look through her father's files. The thought of seeing his signature or any bit of his work made her feel the decay of his body. Some kind of direct connection to the physical presence she knew was rotting away.

She felt the bile rise in her throat and threw up a thick wad of the cheeseburger into a brown-stained sink.

When nothing else would come but dry heaves, she brushed her teeth again, stepped into a stall, and changed into a long-sleeved gray T-shirt and clean underwear. At the sink counter, she carefully folded her dirty clothes on top of the duffel bag and stared at her reddened eyes.

For a few moments she cried until a hillbilly-looking woman, who didn't have a neck and kept a slight moustache, came in and sat down on a toilet. The door was wide open.

If it got too bad, she could always get Maggie to take her back here. Abby grabbed her bag and decided she'd leave with Ellie.

On the way out, she paused and looked down the long hallway. Some video games plinked nearby in a desolate video arcade. A long row of lockers with orange turnkeys lined a far wall.

Abby emptied the duffel bag into a small blue locker and filled it with her old T-shirt and panties. She dropped in her remaining four quarters and turned the key.

Chapter 8

THE GOLDEN LOTUS OOZED with sex and tired Chinese food. Just sitting in the parking lot with the sound of my Bronco's motor ticking in my ears, I could tell that the vegetables would be overcooked, the snow crab frostbit, and the egg rolls soggy. Of course, the patrons probably didn't give a shit. The little cinder block building topped with a pagodalike tile roof near the airport also offered table dances with your egg foo young and a shower show with your moo goo gai pan.

I shut off my engine and walked to an ornate red door guarded by a teenage girl in a bikini top and hip-hugger jeans. She wore stiletto heels with rabbit fur straps, and an angoralike sweater hung loose off her bony shoulders. She smiled briefly at me, remained perched on her barstool, and took a five buck cover.

Her fingers slowly traced a vertical scar that ran from her navel to the clasp of her bikini top as her gaze drifted to a long black row of clouds rolling across the flat land of the airport where a 727 rumbled overhead.

Inside, the floor was concrete and the room smelled of clove cigarettes and cherry air freshener. There were three amoeba-shaped elevated stages throughout the shadowed bar pumping with a slow Ann Peebles song. *Couldn't stand it, baby, if you said we were through. That's what you keep on doin' to me. Heartache. Heartache. Heartache.*

A brown-haired, brown-eyed beauty wearing only pearls looped in a knot like a man's tie stooped to the floor of the center stage and pulled off a balding patron's glasses. She crushed the frames between her breasts and placed them back on his head upside down. Throughout the bar, there were only six guys—most eroded businessmen with wrinkled shirts, slightly untucked—watching the matinee show. Pink and green neon glowed in the dark cave while a soft gray rain began to patter the sun-bleached parking lot framed by the open door.

I lit a cigarette and took a seat at the long bar and ordered a cup of coffee. The waitress was about my age, somewhere between thirty and forty. She had short brown hair, not boy short, but cut just below the ears and tosseled in her eyes.

"Mr. Cook around?" I asked.

She shrugged. She had a sharp nose and full lips. I could tell she worked out by the shape of her biceps as she poured the coffee and firmly shoved a cracked mug before me.

"Could you check?"

"Why?" she asked.

Her man's ribbed tank top didn't quite touch the edge of her dark blue jeans held together with a Western belt.

"Health inspector," I said. "Somebody found a G-string in his wonton soup."

"That's funny," she said. She chewed gum, keeping her eyes trained to a soap opera. The television was muted and suspended by chains from the ceiling. "I never heard shit like that before."

"It's true, and the other day someone reported the indecent use of a fortune cookie."

"How would that work exactly?" she asked. She turned away from the television and wiped off the angry head of the dragon carved into the cherrywood bar. The bartender's eyes were deep blue and the whites had the clarity of someone who didn't drink.

"I'm not sure," I said. "But I bet it could be done."

"You want to tell me what you want, or do I just introduce you as the funny guy at the end of the bar?"

"The funny guy works."

I smiled. She smiled back.

The song ended and the naked woman plopped off stage and took a seat next to me. She was sweaty and out of breath and played with the pearls around her neck like a rosary.

"Hey, cowboy," she said.

"Ma'am," I said, tipping my imaginary hat.

The girl behind the bar disappeared and I watched her jeans as she did. I took a sip of the burned coffee and watched the rain beat on the worn streets outside. The thunder growled in the distance as the naked woman sighed and disappeared. A moist print of her butt stayed on the vinyl seat after she was gone.

More Ann Peebles played on the jukebox. I sipped the coffee and watched some bikers play pool in a back cove. All but one stripper had stopped dancing and she seemed to be doing her act completely from a lone brass pole.

The woman inverted herself into a handstand against the pole and a couple businessmen clapped and high-fived each other.

As the rain drummed harder the coffee felt even more comforting in my hand.

I can't stand the rain. Against my window. Bringin' back sweet memories.

"He said give him a few minutes," a voice called out.

I turned back to the bartender. She'd tied her undershirt up high on her stomach and was cleaning the bar again.

She wrung the cloth into the sink and soapy water twisted down her lean brown arms. For a moment I could feel my lungs tighten. She noticed my glance and smiled to herself and continued to wipe down the bar.

"I'm Nick," I said when my voice came back.

"Good," she said.

"You want to arm wrestle?" I asked. "You have great arms."

"Nope," she said, going back to twisting the dirty cloth. Some of the soap brushed across her stomach and she raised her tight shirt even more to wipe it away. Her abs were tight with a small waist and perfect rounded hips.

"I was wondering . . . ," I began.

The dancer with the pearl necklace walked behind the bar laughing to herself like drunk women sometimes do and latched her hands around the bartender. She kissed the nape of the woman's neck and I felt my face flush with embarrassment.

"What were you wondering?" the bartender asked with a cocked eyebrow. The gesture sort of reminded me of my occasional girlfriend, Kate.

"Nothing," I said, feeling for the warmth of the cup. "Nothing."

A few seconds later, I heard a toilet flush over the slow, grinding funk coming from the jukebox and out walked a muscular man with gray hair holding a stack of newspapers. He looked to be in his fifties with the build of an avid weight lifter. His clothes were Italian and tight. Ribbed black T-shirt. Pleated trousers. Tassled loafers. He threw the papers onto the bar and took a seat next to me.

"What the fuck do you want?" he asked. His face was craggy with lines around his mouth. His teeth were yellowed and he wore thin oval glasses that were popular with effeminate yuppies back in New Orleans.

"You Cook?"

"No, I'm the fucking Easter bunny," he said, shaking his head and watching one of the strippers in a Catholic school-girl outfit. "Hell, yes, I'm Cook. So what? April said you wanted to see me."

"I want to talk to you about Bluff City Records."

"Sold that in 'seventy-four," he said. "I guess you're shit out of luck."

The bartender had pried herself away from her friend and was running the blender in between eavesdropping. She poured a pink slushy mixture into a tall beer mug and laid down a handful of pills by Cook.

He swallowed them all and gulped down half the drink.

"Amino acids. Vitamin B, and yohimbi bark. You want the rest of my shake?"

I shook my head.

"April? April?" he yelled. "Shit, go get Lola, would you? Goddamn it. I left her back in my office and she's probably shittin' all over everything."

"Women," I said, shaking my head again and finishing the last of the coffee.

"So, you gonna tell me what the fuck you want?"

"I'm looking for Clyde James."

Cook belched. "He's dead. Shit out of luck again." He smiled. "You're oh for two, fella. . . . What are you, one of those crazy collector types? Had this British guy come in here once and offer me two thousand dollars for some of our recording logs. Now, that's just fucking sick. Or is it sad? April? Goddamn it."

April walked back to the bar tugging on the leash of a Boston terrier wearing one of those inverted-lampshade looking things that kept them from licking themselves. Didn't help the dog's looks any. The dog was just plain ugly with a severe crooked underbite and low-hanging tits.

And damn if she didn't smell funny when Cook plopped her on the bar and let her lick the glass of his protein shake. She smacked and licked, facing her butt to me until she finally gave a grunt and farted.

"Ain't she a beaut?" Cook said.

The dog turned and gave a cross-eyed stare at me, waiting for an answer.

"I don't thing I've ever seen a dog like her. Makes Lassie look like a skank."

When Cook turned away I grimaced at April. She grinned.

"Listen," I said, watching Cook push the sleeves higher on his Italian T-shirt to show the world his biceps. "I heard you found him."

"C'mon, podna. What do you want to get into that mess for?"

"I work for Tulane University and I'm working on a project about the last of the soul singers."

Cook turned back to me with a look like he was just starting to take this conversation seriously. He nodded and crossed his arms and then unfolded them and scratched his dog's flank. The cross-eyed dog twisted her head when she heard a high-pitched woman begin to sing some tired-ass Chitlin' Circuit soul ballad.

"He was good," Cook said. "Best I ever heard."

"You saw him dead?"

He nodded and cleaned off his glasses.

"When was that?"

"Oh, shit, I don't know."

"Months, years, what?"

"I don't know. Four years maybe."

"Where was he?"

"Why do you care? You work for who?"

"Tulane University."

"He's dead, what the fuck's the difference?"

"I need to know when and where," I said. "Did he shoot himself?"

"Goddamn," Cook said. "Get out of here."

"C'mon, man, these aren't hard questions."

"I said get the fuck out of here."

"You know Loretta Jackson?"

"Hell, yeah, I do. So what?"

"She sent me."

"Why don't you make up your fuckin' mind why you're here."

"She wants to know what happened to her brother."

"He's dead."

"I need some help, man. Give me something."

"Get out," Cook said, rising to his feet and puffing up his chest. He was one of those men who believe weight lifting has made them invincible. They have so much testosterone pumping through their body that it messes up their perception of reality.

"Five minutes," I said.

"Now," Cook said, his face full of blood and anger.

April shrugged and turned back to her soap opera.

Lola continued licking the last of Cook's drink.

And I left the bar smiling. For the first time, I knew I'd find the answers that Loretta needed.

Chapter 9

RAIN SPLATTERED the hood of my Bronco while I waited at an Amoco station across from the Golden Lotus, watching a couple of strippers in black kimonos walking to their cars. To pass the time, I whistled along to Johnnie Taylor's *Wanted: One Soul Singer* album and examined a patch of hair I'd missed while shaving and emptied my truck's lockbox. I found a carton of Bazooka bubble gum, a spent Bic lighter, a dirty Scooby Doo coffee mug, a pair of red lace panties bought at a Clarence Carter concert, numerous cassette tapes, and a copy of *Texas Music* by Rick Koster. The book still had sauce stains from Stubb's in Austin.

I'd been waiting on Cook for the past hour and a half. Sure, I could leave, go back to the Peabody and watch reruns of *Josie and the Pussycats* on Cartoon Network. But what would that accomplish? Maybe Cook had told me to fuck off and *said* he didn't know anything. So what? I remembered trying to talk to this old man in Algiers a few years back and getting met at the front door with a shotgun. Man knew something about the death of blues legend Robert Johnson and I'd wanted his story pretty badly.

Getting a gun in the face was a lot worse than some jackass trying to be rude.

Cook had worked with Clyde James in 1968 and was rumored to have claimed the body. He had every answer I needed. So I'd wait it out and harass the son of a bitch until he told me what he knew. Loretta deserved that.

My gaze turned to a high pile of rusted cars in a nearby auto salvage yard and across the highway was a church built in a defunct stand-alone bank. IS THE DEVIL GETTIN' YOU DOWN? its small billboard read.

I answered under my breath: "Bet your ass."

I cracked the window to blow out smoke from my Marlboro Light. I'd just started re-examining the spot of hair on my cheek when I saw a purple Cadillac—looked to be brand-new with shiny chrome rims and white-walls—pull from behind the Golden Lotus and turn north toward the airport. I cranked the Bronco and followed.

I could see the top of Cook's gray spiky head through his rear window as he took Airways Boulevard north for what seemed like forever past fast-food franchises and pawnshops until the road turned into East Parkway. He cut west by Overton Park on Poplar then down Evergreen to Madison.

The whole way I watched Cook playing with his hair and performing neck exercises by pushing his head against his palm. Cook was so busy working himself out that he didn't notice the gunmetal-gray truck following his ugly-ass purple Cadillac across Midtown Memphis.

I just smiled—a wad of Bazooka now working in my back teeth—when he made a left turn into a Piggly Wiggly. Maybe I'd grab Cook in the frozen-food aisle and lock him inside a freezer until he gave it up.

I pulled into a parking space as Cook parked, got out, and strolled past the entrance to the grocery store—PORK TENDERLOINS $1.49 A POUND/SIX PACK OF DR PEPPER $1.99 painted across its plate glass windows. Cook kept walking beside a high brick wall and around a corner.

I decided to cut him off and drove back behind the store into an alley where men unloaded tractor trailers. I slowly pushed the brake, the Bronco's engine growling under the hood, and stuck the truck into neutral, gassing the motor, scanning the loading dock and back street. A couple of butchers in white shirts splattered with blood hung their legs off the dock and puffed on cigarettes. A homeless man pushed a shopping cart full of tin cans toward a Dumpster.

Maybe Cook had spotted me, doubled back, and was spinning away in the Cadillac right now. *Shit.*

As I turned the corner, rain splattering harder on my windshield, I caught a glimpse of Cook walking down a stairwell from an elevated brick enclosure next to the grocery store. He held a newspaper over his head and ran in a fast jog down to the store, where he ducked inside out of the rain.

I revved the motor again and wheeled toward the stairwell. I got out and bounded up the steps to a grassy hill. The hill looked as if it had once been part of a great mound cut away for the construction of the Piggly Wiggly.

I followed a narrow entranceway cut into a wall wrapping a large square of earth. Looked almost as if it had once been some type of garden. The ground was uneven and covered in grass. Old brown cords, tattered blue jeans, a single mattress, and numerous empty Miller and Colt 45 beer bottles were strewn on the ground. I almost tripped over a foam plate of molded chicken covered in maggots as rain beat into my eyes.

Thunder cracked in the distance.

I'd been in homeless camps before but couldn't quite figure out the purpose of the dirty garden until I saw the marble slab. DRURY LYON BETTIS— AUGUST 21, 1814, TO AUGUST 9, 1854. More toppled headstones and marble slabs were hidden among the heaps of trash.

Several plastic lighters lay upon a cracked slab in the far corner. I kicked away a dirty sheet that obscured its purpose. DANIEL HARKLECADE— JANUARY 15, 1803, TO APRIL 5, 1845.

The man had been buried beneath a quiet oak tree more than 150 years ago. Now he was spending time with crack addicts and the city's unwanted. I dropped to my knee and began clearing away the dirty bottles, cans, and a stray boot. I used the leg from a pair of discarded jeans to clean off the mud.

I scanned the uneven ground again, unsure what I wanted to find. I backed out of the cemetery surrounded by concertina wire and gang graffiti and walked into the Piggly Wiggly searching for Cook.

I found him in the fruits-and-vegetables section feeling up a softball-sized tomato and admiring his reflection in a long silver mirror that wrapped a far wall. The air was cold against my wet face. I stood next to him and picked up another tomato.

"You might need two," I said. "Yours looks a little small."

Cook looked over at me with lazy eyes, his wet gray hair metallic and false in the harsh fluorescent light. His jaw muscles twitched and I could see his hand wrap tighter around the tomato.

"Look, man, just help me out," I said.

Cook nodded and walked over to a huge pyramid of rattlesnake watermelons. He was trying to be cool, ignore me as if I were of no more importance than an unwanted itch. He even whistled along to some Muzak version of "LaBamba." I followed him, my hands in my Levi's jacket, and smiled.

"You tell me where he died and when and I'll leave."

Cook pulled out his pair of yuppie glasses and slipped them over his nose. He inspected a fat green watermelon and tucked it under his left arm. He was quiet for a moment and then ushered me close with a head movement.

I moved closer. He smelled like a wet dog. His breath of dead fish.

He whispered, "If you don't get the fuck out of my face in five seconds, I'm going to make a fuckin' hat out of your ass."

I smiled back.

"My ass would make a terrible hat."

"Then I'd get the fuck out of here."

"What's your problem?" I asked. "I told you, I'm a friend of Loretta Jackson. I'm sure you fucked her out of plenty of money back then, too, so why don't you—?"

"I treated her with respect, you little shit. Don't you even mention her name to me."

"She's my friend."

Cook snorted out a laugh.

"Clyde isn't dead. Is he?"

"Hell, yes, he's dead."

"Did you see him?"

"Yes."

"Where?"

Cook shoved the watermelon at my stomach like a medicine ball and tried to hook me with his left fist. As the watermelon splattered in a red mess on the floor, I ducked the punch and gripped the front of Cook's shirt, tossing him into a table piled high with okra. The okra scattered and an old woman with blue hair shrieked. A black woman with two kids pushed her cart away like she was escaping a nasty plague and an elderly man with no teeth wearing checked pants and a Bart Simpson T-shirt yelled, "Fight. It's a fight! Fight."

Cook, his feet dangling to the linoleum floor, grinned at me and for a moment I thought it was over, but he lunged, tackling me at the waist and driving me toward a pile of Georgia peaches. I felt my back smoosh into the pile and could smell the broken sweetness across it.

I quickly grabbed Cook into a headlock. Mother was strong, I thought, and I held his head tight in the crook of my arm before Cook punched me between the legs.

I fell to my knees, pain shooting through my entire body. I felt like I might vomit right there. Cook was laughing and walking away as I gathered my strength and rushed him and wrapped my right arm across his throat. I pushed Cook facefirst into a mound of tomatoes. The wet red mess covered his face and T-shirt like blood.

But damn if he wasn't smiling with red teeth as he picked up a handful of red goop, walked over to me, and rubbed it down the front of my white T-shirt.

I smiled over at the old man in the cartoon T-shirt and took a step back to grab a handful of muscadines.

I gripped the back of Cook's neck and force-fed him a mouthful.

That's when the shitstorm really started.

Cook punched me hard in the ear. I could hear a pop and the air went suddenly electric around me as I connected my two knuckles with Cook's nose. Blood squirted over his shirt and oozed down his lip. He made several jabs to my head and tried to kick out my knees.

Man knew how to fight.

But he was older and slower and I punched him in the ear, took hold of his arms, and threw him into the sweet potatoes. Cook rolled out onto the other side of the bins where plums dropped to the floor in heavy thuds.

A man in a green vest, who looked to be the manager, ran out and starting yelling that he'd called the police.

Cook didn't seem to hear him. He ran toward me, his eyes squinted and his fists face-high. He jabbed again, connecting once with my rib. I could feel the air rush from me as I made a jab to the left and punched Cook hard in the mouth.

"He's alive," I said, gasping for air. "He's alive and you're protecting him."

Cook made a grunt, his face turning purple, and made another run. He tackled me again at the waist, but this time he didn't have the energy to push me back.

I grabbed him at the scruff of his leathery neck and tossed him five yards away, his butt skidding on the floor covered in mushed tomatoes and muscodines.

The Muzak still played overhead through the odd silence that buzzed in my right ear. The manager held up a mop in his hand like it was a sword and he was fending off a pair of wild lions.

"Y'all stay right where you are," the manager said, his swooped comb-over sticking up like a rooster's.

Cook staggered to his feet, walked over to the man, and pulled out his wallet. He counted out four bills and jogged away. With my ear still ringing and my breath labored, I followed.

The parking lot shone with a patch of sunlight striking the pavement, steam rising in a low fog. I pulled a piece of tomato off my shirt and looked through the lot for the Cadillac.

I caught a quick glimpse of the hood as it fishtailed out to Madison, the tires squealing on wet asphalt.

I wanted to get back in my Bronco and haul ass back to the Peabody. I could just hear Randy's voice when he heard one of his professors had been arrested for a scuffle at a damned Piggly Wiggly.

But instead, I walked back up the stairs to the hidden cemetery and sat on the crooked grave of Daniel Harklecade. I smoked a Marlboro, studied the piles of garbage and makeshift beds, and watched a couple of homeless men as they ate cans of beans in the far corner of the lot.

I didn't hear a siren as the dark storm clouds swirled by in broken patterns. A slab of yellow light still beamed on the store.

The men didn't seem to notice me. Maybe I was so silent, so lithe, that they didn't feel my presence.

"Hey, cap'n," a craggy white man in a plaid hat finally yelled. His teeth were the color of old coffee. Beans dripped down off his chin.

"Sir?" I called back.

"Me and my buddy was wonderin' if you gonna sleep here? 'Cause if you is, it's gonna mean that we's maybe have to move on. You don't look real friendly."

I started another cigarette and peered back down on the lot, a stiff fall wind scattering oak leaves on the graves.

"Cap'n?"

"Yes?" I said, watching the cigarette burn between my fingers and feeling my labored breathing.

"You want some beans?"

"No, thanks."

"We ain't shittin' on your relatives or nothin'," the other man said, pulling off an old brogan and smelling it.

"Nope." I took a few breaths and pulled some tomatoes off my boot. "Hey man, you guys don't happen to know a man named Clyde James?"

"Yeah, we know *a* Clyde. Sleep here sometime."

"He'll be back?"

"Prolly down with Wordie," one said.

"Who's Wordie?"

"Some woman who kiss his ass," the man said, smelling his shoe again.

I took a final puff of the cigarette and pulled some soggy peach off my jacket. The man kept muttering, "She only like him 'cause she think he used to be somebody famous."

I smiled.

"You know where she lives?"

"Down in Dixie somewhere. You know, Dixie Homes. Where the po' folks stay."

Chapter 10

WHEN ABBY WAS eight years old, she used to sneak into the woods behind her parents' house in Oxford to make forts from small trees like the Indians once did. She'd read somewhere in a child's science book about how some tribe up north would bend little trees to the ground to make an arc. The Indians would then make a shell by covering the tree with more leafy branches to protect themselves from the wind and rain. When Abby made her little fort, she always chose the most remote location on her parents' land. She didn't want Maggie to find her, or her parents, or anyone. Inside, she'd kept simple things: an old broom to smooth the dirt floor, a few My Little Ponys, and her favorite book, *Where the Wild Things Are*.

Mostly she'd just hidden from everyone, beneath the branches listening to the birds and the rustle of squirrels, believing the animals would keep her secret. No one would know where she was. Abby was invisible and that had given her peace.

On the road with Ellie, Abby wondered if she'd ever know that same peace again as lightning cracked a veined pattern across the flat sky of northern Mississippi. Ellie sped through back hamlets to Oxford skirting the highway around Holly Springs. The leather of Ellie's car smelled fresh and new, and the hot coffee they bought at the truck stop made her think of home.

She took a deep breath and watched the weathered barns, trailer homes, and convenience stores whip by the car window. Her eyes felt heavy and she hugged her arms across her chest. Ellie was still rambling on about her latest boyfriend and some new restaurant on the Square that served crepes with strawberries. Abby wasn't listening and didn't really care. She was going home. She was leaving the woods.

"Son of a bitch," Ellie yelled, thumping the wheel of her car. "We're going to have to stop in a minute. I'm out of gas and about to pee in my pants."

The blacktop loped into a sharp curve before stretching into a brief straightaway and then cutting through a red mud hill. Ellie flicked on the stereo and started singing along with some old song about "boots made for walkin'."

" 'One of these days, these boots are gonna walk all over you,' " Ellie sang, beating out the fuzzy guitar on the wheel.

Abby tore open a Butterfinger she'd bought at the truck stop, tried to ignore the music, and said, "You still in school?"

"Yep," Ellie said. "You ever hear of a professional student?"

Abby nodded, taking a small bite. Orange crumbs dropping into her lap while Ellie punched the car up to about seventy.

Abby's fingers clawed into the leather of the seats. White lights in the buildings shot by almost as if they were in a dark tunnel. Rain splattered her windshield and in the headlights the highway asphalt looked like glass.

"So you met Maggie through your boyfriend?"

"Yep."

"Who is that?"

"Jamie Jensen."

"Don't know him."

"He was a backup quarterback a couple years back, now he's a bouncer at the High Point."

Abby laughed. "For Raven?"

Ellie nodded in the passing light of the road and mashed the accelerator up to eighty-five. Everyone knew Raven "Son" Waltz. At twenty-eight, he was the biggest dope supplier for most of Oxford and north Mississippi. Kid had black eyes and dirty fingernails and ran this cinder block roadhouse at the county line where you could drink on Sunday.

Ellie's fingers rolled over the steering column and the back wheels slightly fishtailed turning a corner. Suddenly, a deer sauntered out to the middle of the road and Abby shut her eyes tight as Ellie took the car up onto the muddy shoulder, punched the accelerator again, and careened around the animal.

"Jesus," Abby said. "Could you slow it down a little?"

"I told you, I have to pee. All this water is pushing at me."

Ellie slowed the car and turned down the stereo as a song came on about a bad dude named Tony Rome.

"Abby, I hate to ask this, darlin', but do the police know what happened to your parents?"

"Police say they were robbed."

"You believe 'em?"

A tow truck barreled toward them in the passing lane and cut back about twenty yards ahead. Ellie gave a short burst of the horn but otherwise seemed to ignore the fact she'd almost crashed.

"No," Abby said.

"What do you think happened?"

Abby shrugged.

"Was your father workin' on anything?"

"Look, Ellie, I get real sick to my stomach when I talk about this."

"Sure, sure." Ellie smiled and patted her thigh. "It's just that sometimes holdin' on to somethin' so tight can make you sick inside. You know? Holdin' on to things that aren't healthy. I saw this movie one time where this man got real sick. I think cancer or somethin'. I'm not sure. Well, anyway, he goes to see this Chinese fella. You know really wise and old? Well, the Chinese fella tells him the sickness was caused by holding on to negative things. All the bad stuff he knew in his life lived in his insides."

Abby watched the front of the car swallow the yellow passing lines, the soft blue glow of the car's console lulling her to sleep. She turned away from Ellie, tucked her hands under her ear and stared out her window. A sickness passed through her like it was eating her insides. She could feel it like acid dripping through her heart and liver, yellow and burning. She shut her eyes as tight as she could.

A few minutes later, the car slowed, turned off the highway, and bumped along a dirt road before stopping. Abby opened her eyes, pellets of rain rolling down the passenger-side window. Outside, there was a 1940s gas station with those tall glass pumps rusting underneath a drooping overhang. The doors were sunbleached and padlocked. Windowpanes broken.

"Ellie?"

"Hold up, doll, just need to use the little girl's room."

"I don't think . . ."

But she was gone and skirting around the edge of the old gas station. Abby stretched and looked across the highway to see if she recognized anything. A bright orange and red glow broke through some leafless trees as wind scattered pieces of loose trash across the window. The radio played some more of Ellie's oldies.

Abby bit a piece of cuticle and turned down the stereo.

A few minutes passed and finally she opened the door, stood on the frame, and searched through the woods. She called Ellie's name three times. Her heart began to beat strongly in her ears and even though it was cool, she could feel a bead of sweat run down the back of her neck.

"Ellie!"

She left the car door open, a warning bell sounding, and walked beneath the gas station overhang. Weeds grew at the base of a rotting gutter and a double-sided STP sign clacked against a rusted drum of oil.

The weeds ate past her sneakers and the bright light cutting through the darkness reminded her of dawn. A motorcycle whizzed by. The car's warning bell kept sounding.

Abby skirted the corner of the store, loping down a red mud hill, rich with the storm's runoff. The afternoon was almost electric in the rainy blue-gray light.

"Ellie?"

Abby heard the sound of skittering around the back edge of the building. Her breath came labored through her nose and she felt a dampness underneath her arms. A man's voice mumbled somewhere deep into a patchy pine forest where branches clacked together like bamboo.

"Ellie?"

A piece of wood splintered.

Feet shuffled faster now.

Abby bolted back up the muddy embankment to the car. About halfway up the little hill, she heard an approaching car. Almost to the top, her feet gave out in the orange mud sending her sliding, fingernails clawing into the earth.

She could taste the iron-rich mud in her mouth and feel the dirt piercing deep under her nails. She pressed her palms flat against the hill and dug her sneakers into the ground.

A hand gripped the back of her sweatshirt.

She screamed.

She kicked at the head of a man in a black ski mask but he only gripped her ankle tighter. She kicked again and broke free and scrambled more, her breath working in her dry mouth.

At the top, another man in a mask grabbed her by her sweatshirt, twisted the muzzle of a gun into her ear, and pushed her back to Ellie's car.

Two minutes later, they'd thrown her into the trunk and skidded out. In the weak red glow of the taillights, Abby said her first prayer in months.

Chapter 11

DIXIE HOMES, one of Memphis's oldest public housing projects, stood tired and beaten not far from an insane asylum and a record store once frequented by Elvis Presley. I recognized the projects almost instantly because of an article I'd read in *Rolling Stone* about some rappers who'd been raised there. Name was hard to forget. But these projects weren't even close to being as decrepit and mean as those in New Orleans. They were old but clean and reminded me of the stories I'd heard about what public housing used to be like in the 'fifties. Dixie Homes consisted of several rows of two-story red brick units separated by a common area filled with blackened barbecue pits made from oil drums cut in half, rusted dime-store sun chairs, and clotheslines stretched taught from crooked metal crosses. Through the common areas, tattered clothes dried in the weak fall sun that had replaced the rain.

I parked near Poplar and walked through the projects asking anyone I saw if they knew a woman named Wordie. Didn't feel uncomfortable or uneasy. Most people in the projects were a hell of a lot friendlier than those you'd meet in those yuppie cracker box apartments that lined Metairie. Shit, this was a community. I knew I'd find Wordie within ten minutes. People here actually knew each other. Had to if they wanted to survive. About five minutes later, a little old black woman with enormous—almost Jackie O–sized—sunglasses carrying a walker pointed to the next street over. Said Wordie had a Santy Claus on her porch.

I thanked her, popped a couple of fresh pieces of Bazooka in my mouth, and walked up the winding hill where yellow, red, and brown leaves scattered over me like ticker tape.

I soon saw the plastic Santa Claus, black and carrying a fat sack, standing by a corner unit. A crushed Coke can and stray headless Barbie doll lay at the foot of the Santa like discarded presents. I knocked on the worn wood of the screen door.

At the top of the hill, a group of teens lingered by a convenience store pay phone waiting to sell crack to white kids from the suburbs. At the base of the hill, two black children dressed in starched school uniforms walked by my Bronco carrying backpacks heavy laden with books.

Just as I was about to look in the window, the door swung open revealing one of the largest women I'd ever seen. Even larger than the woman at Wild Bill's. This woman could kick her ass. Her arms were the size of my thighs. Her thighs were as large as my waist. She wore a heavy scowl upon her lips as if she'd been waiting for me to show up all day so she could vent all her problems upon me.

"Hello, ma'am."

She had on a tight black muscle T-shirt, black biker shorts, and pink Jelly shoes. Her hair had been woven and dyed into a mismatched pattern of yellow and red braids. I wanted to ask her where in the hell she got size-forty biker pants.

I didn't. I was scared.

"You Wordie?"

"Maybe. Who the fuck is you?"

"A friend of Clyde's."

She crossed her arms over her massive breasts, the left one adorned with a tattoo of a red rose.

"His sister's trying to find him."

"Listen, I got to go," she said, trying to close the door. I could hear the chatter of Oprah Winfrey inside.

"What's Oprah talkin' about today?"

Wordie gave me a frown. "Oh, I don't know. Some woman givin' advice to women whose got husbands that peckers don't work."

"You married?"

"Hell no," she said, giving a little laugh, then catching herself and then trying to close the door again.

"His sister Loretta sent me."

Wordie put her hands on her massive hips and said, "You know Loretta Jackson?"

"She's family."

"Hmm."

"She's *like* family."

"Really?"

I nodded.

"C'mon in," she said, leaving the wood door to batter the frame. I followed her inside to Oprah and the smell of smoked meat and greens.

The greens were great. Firm and salty, but with that smoky flavor that tasted like home and JoJo's and everything I valued. I liked Wordie, and for the moment Wordie seemed to like me. Well, she acted like she liked me in between commercials and *Oprah*—which did truly feature stories about men whose peckers didn't work—as she showed me old brown vinyl picture albums containing clippings on Clyde James that dated back to 1964 and his work in gospel.

"Do you think I could borrow this sometime?" I asked. "Would love to make copies of these articles."

She looked at me, her face pinched tight, and then back at the television.

I turned back to the newspaper clippings that were yellowed and worn thin from constant reading. I flipped to a page with an article whose headline read WIFE OF NEGRO MUSICIAN EXECUTED. I slowly read the story, the page smelling like mothballs and silverfish:

MEMPHIS—Police discovered the bodies of two Negroes early Sunday morning in what detectives are calling an apparent execution.

The victims have been identified as Mary James, 29, and Eddie Porter, 33. James is the wife of Clyde James, a local singer. Porter played organ in James' band, said Bobby Lee Cook, owner Bluff City Records.

According to Detective Ray Jenkins, Memphis Police Department, the bodies were found at the James' home, 433 Rosewood Ave. about 10 A.M. Both had suffered gunshot wounds to the back of the head.

Jenkins would not say if the department had any suspects. No arrests have been made.

Cook said Clyde James has reached national success with a recent chart topper called "Lonely Street." He said James was devastated when he learned of the death of his wife and friend. Cook said the singer is with family and members of the First Zion Church.

"Eddie Porter was one of the finest musicians I've ever known and will be greatly missed by everyone in the Memphis's recording industry," Cook said.

As a police siren wailed in the distance, I took a deep breath and looked at the mildewed walls of Wordie's apartment. Behind her couch, there was a mosaic of album covers and framed publicity stills of Clyde James. News from *Billboard* and press releases from Bluff City. Clyde James with a palm pressed against his thoughtful face and Clyde James wearing a smile of confidence that betrayed the dark depression.

I felt Wordie walk behind me. I could hear her breathing in the worn room and knew she wasn't staring at me but at her fallen hero. Sunlight broke into the room and covered my face with momentary warmth.

"I tried to get him help, mister. I tried."

"He's alive."

She didn't answer.

I didn't turn to face her, afraid that seeing my eyes would only make her skittish.

"I need to find him," I said.

"He doesn't want help," she said. "People always take him away from me. But he come back. He always come back. This is where he need to be. I know what Clyde needs. He needs love. That's it."

A new show blared from the television, this one about cheating wives and double-crossing and there was a lot of whoops and hollering. She picked up my bowl of greens and walked back to the kitchen.

She only had an old sofa covered in a faded flowered bedspread, one dinette set chair, and a coffee table made of concrete blocks and a piece of warped wood. In the center sat a milk crate that overflowed with envelopes. Must've been dozens of them. Most were marked URGENT in huge red letters.

Wordie waddled back and stood in front of the television and sighed.

"I usually don't do this," I said. "But the most I can give you is a hundred bucks."

She looked back over her shoulder, smoothed the biker pants over her thighs, and licked her lips.

"I've got to find him," I said.

Her face became a mixture of relief and apprehension.

"You say you know Loretta?"

"You can call her if you like," I said.

She looked at the worn linoleum floor and shook her head. A pot in the kitchen rang every few seconds with leaking rainwater.

I reached into my wallet and pulled out five twenties, pretty much my budget for the next few days after treating myself to the Peabody.

I mashed the twenties into her waiting hand. It was oddly small but calloused and warm.

"Lots of folks been lookin' for him," she said. "Lots of folks don't need to find him."

"Like who?"

"People who don't want to do him no good," she said, tucking the money between the thick roll of fat on her waist and the tight pants. "I tole him about the men comin' to see me a few weeks back. And he say he's gone and ain't seen him 'round since. You can go look for yourself, but ain't gonna do you no good. He took off."

"Was he living in that homeless camp 'round Piggly Wiggly?"

She nodded.

"Where else would he go?"

"Don't know."

I nodded at Wordie. Thoughtfully. Deliberately. *You can trust me.*

I asked, "Who was looking for him?"

"Big old dudes with muscles," she said. "I git 'em if they come back."

"How you going to do that?"

"I ain't stupid," she said. "When they was leavin' I wrote down their damned tag number."

Twenty minutes later, after waiting for a call back to a pay phone at a Popeye's on Poplar, I got an answer. The car was a black Lincoln registered to a casino in Tunica, Mississippi, called the Magnolia Grand.

Just thirty miles south on Highway 61.

Chapter 12

UNTIL A FEW YEARS AGO, Tunica was known as the poorest city in the poorest county in the poorest state in the whole nation. Jesse Jackson once called it the Ethiopia of America. Now it's the third largest gambling mecca behind Las Vegas and Atlantic City. A damned county whose only hope for the future was catfish and cotton now has marquees with tiny white lights advertising loose slots and off-Broadway shows.

The late evening sky seemed lower and harder here than in Memphis, I noticed as I drove south along Highway 61 listening to the North Mississippi All-Stars jamming their version of K. C. Jones, *a mighty man dead and gone*. The horizon burned a bright orange, yellow, and blue leaving the tin-roofed farmhouses bleeding with rust and kudzu-covered trees, growing brown, in broken shadows.

Farm supply stores soon gave way to pawnshops and liquor stores blazing with neon. Old diners turned to outlet malls. It was as if George Bailey's nightmare of Pottersville had descended on the Mississippi Delta.

I could feel the needle pricks of a fall chill through the open windows of my Bronco and smell the burning rows of dead leaves outside battered trailers and prefab homes. Agriplanes sat parked outside small hangars while rusted Oldsmobiles and Buicks stood restless outside tired motels.

The horizon soon turned an inky purple and then black. I saw lights flash far from the highway in an image that reminded me of that huge UFO from *Close Encounters*. About a mile from the highway, purple, green, blue, and pink neon blinked and shined in the darkness.

I turned the truck onto a wide, circular drive, lit with staggered wrought-iron street lamps and drove toward a four-story monstrosity that ran the length of three football fields. Intermittent white lights wrapped this faux antebellum building like a Christmas package. A fountain the size of a decent bass pond stood before the casino with about a dozen water jets zapping ten feet into the air.

Magnolia Grand. When I went back to change my clothes at the Peabody, a woman at the desk told me the place boasted about six hundred rooms, eight restaurants, a championship golf course, a skeet shooting center, and a casino with a thousand slots. She said it was "Vegas quality." As if Vegas was a measurement of quality.

The Grand looked like a carnival's midway crossed with a convention center. About the silliest thing about these places was that Mississippi law said all casinos had to be on water. So in Tunica, developers dug a channel from the Mississippi River for each casino to have its own private moat.

Man, I hated these places. They were the opposite of everything I loved about the Delta. Dozens of casinos had been built on the same rich, brown earth worked by sharecroppers for generations. Hell, Robert Johnson grew up about ten miles away. But not much had changed. The people of this county were now as shackled to the casinos as generations before them had been to the land.

I continued driving past a couple of hotels, midget versions of the main casino, and into a large parking lot filled with pickup trucks and weathered sedans. The crickets and cicadas whooped it up in the endless cotton fields while a maroon harvest moon hung low over a clearing of mimosa trees.

Amid some lite crappy jazz that played from hidden speakers, I walked over the drawbridge and into the casino. I strolled over green carpet embroidered with gold magnolia leaves as the sound of falling coins and laughing women echoed around me.

Revolving gold signs read CARIBBEAN-STYLE POKER and SUPER BLACK-JACK.

I found a bar near the blackjack tables, sat down, and ordered a Dixie and a hamburger. I hadn't eaten since breakfast, except for the bit of greens, and my stomach had been talking to me since the Tennessee border. Wasn't a bad place to sit and get familiar with the surroundings. Maybe rest a little before I tried to find who ran security. Ask him a few questions about why the casino would be looking for a homeless man who didn't have a penny to gamble.

I watched an old black man in a flannel shirt, a dangling cigarette in hand, punch a plastic cup of quarters into a slot as if a week's worth of groceries was a spin away. His ancient work boots were coated in blackened Mississippi mud.

The bartender was a wiry white woman with long cherry-red nails and tight permed hair. She was probably in her early forties but had the look like she'd been rode hard and put up wet plenty of nights.

I thanked her for the Dixie and listened to the casino action—a steady beat of applause and crestfallen groans from the roulette wheel, a pinging Casio keyboard-type music beeping from the slots. As I prayed for the hamburger and studied a new gash on the toe of my boot, a woman with an unnaturally large chest and a helmet of blond hair sat beside me.

She gave me one of those smiles when the tongue gets caught between the upper and lower teeth. Her body wasn't bad, but her breasts were so obviously aftermarket that they almost made me laugh.

The woman tosseled her hair and sighed. *Actually tosseled it. Amazing. Maybe she'd do the trick with the tongue over the teeth again.*

"What's your name, partner?" she asked, making her eyes go soft.

"Tom Mix."

"Let me guess: You're not here to play poker."

I kept smiling and watched the woman, who had a hard time keeping a steady gaze as she rocked back and forth. Her breath smelled like a whiskey barrel.

"What do you play?" she asked.

"Mousetrap," I said. "I'm a damned fine Mousetrap player. But I still have a hard time with that spindly bucket thing, always falls down when you least expect it."

She rolled her eyes and cackled without a clue.

"So, Tom," she said, running her hands over the worn knees of my 501s. "You need a date for the night?"

She had on some kind of lacey white bra, more than the Fruit of the Loom type. This contraption had a thick front buckle and little blue flowers on the cups. I coughed and looked away.

"Actually here on business," I said.

"What room are you in?" she asked.

"Don't have a room."

"You have a car?" she said.

Ahh. Ain't ego a funny thing? I thought I was so damned handsome in my black T-shirt and faded jeans that she couldn't resist. I wondered how much she cost.

"Nope," I said. "Just a moped. And it doesn't even have a seat."

She snorted out her nose. No laugh. She turned her head away and flipped back her hair. I looked at the worn bartender, shrugged, and then back at the blonde. She was smooth and pressed but in another five years she'd be just as hard, battered, and tired.

I pulled her hand from my knee as the bartender plunked down a soggy-looking hamburger and cold fries. The meat looked almost like cardboard. I glanced over at the blonde and gave her a wink.

"Want some fries?" I asked, shoving a couple into my mouth.

"Go fuck yourself," she said and almost fell as she got off the barstool.

"Be cheaper," I muttered as I hit the sweet spot on the Heinz bottle.

About ten seconds later, the bartender wandered over and settled her elbows down on the table. She watched the woman walk away with a gentle smile on her lips. The pinging from the slots grew louder in my ears.

"Who runs security around here?" I asked.

"You lookin' for work?" she asked in a hard, north Mississippi accent.

"Maybe," I said.

"Black fella named Humes," she said. "Office is in the lobby."

Abby's ride lasted for about an hour, bumping and jostling her all over the oil-soaked rubber mats in the trunk. When the car finally stopped, a man stuck a pillowcase over her head and stabbed a gun into her ribs. She saw patterns of lights and shapes through the cloth as the man moved his calloused hands over her butt and breasts before throwing her onto some cold concrete and slamming the door.

She tore the pillowcase from her head and began beating on the door and screaming for help. She must've beaten on that door for a half hour before she dropped to the ground, wiped her face with her hands, and looked around.

The room was about ten by ten and filled with stacks of dusty blackjack tables and slot machines. A craps table and old roulette wheel sat by the door. Concrete walls and ceiling. She couldn't hear a sound outside and it was hot as hell. No air-conditioning. Almost like a sauna, she thought, as she moved the hair from her face and tucked it behind her ears.

She felt the scrapes on her elbows and spit out a trail of blood from her broken lip onto the dirty floor. She thought about Ellie and that long stretch of woods behind the gas station while she hugged her knees to her chest and began to cry. She could imagine the men grabbing Ellie and shoving her into the molded leaves. They raped her. She could see them straddling Ellie and choking her. Abby tried to block the thoughts from her mind, knowing it was her fault whatever happened to Ellie.

She heard footsteps approach and closed her eyes as tight as she could. She was away from this place. She was back in Oxford and her parents were alive and Maggie was there.

A bolt slid back with a hard clack.

Two men entered the room. One was a thin white guy about her age with slick black hair and the other was an old black man with gray hair. Both carried guns and wore blue blazers and red ties. Radios squawked on their hips.

"C'mon, let's go," the black man said. He had freckles and high cheek-bones like an Indian. Mean eyes.

"Leave me alone," Abby yelled. "Where the hell am I? Who the hell are you?"

"C'mon. He wants to see you."

The black man grabbed the front of her shirt and yanked her to her feet. He twisted her arm behind her back and pushed her into a concrete tunnel. She gritted her teeth in pain—her shoulder screaming loose in the socket—as they marched her through the narrow passageway. The tunnel took several twists through a dozen curves with fluorescent lights beaming overhead.

At the end of another tunnel, the boy opened a side door into an office with dark wood paneling and dimly lit with Tiffany lamps. The shades looked as if they were cut from shards of colorful hard candy.

The black man shoved her onto a brown leather coach.

When she straightened her head, she gazed right into a shadow sitting in a leather chair. He was hard to see. His features were obscured by bright light and smoke from a cigar. She could see the orange glow of the butt and hear his rapid, uneven breath.

"Hello, Miss MacDonald." His voice country and weathered. Someone who drank too much bourbon and had smoked since he was ten.

She tasted the blood in her mouth and heard the dull sound of locks pinging in the concrete room where they'd kept her. She tried to squint through the hot light.

"You got to be tired," he said.

Abby could hear her own breath now. Way too fast.

"Haven't stopped since the death of your parents."

Abby bit into the side of her cheek and listened.

"Truck stops, cheap-ass motels. Always wondered, why the highway? Why not the beach? Or another country? You like bein' anonymous? You like blending in?"

Abby felt the blood heating in her chest. *This was it. This was it.* "What the hell do you want?" she yelled. It was someone else's voice. Someone stronger.

Above them there was a buzz of laughter and the sound of electronic bells. More laughter. Heavy footsteps.

"We need some help finding something belonging to your father."

Her duffel bag sat open on his desk and her dirty underwear on the floor. She felt naked and embarrassed.

"You killed them. Didn't you? You goddamned son of a bitch."

"Help us find what we need. And let your parents die with grace."

She saw his hands reach for the bag and pull it from view. The light was so bright that even when she squinted she couldn't make out his features. A blue halo pulsed in her vision.

"Where does your daddy keep his papers?" he asked.

She shook her head. "You're just gonna kill me anyway."

"Nope. I don't kill little girls. I just make 'em bleed and hurt like hell till they tell me what I want."

Abby stared down at her hands. She breathed quick, her heart ticking. She began to pray silently again. It was the prayer she'd said the entire way in the car about appreciating every second the Lord gave her.

"Abby?"

She kept her eyes on her hands. She felt the gentle stroke of fingers across the back of her neck.

"Go on," the man said to someone behind her. "Y'all have your fun."

Out of the darkness two people walked between her and the man. One was the older black man with freckles. The other was Ellie.

At least it seemed like Ellie. In Abby's scattered vision, the face and the body were the same. But she looked different and held herself in an unusual way. She even seemed to breathe like another person as she studied Abby with squinting eyes.

"Shall we go get this filthy bitch cleaned up?" Ellie asked.

The door to the security office was closed and I was about to walk back to the lobby when a black woman dressed in maid coveralls sauntered by and jiggled a set of keys in her pocket. She opened the door.

I followed.

The office was tiny with a cheap desk and seascape prints hanging on the walls. Besides the smell of stale cigarettes, you couldn't tell if the place was ever used. No loose papers on the desk. No bulletin boards. No appointment calendars.

"You know where I can find Humes?" I asked.

The woman jumped as if touched by a live wire. Her face was round and flat. Reddish brown skin.

"Sorry," I said, my palms outstretched to show I was cool. Didn't mean her any harm. "Lookin' for my old buddy Mr. Humes."

"*Shiiit*," she said. She was very old and very short. Didn't even come up to my chest. "You up to no good."

"No, ma'am."

"Yes, you is." She smiled. "What you wantin' Humes fer? He fucked up again?"

I smiled back.

"You gonna kick his ass?"

"Just want to talk to him."

She looked up at me and studied my eyes. She squinted one eye and then patted me on the arm. "C'mon, he ain't never in here. But don't you be tellin' him how you found him."

She left the office door open and led me down a long hallway to a metal door by an emergency exit. Hundreds of tourist pamphlets sat in a nearby bin. Everything from Graceland to the Delta Blues Museum in Clarksdale.

The woman unlocked the metal door and held it wide open.

"Go on," she said. "Last door on the left. That's where he sit at, pickin' his ass and lookin' at *Playboys*."

I leaned down to the short old woman and kissed her on the cheek.

Ever since the truck stop, Perfect had had the uncontrollable desire to scrub Abby MacDonald clean. She stank. She smelled of body odor and gasoline and coffee breath. She had stubble underneath her arms and probably had long hair growing on her legs. Her eyebrows were unkempt and long cuticles grew over her nails. How could she live like that? How could she even think this was acceptable?

Perfect hated everything about the girl. She hated her greasy dirty-blond hair and her unmade face and her sinewy little body. Probably some kind of runner or athletic freak. Abby wasn't curvy. The girl didn't understand that women were supposed to be full and rounded.

In the concrete room, Perfect studied Abby. The way her head hung down in her hands, the mud splattered on her wide-legged jeans, and those awful running shoes. And, God, how she wouldn't shut up. The little girl kept on crying and calling her Ellie and asking her to disappear.

Perfect, now dressed in hip-hugger cords and a white T-shirt with a sequin heart, moved closer to the girl and watched her cry. Humes sat on top of a blackjack table, a gun on his hip, drinking a cup of coffee. That bastard was waiting for the show to begin. *Oh, well, guess she'd have to deliver.*

Perfect grabbed a good handful of greasy hair from Abby's head and pulled her to the stainless-steel tub. She tore the horrible-smelling T-shirt from her body and told her to take off those dirty jeans or die.

The girl kept sobbing but did what she said, lightly pulling them down over her knees, shaking.

Perfect knew the girl was expecting rape or some kind of sexual kicks from them. Instead, Perfect shoved her stinking ass down in the tub filled with scalding water. The girl, just wearing white bra and panties, pressed her back to the wall and covered her breasts with folded arms.

Perfect shook her head, put on a pair of Latex gloves, and lathered up a loofah.

She pulled up Abby's armpit and began her long overdue cleansing process.

The room at the end of the hall was more than just an additional office. Think *Mission Impossible* crossed with *Dr. Strangelove*. At least thirty black-and-white televisions showing various scenes from the casino were arranged along a gray cinder block wall. One had a closeup of the blackjack dealer's hands and another showed some kind of warehouse where men unloaded an eighteen-wheeler. A narrow desk with microphones and a couple of rolling chairs sat close to the monitors. A coffee mug stamped with the Magnolia Grand logo and a crumpled pack of cigarettes lay on the desk.

I felt the mug. Still hot.

I took a seat in the chair and picked up the October *Playboy* sitting by the mug. Girls of the SEC and some pretty lame music reviews. I skipped past the reviews and some kind of rich man's guide to stereo gadgets and went right to this month's centerfold before leaning back in the chair and studying the wall of televisions.

A woman stood by a slot machine picking her nose and a young Hispanic boy was sitting on his father's shoulders as the man danced in a disco. Two security guards hung out on the hood of a Pontiac, smoking cigarettes and talking shit.

"Hey," someone said. "What the fuck are you doing back here?"

Perfect ran a towel over Abby's reddened skin, the dirt scrubbed away with the hard loofah. The girl was crying because she'd gotten a little chapped and was bleeding. How else was Perfect supposed to get that stench away? God, that girl smelled so rotten and awful.

Humes had his gun pointed at the girl's chest and licked his lips looking at her wet bra and chest. He smoothed his hands over her little stomach, soaking in the control he felt. Perfect smacked the gun away, told him to go back to his seat, and bound Abby's wrist with handcuffs to a metal water pipe.

The girl now lay lengthwise on an elevated bed the casino used to give guest in-room massages. Abby was still crying and bleeding when Perfect dripped the hot wax into the girl's armpits and spread it with a plastic spatula.

"Abby, don't worry, I'll take care of you. You'll be fresh and smelling like honeysuckle when we let you go. Don't worry," she said, caressing Abby's face in her hands. "You and me will be just fine."

Perfect spread strips of cotton paper on her armpits, smoothing it in the direction the hair grew. She held Abby's face in her hands, feeling the blubbering and whimpering, as she quickly ripped the paper backward, taking away a thick collection of dark hairs by the root.

Abby screamed and cried more.

"I remember the first time my mother made me get all dolled up," Perfect said. "I was eight. She made me sit in a hot bath till my toes turned to prunes, and then rolled me in baby powder. She put gobs of blue eyeliner on me, painted my lips fire-engine red, and dressed me in my Sunday sailor suit. Told me I had to look right for my uncle. Said he liked sweet little girls. Are you sweet, Miss Abby? Are you my sweet little girl?"

The girl coughed and then spit right into Perfect's eye. Perfect just smoothed away the spit and poured more of that hot yellow wax into Abby's armpit. Abby was yelling and screaming and kicking now.

Perfect nodded over to Humes and they tied her legs to the table with some torn bed sheets. She used a short piece to gag the girl. Didn't even know this was good for her.

She applied the wax and another strip just like she was taught and ripped it back away. Abby screamed a muffled scream, her eyes reddened and full of tears.

Perfect found a comb from her purse and then started roughly pulling away the tangles from the girl's wet hair. She whistled a little bit as she worked.

She liked to feel good about helping someone be clean.

I turned to the door where I saw a kid in his early twenties with slick black hair, wearing a blue blazer and khaki pants.

"Sent back here to see Mr. Humes," I said.

"No one told me," the kid said.

"Are you Mr. Humes?" I asked.

"No," the kid said, studying my face.

"Then maybe that's the reason."

"Nobody likes a smart-ass," the kid said.

"You'd be surprised," I said.

The kid's jaw muscles twitched and he grabbed a radio at his hip.

"You stay here, buddy," the kid said. "Don't leave."

I made a pistol with my thumb and forefinger and dropped the hammer. The kid shook his head and walked back down the hall.

Maybe Humes didn't handle collections or maybe they'd already found Clyde. Or maybe I was wasting my fucking time. At least this was better than sitting in my warehouse in New Orleans rearranging vinyl.

I walked over to the cooler and poured some water into a paper cup. Really was pretty cool the way they had all these monitors set up. I laughed at some white dude in a white suit trying to dance and at some old lady who was beating the shit out of a losing slot.

I was about to turn back to the Girls of the SEC when something in the far right corner of the monitors caught my eye.

The scene wasn't in the main casino. Looked like it was in some storage area with cinder block walls filled with old slots. Two people talking.

A woman leaned over a young girl who was lying down on a long table. I stood and walked toward the screen, transfixed and sickened by what I saw.

The girl was almost naked and tied down. Her arms were cuffed above her head to a water main and her legs were attached to the table by some kind of strips of cloth. Her loose hair fell into her eyes and she was twisting her head away from the woman's face. I could feel my heart pound faster and heated adrenaline shoot through my body. The woman mashed a revolver in the girl's eye as she poured something down the length of her legs.

Below the monitor was an imprinted plastic tag reading #102.

Chapter 13

PERFECT LEIGH WANTED to tear into Abby's cuticles so bad that her temples throbbed, but the little girl was flailing about and screaming so much that it'd be tough. Maybe she could work on her hands with them still attached to the water pipe, she thought, as she tore off another strip of hair from Abby's leg causing another muffled scream and another laugh from Humes. He was really getting his jollies watching a young girl twisting about her in her little undies. Sick bastard.

Hmm. It seemed the heaviest concentration of blond hair was on Abby's calves, but that would come off with just a quick spread of wax and a flick of the wrist. Perfect stopped for a moment, pulled Abby's wet, now-detangled hair into a ponytail, and stood back to admire her work.

Yes, there were possibilities. Her armpits were clean and her legs were almost done. She'd work on the cuticles next and then apply the makeup. Perfect found a long strip of what looked like stubborn hair and loosened the gag around Abby's mouth. "Just a word, darlin,'" Perfect said. "Just a word. Where did your daddy keep those papers? Y'all have a bank? Or does he have a hidden safe at his office? Come on. You're about all clean and then we gonna have to start li'l things that are much, much nastier. Mr. Humes over there is kind of kinky, too."

Humes smiled, gave a short bow, and walked out the door. He'd be back. He'd be back because he didn't think Perfect could handle getting what they needed. She looked down at Abby who was turning kind of a bluish color.

Perfect traced her bare white belly with the pistol and watched her try to stretch from her bound hands and legs. "All right, girl, your choice. I would like to put you in a nice little black dress before he starts. And we'll have to burn that nasty T-shirt and jeans you got."

She put down the gun for a moment on a stack of clean white towels and concentrated looping sticky gobs of wax up under the girl's calves as she hummed along. "You're going to be so pretty, Abby. Don't you worry, I'll make sure you are the belle of the ball before you take that last breath."

I ran through the twisted concrete corridors searching for the room I'd seen from the monitor. Everything I'd come for seemed unimportant now. A girl was strapped to a table with a gun to her head. Hell, I didn't know what I'd do if I found her. Kick in the door, pull a fire alarm. Something. I couldn't just stand back and let everything shake out.

Jesus. Most of the room numbers were out of sequence. And most of the ones I looked into were storage filled with cans for vending machines, stacks of toilet paper, or new towels.

Just as I thought I was getting close, hearing my boots clacking on the hard concrete floor, the number jumped from ninety-nine to one hundred eleven. *Shit.* I ran back down the corridor, searching, but the hall was a dead end.

Suddenly, I heard another set of footsteps running down the tunnel and pressed myself close to the wall. A black man in a suit jogged past me, staring straight ahead. I took a deep breath and when I couldn't hear footsteps anymore, I continued the search.

The next tunnel was dank and bare and the floor muddied with footprints. I was about to turn back when I heard something at the far end. Sounded like the feral cries of a wounded animal.

Abby tried to focus away from the pain. With each rip of her hair, she could feel numbness spread throughout her body. She tried to concentrate on that, imagining the dead feeling coat her skin in a protective layer. She bit down on the cloth gagging her mouth again and tried not to scream as the woman worked on her back legs, pulling more hair out by the roots.

She'd never felt such sharp pain in her life. She bit down harder on the cloth, tears streaming down her cheeks.

"My sweet little girl," Ellie said, playing with the edge of a gun in her ear. "Get it all out. Purge yourself of all that filth in your mind. Were you

Daddy's little girl? Is that it? You know Daddy died for something that wasn't his business."

Abby wished Ellie would just shoot her and be done with it. She'd never tell them about the little safe in her father's office, the files she'd found there, or even utter a damned word. This is what happened to her father and she'd let the damned thing rot in that nasty truck stop before she'd say a word to these freaks. She closed her eyes and concentrated away from the pain. They could poke at her some more, rape her, or dump her body into the Mississippi. She didn't care.

"You are filthy," Ellie said. Then she matched her screams with Abby. "Come on!"

She slammed the pistol against Abby's ear, carefully placed it back with the towels, and pulled some makeup from her purse. Abby flexed her body, tied at both ends, and turned her head to the door as it flew open.

The girl was tied to some type of elevated bench. A tall blond woman, who looked like she should be showing cars on *The Price Is Right*, stood over her with a makeup brush in her hand. She seemed frozen, caught in mid-act.

I walked to the table, the metal door slamming shut behind me. The woman didn't move. The girl's eyes stayed trained on me while I circled the bench and saw a gun lying across a pile of towels.

The girl was in her early twenties, blond and petite, and wearing nothing but white panties and a bra. I had the sudden thought that maybe I'd walked in on someone's private game. That maybe among all the piles of blackjack tables and roulette tables, that people came back here to get off.

But then I noticed the tears and the reddened skin. Piles of cotton strips with human hair sat on a pile between the girl's legs. I thought I could smell urine.

I lunged for the gun and the woman reached as well. But I had the jump and pushed her to the ground as she rammed into my chest with her head. She grabbed my leg, but I kicked her away and pointed the gun, a .38 revolver, at her chest.

"Get up," I said, walking slowly back to the girl, keeping the gun trained on the woman. "Where's the key to these cuffs?"

She didn't say anything but then brightened with a smile. "You want to join us?"

I pulled the cloth from the girl's mouth and between sobs and gasps, she said the woman was trying to kill her. I tugged at the cuffs and found an instant release. No key necessary.

The girl pulled her wrists to her body and alternated rubbing them for a second before pulling herself forward and ripping the straps from her legs. She bolted for the door but I stayed in place, the gun still trained on the woman.

"Come on," I said.

"There's more," the girl yelled from the door. "He's coming back."

I reached for a pile of jeans and a T-shirt and tossed them to her. While she slid eagerly into her clothes, I stuck the gun into my belt and used the cloth to bind the woman like you would a hog. I shoved a pile of the hairy strips into her mouth, and opened the door wide for the girl.

All the doors were locked. Every hallway led to a dead end. I heard the squawk of a security radio down the hall and turned back the other way, grabbing the girl's hand. I was sweating now and every step seemed awkward and loud.

An exit sign beamed about fifty feet away down the narrow corridor and we started into a slow jog. Just as we reached the turn, the young kid I'd met in the security room turned the corner.

"Thought I told you to wait," he said as he coolly pointed a rifle at my face. But just as he did, my jog turned into a run and I gave a forearm shot to the kid's nose. The kid fell back and his head cracked against the concrete floor. I scrambled for the rifle, picked it up without stopping, and motioned for the girl to follow.

I kept the rifle in my sweating hands running toward a fire exit.

The hallways soon turned into a humid Mississippi night. A ramp led to a walkway circling the building, and beyond that, off the concrete landing, lay a narrow channel stretching south through cotton fields. We jumped, our feet hitting the murky bottom, knees deep in water that shined with a pink neon glow.

We needed to get back to the parking lot.

Back to the Bronco and back to Memphis.

We slogged through the shallow channel, cigarette butts and Burger King cups floating by, until we tripped onto the banks of a cotton patch. We had to get at least another hundred yards into the field and then cut back to the parking lot and the Gray Ghost. I gritted my teeth as I stooped low and motioned for the girl to come closer.

Over my shoulder, I searched the back of the casino and saw three men with shotguns veering to the edge. My heart was a booming mess.

A fat red moon hung over them like a Halloween decoration.

She let go of my hand as soon as we reached the edge of the field and followed closely behind. I kept the rifle in my hand and slid off the safety with my thumb. "We'll get out," I said. "Just stay with me."

"Who sent you?" she asked. She was pretty. Shoulder-length blond hair. Wide-set brown eyes and full lips.

"No one," I said. "I saw you on a security camera."

"You a cop?" she said, looking at the gun in my belt. Her T-shirt was soaked and covered in mud, her hands plastered with blood and dirt.

"Actually, I'm a college professor."

She looked at the men fanning into the cotton field and then back at me.

I tried a crooked grin. "Music history."

She shook her head and ran ahead of me down a row of cotton. A man yelled out behind us and fired off a round. The heavy blast thudded in my ears and I tackled her to the ground. My elbows stuck into the tilled earth as my hand reached over her mouth.

"Trust me."

She nodded slowly and I let go.

I could see the Ghost from the edge of the cotton field. The girl was by my side, keeping low on her stomach and breathing hard. I peered back and saw a black man about halfway through the field with a rifle in his hands and the kid I'd knocked down approaching to the rear.

I'd killed one man in my life and possibly a second in Chicago. Never made me feel good. But these people would take my life and the girl's without a thought. I didn't know what she'd done or why she was here, but these were evil men. They were rapists and killers and there was only one way through the field.

I looked at the parking lot where a loose swarm of bugs collected around tall yellow lights. The cicadas ticking all around like a million clocks.

I tightened my grip on the rifle, tucking the stock into my shoulder, and aimed at the black man.

"Drop it," I yelled.

The man pointed his gun at me and fired. Clumps of dirt flew into my eyes.

I aimed the rifle for the man's chest and squeezed the trigger, dropping him in the field.

A booming shot echoed behind us.

I grabbed the girl's hand and we ran toward the lot and to the Bronco.

At the edge of the pavement, two large guards with crew cuts ran toward us. I fired off two shots at their feet and they hauled ass back to the casino.

I reached into my pocket for my keys, hand shaking as I tried the lock.

"Shit," I yelled, finally finding the right one. We jumped inside.

I reached over and unlocked the passenger door and the girl hopped in beside me.

The side mirror exploded into slivers and I turned around as the kid was reloading his shotgun. I threw the Bronco into reverse and then spun out of the lot, smelling hot tires.

I swung onto Highway 61, the song "Shake 'Em on Down" blaring from my CD player.

I tried to steady my breath as the cold, black night zoomed past the truck.

I turned to the girl and offered my hand.

"I'm Nick."

The girl managed a bruised grin and took my hand.

"I'm Abby."

Chapter 14

PERFECT LEIGH PACED the casino security room as one of Ransom's goons ran the fast-forward on the video surveillance with one hand and held his broken nose with the other. The tape featured hours of countless cars coming into the west parking lot, close shots of drivers' faces and of license tags. Rednecks with broken teeth and drunken smiles. High-dollar hoodlums from Memphis with greasy hair and sunglasses. The boy had promised Ransom and her that an old Bronco wouldn't be hard to spot. Boy didn't know Ransom too well. If he did, he wouldn't have made a promise he couldn't be sure to keep, she thought, wiping away the yellow wax that stuck to her new T-shirt. The little sequin heart now dirty and spoiled.

She ground her teeth together and looked at the pyramid of television screens. She wondered what Ransom would do with Humes's stupid dead ass. Shit, all he had to do was tell the Tunica sheriff that someone had tried to rob the casino and then shot down their brave head of security. Ransom would then probably bend over and wait for his ass to be smooched.

The boy played with the controls, scanning the images until he found the one they were searching for: gray Bronco, big white guy with a scar across his eyebrow. Dumb grin on his face as he noticed the camera.

"Yeah, keep smiling, fuckhead," she said. Maybe Abby MacDonald had more friends than she thought.

The boy drummed the fingers of his left hand and ran the tape forward to the close shot of the Bronco's license plate. *Louisiana. Sportsman's Paradise.*

She looked at his hand drumming. He noticed when he looked back at her. He stopped and softly felt his nose again.

Suddenly, a pulsing cold air whooshed into the room and she crossed her arms over her body. They must've cranked down the A.C. to about forty degrees. A man put a rough hand on her shoulder and spoke loud. Too close to her ear. She jumped.

"C. J., call Mr. Jim and have him run this plate," Ransom said. *Jesus*. She didn't even hear him come in. "Tell him I need it now."

The boy rewound the tape, pressed the play button, and Ransom inched closer to the screen and studied the man's face in the monitor. He froze the image and kept it wavering there.

"Sit down, Miss Leigh," Ransom said. He took a seat. Gray hair in a tight ponytail. Black crocodile-skin boots. Black jeans and button-down shirt. Concho belt. Even his eyes were black. Dead black pools set into his bony, haggard face. A million cigarettes. A million fistfights.

She sat down. He leaned close as the boy disappeared to make a phone call. He'd been drinking. And smoking. She smelled the Scotch and Cuban cigars he lived on. How did she ever find him appealing?

He held her hand, smoothing his long calloused fingers over hers. His nails were too long for a man. But clean and manicured. "Y'all fucked up," he said. "You should've taken that little girl out to Moon Lake and did it there. This was sloppy as hell, Perfect."

"You knew," she said and drew her hand away. She took a breath and pretended like she was watching the monitors.

Ransom plucked a cigar into his mouth, lit it, and blew out a cloud of smoke that crinkled and curled up into the ceiling. He stayed silent for a few minutes, just studying the wavering image of the man. He kept clicking it back and forth and toying with the video until he pointed to something she could barely make out.

"Parking pass from the Peabody Hotel," he said. His voice weathered and cracked.

The boy walked back in the room, smiling. "Man's name is Travers," he said. "He's from New Orleans."

"I'll head up to Memphis tonight," Perfect said. "He's probably still at the hotel."

Ransom shook his head. "C. J., I want you to call Mr. Jim back. Have him put this thing out. I want someone quick, dirty, and good."

"That bastard tied me up like a hog," she said.

Ransom laughed to himself. "He sure did . . . but no." He took another long draw of the cigar and surveyed Perfect's crossed legs. "You ever killed someone?"

She nodded.

"Maybe some poor ole fool that couldn't see it coming. But this is different."

"Let me go," Perfect said. "Let me learn."

Ransom caressed the back of her neck. She remembered all those nights in Biloxi when she was nineteen. The spending sprees, the cocaine, and all those random blackouts. He still had a spot for her. He'd give in.

He watched her legs some more. She parted them a half inch and saw his eyes move up to her face, scanning for something. Maybe trying to see if she was serious about killing the man who had disrespected her and made her feel so nasty.

Ransom nodded. "Lord help this man Travers," he said, toying with the band around his cigar. He ripped the band away and studied the label for a while as if he were reading a novel. "Tell Mr. Jim to make the hits for twenty thousand dollars. Each."

His face and eyes clouded with purple smoke.

Graceland Too stood in Holly Springs, a good thirty miles from Oxford and about fifty from Memphis. A back city street led to the old two-story plantation house guarded by stone lions. Just like the ones at E's place. But this place wasn't so fancy. A vine grew wild and twisted up over the first floor and by the chimney. And the owner, some heavy guy named Paul McLeod, had stuck a satellite dish out back. All for a good purpose, Jon Burrows thought. This place was jacked into Elvis twenty-four hours a day, seven days a week, 365 days a year.

McLeod charged tourists five bucks to come look at his E collection. He'd take the early shift and his son, Elvis Aaron Presley McLeod, would take the night. Junior was about six foot five and had this "photographic memory." He could remember things about E that Burrows had never even heard of.

The family had pictures of E on their walls, their ceilings, even in the damned bathroom. E played on about twenty televisions all through the house. *Speedway* in the living room. *Change of Habit* in the dining room. And the *'68 Comeback Special* in the kitchen.

Burrows smiled and wiped the sweat from his brow with the black Resistol hat he'd just bought at a truck stop outside Vicksburg. It was there that he'd called Black Elvis who put him in touch with the McLeods. Black Elvis said they'd take care of him until the heat wore off a bit. So he'd stayed there with them for the last couple weeks. And man, did they treat him right. Salty country ham in the morning with a side of hot biscuits. Even had coffee mugs with E's face on them.

Burrows walked down the gravel road, cicadas buzzin' in the trees, a red twilight shining down on rain pools dotting the land. Tonight, everything smelled like sex. Rich and humid. Steam smoking from the hot ground. The air filled with sweet honeysuckle.

Man, he sure missed his woman, Dixie. Black Elvis said her trailer would be the first place the police would look. But, man, he wanted to call his Tupelo honey so bad right now the buttons were about to pop off his fly.

"Mister Jon," McLeod called out into the early night.

Burrows looked up at the porch of the old house. McLeod said it was 150 years old. Maybe that's why it kind of leaned to the right.

"Mister Jon, Elvis 'bout to put on *Viva Las Vegas* and I knowed that it's yore favorite. You was tellin' us about Miss Ann—you know, the Memphis Mafia called her Thumper—liked to get all hot when they was dancin'. You know, rubbin' their noses together and all."

"All right."

"We'd made you a meal, too, Mister Jon," McLeod said, his dentures slipping in his mouth. He held a plastic plate in his hand filled with a fried peanut butter and banana sandwich. McLeod used two sticks of butter for each sandwich. He said that's the only way E would eat 'em.

" 'Preciate it," Burrows said, taking the plastic plate stamped with a picture of E from the *Aloha from Hawaii* special. "Think I'm gonna go hit Smart Boy in the cellar."

"Whatever you want, Mister Jon. Black Elvis speaks real high of you. You holler out you need anythin'."

" 'Preciate it," Burrows said again, walking around to the twin doors of the cellar. He pulled the rusted handle on one of the doors and moved below the unmowed weeds and piles of chipped brick into the cool brick bunker.

He closed the door behind him and walked to the electronic screen burning beneath a framed velvet image of E. It was the holy one. The one where E is crying. A blue halo around his head.

He sat before the computer and clicked his way on to the Internet. The computer burped out some weird sounds before he heard the buzzing connection. He typed with one hand and held the sandwich with the other. What he wouldn't give for an RC right about now.

He smacked on the sandwich, warm butter oozing down his arm, as he watched for the address prompt. Sure glad he'd hooked up with that German chick a couple years ago. When they left Mississippi for Las Vegas, she'd taught him all kind of things about computers.

Burrows pulled out a business card from his wallet and carefully keyed in the address. Within seconds, the home page for LOST YOUTH appeared. He clicked on a photograph of a poor Mexican boy and the face disappeared into another site called BOUNTY TIME. Names of wanted men were listed under regions. Burrows double-clicked on SOUTH. There he had a list of states. Under Mississippi he saw a name, picture, and last known address for a prison rat named Dock Boggs. Only $500. *Shit.*

The other hit was out on a woman named Lillie Fitzpatrick. She was worth $2,000, but was all the way up in Atlanta running a beauty shop.

He clicked on the next best thing. Louisiana. As the computer struggled to pull up the names, he finished off the sandwich and scraped the excess peanut butter off the roof of his mouth with his tongue.

In the past two years, he'd killed over thirty men and women. Made some good money at it, but was always on the run. He felt like E did at the end, when no one understood how hard it was to travel. But he didn't have people to put tin foil on his windows while he slept in hotels during the day or give him special pills to make him feel all happy. He just hit the road with his gift, driving through the truck stops of the South. A hot shower and a country meal were about the only thanks he ever got for his true talent.

The computer screen brightened.

Just as you start to feel all sorry for yourself, E illuminates a man to his true purpose. "I'll never doubt you again, E," Burrows said, crossing his heart with his sticky fingers.

Jon Burrows knew one of the bounties.

He pulled out the switchblade his mama had bought him at Wal-Mart and flicked it open. In the gleam of its sharpened steel, he could see a warped image of himself. Beard. A couple years older. And tougher than ever.

Burrows snapped the blade shut and stared at the screen. The face of a white man with a scar across his left eyebrow appeared. Black hair with gray on the sides. Yep, it was him all right.

NICK TRAVERS.

And damn if he wasn't gettin' more valuable.

Twenty thousand dollars.

Chapter 15

THE NEXT MORNING, I felt brittle carpet fibers on my cheeks and a hot slice of sunlight in my eyes. Sometime last night, I'd grabbed a stiff bedspread and pillow before the girl fell asleep and was slowly waking up sore as hell. I usually tried not to think about how many body parts I'd broken, sprained, or dislocated, but mornings like this made me aware. The girl was still curled up in bed, a loose strand of blond hair in her eyes. Lips pursed. Tightly wrapped in a smooth blue blanket.

Abby. Her name was Abby.

Last night, I could barely get her to eat the chicken sandwich that I'd ordered from the Peabody's room service. Kept on saying she had to go, and made it to the door twice before I convinced her to stay. I showed her my driver's license, scattered notebooks, and even the battered cassette recorder I'd used in the Delta. I tried to make her relax and even laugh.

She never did trust me. She was just beaten and scared. Absolutely no place to go. She spent the few hours before she went to sleep silently watching *Letterman* and then the last half of *Breakfast at Tiffany's* in a worn JoJo's Blues Bar T-shirt and pair of my Scooby Doo boxers. Didn't even blink when Holly lost Cat.

She must've fallen asleep with the television on, I thought as I rolled on my back, still wearing the same clothes from last night but missing a sock, and stared up at Saturday morning cartoons. I got to my feet, scratched the back of my neck, and flipped the channels until I found *Scooby*. One of the originals with the miner 49er and the ghost town. Man, I loved that one.

"It's the innkeeper," the girl said in a sleepy voice.

I turned to see her hugging the pillow, her brown eyes underlined with dark circles.

"He found uranium in the mines."

I turned back to the television and watched Scooby eating Shaggy's sub sandwich topped with whipped cream and olives. I pulled the loose sock off my foot and took a seat by the girl. Canned laughter filled the room.

"You ever see the one with Mama Cass?"

"She owns a candy factory," Abby said.

"Wow," I said. "Thought you had to be a child of the 'sixties to understand."

"Cartoon Network."

"Ah," I said. "Probably watched *Smurfs*."

"What?"

"Blue people," I said, shrinking the distance between my fingers. "Real small."

Abby looked away, her hair wired with static electricity, and clutched the pillow tighter to her chest. She exhaled a long breath as if she were trying to expel a sickness. "You going to tell me who you are?"

"I did."

"What's that then?"

I looked over to my Army duffel bag topped off with the Stones and North Mississippi All-Stars CDs and a stainless-steel Browning 9mm. A leg of clean 501s poked from the top.

She said: "Doesn't look like teacher's shit to me."

I smiled at the girl. "I have a slight inferiority complex."

I covered the gun with the leg of my worn jeans and opened a window. I looked out at the new baseball stadium built for the Memphis Redbirds and lit that first morning cigarette. As soon as I took a drag, the smell got to me.

I suddenly had the urge to wash my hands. Maybe take a shower. I could smell the burn of the rifle on my fingers—I'd later dumped both guns in the Mississippi—and could still feel their heat in my hands. I remembered the sound the man's body made as it dropped with bloated weight into the cotton field. That wicked moon bathing his dead face with a bright glow.

Abby steadily got to her feet and joined me at the window. Small city noises bleated inside. Abby wasn't that tall, came up about to my chest. Her hair was bobbed to her chin. She had the kind of face that could wear her hair like that. Delicate. Chin like the point of a heart. Bet she had a dynamite smile if she'd ever smile.

A warm breath of wind washed over my face and I kept staring at the downtown buildings and the bridges crossing the Mississippi. I'd fucked up last night. No matter what was going on in the casino, I'd killed a man. I'd shot him right in the heart. My head pounded and my mouth tasted like cotton.

I tried to take a deep breath but the air felt shallow in my lungs. I'd been in several scuffles and I'd fired my gun a few times. But each time I awoke not truly knowing myself.

All of a sudden Abby asked me, "You ever feel like you could stick your hand in a fire and not feel a thing?" She was rubbing the reddened marks on her calves and sort of talking to herself.

I listened. A couple of horns honked from down on Union. Scooby and the gang ran from the space ghost. I looked down at my bare toes. I wiggled the ones on the left foot. "Sometimes. . . . You want to tell me what was going on?"

She shook her head.

"I don't know."

"Who were they?"

Abby sat on the floor, pulled her knees to her chest, and started rocking. I came to her, bent down, and put my hand on her back. I dropped into this awkward half crouch, my knees aching like hell, but didn't move my hand.

"I don't know who they are," she said again.

"Why would they want to hurt you?"

"You can't help me."

"Why would they want to hurt you?"

Abby placed her head on her forearms. "You tell me who they are and I'll tell you everything," she said.

"I have a friend we need to see," I said, standing. "He'll know."

"You trust him?"

"Like a brother."

Chapter 16

ULYSSES DAVIS RAN a bail bonds business down off Poplar not far from the courthouse and the Shelby County Jail. The neighborhood had nothing but bondsmen for several blocks, their neon signs advertising in the windows with telephone numbers and assurances: ANYTIME, ANY PRICE. But you couldn't miss ole U's place. At first, it looked like a damned art gallery. A lot of blue neon and pictures of martial arts film stars lining the walls. I once kidded U about it, said it looked like these were the folks he'd bailed out of jail. But U didn't think that was funny. Since the time we played on the same Saints' defense, U rarely thought I was funny.

He was sitting at this big presidential wooden desk when I walked in with Abby. From his stereo, Marcus Roberts played jazz piano while patchouli incense burned from a nearby shelf. He'd tied his braided hair into a ponytail, sweat burned off his dark brown skin. A black leather jacket lay on the edge of his desk where he was filling out some papers.

Almost didn't see the young black kid sitting across from U. Kid had a shaved head and multiple nose- and earrings. Couldn't help notice there was a jagged slot in his left ear where he was bleeding pretty badly. Kid had duct tape across his mouth and was handcuffed to a ladderback chair.

"Hey, motherfucker," I said.

U kept his eyes down on the paperwork and broke into a broad grin. "And how is your momma, Dr. Travers?"

Abby gave me a skeptical stare.

The kid handcuffed to the chair started making groaning noises.

U finished dotting some "i" or crossing some "t" and threw down his pen. He stood up to his six-foot-four, 240-pound frame and grasped my hand. Felt like he'd been working out. 'Course that was all U seemed to do. Lift weights, practice tae kwon do, and eat his health food. Tofu and wheat grass. God. I had spent three years trying to get him to eat some ribs and drink some beer without luck.

"What the fuck do you want?" U asked.

"Tell you that I've always loved you. Make up for lost time."

"Well, wait for me in the lobby, punk. Be through in a second. Antoine here decided to fuck me one time too many. Time to get my money back."

Abby took a seat in front of a huge plate glass window with a view looking onto the gray coldness of the jail. She was wearing a pair of jogging pants I bought for her in the hotel lobby and another one of my T-shirts.

Outside, cops and worn-out families milled about. A couple of women dressed in pleather pants and halters walked by the glass window with a cold, indifferent affection.

"How do you know this guy?"

"Played football together. He was my roommate on road trips."

"What can he do?" Abby asked.

"He knows about every cop and federal agent in town."

Abby was quiet for a moment and picked up an old copy of *Black Belt* magazine. Chuck Norris was on the cover. Dressed as a cowboy. Kicking some poor bastard in the nuts.

Twenty minutes later, U walked back from the jail where he had deposited the kid. He was rubbing his hands together as if he'd finished cleaning the kitchen.

"Come on back," he said, taking off his jacket.

Abby found a seat by the desk. I stood. The patchouli continued to burn although Roberts had finished. Now, the stereo played selections from *Carmen*.

"Last night, I drove out to a casino in Tunica."

"Figured you would after I ran that plate. Now you wanna tell me why?"

"Looking for a man named Clyde James. Some security guards from the casino had been looking for him, too."

"Why do you care?"

"He was a big-time soul singer in the 'sixties."

"New project?"

"He's Loretta's brother."

"Mmm-hmm," U said, rubbing his goatee. "And she's worried."

"While I was there, I met Miss Abby here. A woman had kidnapped her and taken her to the casino."

"Which one?"

"Magnolia Grand."

"I see. I see."

"While I was getting her out, I killed a man."

"Ain't your line of work, is it, Travers?"

"I want to set it right. Where do we go? I don't want to go back to that place half-assed."

U nodded. He folded his massive arms—veined and corded—across his chest. "Tunica is a hell of a place."

"You know what we've stepped into?"

"Looks like, brother, you've just landed in a steaming pile of the Dixie Mafia."

I blew out my breath.

"Oh, yeah," U said. "Buckle your ass up."

Chapter 17

PERFECT LEIGH HATED rich fucks in blue blazers and khakis. And today, she was surrounded by them. Seemed like all the men she saw thought they wouldn't be admitted into the damned football game if they didn't dress alike. She hated the way they waddled because they were full of scotch and the way they held Confederate flags in their hands and gave the ole Rebel yell to passing friends. She was tired of watching them and their female counterparts in flowered dresses and straw hats wander through this oak-shaded part of the Ole Miss campus called The Grove, eating barbecue from toothpicks and finger sandwiches taken from black men dressed in tuxedos as if the 'fifties never ended.

While she sat on the warm hood of her Mustang and waited for Ransom, she tried to figure out who was worse, the men or the women. The men were just plain pathetic, gawking at her in her red leather pants and leather halter. They didn't seem to care if their wives were hanging on their arms or if they were holding their kids' hands. The women were just outright hypocrites, boobs hoisted high in Wonderbras and reeking of perfume, as they scowled at her or pointed from loose circles and laughed.

At least Perfect knew who she was. She didn't pretend to be an adoring wife, a concerned mother, or proud girlfriend. Perfect Leigh was Perfect Leigh. One hundred and twenty pounds of pure feminine power. She didn't need a mask or a label. She felt her power and was damned proud of it.

Two black men carrying silver serving trays passed her. One just growled his approval, *"Mmm-mmm."* A fat white man in a suit and crooked baseball hat licked his lips, and quickly looked away. Two fraternity boys passing a flask between them about fell over themselves as she recrossed her long legs and looked at her watch.

Her hair fell in loose curls over her head, styled and bleached back to platinum. Cost two hundred bucks and the outfit pushed the hell out of a thousand. She deserved it. Sometimes you had to give yourself a little present every once in a while, to let yourself know you were doing a hell of a job at life.

This time eight years ago, she'd just left Clarksdale after winning the Coahoma County Cotton Queen contest. Then, the possibilities were limitless: sleep with the county judge (a fat-necked man who owned several local gins), go to work trying to bring tourism to a dying downtown, or make some high-dollar bucks stripping in Memphis.

Her mother didn't seem to care as long as her daughter finally got famous and ended up on one of her soaps. She always pointed to *Soap Opera Digest* in the checkout line of the Winn-Dixie and said, "Your beautiful little face will end up right there."

But her mother didn't know how the world worked. She hid behind a sickeningly large rack of Disney movies and a jelly jar collection of famous cartoon characters. Hell, she named her daughter Perfect because of a stupid mistake. She told Perfect when she was a kid that she'd heard the name in this Rolling Stone song. Said it went, "I saw Perfect-Ly at the reception, a glass of wine in her hand" and that's not even the way it went. It was, "I saw *her* today." How the hell did she hear Perfectly from that?

When Perfect finally heard the song, she was already in high school. Some dorky pothead made her listen to the real version in his crappy van airbrushed with Viking scenes. When it was finally confirmed that her mother was an idiot, her world changed.

She had thought her name was for a purpose, and that it would lead to greater things. But when that didn't make sense, she thought maybe her whole life would follow into the septic tank. So a couple months later, after graduation and the whole Cotton Queen thing, she ended up moving to Panama City Beach and taking a job at a wacky golf course and bar that featured wet T-shirt contests every Wednesday.

That's where she met this grifter named Jake, the man she'd lost her virginity to at the Flamingo Motel. Within two weeks she'd moved to Biloxi and he began teaching her about faking out old folks as bank examiners, working Pigeon Drops on rednecks at check cashing businesses, and trying out the Sweetheart Swindle on horny old men who had loads of cash.

She was a natural, Jake said. Of course, he loved everything she did. But she was good. Even as a child, she knew just little changes in mannerisms could make people react in a whole different way. Like that one time when she was at summer camp and started speaking in an English accent telling everyone she was a baroness. Everyone, including several counselors, believed her until one called her mother and spoiled the fun.

But she'd learned from Jake that it was more than the voice. It was the eyes and the shoulders and the way you held your hands. "Everybody wears a mask," Jake said one night at Wintzell's in Mobile after they took a bank president for two grand. "Everyone is an actor. See that man? He's the hard-working father. See that woman? She's the loving granny who spoils those kids. And him? That man is the funny guy that everyone loves to know 'cause he don't know shit about himself. See?"

And she did see. Jake showed her all of them. He showed her every species that existed in the world. Probably would have married that smart bastard, too, if he hadn't tried to cross Levi Ransom and disappeared into the parking lot of a Sears.

But she grew to love Ransom, too. Or wear the mask that loved Ransom. It was self-preservation and truly a tribute to that ole boy Jake. He would've appreciated it.

As the P.A. system started droning out today's roster from the stadium, Perfect looked down at the wonderful slickness of her new nails. The sounds of The Grove coming back into her ears as the heat from the fall sun baked the red hood of her Mustang.

"Start talkin'," Ransom said. She looked up and there he stood all weathered and styled like Kris Kristofferson with his shoulder-length gray hair and whiskey-soaked voice. He dressed more like a golf pro than the head of a bunch of good-ole-boy cutthroats. Wrinkled linen shirt, blue trousers, and loafers without socks.

"I want in," she said, biting off a stray cuticle. "I want that man."

"Get over it."

"I want him to hurt bad."

"Perfect, you don't kill people," he said, looking at the crowd milling toward the stadium like goats through a chute. "You have your talents and others have theirs. Really, I need to get back to my guests."

"Levi, you hate those fucks. Don't tell me you don't."

He gave a weathered grin. That's the one thing she'd never fake about liking. Levi Ransom looked as if he'd lived his life twice and on the third time around would just sit back and watch everybody fuck up.

Behind him, she saw loose groups of women in straw hats and more dorks in ties and khakis under a funeral tent.

"Let me go," she said, reaching out and touching his pocket. "I want to learn."

"I don't know this boy," Ransom said finally after rubbing his beard and taking a seat beside her on the car hood. "Heard he's got a mile of experience but kind of cocked in the head. You don't understand that part of the business, hon. These folks get off on watchin' people bleed. They're kind of like baseball players. Real shootin' stars. Burn out real fast."

"Who is he?" she asked.

"First time we used him. Said he knows the man we're looking for and can take him out quick. Good references from Vegas."

"Let me in with him," she said, looking sad and poking out her lower lip. Then she looked into his eyes. More serious. Pressing.

He grinned: "I don't know you."

"I don't know you," she said back.

"Memphis. Hell, go. Call C. J. from there and he'll tell you what you need."

She slid off the hood of the car and planted her Manolo Blahnik stilettos in the grass. She winked at Ransom and said, "We had a hell of a time for a while. Didn't we?"

"We did."

"What happened?"

"You grew up," Ransom said, giving what Jake would have called the Wistful Face. Better times, an older, wiser man that had seen it all. He almost had her until that phony-ass move.

As he turned to go back to the funeral tent and his new collection of friends, a guy with thinning brown hair and a square jaw walked over and clasped his hand on Ransom's shoulder. The man was in his late forties or early fifties. Handsome in kind of a large-teeth, big smile sort of way. He was trim and tan and wore a black Polo shirt and bone-colored pants. A silver Rolex dangled loose on his wrist.

"Thank you, Levi," the man said with authority. He gave the ole two-hand handshake and tried like hell to keep that eye contact going as he spoke. "I've got to make one more party before kickoff."

"Jude, appreciate you stoppin' by," Ransom said. "Jude? This is a friend of the family's, Miss Leigh. Miss Leigh, this is Jude Russell, he's out makin' the rounds today trying to get to some of his Tennessee constituents who've come south. Wants them thinkin' to that first Tuesday next month."

Russell. Yeah, she knew him. Liberal senator out of Memphis who wanted to be governor. His father had been some kind of racist pig during segregation. Guy spent every minute trying to tell people that he wasn't like his dead daddy.

"Nice to meet you," Perfect said, fishing with a sly little grin.

Nothin'. No smile. No warm shake. He acted like she wasn't even there.

About ten yards later, Russell was intercepted by another round of the khaki club. He gave more two-handed shakes and wide big-toothed grins. Ransom was watching. He cleaned his sunglasses with a show handkerchief, squinted one gray eye, and looked out through a clean lens.

"I hate that son of a bitch," he said.

Chapter 18

THE TUNICA JUSTICE COMPLEX WAS remarkable for nothing but its newness. Red brick and squat with the architectural detail of a Ritz cracker box, the building sat on the edge of an aging downtown cut in the center by railroad tracks. Outside there was an American flag that flapped stiff and bold from a high pole and a few immature trees—barely rooted in their soil—sitting brown and dead by the front doors.

As I parked in a visitor's slot, Ulysses jumped out before my truck stopped, sliding his boots on the asphalt. He had on a pair of thin shades and had the collar of his black leather coat flipped up on his neck.

"Hey, Shaft," I said. "You want to hold up?"

"Oh, yeah, man. Guess you ain't in a hurry to go to jail."

I stopped and put my hands in the pockets of my jeans. I looked over at the dead trees and the long shot of the old downtown dressed up with boutiques, antique stores, and a coffee shop.

"Remember that time you locked that weight coach . . . what was his name?"

"Shit," I said. "I don't remember."

"At camp? C'mon. Remember you locked him in that old laundry bin where we used to throw old jockstraps and socks."

"What made you think of that?"

"Last time I seen you worried about anything. They were talkin' about cuttin' you."

"Shit."

"This ain't nothin'. Self-defense. It'll work out."

I nodded.

"And the girl gonna be fine, too."

We'd left Abby in Memphis with an associate of U's named Bubba Cotton. Bubba was bigger than me and U combined and, according to U, had once killed a man using a shrimp fork at a Red Lobster by the airport. I felt pretty confident that Abby was safe.

A curtain of deep black clouds headed east on the horizon and a stop sign at the crossroads beat in the strong wind. The sun was hard and white but swallowed whole in seconds by the clouds. A whistle could be heard through narrow cracks in the shotgun cottages across the road.

U headed on in the complex, like a man strolling into an A&P to buy a loaf of bread, and motioned for me to follow. I kind of wished I was back at the Peabody now. I'd kick off my boots, watch the clouds drift over the river, and order a club sandwich and a Dr Pepper from room service.

U motioned again.

The building's stale air hit us as soon as we walked inside to a Plexiglas window protecting a receptionist. She was white and fortyish and as gaudily made up as a corpse on viewing day. She wasn't chewing gum or smoking a cigarette or seemed to be doing anything active at all. She had her hands flat on a stack of papers across her desk. Her eyes cast downward refusing to admit that she heard us walk through the door.

For some reason, I wasn't sure why, her attitude was pissing me off. I wanted to reach through that little cut-out circle, where you were supposed to speak, and flick her in the head.

"Miss?" U asked.

She continued her daze.

Maybe it was a religious thing. Maybe she was meditating or slowly saying a special Russian prayer to herself over and over like the one in *Franny and Zooey*.

"Miss?"

Her eyes shifted upward.

"We need to speak to the sheriff."

"Sheriff Beckum?"

"Is there another one?" U asked.

She looked annoyed. A reaction. A movement of facial muscles. Amazing.

"He's in a conference right now."

Above her hung a picture of the man himself. Sheriff Beckum. Looked to be in his early thirties, businessman haircut, porn star mustache. Not that I watched a lot of porn or anything. It was just that few people could really pull off the mustache thing and look cool.

"You think we could wait?" U asked.

"Can a deputy help you, sir?"

U crossed his arms across his chest and looked away, annoyed.

I took a huge breath of air and said simply and slowly: "Ma'am, we have a murder to report."

Sheriff Robert Beckum entered the hallway in a way I didn't expect. No creased khakis or frowns or mirrored *Smokey and the Bandit* sunglasses. Beckum was clean-shaven—I made a mental note to compliment the change later—and wearing corduroy pants and a faded-blue flannel shirt. Mud was scattered across one sleeve and he wore a big grin of a man completely and honestly content with his day.

He offered his hand to U and then turned to me.

"Y'all serious about a murder?"

He seemed thinner than the picture, and younger. Maybe even late twenties. Beckum had an intense face with a pointed nose and brown hair slicked back against his skull. He kept your attention like an eager shoe salesman and held your hand longer than was expected.

But I had learned long ago, handshakes truly told you little about a person.

I relied more on eye contact. And Beckum never broke away from my glance.

"There was some trouble last night at the Magnolia Grand," I said. "A young woman was being held against her will. I helped her and in the process of getting away I shot a man."

Beckum shook his head. "Well, goddamn. Nobody tells me nothing 'round here anymore. You'd think a sheriff would know when a man's been shot."

U stole a glance at me.

"Last night, about midnight," I said.

"Y'all been gambling? Drinkin' a little?"

I shook my head.

"I was there to talk to the man who runs their security."

Beckum still never wavered from my glance. Kind of annoying. Had this look on his face like he could read minds and expected you to kind of quake with fear as he gave the ole squinty glance.

"Why?" he asked.

"I was looking for a friend."

"He work there?"

"No."

"The girl's a friend, too?"

"No."

"How'd you know she was being held against her will?"

"She was tied up."

"In the casino?" Beckum asked, a sarcastic smile on his lips.

"In a storage room in the casino. I saw her on a video monitor. When we were running away from the casino a man started shooting at me. I shot back. And I hit him in the chest."

"Why'd you bring a gun to a casino?"

"I didn't," I said. "I took it off one of the guards who tried to stop me from leaving."

Beckum nodded and looked over at U.

"What's your deal in all this, hoss?"

"I'm a registered bondsman," he said. "I'm here to make sure he's treated properly . . . hoss."

Beckum snickered. Out of the corner of his eye, I saw U flex his jaw muscles.

Beckum saw it, too, but glanced away like it didn't register. It did. His face flushed as he spoke.

"Guess it's time we all take a ride to the Grand and see what the hell this is all about."

"Indeed," U said.

Chapter 19

EVEN IN THE MIDDLE OF THE DAY, the scene was the same as the night before. The perfectly dimmed blue and green neon light. The ping-ing electronic music. The hundreds of slots, card tables, and roulette wheels buzzing with the energy of a never-ending party. The scent was the same, too. A musky odor of nervousness and beer breath mixed with cheap cigars and endless cigarettes.

I walked toward the security offices flanked by U and Beckum, scan-ning the crowd for the men we met last night. Didn't matter if I had two or two hundred with me, I still felt a raw nervousness in the back of my throat. I swallowed, ground my molars together, and kept walking.

Somewhere in the crowd, a craggy blond in a red cocktail dress whooped it up with a black man in a red suit after the dice she'd kissed rolled a winner. Out of the corner of my eye, I watched the woman—bloodshot eyes, lazy grin—reach into the man's pocket, give a tug, and then stumble backward.

On the opposite side, I saw two boys with black hair slap the heads of rubber frogs with cushioned mallets. One chewed gum. The other pre-tended he was smoking with a pretzel stick.

My stomach burned. The sound of my grinding teeth buzzed in my ears.

Ahead, two men in green blazers met Beckum by the cash exchange windows. U and I hung back. Beckum clasped the shoulder of one of the guards, a white man with teeth like a rake and a buzz cut, smiled, and pointed to a back door in agreement.

He motioned for us to follow.

"Big boss is over at the command post," Beckum said.

"It's the other way," I said.

Beckum shrugged and kept walking. He had on tan ostrich-skin boots that probably cost a thousand bucks but had been worn like they cost fifty. Scarred and muddy.

"How could they not report this?" I asked in a low voice.

"Maybe you didn't kill him," U said, still staring straight ahead. "Maybe they don't want folks knowing they keep little girls chained in back rooms."

A minute later, we followed Beckum up a staircase to the casino's second floor and into a wood-paneled office dotted with Tiffany lamps and sepia-toned photographs of Wild West scenes. Waxy looking figures in coffins. Hardened women holding six-shooters.

A fireplug of an old man stood as we walked in the door. Wide-jowled face with an Irish-veined nose and pale blue eyes. He had a round body, short legs, and thick stubby fingers that couldn't quite clasp around my hand.

He smiled along with Beckum when the murder was mentioned. He scratched the back of his unshaven neck and stared over at another guard who sat in a far corner.

"Did we forget about a guard getting killed last night?" Fat Man asked.

The man in the corner laughed, too.

"He wasn't a guard," I said. "His name was Humes. Head of security for this whole damned place."

Fat Man shook with laughter. "Not only did I find out a man got killed last night," he said, "but now you're telling me I have a boss."

I felt the blood rush into my face and my right fist tighten. U didn't say a word. I could only hear his steady breath behind me in the paneled room. Overhead, Kenny G played some irritating saxophone. My nails dug into the palm of my hand.

"So you don't know Humes?" I asked.

Fat Man shrugged. Beckum snickered again.

I crossed my arms across my chest and stared at Fat Man's face. Impassive. Slow breath. A sociopath of a liar.

"Sheriff, this man is fucking with you. I want to walk you through what happened last night. You won't mind, will you?"

Fat Man shrugged again and exhaled his boredom. His breath smelled of onions and cigarettes. The red veins in his face a road map of a disappointing life.

The door wasn't there. There was a rack of tourist brochures instead where the maid had let me in the night before. I touched the Sheetrock and found dry paint. I scanned for the outline of a door and even pressed against the wall as Beckum and Fat Man stood by watching.

"You guys are good," I said. "What about your back halls? I want to see them."

"Listen, y'all," Beckum said. "I'm tired as hell. I got off a hunt about six this morning and haven't slept a lick. How 'bout we call this whole thing off? I don't know what y'all want or why and, to be honest, I really don't give a shit. But I don't have time to look for secret doors and dead men who don't exist and little missing girls and that kind of nonsense."

"I want to see the hallways," I said.

"You're in them," Fat Man said.

"No, the ones the staff use. You couldn't have sealed off all of that, too."

"We have some back rooms for storage and employee lounges and that type thing. But, Sheriff, this is getting a little ridiculous."

"You mind?"

Fat Man led the way to a steel door in the main casino lobby. He punched a code on the door and sauntered inside. A cold musty odor exhaled from the open door as we walked through the concrete caves intermittently lit with caged bulbs. I moved on ahead trying to reconnect with the same route as last night.

"Where do you keep the surveillance monitors?"

"Upstairs."

"Bullshit," I said. I kept walking. The walls seemed to constrict as the blood flowed hot through my face and ears. I could hear my own breathing as the clacking of my boots beat a steady rhythm.

The hallway ended with a path to the right and left. This was the path back to the sealed door. I walked about fifteen yards ahead to see the hall blocked with seven-foot stacks of paint cans.

"Clever," I said, brushing past Fat Man and continuing down the hall.

"Mister . . . ?" Beckum called out.

U caught up with me. "They good," he said.

I nodded.

I turned to the first door. This was it. Or at least I thought this was it. Shit, I was so damned turned around, this was maybe the women's bathroom. Felt like this was the turn from last night. I didn't remember any doors along the corridor before the surveillance room. I reached for the door. It was locked.

"Open it," I said.

"Listen, I'll indulge you," Beckum said. "But don't be smarting off to these folks."

Fat Man pulled a set of keys from his pocket, extracted a single one from dozens, and pushed open the door.

The room was filled with dusty blackjack tables and roulette wheels and a few mannequin Southern belles propped armless by the door. Along the back wall was a row of something long and rectangular under a tarp. I walked over and pulled it away.

Slot machines.

"Y'all done?" Fat Man asked, giving a phony yawn.

"Room one-oh-two," I said. "But let me guess . . . it's now a swimming pool."

It wasn't.

It didn't exist at all.

The room sequence stopped at 101. A long concrete hallway continued on without a single entrance. Caged lamps burned in the semidarkened corridor.

"Can't you see what they've done?" I asked, my voice sounding hollow. "They've erased everything. Go interview employees. They'll tell you about the work they put in last night. They sealed up two doors and moved a lot of shit around. Check on this man Humes. He was here last night. People saw him. Someone had to have heard the shots . . . there were witnesses. You can't just pretend that the man never existed. That's bullshit."

Beckum looked over to U. "Best get this boy some sleep. And keep him the hell away from this place."

"That's all you going to do?" U asked.

Beckum ran his hand over his head and looked down the concrete corridor. "What do you want me to do? Arrest the man for murder? Do you really want that for your buddy?"

Fifteen minutes later, I slammed my fist into the dashboard of the Bronco. U reclined the seat back and stared into the cotton fields I had shown him. A quiet splatter of rain dolloped on the hood. The sky was deep black and seemed to stretch all the way to the Gulf.

"I'm not crazy, U," I said.

"Listen, brother, I'm with you," he said. "If you say you seen a chicken smoking, I'll walk over to his feathered ass and bring back a pack of Camels."

Chapter 20

JON BURROWS LOVED the smell of Graceland. Burnt bacon, cheap women's perfume, and Tampa Nugget cigars still lingered more than twenty years later. Maybe because everything in the holy estate was the way He'd left it for His return. Jon's heart just started rockin' in his chest every time he entered that front hall and saw that long white leather couch and them stained-glass windows of peacocks. Jon could see E's piano where He sang gospel till dawn with the boys and them pretty blue curtains in the dining room where Dodger used to serve Him boiled ham and sweet potatoes. He wanted to jump past the velvet ropes and sprint up to E's bedroom so he could lay on that shag carpet and soak up all them smells. This was holy air that seeped deep into your lungs and made you one with Him. Jon took in a big lungful, got loose from the tour of old people, nonbelievers, and fools, and walked outside following a back path to the Meditation Gardens.

The man he'd called from a pay phone in Holly Springs told him to pick a spot to make contact and he figured this was as good a place as any. He knew the layout, the curves, the cracks, just in case the law was playin' some kind of game. Jon pulled the Resistol down in his eyes and stroked his thick black beard.

Today he wore nothin' but black to match his feelin'. Black jeans, a black T-shirt—with one sleeve rolled up to show his tattoo with Elvis wearin' a crown of thorns—and real shiny black boots. Jon kind of felt the way he imagined E did when he was making *Charro!*, back when everyone didn't think He could act. Hell, He only sang the title song and didn't even dance once. If that ain't actin', Jon didn't know what actin' was.

Elvis had to control his power when them men in the movie branded Him like He was a steer and then started firin' their gold cannon at that Ole

West city. If E had danced and sung, it woulda been a different story, brother.

It was late in the day and Jon could feel a rumble in his stomach. He sat on the steps of the garden feeling his knee jump up and down like a piston. Been so keyed up about another killin' job that he didn't even remember to eat.

Maybe he was all worked up 'cause he'd sniffed two rags of lighter fuel before he took the bus across the boulevard. Man, the fountain was lookin' mighty strange through all them blurry flowers and wreaths and things.

But this was a special spot for E and he needed to concentrate. Made him feel important, like them Bible people who used to debate scripture, when he sat along the wall of arches in that little curve of brick wall. Jon heard that first time He'd seen it, that tears of joy washed down His face.

Jon remembered that story he'd heard from one of the ole timers durin' Elvis Week a few years back when he just come up from Hollywood, Mississippi to make somethin' of himself. Heard that E sent a man all the way to Italy to buy statues of Roman soldiers and to Spain to buy all them pretty stained-glass windows set into the curved wall.

He watched the big round fountain beyond the graves, some skinny wrinkled woman bawlin' like a baby, and them gray skies overhead. E left a world that needed Him too much.

Jon folded his hands and bowed his head.

Dear Lord God E, please hear my worried prayer for that I may know the full potential of my worrisome mind. I have wandered from my skills. I have become soft in the eyes of You, much like the days of Hollywood when the government took away Your sideburns and powers over the world. I want to be reborn as You were in 1968 when the Holy Spirit entered You and sat You upon the throne of the world. Lord God E, make me into a man. Brand me with Your knowledge and power so that I am me once again in You. In Your name I . . .

Jon was about finished prayin' when he saw about the most God-darned gorgeous woman he'd ever laid his eyes on walk in front of Jesse Garon Presley's grave, pick a flower from the wreath, and tuck it behind her ear. She was blond and blue-eyed and had this body on her that was nothin' but curves. Had on tight faded blue jeans frayed at the bottom and some kind of tight low-cut white sweater that showed a good bit of chest.

Jon thought he was just gonna burst when she sucked on that lower lip, real impatient like, and looked around the garden. He knew he should just leave her alone and keep on takin' care of the business at hand. But man, those hips, eyes, lips. She was shaped like a God-dang Coca-Cola bottle. Probably could wrap just his hands 'round that little waist.

The woman tossed back her blond hair and sat on the fence as everyone else kept lookin' at the grave. Just a bit of her stomach showed from beneath her tiny little sweater and she looked down at the skin. Jon's blood hammered out a pulse in his ears when her lips slightly parted in a smile.

She then lowered her blue eyes to her chest, sweater stretched tight across her, and smiled some more. Woman was watchin' herself. Watchin' all them curves and bumps.

Dang!

As Jon walked toward her, the wind scattered a thick strand of blond hair across one eye. She blew it away with a quick breath from her movie-star lips.

"Ma'am?"

The smile disappeared. She hooked her feet in the low fence, placed her hands on the rail, and looked away.

"Ma'am, I jes had to come over when I seen you, to tell you you're the prettiest girl I think I ever seen."

The woman raked her long red fingernails over her puffy lips and smiled.

"Well, I'm sure you get tole that a lot. And I'm jes a stupid little country boy. But I was wonderin', there's this little malt shop across the road there called Rockabilly's. Wonder if you'd allow me the pleasure of buyin' you a blueberry milk shake. Taste like a cloud up in heaven, ma'am."

"Are you stoned?" she asked. Real lazy like. She didn't say it sexy, more like she didn't have no time for his mess.

"No, ma'am," he said, feeling himself breathe through his hooded eyes.

She folded her arms across her chest and kept looking through the loose crowd that was floating back to the front of the mansion. Jon always liked this part of the day best. He liked to be the final person to leave the garden and the last to say good-bye to E and the family before night coated their lonely bodies.

"You lookin' for someone special?" Jon asked.

"Maybe," she said. "I don't know."

He watched her eyes move across the crowd and focus on an old man in a blue leisure suit carrying a purse. His hair was dyed so black that it looked blue. He was white and pasty and looked like he'd lain with other men.

The woman shook her head.

Jon smiled, his face flushing with excitement.

"You lookin' for a man called Deke Rivers?"

Her eyes slowly turned back to him, her mouth tight like she was real annoyed, and unfolded her arms. "And what would you know about Deke?"

Chapter 21

AFTER BEING SHOT AT, killing another man, and ultimately being called a liar, about the only thing I could think of that would really soothe the problem, mend my psyche, and possibly motivate me to find the answers I was looking for was simple: a plate of ribs from the Blues City Café. I know most real hard-core barbecue folks swear by Cozy Corner on North Parkway or Payne's down on Lamar. But although I have to admit Payne's makes a truly beautiful pork sandwich, there is nothing like dipping your steak fries in some of that sweet molasses-fused sauce down on Beale.

I ordered a large slab. U refused to eat anything deep-fried or barbecued. Abby ordered a Coke.

"You sure you don't want some gumbo?" U asked, polishing off the last spoonful of his. It looked like a mean batch, but I sure missed Loretta's cooking.

Abby shook her head. She fiddled with the old watch on her wrist. It was gold and tarnished and looked like it was made for a man.

Apparently, she never quite warmed up to Bubba Cotton. He'd kept *Days of Our Lives* cranked to volume eleven while she stared out his window and played a little with his cat. But U said Bubba didn't mind. U said he'd only known Bubba to say a couple of sentences in the last ten years. Bubba grunted all he wanted you to know.

I looked over at U as he pushed away his bowl and smiled.

"Better than tofu?" I asked.

"Much. Although, a little teriyaki sauce can make a tire taste good."

He stared over at Abby and then back at me. He nodded. Slowly, keeping eye contact. It was time.

"Abby, look, I know this is tough as hell. I can't imagine what you went through at that casino. But we need to know about those folks."

Abby kept on with the watch. She suddenly stopped, letting it hang loose, and pulled out a couple of sugar packets from a bin on the table. She poured them into a small mountain before her and then raked through the mass with a fork. A tiny Zen garden on the table.

She never broke concentration as she shook pepper on the pure cane and mixed it through the white. She clenched her jaw as if grinding her teeth would stop whatever pain she'd endured.

"What was it?" I asked. I grabbed her hand and she pulled away. The Zen garden swept away under her hand and onto the floor.

U kept silent. He leaned back in the chair pretending not to pay attention.

"Can we walk?" she asked. "If I stay here another moment I'm going to puke. I need some air."

"Sure," I said, pulling out my wallet and dropping money on the table. She was already gone, through the restaurant and out the front doors to the mouth of Beale Street. I pushed through a couple of drunk businessmen in ties and plastic derbys and found her walking down a pathway. She was hugging herself. Head down.

Beale was the black business district that had recently become tourist central for the city. I loved the stories of the old sin dens, told by blues musicians who'd played Handy Park back in the day. Pool halls. Whiskey joints. Grocery stores. Pawnshops. Now the historic street was just a neon strip mall filled mainly with bars that exuded as much cultural importance as a Gap in Des Moines. Who came to Memphis to eat a burger at a Hard Rock Café? Like my old buddy Tad Pierson always says, people want to see the grit.

Funk pulsed from some no-name bar. Jazz floated from the open door of the next. A daiquiri stand advertised with a warped sheet metal sign like it was an old-time juke.

"Abby?" I yelled, finally catching her at the intersection of Rufus Thomas Boulevard. I grabbed her hand and pulled her out of the road as a horse-drawn carriage passed. "C'mon. Someone tried to kill both of us last night. Now they're jerking me around and pretending like the whole thing was a joke. Please."

"I need your help," she said. "I need your word."

"You got it."

She was a head shorter than me and I could see the darkened roots of her hair, which was loosely parted in the middle and smelled of hotel soap. She didn't wear makeup and her face was flushed with embarrassment like she was about to tell a dirty story that she'd begun but didn't want anyone to hear.

"Will you go to Oxford with me?" she asked.

I nodded.

"I have a cousin," she said, her teeth chattering. "And I can't reach her."

"You're afraid they will?"

She nodded. A panhandler walked up to me and grabbed the edge of my jean jacket as a cold fall breeze shot down Beale like an icy river. He said he'd lost his bus fare and needed to see his sick wife. I didn't turn to him but handed him a couple of bucks.

"What do they want?" I asked her.

"My parents were murdered. I left town and came back a few days ago to get some of my dad's things. They were waiting for me."

"Who was your dad?"

"A lawyer."

"Why would they . . . ?"

"I don't know. I swear to you, I don't know." Her tired eyes grew larger as the din of the music down the street grew into a pulsing beat. The steady rhythm seemed to pick up energy and pace as a saxophonist played to an empty street.

I handed Abby my threadbare jacket.

She accepted it and pulled it onto her shivering body.

Chapter 22

PERFECT LEIGH LOVED good hotels. She loved the way they folded back your covers at night and left little mints beneath your pillow. She loved the smell of clean sheets and tiny hotel soaps. She liked room service and the list of services like massage or laundry or whatever kiss-ass kind of thing they could come up with. Basically, she loved being pampered, loved people tripping over themselves to please her. She wished the world could be one big luxury hotel, she thought, walking through the lobby of the Peabody. She wished everybody could just keep kissing her ass like they couldn't get enough.

The air smelled cleaner here, like rich people didn't fart as much as the farm trash who stayed down in Tunica. Smelled like hot coffee and pot-pourri and new shoes fresh from the box.

Today she was wearing a nice pair of knee-high brown boots with a tan suede skirt and white cotton shirt rolled to the elbows. Her hair shone a honey-colored blond. She smelled good, too. Smelled like body powder and Calvin Klein soap.

She felt so damned good that she even hated to touch the jive-talking bellhop who was handing baggage tickets to a Japanese couple. They were doing a lot of *ooh*ing and *ahh*ing about the marble fountain in the middle of the lobby and all the gold trim and oriental rugs.

As soon as they left, she grabbed the bellhop's hand. He was in his late forties or early fifties. Hard to tell with blacks. He had bloodshot eyes and reeked of body odor. Still she smiled, head back like her mama taught her to do in all those child beauty pageants.

"Hello," she said, pulling him into a narrow hallway that led up to the banquet rooms. It was quiet and cold in there. Fresh paint and cigarettes.

"Hello yourself, miss. Can I get your car for you?"

She hugged him and began to cry. His nametag smashed into her eye.
Renaldo.

"Renaldo, he's gone."

"He? He who?"

"My husband. Left with another woman. Left me with the kids."

"Miss, I'm sorry and Lord, you are pretty and all. But—"

She hugged him tighter, getting a good smoosh of her breasts against
his chest, letting him check out her cleavage and smell her Calvin Klein.
This was too easy. She almost wanted to yawn.

"He's a big fella. Black-and-gray hair. Has a scar down one eyebrow.
Wears boots."

He shook his head. Perfect released her grip and handed him fifty
dollars.

"Find the man who checked him out of the hotel and he'll get a hundred."

"Lord, he musta done you real bad."

"You have no idea, Renaldo. Please."

Renaldo tipped his slanted green hat and disappeared. In a few minutes
he returned with a small black man with ears that reminded her of the
movie *Gremlins*. He had a big grin on his face and almost danced in front
of her as he bounced from foot to foot.

"You've seen him?" she asked.

He looked back at Renaldo and then smiled at Perfect. She handed him
the hundred.

"I seen him. Left with a young woman. Wasn't as pretty as you, ma'am."

Perfect finally yawned and pulled a long thread that had somehow
attached itself to her suede boot. She ran her tongue over her teeth and
made a quick smile that fell. "And?"

"That's what I seen."

"Where did he go?"

He shook his head and looked down at his hand.

Perfect stood up to her full six feet (boots helping with four inches),
tucked her hair behind her ears, and scanned each direction of the hallway.
She suddenly ripped a long section of her blouse.

The men started backing away like they were watching a mad dog circling and foaming at the mouth.

"You tell me where they went or I start yelling rape."

"Lord God!" Renaldo said under his breath, pulling away his hat and pulling the little black boy close to his chest. "You crazy."

"You're right, I'm one crazy fucking bitch. Now tell me where they went." She started grunting and expelling little gasps of air like she was trying to scream. She tore at her blouse again and flashed the men her lacey bra. They averted their eyes but seemed to have their feet stuck in concrete.

"Mi-Mi-Mississippi," the boy said. "Asked if they needed a cab and he asked for his truck. Said he goin' to there. That's all I know. Don't know nothin' about them."

Perfect patted his cheek and straightened the hat for Renaldo.

"All I needed. You boys are so kind."

Perfect seemed to float as she skipped down the hall and out to the car where Jon waited.

Woman seemed to give the ole boa constrictor who lived in his pants a good swellin', Jon thought, as he watched Perfect emerge from the Peabody on Union and walk over to his car by the new baseball field. Lord, she had long legs like his old girlfriend Inga and had this self-confidence about her that made her seem more sexy than anything he'd ever imagined. Kind of like she always knew it'd be the biggest pleasure in his life if he ever got in her drawers and rooted around like a hog. But for some reason, Perfect treated him like the damned mental case at the family reunion. That kid that drooled in his wheelchair as everybody grabbed their potato salad and talked about grandpa's drinkin' problem.

She climbed in beside him and pulled off her shirt. She had on a pink bra with flowers. Man, her breasts were so full they just swelled. Tight little stomach with just a slash for a belly button. *Man, oh man.* If she wanted it here that was fine by him. He crawled over the gear shift feelin' the ole snake gettin' hungrier than hell before she slapped his face, pushed him back into the driver's seat, and pulled on a fresh shirt.

"You touch me and I'll have you back at that gas station from whatever Podunk town you're from in two seconds. I don't give a crap how many people you've killed."

"Sorry, Miss Perfect."

"That's better. Now drive."

"Where to?"

"Just drive, I'll tell you. Head south."

"Like Mississippi."

"No, like Alaska. Yes, Mississippi. Now, go."

She was checking her lipstick in the visor mirror as Jon dropped his gaze to his crotch to make sure nothin' was showin'. She wasn't like any other woman he'd ever known. She was it. She was that special woman that E always found halfway through the movie. And, at first, she always hated E, too.

If she was going to be his wife, he had some work to do. What would E do? Think. Jon pulled onto the highway headed south and ran his mind over some of those sacred scenes from *Clambake*. Shelley Fabares lookin' for a rich man when all she really needed was E's love.

Where was a guitar when you needed one?

Chapter 23

THE LAST TIME I was in Oxford, Mississippi, I had to bail an old teacher of mine out of jail for exposing himself to a group of tourists at the home of William Faulkner. He said he was trying to finish a blues song he'd been working on for the last ten years when the group—retirees on a *Southern Living* tour—descended on the historic site on a day it was normally closed. He was so pissed off that they'd disrupted his peace that he thought it would be a fantastic idea if he unzipped his fly, pulled out his unit, and placed his National steel guitar between his legs. When this portly woman asked him if he could play her a little ditty, a dewy mint julip loose in her fingers, my blues-tracker mentor pulled the instrument to his chest and plucked away. Crazy old fucker was still laughing when I found him at the Oxford jail, explaining how the woman screamed all the way back to Ohio or Pennsylvania or wherever she lived.

I wondered where he was now as I turned off the highway and drove along Jackson and past the chain restaurants and superstores and corporate apartments that had descended on the small town in the last few years. I longed for even a decade ago, when my teacher and I would hit the back highways near Oxford, destination unknown, searching for blues men who'd disappeared into small towns across the state. The homogenization of a place so unique, so American, made me sick to my stomach.

I'd heard about a planned Super Wal-Mart that wanted to rape acres of nearby woods and a freakin' Applebee's that wanted to bring potato-skin cuisine to northern Mississippi, and even of the slack-eyed retirees that longed for three-hundred-thousand-dollar condos with five-foot setbacks along rolling acres of golf courses.

I knew that's why I seldom came back. I wanted to remember the

Oxford I once knew. Greasy biscuits at Smitty's. Samurai films at the Hoka. Blues bands at Syd and Harry's.

It had been years since I'd made it over to the Blues Archive for any work, but that was the first place I drove. I wanted to make the most of my time while I helped Abby. Maybe I could find out something about Clyde that wouldn't have me going back to that asshole Cook again.

Earlier that morning, I'd left a message for Ed Komara, a friend of mine who ran the archive, and another message with a woman who worked at the *Commercial-Appeal* library. I knew the woman from hours of research at the paper's morgue and had recently helped her get some B. B. King tickets through JoJo—a long-time friend of the legend.

In return, the woman said she'd pull any clips on Eddie Porter or Clyde James and fax them to Ed's office at Ole Miss. I told Abby all this wouldn't take too long and then we'd search for her cousin who she couldn't seem to reach on the phone.

But a weird thing happened when we started talking about Clyde James and my work as a tracker. It was all Abby could talk about. She asked me about a million questions on the drive down and even had me play some of his music that I'd burned onto a CD.

"So this is what you do, look for these singers."

"Yep."

"And he was known? Famous?" she asked over my noisy muffler.

"Number-one hit in 'sixty-six. Then, he just dropped out."

Abby sat silent for a moment as we rounded the curve by The Grove and headed to Farley. She pulled her hair into a ponytail and sank it back through the loop in her Ole Miss hat. She wore the sweatpants and T-shirt like some kind of uniform.

"Can I help?"

"I think we just need to get you settled," I said.

"I want to help," she said, and nodded as if just making up her mind right there. The shadows from the oaks played over her face as we darted in and out of the sun. We parked on the street and went inside.

The university housed the Blues Archive in the old law library, a space a good size larger than where I worked at Tulane. At Tulane, we only had a small cluttered room for studying separated from the actual library, mostly dedicated to jazz. At Ole Miss it was almost all blues. Two floors that included more than 20,000 photographs (some the only ones in existence), 7,000 records donated by B. B. King himself, and even the financial documents of the old Trumpet Record Label. Posters, memorabilia, back issues of *Living Blues*, and old newspaper clippings.

As soon as we walked in the door, I saw a table by the staircase already loaded with magazines and manila files. A black woman in a dashiki nodded to me as she talked on the phone.

I recognized the familiar logo of Bluff City 45s with its fanned hand of aces, jacks, and jokers. A can of Community Coffee sat on top of the folders. It would be empty. Always Ed's price for help. A Post-It note said he had to catch a plane to a conference in New York and call him if I needed anything else.

Abby sat down at the table and waited for me to pass her a file.

"Hold on, don't you need to try your cousin again?"

"I used to help my dad with his cases. I'd go through depositions to find out any inconsistencies. He said I was better than any of his paralegals."

"Well, this isn't exactly like that. Really, it's not too complicated. I'm just going to read through some articles and make notes of people Clyde worked with."

"Why not ask people you already know?"

"Better to know everything for yourself."

"They lie?"

"They do. And they forget."

"Then what?"

"Then, after I get you settled, I'll go back to Memphis and start my search again."

"You really believe he's alive?"

"Yep."

Must've been about thirty seconds after I sat back down, after grabbing a couple of Cokes from a vending machine in the hall, that I sorted out the gold from the mud. Two articles on the Eddie Porter/Mary James murder investigation sent from the Memphis paper. A couple of shorts. The first dated March 1969. It quoted the police director, guy named Wagner, as knowing what happened to Porter and James but that he couldn't press charges because "the south Memphis community wouldn't cooperate." There was no indication as to what the hell that meant. The second had more:

> MEMPHIS—The Shelby County District Attorney's Office said it will not bring charges against a local singer in the deaths of two Negroes killed last year.
>
> Detectives had targeted Clyde James in their early investigation. His past criminal record includes burglary.
>
> James worked in a musical group that also featured victim Edward Porter. The other victim was James' wife. A spokesman for the district attorney's office said although James was at home at the time of the shootings, several people were questioned about the murder.
>
> The case remains active, he said.

I wondered how this small detail passed by Loretta. *Shit.* And no wonder Cook didn't want to talk if he was close to Clyde. I put on headphones and placed a 45 on the turntable. "Pouring Water on a Drowning Man."

Abby read through the clip, made a few notes on a legal pad she'd borrowed from the librarian, and waited for me to pass the headphones. I did.

"Like it?" I wrote on the legal pad.

She nodded and closed her eyes.

I continued to read through the bios on Clyde. Still the same. The early days with the Zion Ramblers, the crossover to secular music, and the first releases for Bluff City. Found a nice press release about Clyde, his relation to Loretta, and his early days as a bricklayer in south Memphis. Writer tried to tie in the manual labor with laying the groundwork for success.

I began searching through another pile and found a publicity shot of Clyde. He was smiling and wearing a sharp leather jacket. But the smile showed just a trace of an upright curve and the eyes seemed hazy and out of focus, like he'd been caught at an awkward moment. Like someone had intruded on his sadness.

I took off the headphones and looked back through a few magazines. Nothing. Small profiles. A few record reviews.

Abby passed me a yellowed piece of paper, holding the edge like you would a dead fish. She seemed afraid she'd tear the worn newspaper print.

And, at first touch, I knew why: the paper was brittle and thin, almost translucent.

I unfolded the article and lightly flattened it smooth with my palms. Abby smiled. Proud of her find. Article was stamped on the back as coming from the *Tri-State Defender*, a black paper that was a subsidiary of the famous *Chicago Defender*. It was an editorial on the Porter-James murders called FACING FACTS NOT EASY FOR SUPERSTAR.

It's been two years since someone took the life of a talented man and a beautiful young lady. Still, no one has been found guilty by those who call themselves our police. To those who've had previous experience with our local guard, they will recognize the apathy. But as one who knew Eddie Porter as few did—I was his pastor and the first to hire him to play organ in our little church—I'm enraged that perhaps the problem lies even further from police and into our own community.

Porter's supposed "friend," soul shouter Clyde James, was home at the time of the attack. Still, Mr. James told police he didn't see anything. Both his wife, who I'm told was carrying his child, and Porter were killed by gunfire. How does a man not hear gunfire in a quiet neighborhood on Rosewood Avenue? How does one not hear violence in one's own home?

I wanted to ask these questions myself to Mr. James, but it seems nobody can find the superstar. It seems that he's been going from bar to bar leaving reality far behind. I've even heard rumors of drugs.

If you read this, Mr. James, stand up. Tell what you know to Mr. Wagner and the police.

I'm told on good authority that at first Mr. James claimed he saw two white men leave his house and drive away in a station wagon. Now it seems that he's changed his story.

Stand up, Mr. James. Stand up.

The story was written by a local preacher by the name of O. T. Jones and was followed by an advertisement for his Sunday sermon. A black-and-white rainbow had been crudely drawn over a church steeple. The motto read: THE FREEDOM TRAIN NEVER STOPS.

"He killed them, didn't he?" Abby asked.

"You know, I don't care. All this shit is telling us is maybe why he split. But I'm just trying to find him. If I were profiling him, I'd probably go back to Memphis and see if I could take a look at the Eddie Porter murder file. Tracker lesson number one: Use your public record."

Abby was tearing the corners off a yellow sheet of paper. In my rush to make the most of a side trip from Memphis, I'd forgotten what this girl had been through. Her parents had been killed and I was sitting around discussing another pretty nasty murder like it was an old movie. I felt like a complete asshole.

"I'm sorry," I said.

"For what?"

"We need to go."

I returned the records and clips to the librarian and watched her as she walked to the caged doors and locked away Clyde's legacy. I looked up at the walls covered in old juke house posters and concert bills. Howlin' Wolf. Little Milton. Even a musical festival in Memphis with a big picture of soul legend Rufus Thomas eating a hotdog bun loaded with a harmonica.

"My daddy never let me listen to this kind of music," she said as we walked down a wide staircase, almost as if she were talking to herself.

I asked her why.

"Said it was an embarrassment to our state."

"What do you think?" I asked.

She seemed surprised by the question.

Chapter 24

AS WE WALKED under a tunnel of cedar trees, purple shadows dripped over the tin roof of the stables where Abby's cousin, Maggie, worked. Abby scooted ahead in a brisk walk, but I lagged behind, watching a magnolia leaf fall in spindly patterns. The air was heavy with dust still lingering from my truck's tires. Somewhere a woodpecker knocked the hell out of a tree while a squirrel foraged through a pile of bricks covered in green moss.

I whizzed a pebble into the woods and followed Abby into the long building where ragged light caught dust motes in a yellow swath. Down the rows of horses, making brimming sounds with their lips, I heard a woman talking. The air smelled of manure and old leather.

The woman was thin with muscular arms, dark tanned skin, short black hair, and brilliant green eyes. She was a head taller than Abby and wore blue jeans and a gray T-shirt. Ancient brown boots. She had the kind of rapid, quick look that processed your appearance and computed her decision within seconds.

She hugged Abby very tightly.

Abby broke away for a moment and grabbed my hand, pulling me forward. I introduced myself. The woman didn't say a thing; she looked at me as if I'd just whipped it out and pissed on the stall floors.

"My fly isn't open? Is it?"

"It better not be," she said. Sweat stained the front of her T-shirt and a smudge of dirt traced the edge of her jaw. A worn-out pair of Texas show boots, decorated with red roses and cactus, sat by the stall door.

"May I ask what in the fuck a man your age is doing with Abby?"

"She's helping me with my yard work. Sometimes she plays dominoes with me and feeds my cats."

Inside, a black quarter horse with a white star shimmied its head from side to side. The woman frowned, strong commalike creases around her mouth.

"What the fuck, Abby?"

"Maggie, calm down. It's not what you think. He's helping me."

"Helping you do what, doll?"

Maggie looked down at my boots and up at my face. I grinned like a giddy criminal in a prison lineup.

"It's a long story, Maggie. Listen, we really need to talk. Do you know a woman named Ellie?"

"No."

"Think hard. Said she knows you through her boyfriend. Said y'all had a time at some crawfish boil."

"I've never been to a crawfish boil. That's for stupid yahoos from Louisiana."

I smiled. "Exactly."

"I tried to call," Abby said.

"Well, sometimes the phone company gets a little pissed when you're late," Maggie said.

"You about done 'round here?" Abby asked.

"C'mon," Maggie said, walking across the smooth brown dirt to the back of the stables. I rested my arms on a battered wood gate and smoothed the white star on the horse's forehead.

"Nick?" Abby asked.

I turned and she motioned me to follow them. I have to admit I watched the way Maggie walked. Enjoyed it. She sure could wear a pair of jeans. There was something earthy and honest about her. Always had a thing for women who said what was on their minds. Don't know why. It just seemed like everyone I'd ever really given a damn about could handle herself just as well without me.

"Never told me that she was mean," I said.

Abby whispered: "She's pretty, isn't she?"

"I hadn't noticed."

At the second-to-last stall, Maggie stood back with a wide smile across her lips. Abby turned to the stall and, within a couple of seconds, started crying. I moved closer and saw her arms around the neck of a chestnut-colored horse with a black mane.

Maggie kept smiling until she noticed me again. Her eyes narrowed and she dug her boots into the brown dirt. As she continued to beat me in a staring contest, she said sweetly to Abby, "You want to head over to Taylor? Only thing open on Sunday."

"That okay, Nick?" Abby said.

Maggie kept staring.

I narrowed my eyes back at her and said, "Love to."

Old Taylor Road stretched out from Oxford like a familiar song. The road bent and twisted over gentle curves framed by barbed-wire fences as a tired sun dipped low through the pines. Cheap student apartments soon became crooked farmhouses and dilapidated trailers. I'd lived near here for two years but hadn't been out this way. I followed Maggie's Rabbit convertible until I was sure we were lost. I thought maybe she was playing some kind of joke on me, now with Abby safely riding with her, or was taking me somewhere where we'd meet a few of her redneck cowboy buddies.

But then we arrived in a loose, brittle collection of storefronts and cottages. Blue and orange light scattered through oaks and slid down onto the tin-roofed shotguns. I pulled in front of an old building with a wide, crooked porch that seemed out of a black-and-white photo from the Depression. Three men sat on a two-by-eight stretched over some rusted paint cans. One played Dobro. The other a fat acoustic bass.

"Evenin'," the Dobro player said.

"Howdy," I said. I liked saying howdy.

Inside, we took a seat at a heavy wood table covered in a red-and-white-checked tablecloth. Maggie brought in a six-pack from a cooler in her car and pulled off two cans. Slivers of ice fell off the aluminum.

"Maggie," Abby said.

"Oh, well." She pulled off another beer and placed it in the center of the table. "Sorry."

The ceiling was wood and sagged along ancient slats. Floor was wood, too, scuffed as smooth as glass. Graffiti covered the walls and gallons of pepper sauce, quarts of cayenne pepper, and fat industrial jars of mayon-naise filled a stocking shelf.

Men in overalls. Women with two-hundred-dollar snakeskin purses. Gray-headed farmers and frat boys. Place was packed.

"Abby said you're going to help her," Maggie said, popping the top of her beer.

"I'll try. Mainly I just want to make sure she's safe."

"She's safe," Maggie said. She lit a cigarette and blew smoke across the table. Muddled static of conversations filled the room.

"You don't have to impress me," I said. "You're tough. I get the idea."

"She doesn't need any more help. You've done what you needed to. You brought her back to me. Thanks. I'll buy you dinner. You drink that can of beer, have a good meal, and then head out. All right?"

Abby closed her eyes and mashed her fingers into her temples.

Maggie didn't say a word for about thirty seconds. A waitress came over and we all ordered the same thing, catfish with pecan rice. I finished the beer and tried another smile on Maggie. It was a good one, too, the kind that made women cling to my back.

"You have something on your shirt," she said.

I wiped some hot sauce from my T-shirt pocket.

"To the left," she said.

I wiped away some more dried remnants of red pepper sauce I'd used at breakfast.

"Messy eater," I said.

"No kidding. I'm sure all the women are impressed."

"You'd be surprised." I turned up my nose. "Do I still smell manure?"

Abby spoke up: "Am I not here? Both of you shut the hell up."

Both doors were open and a breeze washed through the room as if coming from a machine.

"Maggie," Abby said. "Yesterday morning I went back to Oxford for some of Daddy's papers and some woman followed me. She pretended like she was a friend of yours and took me to this old gas station where these men grabbed me and took me to a casino in Tunica. I didn't want to tell you. I didn't want to worry you, but, Jesus, sometimes you can be so fuck-ing hard on people."

Abby didn't seem like the girl who said fuck a lot and the word seemed a hell of a lot dirtier and hard coming out of her mouth. Just kind of hung there for a moment.

"So who is he? You really meet him in Memphis?"

"No, he helped me back at the casino. He killed a man trying to make sure I was safe."

"God," Maggie said, stubbing out her cigarette and looking at my face again.

The bluegrass band began to play outside and we walked to the porch to finish our peach cobbler. I balanced the cobbler and a coffee in my arms and took a seat between Abby and Maggie on the two-by-eight bench. The band had moved onto the back of a 'fifties pickup and was picking out a combination of songs. "You Are My Sunshine" to "You Don't Miss Your Water."

Lately, it seemed that fun had to be engineered. I saw it all across the Quarter, bars that packaged phony Cajun and New Orleans culture in easy, digestible bites. There was something solid about wondering if you'd make it back from a night at the old Tips or playing a game of chance by leaving your car parked near the Rivershack. Now, we had House of Blues and the new Tips and daiquiri stands that had taken over smoke-filled piano bars unchanged since the 'forties. I would've never guessed I would have ended up having a hell of a time with Abby and her surly cousin. But I did. Never plan a thing. A sure route to enjoyment.

Abby stirred melted ice cream around the last peaches and Maggie pulled out another cigarette. She had on those scuffed show boots and a clean white T-shirt that advertised Stetson hats.

The T-shirt was tight. Her breath didn't stink.

When the band hit the last note of the William Bell song, Abby put down the cobbler, her eyes staring straight ahead. She hiked the elastic band of her sweatpants leg up to her knee and rubbed the tiny red bumps that had formed on her calf. Maggie picked up our bowls and walked back inside, the screen door banging the frame behind her.

Abby kept staring into the darkness.

"I want to go with you," she said. "I want to help."

"Let's go down to the police station and we'll talk about getting you some protection. I have to head back to Memphis."

She shook her head and bit the edge of her lip. "You promised."

"I promised to find your cousin and make sure you were safe."

"You need me," she said.

Maggie came back and took a seat, resting her back against the worn wall. She cracked open a fourth beer she'd gotten from somebody inside, and nodded along with the music. The Dobro and the mandolin melted into the crisp fall night, their notes twisting and falling with a sweetness of old memories. The music reminded me of times I'd failed to recognize as being the best I'd ever known.

I looked over at Abby. She'd had on the same old sweatpants for two days and they were stretched like socks over her running shoes. The knees had already become balled and dirty.

"Abby?" Maggie asked, blowing out some smoke. "Been picking up your folks' mail and found something kind of strange. Letter from Memphis to your daddy. Did he always work with private investigators?"

"I guess." I watched her as she wrapped herself tighter in my jean jacket.

I placed the cup of coffee by my feet and stared in each direction at the two women.

"Your daddy's secretary gave it to me and said it was personal," Maggie said. "Maybe you should take a look."

Chapter 25

MAGGIE LIVED JUST a few miles from Taylor, at the end of a twisting dirt road lined with mounds of kudzu and honeysuckle vines. The house was white and old, an elongated box made of clapboard and tin, with fat Christmas lights dangling from the roof. Outside, thickets of rosebushes grew near short rows of corn and tomatoes, now withered and brown. A laundry line hung loose to the side of the house filled with flowered cotton dresses and extremely short pairs of pants.

"You live with a midget?" I asked after we parked and walked through the chilled fall night. The stars above were bright and crisp but a biting wind had kicked up and I saw a dark cloud curtain headed east.

"A son," Maggie said in the darkness. "You know those little things that men help create but often leave?"

"I ain't got no kids," I mumbled, following her. We stepped into a wide wood-paneled room that smelled like burnt Italian food. It was dimly lit with a television flashing a Chevy truck commercial.

A little boy with inky-black hair lay on a tattered couch, a coloring book loose in his hands. An older black woman came out from the kitchen wiping her hands with a rag and exchanged a few words with Maggie before disappearing out a side door.

I stood, afraid to wake the kid.

The floor was buckled linoleum and dotted with broken trucks and headless plastic heroes. She'd lined the walls with frames filled with photos too personal to have been bought. Black-and-whites of headstones and old people on porches and brilliant white suns setting low across cotton fields.

"Yours?" I asked.

She nodded and handed Abby a Golden Flake potato chip box filled with mail. Maggie picked up the boy, slack but grumbling, and left the room. Abby dropped the box onto the old sofa and I took a seat by her.

The woman had been watching Leno and I quickly flipped the channels to Letterman with a heavy remote. The sofa was thick with animal hair. Above the mantel gazed a mounted deer head.

Abby flipped through several letters, mailers, and magazines. I noticed a couple. *Southern Living. Soldier of Fortune.*

She stared at the outside of one envelope longer than the others and then quickly tore into it. She read it for a few moments. Her lips slightly parted and she used her right hand to brush the hair from her face onto the back of her ear. She tucked her legs up under her, shook her head, and then handed the letter to me.

The letterhead was, like Maggie said, from a private investigator in Memphis named Art Copeland. He wrote pretty simply that he intended to keep the deposit that Bill MacDonald had given him. He said he'd exhausted his search through Social Security, criminal, and Department of Motor Vehicles records. Still, he could not find out more about the man Abby's father wanted.

I'm sorry but there is no record of Clyde James since 1974.

"Holy shit," I said.

"Holy shit," Abby said.

The rain hit us as soon as we reached this wide-porched white house on the outskirts of Oxford. Man, it felt like it had been raining since I arrived in Memphis and I just wished it would stop for a few minutes. I was tired of being wet and cold and having to change clothes about every hour. Somehow, the rain felt different here as we ran to the house. Felt much colder and more brittle, little tiny needles angled at my face.

We clamored up onto the porch filled with dead plants in mossy terra-cotta pots. Abby walked ahead of me, pulling out a key from her balled fist.

Crime-scene tape covered the back entrance and it looked like someone had tried to lock up the house. A padlock had been ripped from the frame and it sat dangling and useless.

Abby tossed it aside and opened the door's dead bolt. We ran inside as thunder boomed in the thick night, making patting sounds in the pine forest.

As we entered, thunder boomed again and shook the dark house.

She tried the light switch but nothing worked. I clicked on my lighter and Abby scurried off for a few seconds and returned with two thick candles. She rushed back into the room as if the other rooms lacked oxygen and she could only breathe when she was next to me.

"Where's the office?" I asked.

She carefully held the candles as I, slightly shivering from the cold rain, lit them and followed her to the back of the house. The thunder crashed pretty damned close to us again and Abby reeled but caught herself and kept walking. I knew she could hear the gunshots in her head and it gave me a thick lump in my throat as I watched her trying to ignore the sounds and images.

She rolled back some wide-paneled doors and pointed at a large wooden desk and two tall metal file cabinets. The walls were painted a deep red and lined with prints of Confederate battle scenes. There was a collection of antique guns mounted on the wall.

Abby sat on the couch, teeth chattering pretty badly. Lightning spliced in a blue and purple zigzag outside and she covered her face with her hands.

"Do you have any clothes here?" I asked, trying to get her mind on something else.

She nodded, face in hands. "No."

"Still at the dorm?"

"I don't want to."

"Abby, I'll go with you. Where's your room?"

She stayed still for a few moments and then she wordlessly got to her feet and circled around the den to a short hallway and a room covered in art print posters. Renoir. Picasso. On a long blue bookshelf, she had several trophies topped with gold horses. An old cowboy hat sat crooked on a life-size cutout of James Dean.

The room smelled stale and dead. Almost like some of the museums in New Orleans. Place had the feeling that nothing should be touched here. In the candlelight, Abby carefully opened an antique dresser and pulled out a pair of old jeans and a sweatshirt.

Her curly blond hair hung loose. Her brown eyes looked tired as hell. I folded my arms and studied the spines of her books as she pulled off her jacket and peeled off her T-shirt.

In a short flash I saw her wet bra and tight stomach. I turned my head quickly.

"Doesn't matter. You've already seen all of me anyway."

I nodded and studied the books. Eudora Welty. Willie Morris.

"You like Salinger?" I asked.

I heard her slough off the sweatpants and saw a wet bra tossed onto the floor.

"Haven't read him," she said.

"You should. He has this story he tells in *Catcher in the Rye* about finding an old baseball mitt that belonged to his brother, Allie. He said Allie used to write poems up and down the fingers and into the pocket."

When I turned back she was pulling her wet hair into a ponytail and had on a fresh pair of jeans and a sweatshirt. I picked up the wet clothes and balled them under my arm. She waited for me to finish whatever the hell I was talking about.

I smiled and said, "After a while this stuff won't hurt so much. Keep some of their things so you can remember them."

"You close to your folks?" she asked.

"I was."

"They're dead?"

I nodded.

"I'm sorry," she said. "I didn't mean to make you sad."

"Shit," I said, looking away. "That was a long time ago."

"Were they killed or something?"

"My father was an alcoholic and drank himself to death."

"Your mother?"

I grabbed the candle from the bookshelf and took a deep breath.

"My mother just didn't like living very much," I said.

Her eyes changed as she watched me. They went from sad to soft, picking up her candle and for the first time truly leading the way.

For more than an hour, we tore through her father's twin file cabinets. Seemed like we went through every file her father had ever touched. I'd read through each one and then passed it to her to read by candlelight. A couple times she looked like she had something she desperately wanted to tell me, but at the last second would change her mind and bury her head back into a file.

"What kind of law did your father practice?" I asked.

"Mainly he worked on contracts," she said. "He helped people with their money, set up special accounts. And he did a lot with wills for old people around town. He was always busy when someone died."

"What's the Sons of the South?" I asked.

I tossed her a loose pile of papers and pamphlets with a Confederate battle flag logo. She read along as I did, about a lot of mission statements and quotes from dead generals. Kept on saying they were not a hate group, only preservers of Southern culture.

"Never heard him mention it," she said, her lips still silently reading along. Rallies to save the Mississippi state flag. A battle re-enactment in Vicksburg. Some kind of big convention in Jackson, Tennessee.

"It's a hate group," I said.

"Says it's not."

" 'We don't endorse the Klan' doesn't exactly mean they want to hold hands and sing the world a song in perfect harmony."

"Look right here," Abby said. " 'The Sons of the South does not advocate any violence or malice to anyone outside the Celtic heritage of the South. The SOS will further the sponsorship of stronger states' rights, the advancement of Southern heritage, and the return of Christian morals to our children.' That doesn't sound so bad."

"What kind of Southern heritage?"

"Oh, says 'Celtic,' " she said, frowning at me. "Listen, my daddy loved the Civil War. That doesn't mean he was a racist. Just because you support having a flag with history doesn't mean you don't like black people. My daddy worked with blacks his whole life."

"Abby, it's okay."

"There was one time we were having a dinner party and some asshole from New York was there and talking about how Southerners were racist because we were illiterate. I thought my daddy was going to tear his head off. He said the most racist people he'd ever known lived up north."

"Calm down," I said, prying the pamphlet from her fingers. "Let's just

put this aside. I just wanted to know if your daddy ever talked about joining this group."

She shook her head as I moved the folder to a separate file. We studied
more and placed a few more files with the Sons of the South.

"Did he ever go over to the casinos?"

She shook her head. "Never mentioned them."

After a while, I got up and stretched and shuffled back through the
files, carefully inserting them back into each of the eight slots in the cabi-
net. She noticed I'd pulled out one file that contained a few crayon pictures
she'd made as a kid and looked away.

"Your father owned a lot of property. Looks like he had thousands of
acres across the Delta and up north. Owned some land in Jackson, Tennessee, too."

Abby nodded, really listening, hands wandering over her face with
fatigue. "Yeah, he used to take me out to some of those places. We'd hunt a
little. He liked to hunt. We also used to break into old cabins in the woods
and go find stuff. Sometimes we'd look for arrowheads in creeks."

I smiled at her as I flipped back through four files I'd pulled from the
rest. Outside the dull patter of rain fell from the gutters. The candles shook
light across her face as I stood.

"You want to get out of here?"

"More than anything," she said. "You find anymore about that singer?"

"I'm sure I'm missing a hell of a lot," I said, scooping up some letters.
"There were tons of case files in there that didn't make a damned bit of
sense to me."

"Or me."

"I'd need an accountant to decipher most of those financial records.
Mainly, I found a shitload about Sons of the South and a thick file of personal letters I'll need your help going over if you don't mind. . . . So, you
never heard him mention the Sons of the South?"

She shook her head again and soon walked with me through the dead
caverns of the house, holding the candles, and back out into the rain. She
locked the door behind us, as if it really mattered, and I smelled the strong
scent of candles as the small flames quickly died in the wind and wetness.

As she followed me back to my truck, her eyes on the broken rocks of the road, I noticed a skinny brown lab wagging its fat tail and placing its two muddy paws onto her chest.

"Old friend?"

She nodded.

I held my truck door open and we all climbed inside.

Chapter 26

JON WAS BATHED in sweat and excitement waiting for the skinny guy with bad teeth to call his name and play his song. This was the opportunity that he knew would come since he met Miss Perfect. This is the way it worked when you were courtin' a high-class woman. You sang the song. She saw you had talent. And soon you kissed her under a fake moon. Dang, it had taken him long enough to talk her into calling off their search for tonight. They were in Oxford and they could stand for a little fun. Stretch the legs. Live a Little. Love a Little. He knew what to do as soon as they'd looped through the Square for about the fiftieth time and he spotted the big plastic road sign with mismatched letters reading, KAR-E-OKE TONITE!

She'd said about a thousand times that they needed to get back and watch the house so they could kill that man Travers and some bad little girl. He told her to relax, they could track 'em to Timbuktu tomorrow. He kind of let it hang there between them like that. Kind of like that he wouldn't mind going to Timbuktu with Miss Perfect, if he knew where it was.

Now Perfect was workin' on her fourth daiquiri while she watched this ole goofy cat clock by the door. Swingin' tail. Shifty bug eyes.

The little bar was kind of dark and smelled like the half-eaten pizzas that lay on the tables around them. There was a good ole handful of college kids around them, too, kids about his age, that were drunker than a goat.

One big ole boy had a straw in his pitcher of beer. A couple of girls on stage were belting out some ole song about "Summer Lovin'" and gigglin' like crazy. They were makin' big eyes at a couple of skinny boys in high-collar T-shirts and beaded necklaces. The girls were so drunk they were about stumblin' off stage.

Jon drank a Dr Pepper. E never drank. And neither would he.

This place reminded him of the time down on E.P. Boulevard when a bus full of Yankees come down to sing all of E's Sun songs at the Holiday Inn. Jon didn't think the police ever did find the one who wore E's metal shades and fake sideburns. Funny how he disappeared after he sang "That's All Right Mamma" while eatin' a big ole cheeseburger, laughin' 'cause he thought E had gotten fat. Never understandin' about the replacement E. Not even when Jon choked the life from his worthless body.

Jon shook his head. Man, his mind sure was hummin' along tonight. He popped another pill in his mouth, pretendin' like he was about to cough, and took another drink of his Dr Pepper. He looked over at Miss Perfect who was slunked into the vinyl of the pizza joint's booth. Bored as hell. Playing with the straw in the daiquiri.

She wouldn't be bored when he hopped on stage. She'd see all the people screamin' and yellin' and goin' crazy, like in his mind, and would love him so hard that he'd never be able to crawl out of bed.

"Has Elvis left the building?" the guy with the bad teeth asked, looking into the crowd.

Jon jumped onto the old wooden stage and felt that same power that E had. Even disguised in a beard, he felt stares onto his body covered in black leather and his electric sideburns and even on the gold T.C.B. necklace (twenty-four carat) that hung from his neck.

But the weird thing was that they was kind of laughin' at him. Thinkin' he was some kind of freak. That's all right. That's the way it worked. There was always the big dumb guy by the jukebox that said E couldn't sing. *One, two. One, two, three.*

He looked down at Miss Perfect and she was mad as a pie-eyed snake. Mad he was makin' a scene. That people were rememberin' him. But she didn't know that's what he wanted.

And then it happened. The magic.

Jon held the fat microphone to his lips and called out that sacred song, so haunting and beautiful that he almost wanted to cry, as the words escaped from his lips:

Down in Louisiana,
Where the alligators grow so mean,

There lives a girl, I swear to the world,
Makes the alligators seem tame.
Polk Salad Annie.

The college kids went wild, man, as he dipped his shoulders and shook all over. Perfect just kept watching, jaw dropped down, and cigarette burning between her cherry-red nails. He sang like E would, right to her. He wanted the holy words to float through the air and into her ears twisting through the miles of veins right to her heart. He wanted to see her wiggle that fine heart-shaped butt and crinkle up that little rabbit nose. Man, he could feel himself heatin' up singin' about ole Polk Salad Annie, that woman wild as hell. He started imaginin' as he was singin'—beer splatterin' all around him—that Perfect was like Annie. He imagined her in a bikini made out of animal hide, showin' off her tight little belly, maybe carryin' a spear down in the bayou. She'd have a wildcat she kept like a damned pet and she'd scream like hell when Jon made love to her up in the trees and sloshin' around in the mud.

"Polk Salad Annie!" Jon sang on the second chorus. "Everybody said it was a shame . . . that her mamma was workin' on a chain gang."

Jon sang it like Perfect's mamma was the one who done wrong. And she had. She'd created a woman so damned fine that it was distractin' to men 'round the world.

Jon looked over at her and ignored the college girl runnin' her tongue across her lips or the two women clawin' at his feet. He just kept singin' to *his* woman. *His* Ann-Margret.

Ten minutes later, Perfect had Jon by the arm and was leading him back to her car. She may not be an expert on killing people, but she knew they'd been seen way too much tonight. If there was killing to be done, they would do it outside Oxford.

"That was interesting," she said, not wanting to tell him that he couldn't sing a lick and that everyone was laughing at him. She didn't want to blow the ego thing. She wanted him to think that all those loopy college girls wanted him for his talent, not 'cause he had a bulge the size of Texas in his leather pants.

After he sang, those girls wouldn't leave him alone. They kept sending beers over to him, only to be replaced by Dr Peppers. They passed phone numbers like they were thirteen, ignoring Perfect completely, and making obscene eye contact across the room. But the thing that touched Perfect tonight, really made her feel like she had his balls in her handbag, was that not once did his eyes leave her face. Or tits.

He was droolin' for her. But they all did. They all did what she wanted.

She popped the lock on the car door, feeling a little numb after the daiquiris. The drive-in's parking lot empty and cold. No lights. Paper bags blowing around in the wind.

She felt his arms around her waist, a strong scent of leather and sweat. His thick lips against the back of her neck. She felt a shiver down her spine like before her time with Levi. Before sex became something that was done to her.

A present. *He would do.* He'd be her present to herself.

As Jon's arms wrapped around her, his pelvis rotating against her butt, she said, "Jon, I want you to do something for me."

"Yes, Miss Perfect?"

Miss Perfect done kicked in the door at the Ole Miss Motel surprising the hell out of Jon. All day long she'd been lookin' at him like he rode the short bus to school, now she was rippin' that nice Hanes T-shirt his mamma bought for him. Didn't even close the door, wind and rain just bustin' through, as she pushed him onto a bed like a dang bearcat.

Bed was round and red and had this real fancy canopy above it that reminded him of a little merry-go-round. Red lights ran up and around its four posts like blood workin' in his veins as she crawled on top of his chest and pushed his wrists to the bed. Thought she was gonna tie him up or somethin', until she reached over, still breathin' real hard, and punched on this little ole car stereo on the bed. Country music came out from speakers up by a mirror at the top of the canopy as Miss Perfect got off him to close the door.

Must've been all them Dr Peppers makin' him drunk, cause them little lights flickerin' around the bed made him feel kind of woozy. He imagined the bed was their own little boat and they'd end up on an island somewhere, where'd she have to dress in animal hides like Polk Salad Annie and shimmy up twisted coconut trees so they could eat.

Radio kept playin' all scratchy as she pushed him to one side of the bed and made a face with a pouty lip, like she was all mad at him sittin' on the bed. Her hair was fine and platinum and her blue eyes as big as quarters. She had a cute little pug nose and thick rubbery lips. Man, she smelled so nice. Made his mouth water.

"I'm sorry, Miss Perfect, I didn't mean to do nothin'," he began.

Then, dang, she was on him again, straddling him and licking his face and fishin' her hands down around his pecker. She pulled the rest of his T-shirt off and threw it to the floor. She started lickin' the tattooed face of E that he had on his bicep and makin' these little cooin' sounds.

Dear E. Felt like he could break wood right about now.

He took a deep breath of air and reached up under her shirt, her skin as warm as an oven on Christmas, and tried to unlatch the back of her bra. But he couldn't find the thing and reached around front, 'cause sometimes high-class women got 'em there. But when he got close, she just slapped his hand away and bit his ear. Hard.

"Dang, what's goin' on here? This ain't fun no more. Miss Perfect, what are you doin' to me?"

She rolled him over to the side and yanked open the bedspread. She was breathin' real hard now, her nostrils flarin', and sort of shakin' like she was cold. He couldn't move, like a damned possum in the road, as she stood and pulled her shirt over her head, motioning with a crooked finger.

"Take them off," she said. She had on a real lacy bra with her breasts just spillin' over the top. Her stomach was tight and hard with a waist that tapered in before rounding out into those beautiful hips.

"Ma'am?"

Then she done reached up and got a good chunk of his black hair.

"Ow!"

"Take them off! Now."

Her breath smelled like old fruit and rubbing alcohol and he realized she was crazy as an old monkey.

She grabbed for his hands and put them on the top button of her pants. She didn't have no shirt on and when Jon reached down, staring right into her heavy breasts, he thought he was gonna bust right out his drawers.

He tried to be nice as he pulled the pants down to her knees and let her kick out of them. But he was about to lose his mind. She had on white cotton panties with blue flowers.

"Dear E. Dear E."

"Jon! Pay attention."

She sat back on the bed, her little toes wigglin', as she watched his eyes and then lay back flat on the bed.

"A mirror," she said. Her tongue fat and heavy with all them daiquiris. "I love mirrors. Jon? Did I tell you that?"

She starting rolling her panties down her knees, curling into thin strips like biscuit dough, and over her ankles and Jon couldn't move. He just stared at her beauty. Just beautiful as hell as he listened to her breathin' and the rain and the thunder.

"E told this woman in *Girls, Girls, Girls* that there was somethin' about a storm. It just made you feel so alive."

But Miss Perfect wasn't listenin'. Her eyes had rolled back in her head and she was moanin' somethin' terrible.

Miss Perfect finally called him over to the bed and he kicked out of them ole zip boots and leather pants like they was growin' on him. She was movin' like a snake in the bed, her hands all over her body and then dippin' down underneath the covers. Man, he felt like Captain Marvel. Felt like he should say *Shazam!* and he'd have the power of a hunnerd men.

He jumped a few feet onto the bed, straddlin' her buck-ass naked. He started kissin' her beautiful breasts and moving his hand down south. Then she done slapped him so hard his head reeled back.

Damn it.

He pushed her wrists over her head and straddled her waist.

"Listen to me, woman. I don't know what's gotten into you. But either you want lovin' or not. I ain't never taken no woman in my life, but you're makin' my head hurt."

She got loose from his hands and pulled his head against her breasts, growling like one of them lionesses. She smelled like a patch of flowers from his ole scratch-'n'-sniffs.

He started kissing her breasts again and she held his face in her hands. Real hard like a vise.

"You want to do somethin' for me, darlin'?"

"Yes, ma'am."

She pushed his head even farther south, dippin' down where Jon ain't never been before. He knew all about state laws and things he seen in all them Baptist comic books about hell. But, man, he couldn't help himself.

He stayed down there as the wind and the rain and black clouds rocked overhead. He'd open his eyes long enough to watch Perfect watchin' not him, but herself in the mirror. She had her hands on his head and smiled. Smilin' at herself.

Jon didn't pay it no mind until a mean old wind beat outside, rain hammerin' until the lights cut off all over the bed. She was screamin' in the dark as the wind roared through the open door and she panted and yelled and clawed at his neck. He could feel his hot blood against his skin.

He moved up to get the best lovin' he'd ever had, but then it happened.

Miss Perfect lay there for a moment makin' kissing faces to herself up in the ceiling.

Then she done turned over, pulled the sheets close to her body, and started to snore.

Jon got up, biting the hell out of his lip, and looking at all the scrapes and red marks on his stomach. He slammed the door shut and grabbed a pillow for the floor.

Chapter 27

AT MIDNIGHT, Abby and I stopped off at a Chevron near downtown and grabbed several packs of beef jerky and bottled waters for Hank. The dog chomped down every damn piece next to the gas station's air pump. Abby hugged him close while he lapped water from one of my old coffee mugs. Her face brightened as she squeezed the dog so tight that he grunted.

I watched her and smiled, my mind buzzing with everything that I'd learned.

Abby's father wanted to find Clyde James and had been killed and his daughter kidnapped. Must've been a few weeks after Abby's parents died that a couple of men showed up in New Orleans hassling Loretta. Now there was all this shit about some whacked-out group called Sons of the South.

We drove back to town, wheeling around the Square toward Maggie's. We stopped at a crosswalk for a moment, Hank panting hard in the truck.

Five young girls about Abby's age ran past in heavy sweatclothes, laughing. We could hear their yells, giddy from the cold. Rain beaded down my windshield and made funny patterns in the streetlights.

Abby hugged her dog again and watched the girls jog down a hill and out of sight.

I had hoped to put her up with Maggie and take off to Memphis tomorrow. But after the letter, I wasn't so sure. *Sons of the South.* I turned off the R. L. Burnside CD and flicked on the radio, finding a station that played old-school soul.

Hank jumped into the backseat.

"Library still open?"

"The bar?"

"The real library," I said.

"I guess."

"You want to keep going tonight?"

She nodded. I kept looping around the old courthouse and headed to campus as Abby patted her leg along with a song written decades before she was born.

On the second floor of the Ole Miss library, Abby was at a computer terminal and I was seated beside her. The library silent as hell. Just the buzzing of the fluorescent lights and some guy with a bad cold at the main counter sneezing every five seconds.

The screen got bright as she clicked through SONSSOUTH.COM. Most of what we found was the same old bullshit we'd read in her father's files. We spent about fifteen minutes looking through pictures of middle-aged white guys going to conventions at airport hotels and scheming to return honor to the South. This was the kind of group that hustled in men too educated to be in militias and too arrogant to see they were doing any harm.

"Where do they keep microfilm?" I asked.

"What do you want?"

I looked at her. "Newspaper articles."

"You want new ones, right?" she asked.

"Last few years."

"It's on computer."

"Not everything we're looking for."

"Watch."

She took me to an alcove located on the first floor and plugged in Sons of the South into a computer loaded with LexisNexis software. I'd heard of it, but most of my research dealt with musicians from decades ago.

Abby was really good. She clicked the hell out of the computer and brought up a dozen articles. Most were from the *Commercial-Appeal* but there were several in *The Tennesseean.*

She scrolled through the first few. Most seemed to be quoting a spokesperson for the group about their stance on keeping the Mississippi state flag with its embedded icon of the Confederacy.

This group loved that debate. And so did Mississippi; they kept the flag. It made me think about U telling me about his days playing football at Ole Miss and watching a bunch of spoiled white boys wave the flag every time he made a tackle.

He loved it so much that when the Kappa Alpha fraternity had their Old South parade, U stood on a street corner and burned the rebel flag. He didn't tell me, but I don't think anyone fucked with a man who could bench 485 pounds and practiced martial arts every day.

I laughed to myself and Abby kept scrolling.

There were a couple of editorials about how the Sons of the South were a bunch of privileged white men who wanted to play war games without really getting dirty. One columnist did a satirical piece about how the South should rise again and talked about the attributes of becoming a slave.

The columnist was black.

"Go on," I said.

Abby clicked but before the story disappeared she saw something at the end of the piece that caught her attention.

"Wait," she said. She clicked back and read through it, her nose inches away from the screen.

"What?"

"That man he's talking about. That state senator, Elias Nix?"

"Yeah."

"He was one of my father's best friends. They went to school together or something. I've met him a few times. He was at their funeral."

We read through a few more pieces on the group. Said they had a military compound in Jackson but their spokesman denied it. Once again, the spokesman said they were only community leaders interested in advancing Southern ways of life.

I had a pen in my mouth and had chewed the end off. I felt the ink on my tongue and spit into a trashcan.

"Your mouth's blue," she said.

"On my face?" I asked, rubbing my fingers over my lips.

"Nope."

"Good."

"You have a girlfriend, Nick?"

"Why? You like old men?"

"First off, you're not old. You're, like what, forty? Anyway, I was talking about Maggie. She likes you."

"Shucks." I wasn't forty. *Yet.*

"I can tell," Abby said. Her cheeks pinched tight as she smiled with her brown eyes.

"Is that why she grunts at me?"

"I think."

"Well, I kind of have that department covered."

"You married?"

"Scroll down," I said.

"Are you?"

"No."

"But your girlfriend wants to," Abby said, her face glowing in the light from the monitor.

"Wait, can you pull up only 'Elias Nix' and 'senator'?"

She nodded and the screen flashed with hundreds of hits."

"How 'bout 'Nix,' 'senator,' and 'gambling'?"

She tapped it in the prompt.

Two hits.

"What's her name?"

"Kate."

"You love her?"

"What is this, junior high?"

Abby laughed and socked me on the shoulder.

I smiled. "She lives in Chicago and we recently learned that's a long way from New Orleans."

"Your mouth is still blue."

I spit again into the trashcan.

When I looked back at the computer screen, Abby was scrolling down a story—Nix was running for governor in November. Shit, I knew I'd seen the damned name. His face was plastered all over Memphis, but it was so late and I'd been so into Clyde James that I wasn't thinking. Besides, I rarely paid attention. Louisiana politics were so bad that I usually slept in on election day.

"Look at this," she said.

Apparently, this year, Tennessee was scheduled for a referendum to decide whether the state would have a lottery. And a lot of folks felt legalized gambling would be next.

Nix did, too.

He told a reporter in Memphis he'd like to see riverboat gambling on the banks of the Mississippi by the end of his term.

Chapter 28

I CALLED U from a pay phone at the student union building and bought a Coke to wash the blue off my tongue. Abby had printed off dozens of articles and sat by a long row of vending machines, shuffling and marking pages. A few feet from me, a hippie-looking kid slept with the Cliff Notes for *Crime and Punishment* in his hands. He smelled pretty damned bad and I turned to face the other way, toward a long row of windows as I waited for Ulysses to pick up. He didn't. I tried his beeper number and within about thirty seconds he called back.

"Mrs. Davis's cathouse; may I take your order?"

"Yeah, I'm looking for a punk named Travers. Has to pay for his pussy."

"Hold on," I said in a high voice.

"Nick, quit fuckin' around. What do you want? Man, I'm sitting outside some peckerwood's trailer waiting for him to come back and get some money from his wife. I'm down to my last bottle of water and I've only got that bootleg Marsalis CD you sent me. It's gettin' old as hell."

"At least it's not that shit you listened to on road trips. What was that, Grand Master who?"

"Flash," he said and took a deep breath.

"That and the Sugarhill Gang and Run DMC."

"Man, I'm fine with that. I still love it. I have faith in the old school. And you better, too."

"All right, listen," I said, the hippie starting to stir at my feet. He smelled his armpit, rubbed the peach fuzz on his chin and tried to hug the brick wall. "I'm still with Abby and we found out a few things. First off, her father had hired a P.I. in Memphis to find Clyde James."

"Your Clyde James?"

"Yes, sir."

"*Whew.*"

"Second, her old man was connected to a group called Sons of the South. You know them."

There was silence.

"You're a charter member."

U laughed.

"Anyway, this group is apparently connected to this state senator Elias Nix who's running for governor."

U coughed and I heard the static of his cell phone as he moved around. "You had me for a while. Now your ass is talking about conspiracy theories and governor's candidates and . . . man, I think that peckerwood is coming in. . . ."

"U?"

"Hold on," he whispered. "All right, had to scrunch down in my seat again. Thought that was him."

"Was it?"

"We're still talkin', ain't we?"

"This whole thing connects back to the casinos for Abby and for me and for Clyde. . . . Nix wants to bring casinos to Memphis."

"That's all we need. We're a broke-ass city as it is."

"Hey, man, we have them in New Orleans, too."

"So you want me to go to Nashville and wake up Nix? Ask him why he wants to make money off all these broke motherfuckers?"

"Not yet," I said. "Maybe later. What do you know about Tunica and the Dixie Mafia?"

"What I told you."

"What about property records? Can we find out who owns the Grand?"

"Man, that's a great idea. I'd call you Sherlock but that's more an idea from Larry Holmes."

"So you did?"

"Yep," he said. "Hey, man, look. I got to go for real. Peckerwood is home and he's walkin' up the steps with a Budweiser tallboy and a fuckin' Glock. Shit. All right; real quick: That casino is buried under corporate names so thick it would take your whole life and a NASA computer to find out who owns it."

"You know any FBI folks we can talk to?"

"Let me check into it," he said, sighing. "Adios."

The hippie was wide awake at my feet and petting a small ferret; apparently he'd kept it in his ragged green book bag. He smiled and fed it some biscuit. The ferret took the morsel and then crawled back into the bag looking for more.

Nothing, huh?" Abby asked.

"Not much. He said he'll start asking around this week."

"Asking who? Cops?"

"Yep."

Abby watched me from a little chair she'd found. Wobbly legs. A thousand coats of paint. She said while I'd been on the phone, she'd arranged everything we found in the library by subject and chronology. Sons of the South. Elias Nix. She said she'd look through her father's papers when we got back to Maggie's and talk to me about maybe finding some more. When I asked where, she changed the subject.

"What about criminals?" she asked when we got outside.

I played with the keys in my hand as we walked down a hill and over to a parking lot where we'd left my truck. Dead leaves twisted around in a dust devil and I could hear oak branches clicking above us. The rain had stopped. A mean cold front had dipped all across north Mississippi.

"I know a few," I said, smiling. "But not good ones."

"I do," she said.

"You know criminals?"

"I know one," she said, a slight grin crossing her lips. "And he's pretty good. Runs most of the marijuana for north Mississippi."

"And how does a little girl like yourself get to meet such characters?"

"He used to come out to Maggie's stables last year for riding lessons. He didn't even know how to get on a horse. We taught him. Didn't know who he was till later."

"Who is he?"

"His name is Son Waltz. He's just a kid, only a few years older than me. His godfather runs a pool hall near the Square and set him up with his own bar when he turned twenty-one."

"What is he, your boyfriend?"

"Hell, no," she said, her face flushing. "I just taught him a little about horses."

"And you think he'll know something about the Dixie Mafia and Tunica?"

"Raven knows everything."

"Thought you said his name was Son?"

"He goes by Raven."

I smiled at her. "All right, we'll find him tomorrow. I'm pretty beat."

"Tonight," she said, stopping and tugging at my sleeve. I looked down at her and gave a fake scowl.

"What about Hank?"

"He can come, too," she said. "C'mon. The Highpoint is just over on the county line and open till dawn."

Chapter 29

THE HIGHPOINT ROADHOUSE was packed early that morning with dozens of pickup trucks, German sedans, and motorcycles. The bar was nothing more than an old Quonset hut held together with pounds of battleship-gray paint and spackling. The building stood on a little gravel neck off Highway 6 in Panola County and didn't advertise with anything but a single blue light that burned by the front door. There, a skinny kid with a ponytail smoked a cigarette and seemed to be scraping some shit off his boot.

The sky above us shone blackish blue as a slight patter of rain smacked big chunks of gravel in the parking lot alongside a narrow creek bed. I could hear the dull pounding of gutbucket blues playing inside. Reminded me of all the time I spent at Junior Kimbrough's place before it burned.

The door had been cracked open and the smell of smoke and sweat rushed outside. Almost seemed as if the old building was exhaling a mighty breath. I had on my old boots, now coated in murky gray mud, jeans, a long-sleeved T-shirt, and my jean jacket. The jacket wasn't cutting it tonight. My face felt tight from the cold.

I lit a cigarette, mainly for warmth, and also because that's just what you do when walking in a bar, and passed by the kid at the door. He was a little shorter than me with Indian-black hair and eyes. He looked up at my face and nodded me in as if I'd just asked his permission. I gave him my world-famous what-the-fuck look and brushed by him waiting for Abby.

The boy didn't give the same look to Abby. He just stared at her and, for a moment, I thought he was going to cause trouble. Then his face just kind of broke apart with this really nice smile and he hugged her. He had a St. Christopher's medal around his neck and wore a dirty white tank top under a long black leather jacket.

"Nick?"

I looked back.

"This is Raven."

I shook his hand and he gave me his own version of the what-the-fuck expression looking to Abby for some kind of explanation.

"You have beer?" I was tired as hell and probably a little tired of explaining myself.

"Coldest in the state."

"I'll be right back."

Raven apparently did his business in public. He found a little enclave, far from the stage where a black man in an undertaker's suit played a bright green Fender, and took a seat in a ratty brown plaid sofa. All around the big wide room people sat in folding chairs and recliners and other similar ratty coaches drinking cans of beer and smoking dope. The floor was buffed concrete.

At the bar, a deputy sheriff with a wide grin, his hat upon the lacquered bar, sat watching the lone player on stage hit some notes that just hung in that smoky air filled with sadness, despair, and a world of heartache.

I took a pull off a can of Budweiser and watched the old man knock out some more truly beautiful licks and nod with his appreciation of his Fender, as if the Fender worked independently of him. I knew how he felt. Sometimes I'd hit that sweet spot on my harps and it was almost as if someone else had played it. Like Little Walter or Sonny Boy were doing some serious channeling.

The kid was drinking Coca-Cola from a mug filled with crushed ice. He had a fat, wet paper bag of boiled peanuts by him that was still hot. He shelled them onto the floor as he watched the player continue out his set and snuck looks at Abby.

I lit another cigarette and leaned forward, my elbows on my knees, as a couple of college girls danced by the stage with a drunken laziness.

"They leavin' you alone?" Abby asked.

"They're still around," he said. "See that dude at the bar?"

I saw a black man in a camouflage baseball hat drinking beer. Raven stared right at him and the man looked back at the stage.

"He's DEA," he said, grinning. "Still can't find out how I get it in."

One of the dancing girls, probably in her late teens or early twenties, in tight jeans and short red sweater, walked by, running her fingers under Raven's chin as she passed. Abby studied her hands and took a breath. I smiled.

"So, kid," I said.

"Raven," he said.

"Raven," I said. "How much you know about the action in Tunica?"

"I know they have women there that ice skate in their bikinis and has-been country singers that get paid in prostitutes."

"Really?"

"Really."

I raised my eyebrows and looked back to the stage where the old man launched into some more north Mississippi blues. Ghostly riffs that spun and hung in the air like the patterns of smoke around us. A constant knocking drumbeat that seemed to come from an impatient spirit.

"What about the Dixie Mafia?"

He shook his head and laughed. "No way, man. Who are you?"

"He's cool, Raven," Abby said. "You know what happened to my parents?"

He nodded.

"Nick's helping."

"Why didn't you come to me? Who is this guy anyway?"

I closed my eyes and with a deep breath I said, "Listen, kid, I mean Raven. This is important as hell. Some people kidnapped Abby and took her to a casino. I was there looking for a friend of mine and helped her get out. Now I'm just looking for some information."

"Dixie Mafia? No way." He dropped some peanut shells on the floor and reached in the sack for a handful more. I glanced at Abby and she moved beside Raven and told him a few things I couldn't hear over the music. He nodded and nodded and then looked back at me.

"You lie to her," he said. "And I'll kill you."

His eyes were black and hard and I believed he would try.

"Fair deal."

She patted him on the knee as he finished chewing some more boiled peanuts, the final notes of the blues player swirling around us, dope smoke as thick as ever.

"What casino?" he asked.

"Magnolia Grand."

He laughed to himself and shook his head. "Ransom."

I took another pull of the beer, and leaned closer.

"Levi Ransom," he said. "Runs Dixie Mafia north of Biloxi. Motherfucker would love to run me out one of these days."

"What's he like?"

"Never seen him. Heard he had a man skinned alive for fucking his wife and that he raises pit bulls for fighting out at his farm. Think maybe he's from Memphis. Met people in Angola who helped him. Set him up. My father was there. If he was alive, he could tell you about Ransom."

"Let me ask you this, would he have the kind of juice to influence politics?"

"Where you from?"

"Louisiana."

"You have to ask that? Gambling is money. Money runs the state."

"What about a group called Sons of the South? State's rights. Rebel flags. All that shit."

Raven shook his head and poured more Coke into his mug. Abby leaned back into the sofa, her face tired and worn. Lines of determination under her eyes.

"What about Elias Nix?" she asked.

"Yeah, I know Nix. Some Republican asshole from Nashville. What about him?"

I asked, "Could he be buddies with this guy Ransom?"

"Listen, dude. Ransom is a legend around here. You hear whispers about what he wants and then it happens. If I heard Ransom wanted to move in on me, my ass would be gone. But Ransom is smart. He doesn't let people get too close. Like I said, I know he runs the Grand and a couple of other casinos. Has to be tied to the syndicate in Biloxi. That's all."

My face must've shown a lot of disappointment because Raven asked me to take a walk with him. Abby stayed behind and we went out through a back entrance to a little spot outside where old-time porch chairs lay rusting. I stood watching the patch of forest and all the cars bright in the intermittent glow of the moon. His eyes squinted and focused on me again.

"I wasn't kidding about killing you," he said, showing me two handguns he wore under his leather coat.

I pulled open my jacket and showed him the edge of my Browning hanging in a big inside pocket. "I watch my ass."

"You watch out for *her*, okay?" His breath clouded before him.

I nodded and I could tell even though he was just a kid, he understood what it meant to give your word. I liked that.

"You think Ransom is running the Tennessee election?" he asked.

"Maybe."

"You know, when I'm in trouble or need some information I always find my opponent's enemies. You know all that *Art of War* shit."

"Who are Ransom's enemies?"

"No one alive. But Nix, that'd be ole Jude Russell."

"You know how to get to him?"

"Nope, but I can tell you he's got a farm just north of Clarksdale. If he's not out campaigning to be governor, he'd be there. If there was some shit about Nix and the ole Dixie Mafia, he'd either know it or be glad to hear about it. Besides, I hear he's a just a good ole boy from Memphis. Likes to hunt and fish. Check it out."

I told him I would. The moon cleared from a big black patch of sky. Water hung off pine branches like ice. The weight of all the water falling seemed more than the narrow trees could bear.

Chapter 30

FROM THE ANTIQUE metal bed in Maggie's house where I spent last night, I smelled smoked bacon frying and coffee perking. I'd been awake for a while, still feeling that uncomfortable vibe of being in a house that wasn't my own. I stared up at the bead board ceiling, sagging in a few spots as if pregnant from rainwater, and stretched and rubbed my feet together. Pale white light blanched through the lead glass window and splayed onto warped pine floors.

I wanted to go back to sleep but I finally climbed into my clothes and pulled on my boots, tucking the Browning into my jean jacket. I hadn't shaved for a few days and I hoped I could take a shower.

"Mornin," Maggie said to me at the stove, slipping the bacon off an iron skillet and onto a blue Fiesta plate. "Abby's still sleepin."

She had on jeans and mud-crusted boots with a red checked shirt with snap buttons. Her black hair was wet and slicked back and her eyes were even greener than I remembered. Almost jade. I heard cartoons in the other room and a little boy laugh.

She nodded to a blue-speckled coffee pot on the stove and I poured a cup. Outside, a weak fall sun shone onto a small backyard cut into the woods. A jungle gym. A wooden swingset.

"Abby said y'all had some luck."

I nodded. She was a beautiful woman. One that didn't need makeup or perfume or anything else other than what she'd been born with. You could tell she liked an honest sweat. Her hands were chapped and her skin flushed from work.

We talked for a bit about the Sons of the South and Elias Nix and an idea I had for driving over to Clarksdale.

I said, "Maybe I could track down Jude Russell in Memphis."

"What makes you think he'll talk to you?"

"I'm gonna try and get one of his wranglers to give him a message at his lodge."

"You ride?" she asked, taking a seat and pulling off her work boots.

"Not in a long time. My folks used to have a farm."

"You had your own horse?"

I nodded. "My dad ended up selling him for a case of beer."

"Let me know if you ever want to get back riding. I have trails that go on for acres. Good land with creeks and a nice bit of woods."

She smiled. Perfect teeth. Her hands moved around the edge of her coffee cup and I felt my face redden.

"Something wrong?"

"Nope."

"I appreciate you helpin' Abby," she said.

"No problem. It all goes back to the man I'm looking for."

"Is he a friend?"

"In a way."

"Oh," she said, hopping up and grabbing the plates. "Almost forgot. You want salt and pepper?"

"You have hot sauce?"

She did and we ate for a while. Her son came in and took a seat on his mother's knee. She broke off a piece of bacon and he ate it looking at me the whole time, as if I were a novelty. She bounced him on her leg and he smiled.

After a few minutes, he became bored with us, jumped up, and made airplane sounds while he ran into the TV room.

"Divorced?"

"Yeah, Dylan's dad ran off with one of his students. He taught creative writing."

"Here?"

"Yep. She was only fucking nineteen. That's why when I saw you with Abby I kind of freaked out."

"I only date students if they're in junior high. Candy works, but I prefer furry animals."

"That's not funny."

"Hand puppets?"

She shook her head. "Abby says you're plannin' on getting married."

"Whoa. Man, why is it that every time a woman hears a man *might* get married they hassle him till he does? I said I was thinking about it."

"Known her long?"

"About ten years."

"Love her?"

"Yes."

"Then what's the problem?"

I looked back outside at the jungle gym and the homemade swingset and Tonka Trucks rusting in a sand pile. The harsh morning light made me squint as I sipped on the coffee.

"Distance," I began.

"It's just I was interested. I mean in . . ."

I smiled at her.

"And she knows I hate change," I said, unaware why I was telling all this stuff to a woman I'd just met. But it felt good to get out and talk about things that had been festering inside me for the last couple months. It looped in my damned mind like a record with one groove. No answers. No epiphanies. I wished I was one of those people who heard a fucking song or watched the weather change or flipped to a portion of a book and made their decision. *Yep, that's it. God put that passage right down for me.* But I wasn't and I never would be and because of that I lived a hell of a lot of time in limbo.

"You don't like getting older, do you?"

"It's not that," I said. "I just like keeping my world the way it is."

She nodded and poured the rest of the coffee. It was still hot and tasted the same way as the cup before.

"If you don't move on with your life you may just keep repeating the bad stuff, too."

I drank the coffee.

We were quiet and looking at each other until Abby bounded into the room. She was showered and red-cheeked and smiling and said, "Ready?"

I smiled across at Maggie.

And she smiled back before looking outside at the wide expanse of cotton fields. Familiar and unknown.

I stood and said: "I know a great barbecue restaurant in Clarksdale."

"You mind keeping Hank?" Abby asked.

Just get your gun ready and be quiet, for God's sake," Perfect said, as she checked her makeup in the rearview and blotted her Torch Lily lipstick with a gas receipt. They'd been squatting on Abby's cousin's house for the last hour and Jon had taken more of his little white pills. He wanted to break into the house right this second and kill them all.

Jon unfolded his arms from his chest, his left leg jumping up and down, while he chewed a big wad of gum. "I'm gettin' sick of waitin'," he said, still pissed that she'd slapped his hand under the covers this morning. "Ransom didn't hire me for no baby-sittin' job."

"It's his show," she said. "We'll just wait."

"Maybe I want to make it mine."

She had a damn awful hangover only made that much worse by this rockabilly hit man who wanted to get into her pants. *Again.* All right, so she got drunk. So, she asked him to perform a few duties. So what? She didn't owe him shit.

After a few moments, Jon asked, "Why didn't you tell me last night about this cousin she had?"

"I didn't, that's all."

"No. You was too busy playin' with my mind," Jon said, and rammed his fist into the dash of the car, grunting loud.

"Grow up, Jon," Perfect said. She felt a little edgy but at least clean. She'd taken a thirty-minute shower and shaved her legs, changed into a pink low-neck cashmere sweater, Earl Jeans, and Jimmy Choo stiletto boots. Huge tortoiseshell glasses with lenses so dark you couldn't see her eyes.

Something moved at the front of the old white house. "See him?" she asked, pointing out Travers walking down a crusty dirt road and getting into his truck.

Jon licked his lips as the truck pulled out and disappeared. "We'll catch you down the road," he said to himself.

Perfect cranked the car and followed, hanging back.

Jon spun out the cylinder from his gun, counted the bullets, and popped it flush with the barrel. His leg kept hopping up and down off the floorboard as they curved off a county road to Highway 6 heading west to

Batesville. Seemed like they were running on the bottom edge of that triangle that stretched southeast from Memphis to Oxford and west back
over to Tunica and Highway 61. Or maybe they were just headed back
north to Memphis when they hit I-55.

"I want you to call up Ransom and tell him it's time," Jon said as he
inspected his swollen knuckles and sucked the blood off the scrape. He
must've hit the metal car logo when he punched the dashboard.

She laughed at him.

His eyes were dark and ringed with circles and he stared straight ahead,
rocking. She saw another gun, looked like a little Beretta, sticking out of his
jean pocket. He gritted his teeth when he noticed her staring.

She could always read people. Get that feeling inside her head about
them. But with Jon she didn't feel anything. It was almost as if his head
were blank, only wrapped up in the emotion he felt at the minute. He
turned to her with hollow eyes and she got a chill.

Gave her goose bumps all down her neck. Her mouth dried out for a
second.

She couldn't breathe but then the old instincts came back. She reached
down and grabbed him between the legs.

"Are you really trouble, Mr. Jon?" Perfect asked, gripping him tight,
making promises with her hand that the rest of her body would never keep.

Jon curled his lip and put on a pair of gold metal glasses he'd bought
when they met at Graceland. "If you're looking for *trouble*, you came to the
right place."

Chapter 31

BACK IN THE DAY, Clarksdale was the capital of the Delta's cotton kingdom and the central hub for Mississippi's blacks leaving the South during the Great Migration. They could head out of the fields up to Memphis or purchase that big ticket to Chicago where they could reinvent themselves, as Muddy Waters did in 'forty-three. The town pulsed with energy back then. Down on Issaquena Avenue, you could sell your cotton, rent a woman, buy a bottle of whiskey, or just a sack of cornmeal for your family. Now most of the black downtown was covered in spray-painted plywood and was wavering after a recent crack epidemic. Most folks who could get out went on to Memphis to find higher paying jobs, away from working crops or as maids in the half-dozen motels. But recently, the city had been trying damned hard to turn Clarksdale into a tourist site.

The old underbelly of society, blues, was now the main focus of a town once overrun by white landowners. There was a damned good museum housed in the old train station and a few local businessmen had opened a juke with a Hollywood actor who was born around here.

But the old circuit I remembered from ten years ago was gone. Sunflower Avenue was pretty much vacant and old Wade Walton, who used to cut my hair—telling stories of doing the same for Muddy Waters, Ike Turner, and Sonny Boy Williamson—was dead. His store just an empty cinder block shell down by the museum that sat in the shadow of hulking grain elevators.

It was Monday afternoon and gray and cold. Fat black clouds floated by as if they were in a dirty river. No thunder or rain. Tornado weather. An electric hum in the air and complete silence around the downtown.

I had a lot of friends at the museum. Most of them pretty up-to-date on politics; one was a former raging hippie who knew exactly where to find Jude Russell's place. It was on Highway 61 running down toward a little town called Alligator.

Abby waited in the car while I used a pay phone to call Loretta. I knew she'd been appreciating the updates and I was glad to give them. It made me feel a connection to home that I always needed while I was on the road. It was almost as if I wanted someone to remind me who I was.

The phone rang on a rough connection to New Orleans, wind blowing paper cups and clinking aluminum cans across the street. The phone kept on ringing and I looked at my watch, a warning siren howling in the distance.

Inside my truck, Abby was reading liner notes on some CDs and playing with her hair. Two more rings. Ever since we'd met I had this overwhelming feeling that I needed to protect her. It felt like she was family. The way I imagined a big brother would look out for a younger sister. Like if some boy went too far with her, you'd feel the need to put his head through a wall. It was like that. I wanted to put someone's head through a wall for Abby. Being with her in Oxford at her house and meeting Maggie only made that more intense.

I waved. She waved back.

The phone kept on ringing. Nothing.

The hunting lodge wasn't hard to find at all. It was just hard getting into. My buddy at the Delta Blues Museum had told me I'd have no problem finding it because of the wall around it. I asked him to describe it and he simply said, "You'll see."

And I did. A log fence surrounded the property, probably about fifteen feet tall, with pointed edges on the top like the old cavalry forts, or the gate in *Jurassic Park*. There was a dirt road that followed the wall for about a half mile until a break where I saw the outline for a retractable door. An intercom with a keypad looped from a metal post and I drove next to it.

I thought about pushing some buttons and asking for a Whopper with fries but that kind of shit usually made people mad while I laughed at my own joke. Maybe I could do a different voice.

"Do you think they'd like me to do an impression?"

"Who?"

"Usual stuff. Sean Connery. Angry Chinese man. Scooby Doo's country cousin."

"Scooby Doo's country cousin."

"Really?"

"No."

I punched a few buttons and for a while nothing happened. Just a few fat drops of rain intermittently began to pound the hood. Finally, the intercom crackled to life.

"I'd like a Whopper with fries. No, make that onion rings."

"This is private property," the voice said. Sounded like a woman.

"I'm here to see Jude," I said, you know, using the whole first name thing. They'd think we played golf together, drank Heineken, and slapped each other's butts in the shower.

"Sir, security has been called."

"Everything's under control. Situation normal. We had a slight weapons malfunction."

Abby shook her head and kind of laughed, burying her face into her hands. I was laughing into the rain, too. Laughing at how damned stupid I suddenly realized I was for thinking I could knock on the front door of a house owned by a man running for governor. I'd put the Ghost in reverse, my arm on the back of the passenger seat, when three men holding shotguns blocked our path. They wore yellow rain slickers, hoods obscuring their faces.

My heart beat a little faster.

A man knocked the shit out of my window, so hard I remembered how much it cost to repair it. I rolled it down and looked at him, water twisting off his wide-brimmed cowboy hat. He had a gray goatee and hard blue eyes. A plug of tobacco in his mouth.

"No onion rings?"

He just looked at me.

"Not a *Star Wars* fan?"

"What?" he asked, just plain out aggravated we were wasting his time.

"You know Obi-Wan? Luke? Chewie? The Force?"

"Out. Get out of the car."

"Sorry, I was just curious. Saw the road."

"You lookin' for Mr. Russell?"

I glanced over at Abby and she was shaking and staring at her shoes. Her back was hunched as if it would hide her from the men.

Pissed me off. Pissed me off these motherfuckers would do that to her.

"Hey man, fuck you. I came here to see Jude Russell and if he's here, great. I got something to tell him. If not, kiss my ass."

I heard the clack of a shotgun and he reached for my door handle.

Without thinking, really acting more stupid than brave, I pulled out the Browning and leveled it at his head. Other shotguns clacked around me as he dropped the gun and took a few steps back. His face white and his mouth open.

"I don't want any trouble," I said. "I have a message for Mr. Russell about Elias Nix. It's something I'm sure he'd want to know."

The man nodded slowly.

"Put down the gun, sir," he said. "Then we'll talk."

I did and the men jumped to each door pulling me and Abby out into the rain. The thunder cracked way over a cotton field as they opened the mammoth doors, yawning like a whale, and pushed us inside.

Chapter 32

INSTEAD OF CUSSING out the men who stuck guns in our faces a few minutes ago or demanding to see Russell, I asked for a cup of coffee. I smiled pleasantly at these hard-core rednecks in flannel shirts and duck hunting boots and told them just three sugars would be fine. The man with the gray goatee, who had first pointed the shotgun into the car, then nodded to an old black woman. She left and reappeared a few minutes later with a steaming mug stamped with a Labrador's face.

"Thanks," I said. "Got a little wet during the whole Bataan Death March up to the lodge. Nice place though. Very Ralph Lauren meets Ted Nugent."

I glanced around at the deer and boar heads on the wall. A full-sized black bear, various large-mouth basses on plaques, and even a bald eagle. Man had actually stuffed a bald eagle.

I sipped my coffee—not bad—at a hardwood table that sat about twenty. A black chandelier with thick unlit candles hung overhead, reminding me of paintings I'd seen of the Spanish Inquisition.

The man with the gray beard didn't say much to me but had been nice to Abby. He'd immediately offered her a sweatshirt and a towel when we walked inside. She took the towel and was patting her hair dry when a momentary flash of lightning knocked off the lights for a second.

The man took a seat by me and finally introduced himself. Easy to remember. Royal Stewart. I shook his hand and sipped the hot coffee while the other men loaded up their guns among dozens in racks by the front door.

"Didn't mean to scare you; we were all out hunting when we got a call," Stewart said. Had a pleasant deep hum to his voice with a dose of Memphis in it. "Kind of my job to look out for the place and Jude. So, no misunderstanding. All right? Just finish that coffee and head on."

"Didn't come here for the coffee. But it is good. Do I detect a little nutmeg?"

"What is it?" Stewart asked, the pleasant hum with a mean quiver in it. "You want Mr. Russell to pay out for a little gossip? He doesn't do things like that."

I put down the coffee. "Tell him it's about Sons of the South."

Stewart laughed. He combed through his wet gray hair with his fingers and kept laughing. "That's it? You want to tell us that Elias Nix is in with those nutcases? Don't you read the paper? Hell, he brags about it."

"Listen, let's quit fucking around. All right? See that young lady over there? Her parents were murdered a few weeks ago. I found a hell of a lot of personal letters at her house that shows her dad was working for Sons of the South when he died, at Nix's instruction. If I were a cop and I learned about that, I'd want to talk to him."

Stewart scratched his goatee. "Let me see the letters."

"Let me see Russell."

"Shit. He's running for governor in an election that's two weeks away. He's at a rally in Memphis right now with another scheduled for later tonight. He has television appearances and speeches. Don't you read the paper? Besides, I'm sure whatever unfortunate thing happened to this girl's parents is being appropriately looked into. Who are you anyway?"

Abby spoke up: "Friend of the family."

I smiled. "It will be worth his time. Besides, wouldn't he want to know before reading it in the paper?"

"What?"

"What's in the letters. A whole box of them, from Nix himself."

Stewart stood and left the room for several minutes. When he returned his face was reddened and he seemed a little more jumpy. He chewed at his cheek and twisted in his seat before finally leaning across the table. "If this is some kind of bullshit, I'll have you arrested for trespassing."

Two-and-a-half hours later, Jude Russell walked through the hunting lodge's oak door and shook the rain from his slicker and removed a wide-brimmed hat. He was younger than I expected, or just seemed younger. Slender boyish face with a lot of lines through his deeply tanned skin. He had thin brownish-gray hair and amber-brown eyes. He wore frayed jeans and beaten work boots that he slipped out of at the front door. He smiled to everyone seated in the kitchen as he padded in and opened a mammoth stainless-steel refrigerator searching for a beer. He found one and came back to the head of the table where he propped up his bare feet, smiled again at everyone seated around him, and said, "Now what the hell is all this about?"

The room had a pleasant energy as most places do during a storm. It felt good just being inside as a true shitstorm pounded the trees outside and batted the hell out of the windows.

"Hey, wait. Royal? Tell Rance to go get Muddy out of the pen and bring him here. Hell. So, what is this all about? Who are you?"

I introduced myself and Abby. I briefly told him about Abby's parents—trying to get through it without too many details—and how we believed that Nix was connected.

"So why come to me?"

"We want to know about him."

"You want to know if he's just a good ole boy or a fuckin'—excuse me—Nazi," Russell said as a fat Lab came into the room shaking its wet coat and rested its snout in his lap. Russell rubbed his head and picked up a towel to dry the dog.

"Who is he and who are the Sons of the South?" I asked.

"Christ. I drove about an hour out of my way and am gonna have to haul ass back to some rubber-chicken dinner tonight because you want to know about my opponent? Shit, Royal, way you were talkin' made it sound like this boy might have pictures of Nix screwin' a goat."

Everyone around the table laughed except Royal, who looked a little pissed. Russell tossed the towel on the ground and leaned back in his chair. He placed his hands behind his head and looked at the ceiling.

"Letters?"

In the rain, Royal and I walked back to my truck for the papers we'd found at Abby's. And for the next thirty minutes after we returned, we sat around and read useless memos and congratulatory messages from Nix to Abby's dad. I knew she felt invaded and uncomfortable, and I was sorry for that. But I also knew this was the only way to get him to talk.

"Well," he began. "You want to tell me your deal in all this, partner?"

"I'm a friend of the family."

"How'd you know her father?"

"I didn't."

Abby said, "He's my friend."

Russell was good, an old poker-player type who could watch a man's face and see what was clicking behind the facade. But I was pretty damned good, too, and stared right back. JoJo had taught me well.

"She hire you?" he asked.

"No."

"What do you do, Travers?"

"Loaf."

He laughed.

"I teach blues history at Tulane."

"No kidding," he said, a big smile crossing his lips. "Been to the Sunflower Festival, I'm sure."

"Yep."

"You know we're not too far from the Stovall plantation where Muddy made that record for that man with the Library of Congress."

"Alan Lomax."

"You know him?"

"I met him once in D.C."

"He still around? I bet he's got some stories goin' back into Clarksdale in the day when white folks kept to their side of town."

"He's in Florida. Been pretty sick."

Russell had gotten me way off subject. I was used to people answering questions with a question or trying to angle the conversation so they could learn about you. That kind of talk usually came from oily record company types who got pissed when I asked them about royalties for some of the blues players I've worked with. But this was different, Russell seemed to have a genuine interest in the history of the Delta and had apparently done more than just read a few liner notes.

The politician scratched the ears of his big dog and finished off his beer. He offered me one and I refused.

"So," I said, trying to get back to Nix. "Is he a Nazi?"

Russell clenched his jaw and rubbed his bare feet together. One foot was bruised and swollen purple around the big toe. He looked over at Royal and the older man shrugged. Apparently he did more than just look out for the place. He was an adviser of some sort.

I smiled for a minute. I'd bullshitted my way into a lot of things, mainly to find musicians or people who owed them money. But here I was sitting with the man who could be the next governor of Tennessee and I had to keep smiling. My ole tracker mentor would be damned proud. Rule one: *You can bullshit your way through anything.*

A maid placed a silver tray of pickles, salami, cheese, and sausage in the middle of the table. We all took a few things off the tray and sat back while Russell seemed to contemplate me.

"Is she one of your students?" he asked.

I shook my head.

"Girlfriend?"

"No."

"So what does this have to do with blues?"

I thought about telling him about Clyde James and Loretta and my time in Memphis and the casino and everything leading up to the meeting. But it was one of those things that I knew would only make him more suspicious. It was better to keep it clean. Friend of the family. New information on Nix.

"She's a friend, man. I don't know what to tell you. The Oxford police aren't listening to her and we wanted to know more about Nix and the Sons of the South."

"And you thought, 'Let's just knock on the door of ole Jude'?"

"Yeah, something like that."

He studied my face again.

"Well, nothin' I can tell you can get me in trouble. I tell some of the media, ones I can trust, the same thing. First off, if you tell someone else what I say I'll deny it. Not 'cause it's not the truth but because it could get me sued."

He sighed. Rain pattering on the metal roof the only sound in the room.

"Sons of the South is dangerous as hell and Nix's connection to them scares me for our state. You care about blues and the heritage of black folks around here? Nix doesn't see that. The South is white. The music. The culture."

"Celtic."

"Yep," he said, pointing the nose of his empty beer at me. "Exactly. Their favorite word."

"And—"

Royal broke in: "This will illustrate our point," he said. Not even looking at Russell as he spoke. Almost like a father. "Two years ago there was some trouble in Biloxi during spring break. Remember? It was national news. Well, some black college students were accused of raping a white girl and tearing up a bar. Turns out the girl was in some wet T-shirt contest and had brought five men back to her room with her. I don't know the particulars and don't want to. But when it made the news, we know some members of Sons of the South went to Biloxi looking for the boys when they were released from jail. They dragged one behind their car on a country road and crucified him on a barn door with a nail gun."

Russell looked at my face as I listened. He nodded and gave it the proper pause before speaking again, to let the weight of the story sink in to both of us.

"The thing that makes them dangerous," Russell said, "is that the makeup of the SOS isn't a bunch of truckers and pig farmers. We're talking about college professors, lawyers. Big-time Nashville businessmen. You ever live in Tennessee?"

I shook my head.

"Tennessee is really like three states. You have the east around Nashville that is blue-blood and conservative as hell. Voted against Gore in the election. Then you have the west that's more rural and usually aligned with us. Then you have Memphis. Memphis is another world. Mostly black. Democrats till they die. The worry comes from the swing Nix could have in those western counties. His speeches sound awfully good to the Bible-thumpers."

"But what about the gambling?" I asked. "I mean, he supports a state lottery and gaming on the river. Why aren't the Bible-thumpers opposed to that?"

"They are. But he talks about how gambling could attract big money and skirts the issues, bringin' up rhetoric about family values and a return to the Tennessee he knew as a child. He's charming as hell and keeps the SOS just enough in the shadows that no one really attacks it, besides some good reporters who understand how damned dangerous this could be. Shit, today there was a whole profile on him in the Nashville paper and the reporter only mentioned the SOS in one paragraph. The SOS *is* Elias Nix. Founder, member, and demagogue."

Russell made a little sandwich from the remaining cheese, pickles, and salami from the tray and folded it into his hands like a magician before taking a bite.

Royal looked at his watch and stood up. He stared down at me and put his hat back on. "Mr. Russell has to get, folks. We appreciate your time and hope it's helped you some. If you do find anything that connects Nix to what happened to your parents, you let us know."

Russell stood, too, and wrapped one arm around Abby's shoulders. At first, the move made her stiffen, but as he pulled her closer, she relaxed a little and smiled back.

"I'm so sorry," he said. "I lost my mother when I was in college and had to drop out for a year. Didn't understand how I could ever make it without her. But you do. You will."

His brown eyes softened and he squeezed her even tighter.

"Y'all be careful out there," he said.

I said we would and walked out of the hunting lodge and back to the Gray Ghost, to head back up Highway 61 to Memphis. Abby was quiet after we left. She just stared into the long gray curtains of rain and the red taillights stretching far in front of us. In the corner of my eye, I saw her pulling the sweatshirt over her hands like mittens as my radio played an old Peetie Wheetstraw tune.

"Nick?" she asked. "Would they help us if we found more papers of my daddy's?"

Chapter 33

PERFECT SNAPPED HER CELL PHONE shut and told Jon that Ransom had finally given the word. She immediately started thinking of ways they'd take Travers and the girl, most of her plans with her distracting the hell out of Travers while Jon shoved a gun in his face. She could play the sex kitten, the confused tourist, or maybe the victim. Maybe she'd teach Jon about the big game: *wife beater*. That wasn't too bad. She could scream and yell while Jon grabbed her by the front of her blouse letting everyone know she'd screwed another man. Shit, the part was made for that jealous country boy and she knew Travers would jump up, wherever he was, and try to help out.

But, then again, what if other people were around and tried to stop Jon, too? They could have some serious monkey in their works. No, it had to be simple. Separation of li'l Miss Abby and Travers would be the key. And it all depended on where they stopped and how many people were around.

Perfect looked over at her partner while the Taurus kept on swallowing up Highway 61 blacktop heading north. He was still talking. Not to her, more to himself. All about Elvis and how he felt he was just like Jesus and how she should start off seeing some movie called *King Creole* because the later movies only made sense to the devout.

Lord, that boy was wired today. He'd downed a bottle full of white pills and had been talking a whole mess since they left Clarksdale. He was funny like that. Silent as ole Lurch, then little Chatty Cathy all the way north. He was talkin' about his mamma and some big motorcycle he bought and then about going to some crappy amusement park in Memphis called Libertyland.

"Thought you said your mamma left you for a while?"

"I never said that."

"You said she spent some time in Canada and that a woman named Erdele looked out for you." She never forgot a word that was spoken to her. Sometimes she wished she could.

"My mamma never left me," he said, drumming his fingers on his knee. "My mamma would never leave me. You heard me wrong is all."

"When did you lose your virginity, Jon?"

"Miss Perfect, why you ask questions like that?" he asked, slipping his metal sunglasses back on. "You like to shock me with that kind of talk? Don't you? You think you gonna make me embarrassed, woman?" He began playing with some gold rings on his fingers. "I had my first when I was nine years old."

"That's impossible."

"That's the truth. She was fifteen."

"Can you handle a woman?"

"You'll never know."

"Oh, Jon," she said, her eyes keeping on the road as she ran her fingers over his chin. "You want to find out? Here."

She placed his hand on her knee.

"You keep going till you get scared," she said. "I'll put my hand on yours. It's called chicken."

"I know what it's called," he said, curling his lip.

"We gonna shoot 'em?" she asked, moving her hand an inch to his thigh.

"Yeah, I'm gonna use this ole forty-five, same kind that E had with Him when He visited the President," he said, moving about the same. "When the President made Him a federal agent so He could fight crime. What you got?"

She moved a little more, raking her nails against his tight jeans. "Me? Oh, just a Smith & Wesson that an old boyfriend gave me. Poor bastard. Somebody threw an electric fan into his bubble bath."

He moved up thigh-meets-crotch level. She could feel his hand trembling and vibrating. She liked it. Good humming in that hot blood. She moved her hand to the same spot on him. *Damn.*

"I once killed a man with three feet of twenty-pound-test fishing line."

"Once shot a man in his . . ." She moved her hand all the way getting a good piece of Jon's ole boy.

"Dang!" he shouted. "Watch the road."

She swerved back into the right lane, barely missing a semi that roared past her. She smiled, checking out her eyeliner in the rearview and puckering her lips. Nice job. Black outlined to make them seem more full. "I won."

I peered over at Abby to see if she'd noticed we'd cut across from Highway 61 and finally curved back onto 78 heading to the truck stop she'd told me about, but she was sleeping. Lips slightly parted. Hands tucked between her head and the door. I turned down the heat in my truck and lowered the stereo, just hearing the steady bump of my big tires on that straight shot to Memphis.

I didn't feel like we'd gained shit from Jude Russell. He was affable and had confirmed my ideas about Nix being a racist moron, as well as a Republican. But about the only thing I could figure out was that somehow MacDonald had something on the casino business coming to Memphis that would seriously affect the campaign. But what about Clyde? A forgotten soul singer didn't make a bit of sense. The casinos were the only common link.

The wind buffeted through cotton fields and made howling noises against the truck's frame. The sky was dark as hell and I watched a large cardboard box cartwheel until finally slamming into the side of a crooked trailer.

I thought about my conversation with Maggie earlier that morning, about my problem with change, as I listened to Delbert McClinton.

I mean, did I ever think I'd be mature enough to raise a child like she's doing? What about attending Little League games, looking for good deals in the Sunday paper, taking pride in my lawn, worrying about property values and gas mileage, exchanging wine with other couples, wearing Dockers or other sensible pants, wondering about the market's effect on my 401K or ever believing the music was getting too loud?

Just the thought of those things made me nauseated. But, of course, I never thought I'd be approaching forty and running all across the Delta trying to solve other people's problems either.

Abby stirred beside me and I turned up the music just a bit. Delbert's new album made me want to drive forever. But the gas tank needle had been dropping mighty low ever since I cut off Highway 61 onto Highway 78.

"Abby? We getting close? Which exit was it again?"

Off," Jon shouted, pointing his finger at the exit. "There they go."

Perfect followed the Bronco past a Kentucky Fried Chicken and Hardees and into this huge-ass truck stop. Place advertisin' Western Wear and Country Cookin'. He liked that. Two of his favorite things. Place was real honest.

Jon watched them park underneath one of them big ole overhangs for semis. Travers started smokin' and pumpin' gas like an idiot and the little blond girl, cute as all get out, walked on into the place like she was in a heck of hurry. Probably had to pee.

Peein' and Coca-Cola. That's what these places should advertise. That's what people wanted. Jon reached in to the backseat for his Resistol hat and pulled it low over his eyes.

"You goin' in?" Miss Perfect asked.

He nodded.

"Watch her. She's a tricky little bitch."

"What you gonna do?"

"Distract your boy here," she said. "Let you get where you need with the girl. We can do it at that pump if we have to. Get them in the car. We'll handcuff both of 'em and keep 'em in back."

Jon jumped out and walked through a mess of puddles into the long shot of bright lights and rows and mesh hats and cowboy boots. The girl was walkin' back to the bathroom, near an old arcade. Jon jingled the change in his pocket and muttered to himself, "Let's play."

Iwas almost done filling up the Gray Ghost when I noticed this blond woman in an uncomfortably tight pink sweater and jeans with tall stiletto heels. I was sure she was a professional. If not a hooker, maybe a dancer who specialized in brass poles. The woman kept walking toward me. Really nice smile. Blue eyes. Her hair in blond curly locks. Beauty mark on her cheek.

I checked her out; I like to look at women.

I kept smoking my cigarette and instantly found myself kind of posing. Chest out. Cigarette dangling. You know, the whole Marlboro Man thing.

"Hey," she said, toying with her little finger in her mouth.

"Hey," I said, coughing and dropping the cigarette onto my new T-shirt. "Shit," I broke from my pose, brushed off the burning ashes, and quickly crushed the cigarette with my boot.

"That's stupid," she said.

"I try to keep the sparks away from the gas."

"Knew a man who died like that," she said, squinting her eyes looking into mine.

"I'll be more careful," I said, glancing at the asphalt for any gas leaks.

"Sometimes just a little spark can lead to an explosion," she said. She rested her forearms on the gas pump, price spinning higher, and looking at me. Her eyes were an unnatural blue. Beautiful, but a color not found in nature.

"I've heard of such things."

She sighed and licked her lips.

"Where you from?"

I pointed south.

"Where you headed?"

I pointed north. I wasn't being coy. I really had a hard time speaking.

"You don't like bullshit, do you?" she said, motioning for me. "So, let me tell you a secret."

Jon liked games. Mostly pinball. Games that weren't too complicated, like video stuff with trucks or guns or fast cars. He didn't like games that made you add things or play out some kind of strategy. He just liked kickin' the ole horse in the side, mashin' the pedal to the floor, and seein' what it meant to be balls to the wall.

Real life wasn't a dumb-ass game of Battleship. Real life was takin' chances and playin' out the consequences. You just hit it hard and things would shake out.

He stuck a quarter into Police Trainer and watched the screen explode into different ranks. He chose captain. He could be a captain. Captain. Captain America.

He aimed the gun and fired off a shot, feeling his real gun, that .45, poking him in the ribs. He pointed the plastic pistol at little balls flippin' up in the air and cracked them in half like eggs. Kept on shootin' as he watched the girl walk toward the bathroom and stop by some lockers.

She pulled out a key and cranked open a small compartment.

More eggs exploded for points, bells went off for passing the test, and the screen exploded into another game. This time people popped out on the screen. Good people and bad. But sometimes Jon found it hard to tell the difference. Little old woman with groceries. Scruffy guy with a sawed-off. Who could hurt you more? Who'd take you in when it was all over?

He shot everyone in sight. Shootin' up the score and bringin' it on back down.

The girl walked past him, a bunch of thick files in her hands, and back to the front of the truck stop.

He stopped shootin', let the gun dangle from his finger, and tucked it back it into the slot like he was one of them ole time Japanese swordsmen.

Perfect made her voice get warm inside her lungs and blew it all out in a steady stream of breath and words. She rubbed her lips against Travers's ear and said, "Don't you ever fuck with me again."

He took a step back as if seeing her for the first time while the portico lights came on and shone on rainbowed pools of oily water. She turned as he stared and saw Abby walking from the truck stop toward the Bronco.

Perfect, backing away from Travers and the pumps, pulled out the gun.

Jon was following and made a quick cut to the Taurus. She could see Jon's hand already tucked into his leather jacket. He was chewing gum like a madman as he crawled in, started the car, and looped back to the pumps.

She didn't say a word as she spun around and pointed the gun into his scruffy, ugly face.

Jon ran the car hard for about fifteen yards, braked, and jumped out. He leveled his gun at Travers as she went for the girl. "She's got it," he said. "She left it in the lockers."

Travers put up his hands.

Abby had locked the Bronco's door. Screaming and yelling, Perfect rammed the gun against the windows but nothing happened except a hard knock.

Perfect kept banging the shit out of the glass and yelling for that little bitch to open the fucking door. She was frantic and for the first time in about two years felt like she was really losing her shit. Her face heated up and she just wanted to tear into her with her long red nails.

Teach her something.

Jon didn't speak as he moved slowly to Travers, Perfect watching while she tried to catch her breath, and pulled a big handgun from Travers's jacket.

Travers just stared at Jon and clenched his right hand that stayed pointed in the air. His boots were submerged in the oily puddles and he held his face as if he were absolutely freezing. Like his feet were stuck in blocks of ice.

She waited for Jon to say something about revenge or the Bible or Elvis or announce to Travers he was back to punch out his lights. But he didn't.

Instead, he breathed and looked around him as if this were some kind of holy fucking moment. That he wanted to soak in everything he saw.

The air smelled like burned bacon and diesel fumes.

"Open the door," she said. Lightly tapping this time. Barrel pointing to the girl behind the glass.

Travers shook his head.

"What do you mean? No? Jon, shoot the bastard."

Jon cocked back the hammer, gun outstretched in his hands. But instead of pulling the fucking trigger, he let the gun drop onto his finger and tucked it inside the leather jacket.

She followed his eyes to the lot where two state trooper cars had parked near the restaurant. One patted his belly and laughed while the other double-checked locking his door. They started to walk on inside.

When she turned back, Travers was watching Jon and stepping backward to the Bronco.

The locks went up. He opened the door, scooted inside, and started the engine.

Then it was Perfect and Jon's turn to feel that oily ice up to their knees as Travers pulled out and took a left over the highway bridge. Damned if he didn't miss the on-ramp and kept speeding down some winding country road. Shit. He'd lose them. A million country roads on this side of the state line.

Jon jumped back in the running car and tossed her Travers's heavy gun. She liked the weight of it in her hands as Jon opened the windows and cranked the stereo.

"I'm too damned good to lose," Jon said. "Let's take care of business."

Chapter 34

I FIGURED I could lose them on a back road to Memphis. The old roads and country trails stretched into the northern hills like a million fingers, the highway providing a damned clean shot without the bends and twists of road. Besides, they'd taken my gun and I knew both of them were armed.

I took the Bronco to about seventy, before braking and downshifting, looking for more arteries to get lost. At first, I'd thought about trying to get the attention of the two troopers at the truck stop but didn't want to risk getting killed while trying to get close.

I glanced in the rearview mirror, wondering how I hadn't recognized the woman until Abby screamed as we peeled out. *That was her. The girl from the Grand.* But what bothered me more is that I knew the man, too. As I flew through a small nameless town and turned on to another road, I remembered him.

He'd worked for a California record producer who'd been killed by a friend of mine a few years back. The kid, who'd looked like a waxen replica of Elvis Presley, was supposed to be dead, too. I'd read it in the newspaper. But even with a beard and a few years on him, I recognized the pompadour, glassy eyes, and slack jaw.

Shit, the damned snakes in my head were loose from the box. Being chased by fucking ghosts.

Abby had wedged herself against the roll bar and had the seat belt gripped tight in her hands. She had her eyes closed as we went airborne for a second over a rutted back road and followed the outline of a muddy creek. Tree branches shook over our heads like an old crone's fingers in the hollow black light that surrounded us.

We whizzed past about six trailers in a little court, found another back dirt road, and slowly drove to a muddy embankment before I stopped the truck. The heat of the engine ticked and burned as I watched Abby. Her fingers became unclenched, reaching down on the floor for the papers that had been scattered.

I took the pile from her but before I could glance through them, the Taurus roared past and I heard the slam of brakes and the deep whine of a transmission reversing.

I opened my lockbox and tossed the papers inside before U-turning, reddish dust twirling behind us, and hitting about sixty down a rutted road to nowhere.

You can't drive," Perfect said. "Hit the accelerator. We'll never catch 'em. Go. Shit, kid. Go."

Perfect ran her leg over Jon's and mashed the damned pedal herself.

"Woman, let go. Woman. Gonna make me have a dang wreck."

The rented car's back tires fishtailed behind them on the dirt and rocks as the Bronco dipped around a corner and out of sight.

"Left," she yelled. "The dust. Follow the dust."

Jon did and she gritted her teeth watching the red taillights flash before her. They were in some kind of fucking tunnel of trees. Maples. Cotton-woods. Oaks. Colors on fire. Yellows and reds hot as hell against the blackened sky.

"What he got under that hood?" Jon asked himself. "That thing's been jacked up, I do believe."

"Catch him," she said, pulling out the Smith & Wesson and finding two speed rounds in her purse. "This is the place. We'll shoot both of 'em. Drop both of their bodies where they stand and then make sure that truck can't be seen from the road. Be spring till someone finds them."

Jon pushed the accelerator hugging a turn, fishtailing again, a hell of a grin on his face. He gave a rebel yell as they bounced off the ground and landed with a fast, hard thud. At that moment, Perfect knew Jon didn't care about dying.

She clutched his knee and watched his face flush with excitement.

"Get close," she said, letting her window down and pointing her gun at the truck. "I got 'em."

The shots came just as we rambled over a short wooden bridge, bumping and jostling, and turned onto another dirt road that I hoped led back to the highway. I figured we were racing through some kind of state park; every few miles, I saw wooden markers and signs that outlawed hunting. No people. No buildings. Just these smooth dirt roads cut into the Mississippi hill country.

The shots came again.

Two more harsh echoes cracking behind us. I didn't hear a hit but that didn't stop me from punching that 302 V-8 hard around the twists and straightaways. I told Abby to get on the floorboard, and she did, with her hands over her ears and her face buried in her knees.

I could see the Taurus in the rearview, the woman aiming a handgun at the back of the truck. As I punched the pedal around another long straight shot, my rear window exploded.

"Shit," I yelled, mashing the brake and banking the truck hard to the side, praying that we wouldn't flip.

The road had ended.

Only way back was through the Taurus.

Hot damn," Jon yelled, feelin' the same way as when he won the potato sack race back in Vacation Bible School. He'd won. Just shoot 'em. Let Perfect get them papers and he'd be forty thousand dollars richer. Hot damn. He could finally get that Cadillac for Miss Erdele. Miss Erdele. Mamma. Jon Burrows/Jesse Garon.

It all made sense now. Everything was looping back to his past and his future and the holy numbers that Black Elvis told him about. Said he was born under a moon sign. Moon dance. Moon child. Hell, he was shiftin' and changin' like that spotlight that never really disappears from the earth.

"I'm full force," Jon said.

"What?" she yelled.

Jon slowed, ran the car into neutral, and watched the old Bronco just idling there waiting for them to come and take what was theirs. Travers was in there, just a damned wreck after seeing ole Colonel Jon Burrows. *How did he live? Why had he come back?*

Damned comeback. 'Sixty-eight style, motherfucker.

He jammed the car into drive and mashed the pedal.

"Jon!" Perfect yelled. "No, we got 'em. We got 'em."

I saw him coming and dropped it hard into first gear, hearing my tires spin behind me, and headed right for the grille work on the Taurus. Hard gunning and waiting for him to drop away. My teeth ached they were clamped so hard.

I could see the car getting closer and closer as I headed up to about fifty.

"Holy shit, holy shit, holy shit," Abby said, softly over the gun of the engine.

I gritted my teeth harder and punched the 302, juicing out every bit of muscle she had down a single rutted road only made for one car.

I could see the boy doing the same. Almost could make out his eyes, maybe ten yards between us, when I broke hard to the right, jumped up on a long embankment, darted around him, and kept on flying by.

I pounded the roof of my truck three times and kept on moving around the curves trying to find my way out.

I was smiling and laughing. Really just relieved as hell, with my damned heart in my throat, as I reached down and pulled Abby back into her seat. I knew they were gone. I was too far ahead and they'd never catch up.

She buckled back in and I took another road.

I'd gone too far. Too many choices for them.

I kept on smiling and laughing, rubbing Abby's back for reassurance when the ground disappeared from under us.

We must have been going about sixty, no road, just air below, when we came crashing back down.

It was a hard landing. My back exploded with heat, black amoebas crawled over my eyes as my seat belt yanked me back hard.

Then I closed my eyes.

Never more in my life had I wanted to sleep so badly.

Chapter 35

THE LEAVES SMELLED of death. The sweet aroma of moist dirt with the tang of old copper pennies. Fresh blood. Even before I opened my eyes, I felt the warm, sticky wetness on my head. Everything was muffled and silent and soft. Coated in leaves. Buried beneath them. Over my face and in my mouth. Some kind of bug with a million legs crawling on my arm. I spit out some dirt, my head absolutely swimming. That same feeling of getting off the big roller coaster and bringing the curves home with you. I felt like I needed to throw up.

A small hand held my face. I opened my eyes to darkness above me. Seeing nothing. Small lips pressed close to mine.

"Shh," Abby said. I held my body still. Wasn't hard. I wasn't sure I could move my toes.

I heard the crunching sound of feet running on old leaves. Branches breaking. Voices. A man and a woman. Too far away to make out the words. Just voices. Connotations from the sounds.

It was night now. Was sure of it. Goddamn, my head hurt, I thought, trying not to move my eyes or budge a finger. Everything moved in the haziness of the worst hangover I'd ever known.

Abby's arms wrapped around me and pulled me toward her chest. I could feel her breasts against my neck and her nails digging into my skin. Before me was a mouth of a narrow dirt cave. The moon's gray glow shot through the trees and onto a thick, wet carpet of forest floor.

I moved my arms. Maybe not a cave. A little opening in a hill. A concave mound of dirt and rock that had been eroded into a little burrow. Somewhere a dog would hang out during a storm.

I didn't speak. I didn't move.

The voices were clearer now.

All of it coming back. The woman from the casino. A man I knew. A hired gun. The wreck. The blackout. Jesus, how long had I been away?

Abby's chest rose and fell in quick bursts. She held me even tighter. Her hands coated in wet black dirt. Leaves dissolving back to earth brushing across my face. I suddenly had the thought that this was what it was like to be dead, but awake. I was just getting loopy. I wanted to stay still.

I wanted those fucking voices to go away.

Shit, no gun. No car. No place to escape. Miles and miles of anonymous woods.

I took a breath and felt a groan coming on, the wet plink of rainwater beating some dead kudzu at the mouth of the burrow.

Two black boots appeared.

"I bet they followed the god dang creek," the man yelled.

The woman yelled back.

He stood there for a moment. Not more than three yards away from my feet. Almost playing with us. Toying. Just make our hearts explode until he stuck the muzzle in the shallow dirt grave and finished it.

I remembered him. I remembered how he'd tried to rape a woman I knew and how he'd tortured an old hermit who was so shy he could barely look you in the eye.

I gripped Abby's knee.

The rain plinked on a fattened brown leaf again.

The foot disappeared.

The crunch of boot soles on smooth creek bed fading into the distance.

"Do we stay here?" she whispered.

I held my head in my hands and wiggled my toes. They worked.

Sickness. Vomiting on my shirt.

I held my head some more and pushed myself from the muddy hole, with the arm that didn't hurt, and out into the forest. A million raindrops sliding off trees and across saplings and down into decaying leaves and puddles. Little slivers of moonlight, almost too weak to notice, making the distant surface of the creek look gray. Cold as the air around us.

God, I was soaking.

Abby helped me to my feet. I wiped the puke off my face with my jacket and straightened my back and felt my arms. My left arm hung loose at my side and I felt a numb tingling in my fingers.

We walked. Each step something to concentrate on, until I saw a fat pine. I listened to the flow of the creek and the rain patter. Convinced they were gone, I thrust my shoulder into the trunk and heard a sickening pop—pain shooting through my torso and into my bruised head—until I fell to my knees, biting the inside of my cheek so I wouldn't howl.

"God. God. God." Abby was on her knees now, too. She was smoothing the wet hair away from my forehead. She held my head in her hands and spoke some kind of low, mumbled prayer.

"I'm fine," I said. I moved my fingers and felt the shoulder rotating as it should in the socket. "Used to do that all the time. Always comes out."

"God," she said, again.

I got to my feet. Abby watched me from where she squatted and looked at my face for a second. She soon got to her feet, too, and pointed to the road that had ended so abruptly.

She held my hand.

Made me want to lead the way. Made me feel a little stronger than I did.

We walked as quiet as we could. Abby listened. She watched.

She'd probably been in the woods more times than I could imagine. She knew the rhythms of forests from deer hunting with her dad. I was sure of it.

We followed a little gully, once losing my feet and thudding down on my ass, until she showed me the narrow bed filled with reddish pine needles and leaves. She pointed to the crumpled piece of machinery that I used to love spending my Sundays waxing. Chrome that you could smile into.

Apparently the roadwork had only gone so far. It ended over the gully where my Bronco had simply dropped down into its muddy bucket, struck a fat little oak, and slammed to a stop. My front windshield was cracked pretty badly on the driver's side and the front end was smashed in pretty good, too.

"I'm so sorry, Nick."

"How far do you think we're in this place?"

"Couple miles," she said.

"Yeah," I said, looking back down the road we had traveled. "Let's follow the edges but keep out of sight. Okay?"

I walked over to the Bronco, feeling pretty damned bad about what had happened to her, not thinking about me or the two psychos that were tramping around the woods looking for us. Nope, just thinking about the old Gray Ghost and wondering if she was salvageable.

I pulled open the passenger door; it rocked open slightly ajar and completely fucked up, and leaned inside.

I grabbed my Army travel bag and for some reason the stupid face plate from my CD changer, like theft was my biggest worry, and opened the lockbox for the papers.

But it had already been opened.

The metal top ripped from the hinges. My CDs were there. My old Ford manuals. My coffee mugs and crap.

I felt her behind me looking over my shoulder. She began to cry.

I snaked back out of the truck.

I felt like crying, too.

Whatever it was, they had it.

Chapter 36

LEVI RANSOM WASN'T so scary. He didn't talk in a whisper or have some kind of weird quirk like rattling off the names of venomous snakes or collect stories of particularly gruesome suicides. He didn't like to watch videos with little girls wrestling in their panties or have a fetish about smelly feet. Nope. Levi Ransom was just a man. Maybe a cutthroat bastard. Maybe the kind of guy who'd bury you in three southern states if you lied to him. But he also liked good bourbon, cheap drugstore cigarettes, and quick meaningless sex. He had his sex like some ate a damned cheeseburger. Didn't even taste it, just devoured the whole thing as fast as he could.

When old Jake died, Perfect didn't have anybody. She'd been stuck at that stupid carnival he was running in Biloxi for almost a week until Levi showed up. She just remembered sitting in that L.S.U. beanbag chair and listening to Ransom run down her options. Most of them sucked. Dancer. Hooker. Back on her own.

But then he asked if she'd come with him to Jamaica that same day. His voice was so damned warm and it was hot as hell outside. Jake hadn't paid the electricity for the carnival to run and most of the carnies had moved back down to Gibtown or wherever they lived. She had on a dirty tanktop with no bra and red silk panties.

He just kept looking at her legs, waiting for her to decide.

"Beach or shithole city," he said, opening the door, allowing the hot-ass air that smelled like stale cotton candy to brush into the room.

The next day, he'd mounted her. He pressed her face into a pillow and took about five minutes to do his work. Then, he jumped up and told her to get dressed, talking about steaks and whiskey. She barely had time to catch her breath.

The dominance and the short sex continued for two years till he found a cocktail waitress with thirty-six double Ds and rusty-red hair.

Tonight, in one of the thousands of honeycomb rooms at the Grand, he had the same look on his face as he did that day in the trailer. She had no false notions that he was recalling that walk up the long waterfall when he swatted her ass and told her dirty jokes or when he was arrested after shooting an alligator in some run-down zoo.

No, he was just thinking about eating another cheeseburger. And while he flipped through those papers Jon had pulled from that wrecked Bronco, she knew she'd done pretty good.

He stubbed out another Vantage. A dozen already curled up like little blackened worms in the ashtray.

"They're alive?" he asked.

He was alone with her and Jon. The room was just a double. A lacquered two-seater table. Bolted-down television and phone with a red bubble light for messages.

Jon looked at his zip boots. She looked at Ransom's eyes. Pissed off, but not really. He just kept watching her damned tits.

"We walked those woods for two hours, Levi. Don't give me any shit. I have leaves in my hair, blisters on my heels, and dirt up my ass. So don't start."

He cackled out one of his bourbon-soaked laughs and gathered the papers before him. His gray hair dropped over his skin, weathered the color of an old horse saddle. His eyes blue and hard.

"Y'all did fine. Kid?"

Jon walked forward.

"Ten thousand sound all right to you?"

"No."

"No? For not doin' shit."

"I don't want nothin'. I always finish."

Ransom, dressed in a white suit and black linen shirt, got up with a groan and walked into the bathroom. Place smelled of plastic and fresh paint. She didn't believe it had ever been used.

She followed and watched his back and heard the click of a lighter. He turned and she saw the papers starting to brown and curl in his hands edged with orange and blue flames. The air now smelled rancid.

Not like paper. Like some kind of animal cooking.

She walked back to the two chairs and the small table overlooking the Grand's parking lot. She wondered what it had all been. What was so damned important that he'd had two people killed and wanted to do in two more?

Perfect watched a real junker car turn into the lot. Car held together with duct tape and Bondo and glue. A man in his early twenties got out. White. Blue jeans and NASCAR T-shirt.

He stood for a moment watching the neon twirl round that silly fake *Gone with the Wind* facade as a teenage girl, pregnant as hell, followed and came around behind him. He snapped back to her and fired off some mean words. And the teenager kept moving to him. She reached out and held his hand. The man turned to watch her in the glow of the parking lot lamps.

Perfect couldn't quite see what was happening. But she thought they were both crying. Yeah, pretty damned sure.

"Perfect?"

She turned.

"Y'all have two hours to get to Memphis for a flight."

Jon hung back. His face half hidden by shadows, split down the middle by a tableside light.

Levi said, "New Orleans."

She looked at him. Her mind still kind of on the sad little couple.

"One last piece."

She looked back at Jon. Nothing. Just the split face.

"Last week, I sent some people down to take care of a man I should've killed thirty years ago. They didn't get shit. But I know his sister is shielding him. I know it. You get her. All right? You find out. This is your thing, Perfect. They always open up their damn souls to you in five minutes. Find out where he's hidin'."

He smiled.

Thirty years ago. That was a long time to be pissed off, she thought. But it made sense. Those papers were a bunch of police reports and court files from Memphis.

All seemed to be from December 1968.

The Waffle House was the place to be when people were trying to kill you. I mean, you'd really have to work at it. Shoot through about a dozen grizzled old fuckers cutting waffles and greasy eggs. They'd probably catch the bullets in their teeth and keep on chewing, I thought as I pressed a wet napkin filled with clumped ice to my head. I still felt sick as hell. Almost as bad as when this 330-pound tackle for the 49ers sat on me during an exhibition game and kicked me in the helmet as he walked away. I remember trying to jump on his back but someone yanked me off. Then I blacked out.

Abby watched my eyes, her brows drawn together.

"You ever been kicked in the head?" I asked.

She shook her head.

"Kind of feel that way."

She shrugged and finished her cheeseburger.

A cheeseburger. A Coke. A pat on the head. Sorry someone was trying to kill us.

Man, ole Abby was taking it in stride, though. You'd think she'd be pissed off as hell, or frightened. But she wasn't. She was resolved. Fucking resolved. Wanting to track all her worries to the source.

"You look terrible," she said.

"Thanks."

"No, really. Your forehead is all swollen. You look like that kid from that movie. You know, where he wants to drive motorcycles across Africa and Sam Elliot is his adopted dad?"

"*Mask*. And thanks again."

"No problem," she said, and smiled.

"That's the second truck I've killed in as many years."

"What happened to the other one?"

"Some old man I'd been tracking paid a couple of Haitian guys to ram me. Broke my arm. I guess I'm lucky tonight. Just broke my head."

"You look terrible."

"You said."

"So what do we do now?"

The waitress walked over and plunked down the check in front of me. Kind of surly about it. One of those you-cheap-bastard-for-not-ordering-a-thing looks. She had, honest to God, two gold teeth, a tattoo of Jim Morrison on her neck, and a nose ring. This was Mississippi, not Los Angeles. Everything was a mess. Cable television had fed us into a blender that made social clusterfuck cocktails from pop culture.

She chewed gum. Stared for a second, gold teeth bright as hell, and walked away.

"Peace," I said to myself.

"So?" Abby asked.

"I called U."

"What did he say?"

"He made fun of me."

She looked concerned.

"Oh, don't worry. It's what we do to each other. One time this little sawed-off halfback cut-blocked me while I was rushing a quarterback." I smiled at her. "Just a footnote, I'm not going to talk football with you a bunch. Who gives a shit, right? Just about U. Anyway, this little sawed-off dude cut me at the knees and really made me twirl in the air. Quarterback ran around my end for a TD. U bent over, offered his hand, just smiling and laughing like hell, and said, 'Man, I never knew you could fly, Travers.'"

I laughed, pain shooting through my head, and dropped the iced napkin to the floor. "Shit."

Abby grabbed my hand. "You all right?"

I nodded. The world stopped spinning. For a second.

"He also thought it was pretty damned funny that I'd drive the old Ghost into a hole. Why did I tell him? *A hole.*"

Abby watched me.

"He'll be here soon and we'll go back to Memphis."

"And then what?"

I watched the road waiting for my friend. Nowhere, Mississippi. For some reason I thought about one of my favorite lines from *The Magnificent Seven.*

"You hear what the man said right after he jumped from the twenty-story building?"

She shook her head, eating her cheeseburger. Dirt all in her matted hair and in loose clumps over her shirt.

I smiled at her. "So far so good."

Chapter 37

WHEN WE GOT BACK to Memphis, U had a big surprise for me. He had me kind of wondering anyway; I thought he'd at least ask Abby and me to stay with him at his place in Midtown. But when he didn't, looping back to the Peabody after getting my head checked at some doc-in-the-box, I should've figured he was up to something.

Man, we looked terrible walking into the hotel lobby, some kind of convention just breaking up around the bar. The Peabody was all dark wood and marble, brass rails and oriental carpets. The smell of aged whiskey and the gentle notes of a jazz piano. The kind of place that made you feel you had a couple more zeros in your bank account. The hotel had given lodging to Faulkner and Robert E. Lee, and local legend says the Delta begins right in its lobby and stretches out to Vicksburg. Still, most tourists just remember their mascot ducks that paddle around in the fountain all day before returning to their rooftop roost.

But the ducks were long gone by the time we got back. It was late, approaching midnight, when we tracked mud over those oriental carpets looking for a place to fall asleep. U's truck would've done nicely.

But instead of heading with us to the front desk, U stopped cold and pointed to a couch in the center of the lobby. I could barely make out who was waiting for us. I mean, it was a convention of real jackasses. Laughing at bad jokes. Drinking that free company alcohol. A couple slow dancing without music.

But then she turned around.

Loretta.

Dressed in a floor-length black suede coat, a black turtleneck sweater dress, and tall black boots. She was smoking; Loretta hadn't smoked for two decades.

Suddenly, I felt like I was about ten and my mother had come down the street to make me come home for dinner. My face and neck heated with embarrassment.

"Said not to tell you," U said.

"Thanks."

This was all I needed, Loretta coming up to check on me. She did the same damn thing when the Saints threw me off the team and about everyone I knew had quit me. My girlfriend at the time was sleeping her way through New Orleans social hounds and I had gotten myself into an intimate relationship with bottles of Jack and Beam.

Loretta found me at this biker bar by the Riverbend puking in some bushes. She didn't say a word but grabbed my ass, stuck me in the back of JoJo's El Dorado, and drove me back to my warehouse. Never did ask how she knew I was there.

"What, you ain't happy to see me?" she asked.

"Yes ma'am," I said. My head beginning to throb. "Where's JoJo?"

"Lord, look at you. Ulysses, you do this to my boy? I told y'all, you ain't young men anymore. Fightin' like kids."

"I was in an accident."

She touched my head and then patted my face. "You'll be fine. And JoJo ain't here. I took the train myself this afternoon. He had the damned nerve to ask me how he was supposed to eat. I told him to serve himself some of that "jump up" breakfast. He asked what it was and tole him that was the kind where he jump up off his ass to make it."

U laughed. My head kept throbbing so I didn't try.

"And who is this?" she asked, looking over at Abby.

I introduced her to Loretta, and for a moment—knowing every one of her facial expressions—she thought I was scamming on one of my students. Abby was in her twenties, but I was well aware she looked about fifteen. She was polite to Loretta, even offered her hand while looking at the ground.

Loretta just reached over and held Abby to her fattened bosom. Loretta always had the ability to find people who were in pain. Sometimes in her show, she'd spot some poor bastard who truly was living the blues and start making him laugh. It was beautiful. It was a gift.

U said, "Good to see you, Loretta. You got him now?"

She smiled and wrapped her other thick arm around my waist.

"Hey, man," U said. "Come on with me for a second."

I got untangled from the family hug, Loretta already seated with Abby and plying her with questions, and followed U back out to his Expedition parked in the Peabody's mammoth parking garage.

"You sleep," he said. "I'll watch."

"Go home. I'm fine."

"Woman got your gun?"

I nodded.

He laughed again. Maybe even harder than when he found out that I'd driven the Gray Ghost into a hole. He punched a button on his keychain, the truck chirped, and locks clicked in his doors.

"What were you packin' anyway?"

"Browning nine."

"What the fuck did you have that for?"

"Worked great for me."

"How'd you keep that under your coat? I mean, you got to holster the damn thing and you can't move and anyone with any sense can see it. This ain't the *Wild, Wild West,* man. Get in."

I got in the passenger side. The parking lot bare and quiet.

He opened his glove compartment and pulled out a Glock 9mm. Smaller than the ones I'd seen. Must've been a new model.

"Stick this in your coat. Don't know where you found it. Understand? Has a hell of a history I'm sure. Took it off that peckerwood from the other night." He widened his eyes. "Holds seventeen motherfuckin' rounds. Take both clips."

I did.

"Be careful, brother."

Loretta had already gotten a suite for us. I always knew Loretta and JoJo made a nice living but they usually lived pretty simply except when Loretta traveled. When we played the Chicago Blues Festival last year she'd rented out a hell of a room at the Palmer House. She said life was too short to stay in those "Holidaze" Inns.

I agreed. It was nice to be in the big sprawling room filled with heavy wood furniture and gilded lamps. Big-ass bathtub where I took a thirty-minute shower cleaning dirt from every inch of my skin. Loretta had ordered me a couple beers and a sandwich from room service.

I thanked her, but the thought of food made me sick as hell.

I exchanged places with Abby and a quick silence fell between me and Loretta. Her face had been in such a tight grin since she'd met Abby that it took it a few seconds to fall. She had her long coat draped over her chair and had propped open a window listening to the sounds of the city where she'd made her name.

"You want to tell me why you're really here?" I asked.

"You need help."

"Shit."

"Watch your language, boy." Her face didn't break, just kept on listening to those city sounds like it was music.

"Bluff City was a long, long time ago. All of us in that same neighborhood. Stax. Hi. Called it Soulsville."

I watched her as I took off my boots. Then I stretched out on a rollaway that had already been laid out, smelling of the bleach in the sheets. I closed my eyes still listening to her stories.

"Why are you here?" I asked in a groggy voice. "I can handle it."

"You need me, boy. They ain't talkin' to you. Are they? Tomorrow we'll find Clyde. All right? Tomorrow let's go get my brother."

Chapter 38

MEMPHIS MUSIC IS not dead. Although it's pretty damned hard to get away from the past. The droves of Elvites to Graceland, the well-known mantra of Sam Phillips's contributions to rock and roll, and even the B. B. King imitators playing covers in nameless, soulless bars along Beale. But beyond the history, the tributes, and even the fiction, there is a real, breathing music scene at little clubs in Midtown with singer-songwriters who've come to the city as if it were Mecca, hoping just to soak up a little bit of what has inspired musicians for generations. Knowing that the name Memphis attached to you somehow makes you more interesting, more soulful, more real.

One of the best places to get immersed in the local scene was down at the Hi-Tone on Poplar. I hadn't been there since the bar screened a documentary of local bluesman Will Roy Sanders a few years back.

Tonight, men with sideburns and wallet chains prowled the bar, smoking as if the surgeon general had suddenly changed his mind. Women in satiny vintage dresses and funky 'fifties glasses shaped like cat eyes sat around small tables with mismatched chairs sipping imported beer and listening to the music.

That was the thing about the Hi-Tone. People *listened* to music. They didn't come to be seen or to pick up, or, for the most part, just to get drunk. They came to respect the music.

The interior was a funky mix of early Fred Sanford: kitschy ads for Chesterfield cigarettes, a bullfighting poster, a cow skull, a poster for an Elvis movie, Japanese lanterns, and a Schlitz beer sign, circa 1972. Loretta and I walked under drooping Christmas lights that had been snaked overhead.

"In Memphis, you don't throw away shit," Loretta said.

I kind of liked it. Memphis, a blender of the last five decades.

On a low stage near the front of the darkened bar stood one of those twenty-something punks. Wallet chain, check. Sideburns, check. Even had one of those grease monkey workshirts with some improbable name on the pocket. *Earl.* Every garage has an Earl.

"That him?" Loretta asked.

"Could be. Don't see his father."

"He'll show. Tole me he would."

I hadn't woken up till about 2:00 P.M. with a massive headache and a sore-as-hell back. Loretta, God bless her, had gone downstairs and bought Abby some new clothes in the Peabody's shops, and brought me back a club sandwich and a Dr Pepper. As I ate, I told her more about my days in Memphis and what I believed and what I still needed to know. She was particularly interested in Cleve. She seemed to think he'd been bullshitting me because he didn't talk that much about her. I said it was probably an oversight, but she called it bullshit. She said Cleve, a former member of *her* band, too, should have been kissing my ass if he knew I was a friend.

"I get uncomfortable with the ass kissing," I had said. "I can chafe."

She ended up calling Cleve from the hotel and he said he'd meet us at the Hi-Tone to talk some more. Once again, he told Loretta the same story that he'd told me about Clyde probably being dead and about getting in touch with Cook. But Loretta was pretty damned good. Without another question, she said she looked forward to seeing him at the bar.

Loretta had a tall glass of ice water and I had an Abita Purple Haze, somehow that raspberry ale kind of having a tonic effect on me. Or maybe I'd been knocked loopy yesterday. Anyway, that slight fizz felt pretty good.

The kid on stage was singing an acoustic ballad about meeting his teen love at the Wal-Mart and the girl's mouth tasting like honeysuckle. He wasn't bad. Had a nice talent for images and words and sang in a rough, gravelly voice that spoke more of his experience than his age.

"You remember when you first started playing?" Loretta asked, carefully folding her long jacket over her arm and taking a sip of the ice water.

"Sort of."

"You were scared shitless, Nicholas. Remember, you were playin' those licks for JoJo out back makin' sure they sounded in key? And he was laughin' at you and blowin' 'em back in D instead of C to make you fret 'round."

Loretta laughed.

"I got over it."

"Kid's good," she said.

I nodded.

"I always said, blues about lots of things," she said. "People can play blues music but not play blues. You see? Kid has soul. He knows pain."

"How about you? What was your first gig?"

"Beale Street, nineteen fifty-seven. Sang 'Things I Used to Do' with a little combo. My little brother came with me but they wouldn't let him in. Had to watch the show from a stack of beer crates out back. He was lookin' through a little window."

I smiled. "You did good."

"Hell yes, I did good. Kicked the crowd right in the nuts. Bar owner, little midget with dandruff, offered me a deal singin' for eighty-five dollars a week that night. I was cool back then, son. Had that platinum hair and cherry-red lips."

"You knew JoJo?"

"Not yet. That fool had no idea what was waitin' for him."

"And then you met him when he joined your band?"

"We met at a Fourth of July church party. He'd churned some ice cream and I just looked at those arms and hands streaked with cream and knew that was a man. You know how JoJo got them knuckles with scars on them? Don't know why, but always kind of turned me on. Had the preacher introduce us. His country ass had just come up from Clarksdale."

The main entrance to the Hi-Tone was cracked and I felt a broad chill when it opened again and Cleve walked in the door. He had on a mustard-colored rubbery-leather jacket and plaid slacks with white shoes. His shirt was satiny and tropical and wide-collared and about thirty years out of style.

I knew he'd just raided the back of his closet for something clean. But here, he was vintage and hip. A few people stopped him at the door and shook his hand but then he quietly found a seat next to a small lounge table topped with a glowing red candle. I could tell he didn't want anyone to pay him any attention. He sat down and intently watched his son finishing out his song about animal crackers and foul-tasting beer.

"Look like he stole them pants off a dead man," Loretta said.

I laughed and walked over to Cleve, tapping him on the shoulder and pointing out our table. As soon as he saw Loretta, he got up off his ass and came over and gave her a huge hug. Laughing, no longer paying attention to his son, and holding on to her like he was asking forgiveness.

She held his hand and pulled him down in the seat next to her. She did it almost regally. Like he had his honored time to sit beside the queen of the blues. Loretta took out a silk show handkerchief, probably JoJo's, and dotted her brow.

I could make out a few words of the conversation, trying to hang back and be cool. Let her take the lead to relax Cleve. If I was leaning over the table watching his every breath, he'd repeat the same story, drink up on our tab, and we'd be wasting more time. I wanted to find Clyde. We had to find Clyde.

"So Cook told you he was dead. That was the last you saw him?" I heard her ask during the intermission, Junior sitting at the table now.

Senior nodded. Junior drank two Buds on our tab. I'd had two also. Enough to make me contemplate some cheesy movie poster by the stage about juvenile delinquent drag racers and its deeper meaning to the Hi-Tone. I leaned in closer and joined the conversation.

Loretta asked questions I'd already asked. Sidetracked onto some pretty good stories I'd never heard. Real gems about playing gigs in the segregated South. Black and white musicians trying to sleep in the same hotel.

"You remember that li'l ole sissy man in Atlanta?" she said. "That man actin' all funny when you said you and Eddie Porter were stayin' in the same room. What did Eddie say? Somethin' about not lovin' you?"

"Yeah, that man asked us if we wanted one bed or two," Cleve said. "Guy grinnin' like he'd gotten ole Eddie. Eddie didn't hesitate; he said, 'Listen mister, I like this white boy, but I don't love him.' "

We drank into Junior's next set, the light reflecting off the mirrored shards on the disco ball, white squares crossing over Loretta's face. Felt odd being in Memphis with her and without JoJo, outside our French Quarter patterns. I wanted to be back in that far corner of JoJo's, next to the back exit, a mess of Dixies before me, listening to Felix hum as he emptied the night's ashtrays.

Cleve and Loretta's conversation finally left Clyde altogether and settled into family and life and Cleve's new belief system he'd acquired after watching a cable television show on Hinduism. Loretta was getting tired, too, and her conversations lapsed into a lot of *Mm-hmm, honey*s, and *I know what you mean*s.

I helped Junior break down after his set and carried his guitar out to his green Pinto. He told me about this cool *Dukes of Hazzard* episode when Beau and Luke go to Atlanta to participate in some government conference to find a substitute for gasoline.

"It was Uncle Jesse's moonshine. It was awesome."

But a few feet away, there was another conversation going on with Cleve. Just caught a bit, something about Bobby Lee Cook being a criminal.

"A criminal?" I asked. "You mean with the strip clubs?"

"Shit, he's always been a criminal," Cleve said, smoking a clove cigarette and pulling his hair into a ponytail. "Bluff City was nothin' but a Laundromat for the Dixie Mafia. You knew that, Loretta. Didn't you?"

Chapter 39

WE FOUND BOBBY LEE COOK in a back booth at the Golden Lotus playing Boggle with three strippers. A little girl, looking about fourteen and wearing a gold bikini, shook the bubble and plunked down the game removing the plastic lid. A black woman, who looked as if she'd been stripping since Earl Long's days on Bourbon Street, was the first to yell out a word from the dice-like letters, "There it is: *Cooch.*"

The other two girls, identical blondes with bobbed hair and rhinestone-studded halter tops, squealed with laughter. The young one in the gold bikini protested, "That's bullshit, Tiki. That ain't no word."

Always seemed strange to me when such beautiful people can have such guttural accents. The little girl looked like she should be shopping at some midtown mall with her daddy's credit card, but instead talked like a featured part of an Appalachian documentary, the kind with snake handlers, brother-sister marriages, and kids who thought toothpaste was a rare but tasty treat.

"Sure it is, *cooch*," the black woman said. "Like as in *coochie.*"

"Yeah, but you spellin' it with a K, ain't that right, Bobby Lee? Look. K-O-O-C-C-H-I." The little girl thrust the game in front of him for closer inspection. "That ain't no word. It's some kind of furrin country."

Cook hadn't seen us yet, even though we'd slid into a booth right next to him and his girls. As we waited, Loretta didn't take off her coat, her gaze wandering over the cinder block walls and concrete floor. A half-dozen girls thrust and ground their hips to some Huey Lewis and the News relic on mini stages around the bar.

I kept listening to the women, shaking off a waitress who came over to take our order. A few seconds later, Loretta nodded and I tapped Cook on his shoulder. He was wearing a black muscle T-shirt, the nape of his neck coated in black-and-white hair. Even over the booth he emitted an odor of vinegar and talc.

I stared over his shoulder at the game. "Oh, there's one more," I said. "A-S-S, and on the other side there is a big ole *hole*."

He turned.

"Hey, get the fuck out of here, Travers," he said, pinching the bridge of his nose with his thumb and forefinger when he saw me, being surprisingly cool. "You ruined my shirt. It was Calvin Klein."

He scooted out of the booth, the little girl pulling the game close to her and reading different words she saw. I think she was really looking for asshole.

I remained seated, smiling up at him. But his eyes moved right over me to Loretta, his face softening. All that hard light in his eyes gone as he moved in beside her. "Holy shit. Loretta. Good God. I thought this boy was kidding."

He hugged her tight and Loretta hugged him back. Her thick hands covered in gold rings, patted his shoulder. He motioned quickly over to the waitress and asked us what we wanted.

"Where's the pooch?" I asked.

"Vet."

"What happened?"

"Diarrhea. Got into my protein powder the other day. Shit all over the D.J. booth."

His teeth looked yellow in the low light and I had to bend my ear toward him to make out what he was saying over the pumping music.

"Too bad. Nice dog."

Loretta said something and he nodded. "You want something, buddy?"

"Beer," I said. "Just a beer."

He shrugged, told the waitress, and off she went. The girls remained at the next booth, its vinyl sealed in places with duct tape, laughing and shaking the Boggle bubble. I heard one of them make up another dirty word that I'd never heard but thought I understood from the way it sounded.

Loretta folded her hands before her and leaned in close to Cook. "Bobby, I known you for thirty-five years and I need help. Where's Clyde?"

He looked at me and I could tell he was grinding the hell out of his teeth. The waitress came back and handed me a beer. Miller Lite. The worst.

"Clyde's dead, Loretta," he said in a soft graveled voice. "I'm sorry."

I started absently peeling the label from the beer—much better than drinking it—and watched the neon light flash across Cook's craggy face and blue eyes. I could tell he was holding his breath, his eyes staring straight into Loretta's.

"He's alive," I said, looking at the table. I held my gaze for a few seconds and then stared up at Cook. "I know. I have witnesses. We just want to know where."

"You don't want—"

"To what? Let this woman that you like so much find her only brother? Yeah, that'd be a real shame. Listen, I know you guys were into some pretty fucked-up shit back then. Using the label as a wash for your buddies from Biloxi."

Cook kept his head down and nodded along with a wide grin. He started laughing when I mentioned the name Levi Ransom and said that I believed Ransom had sent two men to hassle Loretta in New Orleans.

"You want to tell me what all that means?" I asked.

He just kept laughing. "Man, you have a hell of an imagination, Travers. Loretta, this boy really your friend?"

She smiled. "We just want to find Clyde. We don't want to get you in no kind of trouble." I felt her hand tightly grip my knee under the table.

"I do that to your head?" Cook asked, motioning at my bruised temple.

"Yeah," I said. "Cook, you are the toughest."

"Loretta," he said, grabbing her hand and massaging her fingers. "Clyde is dead. All right? You understand? He's not been with us for a long time. You remember how he used to get? He left us when all that stuff happened with Mary. Those blackouts and the fits. It got so much worse. Be glad you were in New Orleans. We all tried to help."

I watched Loretta's face tighten and eyes wander to an old jukebox in the corner, lights flashing and neon pumping with music that was a relic from another age.

"If he's alive," she said, "I want to know."

The music faded out and the jukebox started playing Otis Clay's

"Tryin' to Live Without You." That driving Willie Mitchell beat and Hi horn section unmistakable. Pure Memphis.

Cook ran his fingers over his biceps with pride and nodded slowly to himself until the black girl stood before us and tossed the Boggle on the table. "That little bitch broke it," she said. "Redneck can't spell and blame me. She spell tootsie like in Tootsie Pop with a U: T-U-T-S-I. You hire some trips, Bobby."

The woman left and Otis Clay kept singing. Loretta watched his face while I looked away. This was her move. Anything he would tell us would come to her, not to me. He probably just wanted to move our scuffle over to a Winn-Dixie.

"You remember when we first started?" he asked. "You remember how I got that little movie theater over in Soulsville and me and Eddie Porter spent two weeks in July cutting up old mattresses and hanging them on the walls? I thought I was going to be a failure. Thought I'd never have enough money to pay my aunt back, thought I'd have to go back to driving trucks. But you changed it. Those first singles you put out made me. We bought new equipment. Hired a secretary. You remember Mae? Made me. You know?"

"So where is he?" she asked.

Cook ground his teeth some more and softly pounded his fist onto the table. "This is all show, you know? The girls. This isn't me, Loretta. This is money. Got to make that money."

She smiled at him and moved her hand over his, his fingers delicate and manicured.

"Y'all know the Harahan Bridge?" he asked.

Loretta nodded.

"He may still be there. It's been a few years. Little camp where people live on the Tennessee side. I just didn't want you to see what he'd become."

Chapter 40

I WAS THINKING about a story I'd read about Clyde James when, in the glow of the neighboring Memphis-Arkansas Bridge, Loretta and I saw the two Erector setlike tunnels stretching out over the Mississippi. As we neared the bridges, I remembered a short profile of Clyde in the *Living Blues* soul section a few years back. It was an interview with a manager of his who Loretta said had died years ago. The manager talked about how, even before the death of his wife, Clyde would disappear for weeks at a time, already suffering from deep depression. He said it got worse after the events of 'sixty-eight. He said Clyde took off during a tour of south Mississippi and showed up on his doorstep in Memphis a month later. Clyde very calmly said, "I been lookin' all over for you. Where you been?"

I drove the little compact U had loaned me off the main highway, just before reaching the bridge, and dipped down a narrow dirt road. High clumps of weeds lined the path and the little tires of the car bumped and jostled us until I found a decent place to stop by the two railroad bridges. They seemed like relics of a Memphis that no longer existed. Rust and rotting wood. Thick bolts that fastened beams together probably a hundred years ago. In the distance, north toward the city, I saw the two distinctive humps of the Hernando-Desoto Bridge lit with fat white bulbs and the weird glow of the Pyramid sports arena.

"What if I asked you to stay here?" I asked. "Just till I check things out."

Loretta opened the door and pulled herself out, smoothing down the suede of her coat. A hard fetid wind broke off the Mississippi and washed up the dirt bluffs to us. I lit a cigarette as I searched in U's trunk for a flashlight. I found one and moved the Glock to a better position in my hand-tooled belt.

"Why you smoke those things?" she asked. "You want to die early? Don't be a damned fool."

"Yes, ma'am," I said as she pulled it from my lips and ground it under her foot. Her shoulders shook just a little and there was a little quiver in her voice. I put my arm around her as we made our way down an embankment, smelling burning wood and hearing the muffled grumbling of men.

Right below where the Harahan jutted out from the bluffs, I saw fire sparks catching in the wind and dying out below the bridge and far above the swirling black water of the Mississippi. Felt like we were hanging on the edge of the earth, the split in America, a place where Old World explorers marveled.

I offered Loretta a hand as we scooted down the hill, making sure she kept her balance. The heels of my boots ground in the soft mud making it easy to track down. The sound of the men grew. More smoke. Wood. Cigarettes? Bottles clinking. Grunts. Bizarre moaning.

The men had found a little cove in the groove where the bridge meets the hills. Four nasty recliners, a sofa (more springs than material), several refrigerator boxes squashed flat and used as pallets, and dozens of men warming themselves over little campfires. Drinking labelless whiskey and talking. Several were white with long, yellowed mountain-man beards but most were black, sallow-eyed, with nappy hair.

Toward the edge of the firelight, one man was leaning over the concrete embankment singing like hell and pissing toward the Mississippi like it was his own personal toilet.

"Loretta," I said, grabbing her arm.

She looked over at me and shrugged. I moved ahead and began to search for a face that I only knew from a thirty-year-old picture. No one said a word to me. A few quit talking. Most just ignored us.

"Clyde?" Loretta yelled, like she was calling her cat home to dinner. "Clyde."

Most of the men I saw would actually be younger than Clyde. A few too old. No one responded to her calls. I let out a steady stream of air and turned as I saw a wiry white man with an ax handle trying to sneak up from behind.

I dodged his blow, the handle raking across the concrete ground, and pulled his shoulders forward, making him smack the ground facefirst. There was an audible pop.

I yelled to the group that I didn't want trouble. I told them that Loretta was just looking for her brother. "Clyde James. Any of y'all know Clyde? He used to sleep down at the Piggly Wiggly on Madison. The graveyard, right there."

A couple of coughs, a grunt, the old man still pissing into the Mississippi like he had attached a hose inside himself.

"Look, I got twenty bucks for someone. Buy a lot of whiskey or Eight-Ball."

"There," grunted a little black man wearing a worn Confederate battle hat. His face covered in short silver whiskers and wearing a bright pink trench coat. "Y'all can see him right there."

"Where?" I asked.

"There," he said, aggravated as hell that he'd had to stand. "Look, I'll show you. Just give me that twenty."

And I did.

We crossed over a weedy lot strewn with empty beer cans and torn pieces of clothing. The man leading us down below the next bridge, identical to the Harahan, walked stoop-shouldered and slow. His face was gray, as if oxygen didn't circulate above his neck. Bloodshot eyes. If I'd seen him sleeping on the street, I would have thought he was dead.

I pointed the flashlight down the path, every click and shuffle making my heart pound, until he pointed to a collection of grayish-black mounds gathered in the fall cold. A tin drum of old rags and driftwood had been lit at the base of the bridge as if marking an entrance to some kind of feudal castle.

I kept my fingers close to the Glock and I took comfort in the seventeen-shot capacity U had bragged about. Loretta wandered ahead and I soon lost our guide as I followed her underneath the bridge.

There I was greeted by a tremendous smell of piss and shit. I wanted to gag and buried my nose in my jacket.

"Good Lord," I said.

Loretta took the flashlight out of my hand and swept it over the mounds. They moved.

All dirty. Blacks and grays and sun-bleached browns. People under mounds of rags. Boxes of chicken bones and empty dog food cans. More bottles of whiskey. Pits bordered by barbed wire. Some slept in the pits, others in boxes, and even more just on the ground in heaps. There must've been thirty, forty of them.

"Clyde!" Loretta yelled. Just blind. Absolutely blind. I moved my hand away from the Glock and felt for her fingers. I had a hard time swallowing. God, the smell was absolutely awful.

Everyone was sleeping a hell of a hard sleep.

No one moved as we searched for about ten minutes. She'd stop, flash a light into their faces, and move on. One old guy sprang to his feet and tried to knock my teeth in. But these were weak people. Their bodies barely functioned; their minds were completely fucked up. I just sidestepped the old dude and he fell back to the ground.

Between the gaps of the massive supports of the bridge, I watched a tugboat pushing a barge upstream. The moonlight broke and swirled on the brown water in its wake. I spit on the ground, trying to remove the smell from my head when I noticed Loretta had stopped and bent down to the ground.

I followed.

She was crying.

I looked at her; she nodded to me.

Clyde James opened his eyes.

Chapter 41

AT FIRST, CLYDE thought Loretta was his mother. Kind of strange and Freudian but he did. Thirty years. It had been thirty freakin' years, I had to remember. His hair was almost straight, gray wisps. High cheekbones and blackish-red skin. Fingernails like daggers. As I watched his face, he moaned. His eyes bloodshot as hell, and his mouth smelling like a septic tank but asking for forgiveness. He just kept asking her to find pity on his soul. He then curled himself into a ball and started crying. Around him lay jug bottles of malt liquor and crushed soda cans punched with holes. His head lay on a tan vinyl suitcase and he'd wrapped his body in a plastic tarp. A Memphis winter wasn't far away and I wondered how anybody could ever survive out here. I felt like we were on the bottom of an ocean.

I watched Loretta crying and felt a thick rock form in the back of my throat. She lay her hands across his cheek. "Oh, Lord. Clyde? Clyde?"

He said something about the cold as if reading my mind. His eyes wide open now, a feverish light cast across his face.

"It's Lo. Baby. Clyde. Come on. Clyde?"

He rolled to his elbows. I cast a quick glance to the stirring mounds around us, the tug fighting the currents and the whipping strands of fire licking the base of the bridge. I wanted to grab him and get the hell out of here. I fingered the butt of the gun. I tried to steady my breathing.

Loretta moved by him and sat down in the dirt in her five-hundred-dollar jacket to cradle his head. The ceiling above us, seeming to close in even more, shook hard as a train passed for several minutes. Light from the train splintered in across the floor and over Loretta's face and her lips moving with words I couldn't hear.

Clyde was crying as she held his head like you would a child's.

My ears rang with the sound of the train, looking for anyone moving around us.

When the train passed, Clyde was talking: "The rain. It was hurting, too. I could feel the rain hurting but it wasn't really me. I was there, in sight and soul and everything, but my body wasn't there."

"Clyde, come with us."

He flopped his head around in her lap. Violently.

"Some men are looking for you, Clyde. They want to kill you. It's all about Mary. Clyde, what happened that night with Eddie and Mary? What?"

He rolled his head.

"It's raining. God is raining. God's face is raining. Black rust. Black rust all over my face."

I put my hand on Loretta's shoulder.

"Uh-uh. I ain't leavin' here without him. Grab him and let's go."

I nodded and reached around his waist. His body buckled and he rolled to his feet scattering leaves and torn-up pieces of yellowed newsprint in the air.

"We're just trying to help," I said.

He was crying and rocking and he beat his fist into his leg. "No!"

Somebody yelled at me and I felt a harp thwap at my back. More little hard hits on my legs. They were stoning us. I covered my head, reached for the Glock, and fired off a round.

The throwing stopped. I saw Loretta wiping blood from her ear and I gritted my teeth.

"Come on, Clyde. Come here." I moved toward him and he snarled at me. I lunged, got a good hold of his arms, and he clawed at my face with his curved nails. I felt the blood heat in my skin as he buckled and tried to bite my arm. He almost chomped down when I pushed him away. It was a hell of a thing to try to grab someone you didn't want to hurt. Kind of like alligator wrestling.

"Clyde," Loretta said. "Let me get you some help. Be just like that doctor we used to see. Remember he gave you those pills? You all right with them pills. Come on."

I lunged for him again, pulled his skinny arms down by his sides, and then he really started writhing. I moved him toward the lot separating the bridges and out from the camp in a bear hug. His head flew back and connected with my jaw sending me reeling, almost making me pass out, as I gritted my teeth and pushed him forward, his feet off the ground.

Then he gave the most god-awful howl I'd ever heard. He was screaming and crying and moaning. His body started convulsing and Loretta screamed to put him down. And I did. He rolled to his back shaking, his eyes up in his head until he flipped to his hands and knees and vomited. I saw a pool of urine collect at his brogan shoes.

"Leave him," she said. Her face impassive. Tears streaking her perfect makeup.

I nodded.

"We'll need some help. He needs to be in a hospital. Lord. Nick, I didn't know. I didn't know. I just gave up on him. I let him go. And I knew. Goddamn me, I knew."

We walked to the car in the weak light, and I hugged her. I heard the horn of the tug upstream and felt a harsh wind blowing across the tips of my ears.

She pushed her face into the crook of my arm and I held her tight. Her words a confusing mix of sorrow and blame.

We drove back to the Peabody, to our suite and warm beds, not saying a word.

Chapter 42

THE NEXT AFTERNOON, we drove a rental car back into New Orleans, Canal Street, and the French Quarter a little after six. A tourist carriage driver had stopped off in front of the bar. His clients, confused elderly women with their new digital cameras, seemed impatient as we walked past them and found the driver drinking a cold one and talking with Felix about the Saints. Felix didn't like him. And neither did I. We'd had some run-ins about the way he treated his horses. As soon as the driver saw me, he threw back the Dixie, washing off his mouth with the sleeve of his jacket, and tromped out the door.

Felix laughed as he continued to slice lemons and absently watch *SportsCenter* from behind the bar. His black bald head so slick and clean the images of the television reflected off his skull.

Loretta walked ahead of Abby and me into the far corner of the bar where JoJo kept his office, a dull yellow light showing from a cracked door. She was tired as hell and pretty quiet on the way home on Interstate 55. Earlier that morning, she'd had Clyde committed to the Memphis Mental Health Institute on Poplar. I'd gone out with some of their wranglers, although they called them something much more official, and I was tired, too. The fight with Clyde had been pretty nasty and the way Loretta's face dropped again at the center was hard to watch.

I sat at the bar. Smiled at Felix. Felix smiled back and absently popped the top off a Dixie and hammered it next to my elbow.

"You thirsty?" I asked Abby.

She nodded. Felix popped another.

"You're in luck," he said. "I ain't askin' for IDs today."

I introduced them as I finished half of the cold beer. I was dead, travel tired. I wanted to go back to the warehouse and sleep for a couple days. Maybe even hibernate. I stretched my legs off the barstool.

The pale yellow afternoon light shot in broken, loose fingers between handbills that had been Scotch-taped in the window. Some so brittle and old that they'd somehow fused to the glass. I heard the clip-clop of the driver and horse rambling away into a French Quarter dusk.

"How long has this place been here?" Abby asked. She tugged on the beer, too hard, and the foam spilled over onto her hand.

"Long as I've been alive."

She seemed okay with the answer as she felt along the edges of the old mahogany bar, feeling the cuts, cigarette burns, and dents as if they were braille markings.

We watched *SportsCenter* with Felix for a while as the afternoon regulars of T-shirt salesmen and Bourbon Street day players rolled in for a cold one before heading home or to begin their night. I hoped I'd see Oz or Hippie Tom. But it was early and I believed Oz may have started his fall ghost tours since it was close to Halloween.

I felt an arm reach across my throat and heard a gruff, weathered voice say: "Gettin' soft when an old man can sneak up behind you."

Without looking up I said, "Shouldn't have to watch your back in your own home."

"Yeah," JoJo said, laughing. "Just like a crazy man to call a bar his home."

I turned and gave JoJo a quick shake so he wouldn't try to crush my knuckles as he always did with his thick bricklayer hands.

"Abby, I'd like you to meet the top male stripper in New Orleans, Mister Joseph Jose Jackson."

He reached out and kissed her hand. "With his legs, he'd be lucky to make a nickel on Rampart Street."

Abby laughed and JoJo motioned us back to the far corner table where he conducted business and occasionally drank with dead men. I wondered how much Loretta had told him as we sat down.

The chairs were mismatched, rickety, and old. I felt a bit uncomfortable stretching my legs again as the chair strained with my weight. I watched JoJo's face grow serious under a big red neon sign for Jax beer.

"Miss," JoJo said. "I am real sorry to hear about your folks. If you get tired of this ole so and so, you can always come stay with us. Always need some help 'round here." He winked at her, his face weathered and very black. "Jes let us know."

Abby thanked him. Felix brought out another round on JoJo's orders and Loretta soon appeared with four steaming portions of her famous soul jambalaya. Reheated but just as good. She didn't tell anybody how she made it, but I knew she always began everything with a thick, smoked ham hock. Even reheated, this stuff was the essence of life: andouille sausage, onions, green peppers, and chicken soaked in Crystal sauce. A big crusty baguette from the market.

You knew food was good when no one talked. No one spoke until every bit of jam was gone and the bowl had been wiped clean with the bread. After that, Loretta began to talk about meeting with Cleve and Bobby Lee Cook and even about our encounter with Clyde at the bridge. As she told the story, she watched my face, letting me know to leave out other parts. She hadn't told JoJo about the men coming to the bar before I left, or that someone had tried to kill me and Abby.

"So the Ghost finally up and died on you?" JoJo asked.

I watched Loretta looking at her hands and said, "Yeah. She finally just fell apart."

"Well," JoJo began, his eyes narrowed. He leaned back and folded his arms, a man just watching what would come out our mouths next. "Glad y'all is back."

Felix dipped by as an awkward silence fell onto the table and lit a candle in a red glass. It was night now and the evening's band, some guys out of Atlanta called The Shadows, were setting up.

The doors had been propped open and a biting breeze shot off Conti and bent the candle's flame.

"Lo, you mind closin' up tonight?" JoJo asked. "Robert Junior down at Tips and asked me to sit in."

"I can help," I said. I guess I spoke too loud and too soon because JoJo raised his eyebrows. "We'll come back for the last set. Just let me get Abby settled in to the warehouse and get some clean clothes."

JoJo nodded to himself and got up from the table.

As he turned his back, Loretta winked at me and pinched my arm. She was actually having fun fooling the old man.

"I'll be fine, Nicholas," she said. "Y'all get home and get rested."

"Don't leave this bar without me tonight," I said. "You hear me?"

"Nicholas, I ain't ever lived my life in fear and won't start now. Besides, we're back home. Memphis is a long way."

I slipped back into my jacket and motioned to Abby. The band launched into their first song, the lyrics about souls slipping off into the *Dark Side*.

Chapter 43

PERFECT LEIGH WAS damned tired of waiting. She'd been sitting on her ass in the stinky French Quarter since noon, most of it in some nasty old burger joint where she'd watched this elderly cook ritualistically pick his nose, and now she wanted a little action. She was bored. And that was about the worse thing that you could make Perfect Leigh. When she got bored she got bad. She clicked her nails together. Nice color. Siren. She whispered the words to herself, her tongue flattening on the roof of her mouth, as a cold wind knocked down Royal Street and into the darkened bar.

Where was Jon? She'd gotten off the phone with Ransom thirty minutes ago and he said to go on and get what they needed. But Jon wanted to get the car ready, said they needed good parking as if they were goin' shopping down at Maison Blanche.

She blew out a long breath, studying the fine curve of her nails in the candlelight.

Bar was called Lafitte's. It was supposed to be some kind of historic site although it looked to Perfect as if it'd been slapped together with a bucket of concrete and rotten wooden beams. They didn't have lights; each one of the tables was dim and yellow from little candles. No air-conditioning either. Its tall creaky doors had been propped open to breathe in the night's snappy cold air.

Finally, Jon sauntered on in from the cold, lanky and determined, and sat across from her. His face nothing but a bearded black grin under his cowboy hat. "What time you got?"

"Almost midnight," she said, studying the way his mouth formed words. She wondered how he'd say *si-ren*. "You park in Mississippi?"

Jon didn't answer. His face pinched in the glow of the table's candle.

Dark circles seemed to grow under his eyes as he leaned close and he played with the rings on his fingers. "Did you see him?"

"He wasn't there, only the black woman."

Jon looked back at the open doors and felt at the side pocket of his jacket. Perfect watched his pistonlike leg and the way his jaw chomped on a whole pack of gum. Juicy Fruit. She hated Juicy Fruit. Reminded her of when she was in Biloxi and thirteen and her mother had paid off the pageant's judge with a visit to Perfect's room at the Motel Six.

"Why do you care about Travers so much?" she asked, trying to turn her head and not take a whiff of the sickly sweet gum.

"He killed me."

She again studied his features under the Resistol's brim.

"Years ago, I died and this man was responsible."

"You're insane. I knew you had some quirks but I refuse to work with a real life walking head case."

A waitress came over and asked if they wanted another couple of Cokes. They said they didn't, but she paid her a decent tip. Decent. Not enough to be remembered. She looked around the bar and noticed the way everyone ignored them. She'd taken a lot of care to look so ordinary. Didn't brush her hair or make up her face. Even tried to slack her shoulders a bit so no one could notice her sculpted body.

"Sweet sister, I'm not crazy," Jon said when the woman walked away. "The man took my holy name of Jesse Garon and my birthright as the brother of E. I died at Graceland one night. All the papers said so. They said I tried to steal E's Sun God jumpsuit and the police shot me in the heart. They said my blood washed against E's leather bedspread."

Perfect listened but she couldn't think of a response. She felt all the air in the bar heat and turn to vapor before floating away as if sucked into a vacuum.

"It wasn't me," Jon said. "It was another True Believer who stole my wallet at the motel. He took all the money I had and thought he could get away with my driver's license because he, too, had the look. I guess he did. He's dead. I'm dead. Now I'm invisible. I'm Jon Burrows who floats on the mist and kills people with a talent that the world will never understand."

"So who are you?" Perfect asked.

"Just a believer on the path."

His jagged curve of a smile and the soaking smell of puke and Quarter beer from the street was too much already. She wanted to get it done.

"Ready?" he asked, pulling out a cheroot and striking a match against the grain of the rickety table. A breeze buckled off the flagstone walk outside and across her face like a slap.

She nodded.

"And he said unto them, I beheld Satan as lightning fell from heaven," Jon said as he stood and began their trek over several blocks to Conti.

When E shot the holiest of messages to his fans, the *'68 Comeback Special,* He only had a few words of advice to D.J. and Scotty who were backin' Him up: "Tell it like it is and play it dirty." It was the first time that E had been in front of a live audience in eight years because of the secret deal He'd made with the government and President Kennedy to make films and help America's youth. That night in 'sixty-eight, He couldn't even sit in the chair with the guitar. All them emotions was bubblin' up to the surface. It was like that now for Jon; he felt an overwhelming need to kill Travers. *Why couldn't he be there, too? That's why he was here. On this path.*

A few minutes later, he and Perfect rounded the turn of a forgotten section of the Quarter at the place Ransom told them about. JoJo's. Jon remembered the place from a dream somewhere. The lights were off with only a couple of neon signs burning purple and green in the long, fat window.

A sad old blues song played from the jukebox and floated out the open doors as a couple of men walked out carrying guitars and drums. One had a saxophone. The man with the sax, dressed like a Sun Records daddy in bowling shirt and baggy pants, hugged the neck of a large nigra woman before piling into the van with the others and disappearing down toward the Mississippi River.

"That her?" he asked.

"Yes," she said. "If he comes back, Ransom said you could."

Jon felt for the gun in his pocket. "It's been a long time, Jack."

"What?"

"It's like a surge of electricity goin' through you when you kill," he said.

"It's almost like making love, but it's stronger than that. . . . Sometimes I think my heart is gonna explode."

"He's not here yet."

"*He* will be," Jon said. "I sense him."

"Jon?"

He stopped halfway across Conti. A gaggle of businessmen in crooked party hats and drunker than a herd of goats filtered by them. Jon rubbed his beard, nodding at the neon lights quittin' in the bar's windows and the front door beginning to close.

All along the street, the buildings were real dark and vacant and seemed to wrap over him in a curve like in *King Creole*. Midnight in the French Quarter. Wooden business signs flappin' from under balconies. Gas lamps burnin' from a corner restaurant. He reached into his jacket for the pistol and nodded.

They hustled inside the bar, front door unlocked, as they saw the nigra woman turning chairs upside down onto the tables scattered by a stage.

"We closed," she said, not even turning to look at them.

The woman moved real careful, unlit, and kind of shadowed across the dance floor. Jon walked backward to the door and slid the dead bolt into place with a solid thunk.

The woman slapped another chair onto the table and sunk her hands onto her tremendous hips: "Money gone, you sons a bitches. Got a couple cops about to roll by in two seconds, so you best get yo' trashy asses back to Bourbon Street."

Jon struck a match to his cheroot.

The jukebox glowed green and scattered twirling patterns across Perfect's face and the woman's. He hung back and waited for Perfect to begin the show. He watched through random spots in the glass for Travers.

Perfect walked four steps forward. The gun inches from the big woman's heart. "No money," she said.

The big woman nodded in the darkness, her face crossed with the knowin'.

"Your brother," Perfect said. "Where is he? We're not leavin' till you tell us."

"Well, then I'll be cookin' y'all breakfast," she said. "'Cause I don't know. Why? He owe y'all some money, too? If you see him, tell him he still owes me from nineteen sixty-five."

Jon clamped the cheroot between his teeth and blew smoke into the green light. Funny twirling patterns of color and grayness passed over his eyes.

Perfect pressed a gun into the woman's ribs and the woman held still. She glanced at Jon's face and then returned her gaze to Miss Perfect. She nodded slowly and pressed her palms flat upon a barroom table. Leaning. She kept nodding.

"Okay," she said. "I got you. . . . But what you want Clyde for? He's a sick man."

Perfect ground the gun into her ribs. "Where is he? Where in Memphis? You give us an address, we have someone check it out and we're out of your life. All right?"

"Okay," the woman said. "Okay."

"Where is he?" Perfect screamed. Then she looked over at Jon and the woman and shook her head like the whole dang situation made Miss Perfect sad. "I'm way too good for this," she said.

The woman gave Perfect a good ole once-over from the shoes to her uncombed hair. She shook her head like Perfect wasn't fit to spit-shine the bar's toilets. "Sister, I don't know what your man got on you, but you need to get your trashy country ass out of the big city. It's showin' all about you."

Perfect gritted her teeth and rammed the handle of that old Colt she was carryin' into the woman's stomach, making her drop to her knees and start coughin'.

"I ain't trash," Perfect screamed. "Now where is he?"

Jon knew time was short. Answers had to come.

He knelt down and whispered, "Ole woman, where is he?"

Perfect grabbed Jon by the edge of his collar and yanked him away, "This is mine. Go outside!"

She pushed the gasping woman onto her back and began knocking beer bottles and half-filled glasses to the floor. Perfect kicked the jukebox, stopping some sad blues song cold, and walked over to a row of black-and-white photos of people Jon guessed were famous singers. She started cracking the glass frames with the butt of her gun. A bunch of 'em came crashing down and Perfect kicked and skidded them in jagged pieces across the floor.

She yelled again, "Where is he?"

The old woman got to her feet and smoothed her dress over her hips. Jon wandered over to the two, big ole roughshod doors and looked out the window. No one. Dead street. He crossed his arms across his chest and looked at the floor.

"We know he's in Memphis!" Perfect said, walking real quick like across the wooden floor and aimed the gun straight at the woman's forehead. "You have two seconds."

"Sister, you trip on power. Don't you?"

"Shut up."

"Think it brings you out of that backward upbringin'?"

"Shut up!"

"Look at you, gun in hand. Greasy-ass boyfriend. No five-hundred-dollar shoes can change what you are. You left the country but that pig shit sure stuck to you."

Miss Perfect looked down for a moment at some fancy shoes she'd been wearin' since Memphis, her mouth forming a big O.

She jumped a step back in surprise before she shot that big ole nigra woman right in the chest.

The woman reeled backward, knockin' down and crackin' chairs as she fell. Her scream deep and throaty and seemed to shake the whole dang bar. Everything vibratin' around Jon's head.

His head jammin' and heart jackknifin' in his chest.

Perfect looked down and admired the gun in her hand. She watched the fallen woman, loose and bleedin' on the floor, and started to grin. She didn't know she had it in her.

"Miss Perfect," Jon yelled. "We didn't come for that. Dang, you screwed us all now. We ain't got squat."

He ran to the window and looked outside. All right. They hadn't worn gloves and he didn't know what kind of gun she'd used or who owned it. This wasn't a hit. You set a dang hit up real different. If he'd killed Travers tonight, his gun would come back to a crack dealer in south Memphis.

"Miss Perfect. Miss Perfect."

"Let's go."

"We can't. That your gun?"

She nodded.

"Where'd you get it?"

"I bought it."

Jon's leg started aheavin' and jumpin' right where he stood until he ran over to the long wood, Mardis Gras beads drippin' down from glass rack like a fancy curtain. He plucked a couple bottles of gin and whiskey from a row of booze and started pourin' all over the place. Over the scarred ole bar and the floor and the jukebox and even the old nigra woman who lay still on the floor.

"Goddamn," Perfect screamed. "What the hell are you doin'?"

"Savin' your skin, woman."

He kicked the backdoor with the heel of his boots. His mind racin' back in time to a day locked away in his soul. *Mamma wasn't breathin' either. Mamma wasn't breathin' either.*

"It's all clean," he said, tossing the cheroot onto the bar and watching a bluish-yellow blaze kick up and begin to smolder and burn in the wood. A poof of air sucking from the room.

A couple of them old, dusty-as-hell photos began to crack and fall as if the old woman's scream had awoken them dead singers one last time.

Jon yelled to Perfect to follow: "Last train to Memphis, sister."

As the smoke gathered and flames grew, the jukebox sputtered and crackled to life one last time. Its weak lights pumped and dimmed with a scratchy, slow-moving 45 record that seemed to mirror that of a weak woman's heart.

Chapter 44

I HEARD THE SIRENS about halfway across Canal Street while I walked toward Royal and back into the Quarter. I'd left Abby at my warehouse, locked up tight and watching reruns of *Josie and the Pussycats*, after I got the call from Loretta that she was closing up. I'd hopped a streetcar and was even planning on seeing if Loretta wanted to get a cup of café au lait down at DuMonde—it was that kind of cool night—and talk about the things that we couldn't discuss around JoJo. But as soon as I rounded the turn in a swift jog down Conti and saw the smoke surging above the high rooftops, I felt my stomach drop from me and my throat clench. I broke into a full run down the crooked sidewalk and past the all-night bars and executive strip clubs.

Outside, there were two fire trucks and an ambulance. Two hulking firemen were lashing their hoses to a hydrant when I yelled that there was someone inside. I didn't even see their reaction as I kicked in the two big Creole doors, the battered wood breaking away as if paper, and running inside. The smoke was so thick and bulging, blackened and coiled, that I dropped to my knees and squinted into the room lit by the orange flames eating away the walls and crawling live and blue on the brick in a crisscrossed scrawl.

I saw a hand.

I crawled for her, almost touching her fingers, when three men pulled me away. I saw two others picking up Loretta and dragging her from the building. She wasn't moving.

In the clearing of tearing eyes, ragged and stinging, I saw the blood across her dress.

I crawled away from the men trying to give me oxygen and ran to her as they loaded her into the ambulance and sped away. I ran after the ambulance for a few blocks, coughing in spasms, until I bent over and tried to steady my breathing with my hands on my knees.

The ambulance screamed, lights twirling and scattering on the old buildings, all the way to Decatur and heading to Charity.

I ran back to JoJo's and a fireman confirmed that's where they'd taken her.

I stood at the bar for a moment watching the smoke pouring from the broken plate glass window and snaking from the broken twin doors. Dozens of firefighters held firm, washing the fire down as it continued to eat away the chairs, tables, jukebox, bar, and vintage photographs and posters. All that heat. The heat felt like a sunburn across my face where I held myself. Paralyzed.

The sound of cracking. Brick buckling.

I turned to find a phone.

But he was already there.

JoJo watched his business of thirty-five years curl and bend with that pressure and heat. His expression dropped and froze as I watched someone that he didn't know tell him about Loretta. As I walked to him, he saw me.

JoJo turned his back and got into his Cadillac, speeding away.

Abby and I found JoJo a little after 3:00 A.M. at Charity Hospital. I'd picked her up, worried they'd head over to the warehouse next. He sat in an anonymous room full of dozens of vending machines and scattered tables and chairs sipping coffee from a paper cup with an old teammate of mine, Teddy Paris, and his brother Malcolm. They owned a small rap label called Ninth Ward Records and were a hell of a nice couple of guys. But lately they'd been making quite a chunk of change. So much that I overheard 300-pound Teddy telling JoJo he'd pop a cap in the bastard who torched JoJo's bar and shot Loretta. "Just a word," Teddy said. "And it gets done."

Teddy was no gangster. But it was that kind of night.

Abby and I joined JoJo.

The Paris brothers politely left, swearing their return.

"Teddy shoot himself if he tried to use a gun," JoJo said, lazy and unfocused to no one in particular.

"I don't know who called him."

JoJo nodded.

I felt raw and beaten. I'd had to wake up Abby from the couch where she'd fallen asleep. Her eyes were dazed and unfocused. But she seemed determined to go with me the same way victims of crimes want to help others to ease their own pain.

I got a cup of coffee. Abby just sat there and tried to smile at JoJo.

JoJo watched the wall.

"Heard the surgery went fine," I said.

He nodded.

JoJo had on a gray cardigan over a black golf shirt. As I reached for his shoulder, I noticed he was still wearing bedroom slippers.

My hand weight felt dead and useless. He wouldn't look at me. Hadn't looked at me since I'd walked in.

A cleaning crew of three men in gray coveralls propped open the doors to the cafeteria and began swishing their mops all around us. They worked as if we lived on this tiny island and were forbidden to move.

I leaned back into my chair and smiled at Abby.

I hated hospitals. I hated their smells and sounds. They reminded me of spending the night in one when I was twelve. My mother had shot herself and I'd spent five hours in a waiting room alone while my father disappeared to drink himself into a world of shit. I had to be told my mother was dead by an arrogant surgeon who felt himself morally above anyone who would end her own life.

I asked JoJo if he needed anything.

For a while he didn't answer.

The cleaning crew soon left, the floor wet and shining like glass but smelling putrid.

"Why you bring these people in our lives?" JoJo asked. He slumped forward and folded his thick, scarred hands together. He stared up at me with such an intensity that I felt bumps form on the back of my neck. "Why, Nick?"

I opened my mouth but words wouldn't form.

"That detective said you knew who did this. Said you tole him they were folks from Memphis following you."

I wanted to tell him about Clyde and the men who had harassed Loretta before I'd even agreed to help. But it didn't seem appropriate. It was a deal I'd made with Loretta, and although I didn't see how it could possibly cause anymore pain to JoJo, I just nodded with him.

"Loretta's gonna live," JoJo said. "Has to. Don't nothin' work without her. Understand?" He raised his voice. "I said, do you understand, boy?"

"Yes, sir."

It was me that couldn't look at him now.

"I worked my whole life to own that bar. Been open since nineteen sixty-five. Do you know what it means to pour your soul into something and see it disappear?"

I watched the toe of my boot.

He knocked the coffee away with his hand. Some of the brown mess scattered across my face and poured toward Abby's lap. She stood quickly and walked into the hall to leave us alone.

"I want you to stay away from my family," JoJo said. "We didn't do nothin' but open up to you. Give you a place to be. That old woman, tubes coming out of her lungs, love you, man. Love you like her child."

I watched him. "You have no idea how sorry I am."

He reached out and grabbed the front of my blue jean jacket, twisting the cotton into his hands, and pulled me close to his face.

JoJo loosened his grip and broke from his flash of anger, pushing me away with disgust and pointing his finger. He yelled: *"Stay out of our lives!"*

I told him I was sorry again.

The sound of his breathing matched my own blood before I got up and walked from the room. I knew it was the only thing that would help him tonight. And I hated that. I hated myself for not being more observant if someone was following us or for not arriving five minutes earlier.

Out in the hall, I grabbed Abby's hand and dragged her down a linoleum hallway to the elevator. "I want you to pack your things," I said. All the different rooms and hallways made me feel dizzy and small. A rock formed behind my voice box.

"What about—?"

"We're going back to Memphis."

Chapter 45

RANSOM WAS PISSED. In all the years Perfect had known his broken-down butt she'd never known him to take a loss so hard. So she shot and killed some old black woman. Who cared? She knew Ransom wanted to find out about where to find her brother, but it was his damned fault he didn't allow Perfect to work with her own talents. His moronic hick-ass thought a gun could do all the work. She wanted to tell him this wasn't the 'sixties as he continued to lecture them from the flatbed of his pickup truck parked in some Tunica cotton field. She wanted to tell him she needed time to learn about that old woman's faults and desires. This was sophomore crap and she would not stay here and listen to how it should've worked.

"Goddamn it!" Ransom yelled, throwing a rock into a few acres of flat poured concrete as dawn crept over the cotton fields and his casino to the east. Early day was a strange time. They were tired as hell from the drive from NOLA but dawn brought a weird electricity to Perfect, almost like those tingling vibes before you make love.

"If that's all you can say, I'm gone," Perfect said, walking back to the rental.

He leaped off the flatbed, black leather jacket and one of those silk black shirts old men prefer, and came right to her, gripping his fingers into her shoulders, so hard it made her jaws clamp. "That boy saved us back there. We don't need a damn screw-up right now. Do you know how big this is?"

"No," she said, clawing her long red nails into his hairy hands. "No, I don't. Why don't you tell us. Why don't you tell us why you're so fuckin' obsessed with some street-walking nigger?"

He grunted and walked back to his truck. The haze of the morning all dewy and crisp. The cotton popped and made swishing sounds in the rich dirt.

"I'm through with this," she said. "I don't work like some kind of street-trash criminal. When have I ever lost for you? Ever? What about that family who sold you the land where we're now standin'? What about the Baptist preacher who knew all about that police detective and his problems with little girls?"

He shook his head. "There is no time."

"Time for what? For doing a job right?"

"I don't know who my enemies are," he said. She studied the acne scars on his reddened skin. "I don't know who they are. But the one thing I know is that they can use this man against me. He should've been dead thirty years ago."

"I'm done," she said. "This is not what I do."

"You selfish little bitch. Aren't you the same one who got your panties all wet at the Grove wanting to kill? You said you wanted to learn another talent, or some shit."

"That was different."

"Why?"

"That was one man," Perfect said, chewing on a loose cuticle. "He disrespected me at the casino."

Ransom let out such a laugh that it echoed all around them in the clearing of trees. He put his hands on his hips, all loose and craggy in the face, and said, "Well, shit. You want to put a bullet in that boy for hog-tying you? That is professional . . . Miss Coahoma County."

She looked away.

Jon remained on the hood of his rental. He toyed with his beard; he'd lost the hat and rain slicker around Vicksburg. His movements jolted and jumpy after he'd taken about fifteen more of those white pills on the way back. Singing Elvis songs along with a tape he'd bought at a truck stop over the Louisiana border. She told him if he didn't slow down his heart would bust.

Ransom walked to the edge of the poured concrete and looked into the air as if he were imagining the way the new casino would take shape, like he could see all the neon, hear the slots, and smell all that nasty money in his mind.

"I quit," she said.

He nodded, toeing the edge of the concrete. It wasn't all the way dry and he made an indentation with his crocodile boots. He smoothed the edge away with his heel and grinned that all-knowing crooked smile at her.

"Them ripples kind of disappear."

Her heart kind of changed gears for a moment, like a transmission shooting loose in her chest.

"How 'bout you stay the night?"

"I have to go."

"With what? My boys are takin' that car right now and lettin' it loose in the projects. You been on the road all night. Take a room."

"Where's *my* car?"

He shrugged.

She said: "Your mind is crippled."

"I don't like fuckups. I talked to the boy. I don't like folks who can't control themselves. You gonna make me screw up this whole thing. That man is lost in Memphis and she was the only damned link."

"What about Travers?"

"Our boy is takin' care of him."

"You don't even know Jon. He's crazy. He takes pills like vitamins and prays to Elvis like he's Jesus Christ. Yeah, boy, that's gonna work out just great."

"Take a room, sister," he said, cleaning the gray concrete off his polished boots.

He moved his hand up to her waist and she caught his wrist in her long, narrow fingers. He stretched his hand over the rim of her low-riding pants and hooked his thumb into her thong underwear. "Think we could all use a rest."

She looked at the concrete.

She looked at the road map of a face and the brittle black beard. His breath smelled of cigars and butter.

When she glanced back to the car, Jon had noticed Ransom.

But he looked away the only time she really wanted to see his eyes. Needed to see his eyes.

Jon Burrows had cast her away.

Even before he saw her walk from the room later that morning, Jon could smell her. That sickly sweet smell like magnolia leaves when they get all mushy and brown. Decaying and ripe with tired sex. She wore a real slutty look about her, too. A halter top made out of black leather, and matching pants. High heels made out of clear plastic. Her blond hair was moussed up and combed straight back and behind her ears. Every damned thing about her looked fast. Speed. All slicked up and ready to go.

He felt his leg start twitchin' in the little cove where they kept Coke and candy machines. That ole ice maker hummin' at the same speed as his heart.

He watched her walk down the long hallway and take the stairs, silent as hell because none of the rooms on the floor was bein' used by payin' folks. He followed. The carpet of gold flowers swimming in blue made his head hurt. He imagined he was walkin' on the sea as he caught the door before it clicked shut. Barely. Just a low tick as he pulled it wide and heard Perfect's heels clicking down the stairs.

He watched her head getting smaller and smaller. Two floors. Three.

Blood in his ears. Teeth grittin' in his head.

Three floors down in this damned motel. Ransom's room.

He waited till he heard the metal door click and he ran down the steps. His bare feet not makin' a sound. He was invisible. Floatin'. Peformin' the miracles and usin' the talent He'd left him.

He opened the door, peered into the long hallway. Same carpet. White, low walls. Smell of fresh paint. Same hum of the ice maker. Same hum in his heart.

Miss Perfect. He saw her beautiful back, shoulder blades movin' up under her tanned skin and that heart-shaped butt wigglin' in those leather pants.

The door opened down the hall; Jon ducked back into a little cove. Listening. Long caves of sound. A thousand rooms not yet used. The building just a castle for Ransom.

Bristlin' fibers. Hands over flesh and body. The smack of a kiss and a moan of pleasure from Miss Perfect. He didn't care. He had to see it.

Jon gave just enough of himself to look into the hall and see craggy-ass Ransom in a blue velvet robe pushin' Miss Perfect against the wall, pinnin' her arms over her head and buryin' that nasty wrinkled face into the two most perfect scoops of flesh he'd ever seen.

But Jon knew who'd started the business. He knew Ransom was just followin' her lead. That woman knew how to control the action.

Jon heard a pop in his own head and saw Perfect look down the hall.

He ducked back, sure she didn't see him, and tongued a bit of tooth out of his mouth. He felt a wash of blood on his tongue, his heart racin' like an overused mule's. He tried to think about that cool ice in the metal bin before him and the way it just lay there, cold and unchanged. He fingered the chip of tooth off his tongue and spit out a long string of blood. Makin' it loop back up to his lip, tastin' himself and likin' it.

Down the hall the door shut with giggles and laughter.

Jon walked back to his room, closed the door, and flicked on the television. Nothin' but three channels and dirty movies. He watched a couple featurin' Asian women and waterfalls and things. Didn't help. He flipped back through to *Spiderman* and that only bored him.

He pulled the curtains, makin' it dark as hell, slipped on his metal shades and picked up his Beretta. Jon swallowed some more blood, movin' his mind away from Miss Perfect and them things that troubled him.

Hidden people laughed and squealed from the bolted-down television. Some boy in high school named Screech who kept screwin' up. A blond girl with a tight little ole stomach who did nothin' but roll her eyes at him.

The laughter playin' over and over in his mind until his temples started to hurt a mess.

That was it.

He felt the silence of the vacant hall—TV light flickerin' over his face— and pulled the trigger.

The television exploded into white, blue, and yellow sparks sending the smell of burning plastic swirling around him.

Chapter 46

THE CITY OF NEW ORLEANS rolled into Memphis a little after 3:30 P.M. I'd spent most of my trip awake on the train watching the Mississippi Delta flash by in scattered bits of old rusted trailers, eternal acres of fattened white cotton ready for the gins, and crevices of cypress swamps, morning light hard and gold on the green skin of the water. I prayed a little, thinking about Loretta, wanting God to help. Help me put things back in order. Help me, knowing I shouldn't ask, find whomever was responsible and take them out. I couldn't stop seeing the face of that Elvis freak in my mind. He'd been there. That piece of shit broke into JoJo's. Set fire to my second home.

I could still smell the smoke on my shirt as I reached up and grabbed Abby's bag from the overhead bin. She thanked me and I followed her off the train and onto a wide concrete platform with a tall view of short buildings built along the bluffs. Mostly old warehouses, a few bars, and art studios.

We followed the herd down some marble steps into a wide train terminal filled with long wooden benches and lit with green neon signs marking the ten tracks out of town. U was at the foot of the steps, arms crossed over his body, broad smile on his face, as he walked up a few steps to meet us. He surprised me with a huge hug—U wasn't what I'd call an emotional man—and yanked the duffel bag from Abby's hand.

"I got it," I said, taking the bag back from him. Carrying both outside.

"Just talked to JoJo," U said. "Said Loretta's awake. Said she was sorry about the bar . . . but glad she got the day off. She asked 'bout you, thought those people coming for your ass next."

I felt my breath drain from my body, thick and polluted. I took in some new air, watching the uncluttered blue sky. A perfect crispness seemed to be wrapping the whole world. But I felt stale. I couldn't fall asleep or focus on anything but my anger.

He'd parked across the street at the Arcade diner and we found a little cove by the kitchen where we ordered a couple plates of sweet potato pancakes and coffee. Place hadn't changed in fifty years. Same torn vinyl booths. Squiggly 'fifties Orbit impressions on tables worn out in spots by years of elbows and coffee mugs.

"How you doin', Miss Abby?" U asked.

"Fine, when one of y'all tell me why we're back in Memphis," she said. She sat taller in her seat. Hair in a ponytail. My Tulane football sweatshirt. "Whatever it is, I'm in."

U raised his eyebrows. A green-haired waitress in a black T-shirt poured us some coffee. I passed U the sugar first. He watched me. He watched my hands shake.

I drank some coffee. I said: "Obviously you got my message."

"Big job."

"At least point the way."

Abby picked at her food. Her fork clanked to the rim of her sticky plate. The green-haired waitress refilled our cups. A kid in the booth behind us sported a nose ring and a Britney Spears T-shirt. He looked like he liked Britney about as much as I liked the Dave Matthews Band.

"Said it was big," U said. "Didn't say I wasn't coming."

He looked over his shoulder, the leather of his jacket squeaking along the booth. The Britney kid was watching the green-haired waitress's ass. U turned back and pulled a map of southern Tennessee before us, already marked in red pen. A big red circle had been drawn around an area south of Jackson.

"That's it?"

He nodded, and as quickly as he slid it out, folded up the map carefully and stuck it back into his pocket. "We could be there by sundown. And that's what we want."

Abby was quiet. But she watched. I looked at her eyes; she stared back.

"How'd you find it?" I asked, still watching Abby. I smiled. She didn't.

"Heard it was near Bemis, this little town that was some kind of social experiment around the turn of the century. Yeah, I checked it all out. Anyway, I called in a favor from a good ol' boy I just keep on bringin' back to jail," U said, dropping into an imitation he believed sounded like a redneck. "Met this peckerwood at a bar. A biker bar. Imagine me in a biker bar. It was like Eddie Murphy in *48 Hours*. 'There's a new sheriff in town,' and all that."

"So peckerwood–biker boy told you where to find the compound?"

"His nasty ass—and I do mean nasty—wore a leather vest and no shirt, even drew a little map for me. One electric fence. Some surveillance."

"Two of us can do it?" I asked.

"Hold on," Abby said, pushing her plate out of the way. "What are you going to do with me? You're not leaving me here. I'm the one whose parents were killed. I'm the one who found Nix. What are you going to do, drop me at the mall with your credit card?"

"Nick ain't got no credit," U said.

She made a grunting noise. "I want to go back to Oxford."

"Not till this is over."

"I'm not moving in with Bubba so I can sit around and watch *Ricki Lake*," she said. "Besides, do you even know how to shoot that gun?"

"Yes."

"How? I hunted with my father; what did you do?"

"I used to—"

"Hold up," U said, raising his palm out. "I got this. See, Nick is from Alabama."

"So?"

"That about says it all."

"Give me two days," I said to Abby. "I'm sorry, but this isn't up for committee."

Abby grunted again and tromped to the bathroom to cool off. I got up to make sure she was all right. For some reason I wanted everyone to be okay with everything.

"Nick, cool out," he said. "We got it."

I sat back down and asked, "So, you're in?"

"Me and you are the same, brother," he said, looking out the window. Maybe seeing that same blue crispness but feeling better about it. "You know that. We just a couple of Zen cowboys, Travers. What else we supposed to do with our lives? Ain't many of us around."

"Thanks."

"Listen, man. Loretta and JoJo have been real good to me, too," U said, his head nodding with his own words. "Somebody mess with Loretta? Come on. You got to ask? You wanted backup on one thing, said you wanted a meeting with Elias Nix. . . . Well, I'm gonna get you that appointment tonight."

We didn't go alone. On the way out of town, U picked up Bubba Cotton in, of all places, Dixie Homes, where he'd been baby-sitting his sister-in-law's twin boys. The boys had pulled out every pot and pan their mother owned, using them for drums, as we stepped over their mess and found Bubba swilling a forty and watching a little *Ricki Lake*.

His sister-in-law had gotten home before us and Bubba was glad to leave because she was cussing his ass out. He sat in back of U's Expedition on the ride north with earphones on and silently bobbed his head.

We soon dropped off the highway and away from the commercial roads and hotels and restaurants and hit a long straightaway of curving hilly blacktop. A lot of cotton fields soon turned to woods. Maple trees with yellow and red leaves. Pin oak. Cedar. A lot of pine trees coated in kudzu, almost looked like a 'fifties horror film, *It Came from the South*. Kudzu everywhere. Telephone poles. Abandoned shacks. The growth had even snaked its fingers and arms through several old rusted cars.

We traveled along the road for another thirty minutes with only the sound of Bubba's Walkman and the roaring of tires on the blacktop. We passed some corn fields, yellowed and mowed flush, and then got into more woods with gullies of bottom land where rainwater stood in stagnant rows. Turtles slept on floating pieces of wood and trash. Red bud willows draped their branches across pools, catching the final reddish-purple light of the day.

U slowed, pointed out an anonymous dirt road, and kept driving.

"Let's get some more coffee, stretch, and check our plan. Again. I found us a campsite up the road and we'll go through the final details." He looked over at me, taking off his sunglasses as if just realizing the sun had been down for a while. He yawned and ran a big hand over his face. "You still cool with this?"

I checked for the Glock he'd given me and smiled. "Yeah, everything is cool."

But I remembered some graffitied words on a decaying brick wall in downtown as we headed out. It was one of those times when the message seemed to be written just for me: SUPERMAN IS A DAMNED FOOL.

Chapter 47

NIGHT HAD ALMOST FALLEN in backwoods Tennessee and Bubba Cotton was smacking the hell out of a tin of Planter's roasted peanuts and eating a Nestlé Crunch. He hummed along to some song I couldn't quite make out as he stuffed another handful into his mouth and moved his head to the music. The sound must've been too much because U put down these night vision goggles he'd been bragging about for the last hour, Baigish B-21s with clear vision up to 250 meters, and looked into the rearview mirror at his big, silent (with words anyway) buddy shaking his ass while on recon.

U glanced over at me in the front seat of the Expedition, his hair braided tight against his skull and wearing the same Saints grays that we'd been issued about a decade ago. Number ninety-three stamped in the middle of his chest.

"Mystikal," U said. "Kid out of New Orleans. Don't look so damned confused, Travers. You know there's got to be other music besides blues."

"Name a truer music."

"Jazz."

"And you'd be wrong."

"How can music be wrong or right?" he asked. "It's what is true to me. If I say it's Toumani Diabate or Ali Farke Toure, would that be better than blues, more roots for you?"

"If I said that I liked Cap'n Crunch better than Lucky Charms it would be a fact," I said. "Lucky Charms has sweetened crap in it, yellow moons and blue diamonds, and Cap'n Crunch is simple and damned tasty. I'd say it's downright Zen-like. Besides, why don't those kids leave that poor leprechaun alone? Little bastard can't even take a piss without being harassed."

U nodded, switching out the batteries in his binoculars. "Yeah, that is pretty messed up."

"Damn kids," I said, waiting for darkness to drop on us. Still a grayish red burning through the branches, a light purple glow to the air around U's truck.

U agreed: "Can't even take a piss. Plain messed up."

Bubba kept munching on the can of nuts till he was done, and then swigged down half a bottle of Mountain Dew.

"So you saw Nix?" I asked.

"Little pointy-eared mother was out for a night jog with a couple of beefed-up dudes in camos. They took a little run around that lake," he said, handing me the binoculars. "They'll be back."

"Don't see the lake."

I felt him push the binoculars to the right and the lake came into view in a bright green image. On the other side of the water, I saw ropes hanging from a twenty-foot tower and some rutted, narrow tunnels underneath barbed-wire grate. A longer, more advanced version of monkey bars stretched out by a small stucco hut.

"Just in case being governor means storming a third-world country."

"Exactly," U said.

"So, how many?"

"Saw about six so far. Shouldn't be much trouble. Big boy behind us acts stupid as shit but he's a great shot. You got all the clips I gave you?"

I checked the inside pockets of my leather jacket, trying to keep a cool face as my blood rushed around my head and heart. I had a hard time breathing. But the thing that bothered me most is that I felt more excited than scared. Sure I wanted to talk to Nix, have him fill in some holes about Clyde James and the casinos, and some man named Levi Ransom. Find out how much he was going to make out of this deal. Find out why the most good-hearted human being I'd ever known had been shot in the chest and left to burn up along with my best friend's bar.

I must've started shaking a bit because U reached over and grabbed the binoculars back from me. "What about that Trix rabbit?" he asked me. "Ain't he a motherfucker?"

I tried smiling and poured some more coffee from a thermos we'd filled at a convenience store into a foam cup. I looked into the darkness around us and listened to the unfamiliar sounds of crickets and more bugs. The kudzu wrapped the trees in such a way that they became giants. Looming ten feet over us, green mouths open wide, fingers branching out like claws.

I spit out the window, checked the clip in my gun, and tried to be cool, slinking into the warm seats and sipping my coffee.

My fucking hand would not stop shaking.

Our recon mission failed to spot at least fifty guys who'd apparently shown up in the last twenty-four hours. At 8:00 P.M., they flooded from a long ranch house with barred windows and metal doors and formed into columns, their breath warm clouds before their determined faces. They dressed in military pants, jackets, and boots. Some loaded into Hummers, black and green, all the stylish colors for paranoid wealthy men with small penises, and drove down rutted paths shining yellow spotlights into the woods.

"Hey," U said, in this high-pitched old-black-woman voice he sometimes used. "We's up here. All us black folks would love to meet such nice young mens."

Bubba snorted out a laugh.

"Does he ever talk?" I asked.

He looked back at Bubba. Bubba shrugged.

"Guess not."

"Let me guess," I said, straightening myself into the seat and crushing my cup. "I crawl over that twenty-foot fence, slide by that razor concertina wire, and then jump into the middle of those God-lovin' white boys and start raisin' hell. You and Bubba can come, too. It'll be a blood bath, man. Bullets everywhere. I'll mow 'em down, reloading like hell, and then you'll shield me as I run in and find Nix. Nix will get down on his knees as I kick the pole from their rebel flag up his ass."

"Well, goddamn, Travers, you done figured it out." U opened his door and walked outside. I followed, our feet crunching on the rotting earth. It was cold and I turned up the collar on my jacket.

The sound of Hummers and gunfire at a nearby target range drowned out our movements. I looked down the hill into a bowl where they'd formed their little training ground. All around us, orange signs warned NO HUNTING ALLOWED.

I asked for the night vision binoculars and scoped out the main building. It seemed just like an extremely long ranch house. If I'd seen it from the road, I'd have thought it was another hunting lodge. Of course, that's what U said most of the people around here believed. A place for rich men from Nashville to come out, drink some Wild Turkey, and raise a little hell.

A long *rat-a-tat* erupted down in the bowl and U quickly grabbed the night vision back for another scan of the ground. "All right, we're out of here. Man, that's a damned M-60."

"That's bad?"

"You see *Rambo*?"

"Yeah."

"You know that big mother gun he carries?"

I nodded.

"Let's go."

Bubba was behind us now, peering over my shoulder. He had on black sweats and high-top Chuck Taylor's, looking like a wayward ninja. I smiled at him as we fast-walked back to the car. He wouldn't look at me, he was transfixed by the sounds of the miniwar being played down the hill. I know he was wondering how he could have ever gotten this close.

"Those are fifty-caliber machine guns strapped on top of those Hummers," U said. "They'd make hamburger out of a deer before it hits the ground."

We'd almost made it back to the truck when three men walked from the brush, almost like they'd evolved from the night and trees, dressed in all black with blacked-out faces. They came to us with AK-47s pointed at our chests.

"Ladies and gentlemen," I said. "A tribute to Al Jolson."

"Nick," U said under his breath. "Shut the fuck up."

Bubba Cotton froze. If I hadn't been so scared, I'd have laughed. His big ass looked like one of those men in Jackson Square who asked for tips for standing still.

U spoke a little louder when the muzzle of their guns came inches from our chests. "Hey man, saw your fire. Y'all wouldn't know where a brother could find some decent barbecue?"

Much better, I thought, blood now swimming through my ears. Heart lodged behind my larynx. At least Al Jolson confused them.

Chapter 48

"THRILL KILL," Ransom said to Jon Burrows as they continued to hunt the wildcat in back of the casino. "Is that what it's all about for you?"

"No, sir," Jon said, takin' good aim into the edge of cotton fields, where they'd seen the skinny ole cat disappear. He sighted down his arm and along the straight edge of the Beretta. For a moment, he wondered what would happen if he turned the gun around to Ransom and shot that grizzled fucker right in the throat. He rested the gun at his side, the grip loose in his fingers. Might as well hear what he got to say.

"Seems to me you know the difference," Ransom said, smashing cotton plants under his muddy boots and tracking the wildcat into the woods. "You know when I was your age, I ran most of south Memphis. Took me about six months to figure out the players and then how to play them. Make them turn against each other. Make 'em afraid of me. Sometimes you got to crawl up high in a tree and watch the animals below you. It's not hard."

Ransom pulled out a cigar from a deep pocket in his heavy hunting coat. He snipped the end, offered another to Jon, snipped that one, and lit both. Jon took a good draw, trying to make sure he didn't cough none and show he didn't know nothin' about cigars. He did. He'd been through his share of Tampa Nuggets and Swisher Sweets.

It was night and kind of cold. His face felt all funny every time the wind blew out of the trees and cut across his face. He'd shaved off his beard a few hours ago, leavin' a pair of perfect sideburns just like E in sixty-eight, and splashed all his pores with Hai Karate. That wind 'bout tore his face up when they'd walked out back of the hotel and tromped about a half mile to that new site, lookin' for some wildcat a guard had seen.

"How far you want to take this?"

"What you mean?" Jon said, spittin' out the smoke from his mouth. Much more blue and heavy than them Nuggets. Felt rich.

"You travel a lot?"

"Yes, sir."

"You taken lots of jobs?"

"Yes, sir."

"How'd you like to get out of that mess?" Ransom said. "I liked the way you took care of that body in New Orleans. You took care of any evidence real quick. If you'd moved that woman, we might have some folks breathin' from behind. . . . Did Perfect really go crazy?"

"Yes, sir," Jon said. He thought he saw some movement along the edge of the high grass, right near that clearing of maples. "You see it?"

Ransom aimed his Browning and fired off three quick hits into the grass. They ran over to the clearing to find an opossum, about the size of a fat squirrel, bleedin' from the mouth. Ransom kicked it over and Jon saw a dozen little tiny babies, like pink worms, wigglin' all about.

Ransom didn't notice and kept walking along the edge of the woods, turning inside on a narrow path, all the way clearing away the branches for Jon. Ransom was showin' him respect. Showed respect for his talents. Jon's hands quivered along the handle of the gun.

Felt like he could run around the woods about a million times and not get tired. Ride into daylight without a lick of sleep. He was E.

"I could use you permanent," Ransom said.

"Yes, sir."

"So . . ."

Jon suddenly had the vision of Colonel Tom Parker and Hollywood and record deals and spreadin' the word of E in every language on the gosh dang planet. E on cologne and shampoo bottles and bumper stickers. This is what Jon needed, someone to take his skills to the next level. Someone to get him them high-level killin' jobs to make him a legend.

"Yes, sir," Jon said, smiling, leg just ashakin' at his side.

They were surrounded by darkness now. Nothin' but woods and a narrow path. Tree branches swattin' into their faces with every step. Barely even hearin' the semis rollin' off Highway 61.

A cry.

A dang wild animal in heat.

Jon followed Ransom down through a loose gathering of small trees. Small moon above beamin' down some pale silver light that reflected off the leaves and the back of Ransom's leathery neck.

Ransom crept along, listening.

"Kid, you know much about politics?"

"No, sir."

"You know Tennessee is gettin' a new governor next month? The first Tuesday in November?"

Jon listened for another wild cry.

"I don't want to lose," Ransom said. "You get back to Memphis tomorrow. All right?"

He looked back at Jon. Jon felt a heat spread through his body. Real warm. Man appreciated him. Colonel Ransom.

"Yes, sir," Jon said, biting into the cigar and taking a long puff. A nice old buzz mixing with the Benzedrine.

Another wild cry. The fast rush of leaves and little twigs cracking under paws.

Jon saw the dang cat first. Didn't even wait for Ransom, just squeezed off five rounds from his Beretta. That cat crying and wrigglin' on his back, screaming wild as hell and swattin' that ole tail.

Ransom laughed and ran to the animal. "Hot damn, boy," he said. "That was a hell of a shot. See what I mean about lookin' around you. Can you do that fast for me?"

Jon nodded as Ransom aimed at the wrigglin' cat, ears pinned back and teeth exposed with fright, and fired off two rounds into the animal's skull.

He kicked the cat in the side. "Mean bitch, too," he said.

"Can you do that again?" Ransom asked.

Jon didn't understand but didn't want to say it. He looked down at his cigar; it had gone out and sat wet and useless in his mouth. He wanted to relight it more than anything in the dang world.

"Can you take care of another mean ole bitch?" Ransom asked.

The cat's blood was scattered and red on Ransom's boots like a crazy painter's dream.

Perfect walked back to her hotel room adjoined with Jon's and noticed the connecting door was cracked open. She heard the buzz of a television on some kind of teenage sitcom where this little girl was a witch and had a damned talking cat. The cat made some kind of crack about the teenage witch's boyfriend being stupid and a sissy and was shut up into a pet kennel to the delight of a laugh track.

She called out Jon's name. Nothing. She checked the bathroom and even the closet and made sure the hall door was locked. Even if he was at the door right now she could scoot on out of Dodge before he knew she was in there. Nothing much in the bathroom. A toothbrush and a bottle of white pills. Wet towels on the floor. A wrinkled JCPenney catalog, opened to the teenage girl's underwear page, lay wide open by the toilet along with a couple *Captain America* comic books and a Gideon's Bible with a crude hand-painted image of Elvis on the cover.

The drawing was so bad that she could barely recognize the singer. His head was kind of lopsided and he had on a high, white collar studded with jewels and thick black sideburns. Below were the words: *My name has Evil and Lives. It's probably better not to worry too much about it.*

Back in the bedroom, she opened the drawers in a long chest. Nothing. Not even lint. She looked under the bed and in the nightstand. Some stray socks and a book on numerology and sexual positions. But tucked behind a long row of curtains, standing on its side, sat a little Captain America suitcase. Something seriously made for an eight year old. It had been buckled tight, its plastic hide ragged and worn at the edges. She pulled it up to a coffee table, loose beams of sunlight breaking through the blowing curtains, opened it, and rifled through.

Inside: four pairs of dark-indigo unfaded Levis, five white T-shirts (crisp and ironed), four pairs of tube socks, a couple leather wristbands, a couple Polaroid shots of a naked woman with dark hair and long legs in a shower stall (on the back, words written in German), a couple more *Captain America* comics, Vitalis hair oil, a dozen identical postcards of Graceland, a beat-up cassette of *Elvis: Live at Madison Square Garden,* and a full bottle of Hai Karate cologne.

She thought she'd unearthed about every weird object that li'l ole boy could have until she found a purple Crown Royal bag under the Vitalis. Inside the bag, she discovered three books tucked away like holy texts. *Elvis*, by Jerry Hopkins; *Elvis, What Happened?*, by Red and Sonny West; and *The Private Elvis*, by May Mann. Each of the books had been charred at the edges and broke off in blackened pieces when she touched the ragged pages. Almost every line underlined in blue or red ink with paragraph sections in yellow highlighter.

> It was Gladys who inspired him and encouraged him when the going was so brutal, so rough, when he was disclaimed, when he was ridiculed. It was Mama who made him believe that he could be a great star! Those people making fun of him, yelling and jeering and calling him "Elvis the Pelvis," resounding in his ear into nightmares, would go, his mother reaffirmed. They would accept him, once they understood what he was really doing.

The paragraph from the Mann book was highlighted with yellow and had scrawled third-grade writing in the margins. Seemed like equations. *Love + Mamma = acceptance/fortune. Acceptance comes with understanding of skills. Gladys's middle name was L-O-V-E. Love is success.*

She tossed the burned book back into the suitcase as if it was still on fire. As if the sickness of the mind that wrote it would somehow contaminate her. But before she could close the top of the suitcase, a little yellowed photograph came flying out. A middle-aged woman with massively huge hair—had to have been a wig—with a bulging throat and pig's eyes held a small boy.

The boy wore a small T-shirt emblazoned with the face of Elvis wearing a lei. It read, ALOHA! The woman beamed like she was holding the answer to the world's problems but the little boy had no emotion at all. Black circles under his eyes. His tiny arms as skinny as twigs with malnourishment. On the back, someone (obviously not the book scrawler) had written *Patsy Roach with son, Absalom. 1939–1983. House fire.*

She heard a key click into a slot, the jiggling of the tumbler, and a hard clack. She closed the suitcase, shoved it under the curtains, and bolted from the room.

She listened at the cracked door as he walked inside.

And for a moment, she thought she heard Jon sniffing the air like an animal hunting for its prey.

She was out of here. She'd find her way back to Memphis tonight if she had to walk the whole way.

Chapter 49

ONE OF THE black-faced white boys made a mistake when he grabbed U's five-hundred-dollar pair of binoculars and tossed them down the hill. The boy, thick-necked with a bristled haircut, then made a crack about the shiny rims on U's truck. With a snicker, asked how long U had financed his vehicle. U smiled and nodded, giving one of those okay-you-got-me looks, his big hands at his sides. But as he dropped his head, U gave me a wink. So fast they didn't see it.

His hands flew from his sides and knocked the AK-47 out of the man's arms. As the other turned, I punched the fucker right in the throat and caught his gun before it crashed to the ground. I turned the gun around and used the muzzle as a handle and the butt for a club. I smacked the guy—a little skinnier than the other, with bad teeth—in the jaw and rammed him hard in the stomach, lucky the gun didn't crackle to life, but not really caring. My face and ears felt as if they were baking in the sun as I threw the gun over my shoulder and straddled the man, beating the ever-loving shit out of him. I hit him across the temples and directly in the eyes and rammed my fist deep into his gut. He puked blood on himself as I reared back and felt strong hands grabbing my arms and pulling me back.

I clawed at the hands and kept punching that little redneck fucker right in the jaw, seeing Loretta lying on the floor of the bar and those tattered bedroom slippers on JoJo's feet at the hospital. More hands reached for me and yanked me away. Spit flying from my mouth, yelling words I didn't feel myself consciously saying. As Bubba and U pulled me away, I kicked the son of a bitch hard in the head.

"Cool it," U said.

I was breathing so hard I almost choked in air. And as U's face came back into focus, I bent at the waist as if waking from a strange dream. Bubba patted his strong fingers on my back and smiled at me.

"It's all right, dude," he said, in this cracked hoarse whisper. "Dude, it's all right."

"Bubba?" I asked. He speaks. The revelation made me almost forget about those stupid rednecks.

As I looked into his face, a white-hot light shined down from the trees and gunshots erupted closer. My body seemed filled with heated blood.

We ran quickly toward U's truck.

But before we got close, about fifty men slathered in camou face paint, carrying rifles, and driving ATVs blocked our path. I slowed to a jog. I heard Bubba's labored breath beside me.

The men told us to drop the guns.

We did.

We just stood there, hands on top of our heads, until they jabbed the muzzles of semiautomatic guns into our backs, and marched us down a thin but old path and into the valley.

An hour later, my knees screamed from standing on them so long. My shoulder, that I'd dislocated for the thirtieth time, ached in its socket so bad that I clenched my teeth in pain. I had my hands laced on top of my head. Bubba's and U's had been lashed behind their backs with rope.

The floor was smooth concrete and splatted with the occasional patch of leaking oil. Over our heads stretched a huge arc of corrugated tin forming some kind of large garage with a retractable door big enough for an airplane. The door was open. I could smell the Sons of the South campfires burning and hear gaggles of men talking.

Every time I breathed, the hot air expelled in a cloudy mass.

I looked over at U. He slowly shook his head and kept his eyes focused on the twelve men guarding us. He was watching hard, taking it all in.

I dropped my shoulder an inch. One of the guards screamed for me to raise it back up.

On the other side of me, Bubba had his eyes closed. He was either meditating or sleeping.

Soon another ATV's engine gunned outside. The sound grew close enough that it rattled the tin above our heads until it pulled inside and shut off the motor.

A dozen or so men formed a line behind the man dismounting from his ride. Short and gray haired. Large, almost comical ears and yellowish eyes. He had an oversized mouth when he smiled, appraising us down on our knees. His hair was cut extremely short with a section on top that struck me as so hard and perfect that it had to be a toupee. His teeth were little, worn-down nubs.

He placed his smallish hands on his waist as he stood in front of me and said: "You with these niggers?"

"Oh, thank God," I said. "The senator will save us."

Elias Nix laughed for a moment with me and then kicked out my knees. I landed on my back and then worked my way to a resting position on my elbows.

"They yours?" Nix asked, looking over at U and Bubba.

Some of his group laughed.

He'd left the square headlight of the ATV shining bright in our eyes. I squinted at his face—smooth, thin skin with bluish veins on his cheeks.

I looked over at U but didn't say anything.

I crept to my knees again, like I was about to get back into the same position, closed my eyes, and waited for Nix to relax. Slowly I opened them, dug in with the balls of my feet, and launched from my knees, grasping for his throat.

I ringed a good grip, feeling the cold, corpselike skin, and yanked him from his feet. The shorter man was level with my eyes. I was throttling even harder when something struck the back of my head and my vision left me for a moment.

I felt a hundred kicks in my side.

U yelled for them to stop.

More yells. Some screams at U to shut up. But they did as he said.

I rolled to my side, coughed several times, and stood as if I were a boxer wavering in the first round. One of Nix's men, I couldn't make out his face, pointed a gun into my ear.

"Why are you here?" Nix said, hands behind his back, strutting rooster-proud now. Trying to make up for being the little toy he was.

"You assholes tried to kill one of my friends," I said, my breath wheezing. "I guess since you killed Bill MacDonald and his wife, you thought y'all were unstoppable."

"You're not a friend of Bill's," he said. "We're his friends."

He said friends as if it had a couple of "e"s in it. Nix jerked his head over at U and Bubba on their knees. "And Lord knows they're not."

"Stay out of New Orleans," I said. "Those people don't know anything."

"Son, I haven't a clue what you're talkin' about."

"Your friends down in Tunica killed the MacDonalds and then sent some assholes to work my friends." I didn't want to say their names. I thought by uttering the words in this place I would pollute their dignity.

Nix let out a long laugh. His breath, clouded and foggy, obscured his face. I couldn't quite make it out anymore. The yellow eyes. Grayed toupee. Nothing was clear anymore.

"Now you're making sense," he said, whistling and pointing to a herd of men at the back. Several ATVs, thick tires coated in mud, kicked to life buzzing away into the night. "Son, you boys are so dang thick in a world of shit that you're drownin' in it. Little advice: Let the big dogs handle the war."

I looked at him. Still everything was cloudy and hidden in the lights. I squinted harder.

Two men stood behind U and Bubba and quickly brandished a pair of Bowie knives. I yelled to them but as I did, I could see their hands were already free.

They'd been cut loose.

My friends stood.

"Y'all have ten seconds to get out of my world," Nix said.

U led the way and Bubba and I followed past the buzz-cut boys, mouths pocketed full of Redman and Kodiak, and onto the same path we'd followed before. We were just walking pretty damned fast, but picked up the pace when automatic weapons sounded from down in the valley.

As we got close to the truck, Bubba's big ass passed both of us as if he were chomping for the finish line. We all jumped inside and U cranked his Expedition.

As he spun away, I heard Bubba screaming in that same low hoarse whisper. He was yelling with volume set at two.

"Goddamn, I'm hit, they shot me right in the ass," he croaked. "Y'all get me to a hospital, I'm bleedin' to death. They got me. They got me with them machine guns."

U didn't look back for several miles. He only stopped for a second before we turned onto another highway heading south to Memphis.

He turned on an overhead light, crawled halfway over the seat, looking for the wound.

Bubba yelped.

"Damn, Bubba," U said, laughing as the truck idled. "That sure was a mean-ass tree." He showed me the broken-off end of a stick and shook his head as we headed south again. "That tree just jumped up and bit him in the ass."

The laughter came again in waves. I must've laughed for five miles.

"Y'all be quiet," Bubba croaked, again. "Ain't funny."

But soon the laughter spilled back into silence and we were left with the feeling of failure. Even though I knew it would've been pretty damned stupid to have stayed, I felt like I'd failed Loretta. I had come to face Elias Nix and left with my tail between my ass.

"Those assholes could've killed us," U said.

"But they didn't," I said.

"Ain't 'cause they're good people."

I could feel U's eyes watching me as I continued to stare out into the darkness and passing signs along the highway. He turned on some jazz and we entered a section of road jammed up with construction and soon I couldn't see anything around us but flashing yellow signs and orange barrels. U checked in his rearview mirror again as we slowed and waited for a semi to merge.

I watched him as he turned the wheel hard and passed on a closed section of highway before darting in front of the semi.

U punched the accelerator up to eighty and with the windows down I felt like I could breathe again. My blood pressure had slowed and my head no longer buzzed like it had been filled with hornets.

He asked: "Why would them boys want some broken-down soul singer?"

"The only man who can answer that question checked out some time ago," I said. I didn't talk for a while, thinking of our meeting with Clyde James. Then I said: "But we could try again."

Memphis shined loose, bright, and broken before us.

Chapter 50

DIDN'T TAKE BUT about two seconds for Perfect Leigh to spot a man in the first floor of the casino, not bad-looking, either, in kind of a bland-businessman way, and get that ride to Memphis. The man was even up about five hundred bucks at the blackjack table, but left it all just for a chance to take Perfect for a spin in his Lexus. He was nice and clean, thirtyish with a couple kids and a wife that didn't like sex anymore, and even opened the door for Perfect when they got back to Midtown. She gave him a phony phone number, said she couldn't wait to see him again, and walked the next two blocks to her real apartment.

Now, thank the Lord, she was drawing a bath while she lit a dozen or so colored candles around the big claw-foot tub. Get Tunica out of her mind.

Perfect removed her favorite plush terry-cloth robe and slid into the warm, soapy water. She wanted to lie in this tub till all of Levi Ransom had been soaked away. Then she'd drain the murky fluids that had filled her, towel off, and clean the tub with Clorox.

Only then could she become someone else and forget about this whole damned mess. Just like when she was a teenager and pretended that winning those god-awful pageants was such a wonderful thing, back when she had to grin so hard her gums and lips hurt. Grin till her mother had grabbed the trophy and they were headed back to Coahoma County.

That fat woman would do anything to have her doll win. She'd coat her in that pancake makeup and foul-smelling Wal-Mart perfume she bought by the gallon and just hug and hug her like a prized pet. The thing that Perfect couldn't understand, she thought as she ran more hot water into the tub, was why her mother had to cheat. Just like Ransom, she had to know they'd won even before she'd taped her daughter's boobs together or watched her perform the Nancy Sinatra baton routine.

Perfect closed her eyes, submerged her head for a moment, nothing but the darkness and candles in the room, that terrific soapy water flowing, swooshing inside her. She ducked under, bubbles pouring through her ears, water flowing into her nose. She let out a long breath, screaming into the water.

After the bath, she lay naked on her huge red couch watching her legs in the seven antique mirrors that hung along the wall by the television and in a little mirrored jewel box she'd picked up in New Orleans. Mirrors everywhere. Gold. Silver. Antique. Some still in boxes. Sterling silver hand mirrors and ones with beveled edges and maybe thirty compacts she'd collected since she was sixteen, in a little basket on the coffee table.

She yawned and stretched, feeling with delight her rib cage and firm ass.

She picked up one of the many compacts and twirled it in her fingers as she flopped onto her back and moved her hands over her breasts, when suddenly there was a thud on her little balcony.

She saw the shifting figure of a man in black. Had to have crawled up three stories to reach her. Perfect had a gun in her bedroom and a set of steak knives in the kitchen. She slowly let her bare toes touch the carpet; she didn't want him to think she knew.

But he saw her. He was watching her with those damned black-ringed eyes.

Jon had dropped to his knees in the cold onto a big pile of leaves that had fallen from a nearby oak. He had on this sad face. Humble as hell and holding some more of those nasty grocery-store flowers.

She shook her head and started to drop the blinds over the window. Her heart ramming against her rib cage.

The window exploded with glass.

A large pot filled with a dead palm tree cracked and scattered dirt all over her floor. She scrambled to her bedroom but only got halfway when he jumped her from behind and started prying her mouth open. He stuffed a handful of pills deep down into her mouth, so far that she started gagging, while he rubbed her throat making her swallow.

He pushed her wrists to the hard wooden floor and stuck a knee into her stomach. He lay his head across her bare breasts, like a child would, listening to her heart. She couldn't move with his sinewy weight holding her. "We just stay here," he whispered. All right? Then I got somewhere special we can go. It's a real happy place."

I'll cut your fucking nuts off," Perfect Leigh said, slurring her words and walkin' crooked toward the exit of Libertyland as an orange-black sky twisted overhead. "I want to scream but it makes me sick. I'm not feeling well."

The little white lights on the trees had just flickered on at dusk. Families pushed strollers and carried huge teddy bears and hustlin' young black kids in Grizzlies jerseys and gold bracelets prowled nearby. The air smelled like popcorn and hotdogs with an edge of baby powder.

"Miss Perfect, let's get on the Zippin Pippin one more time," Jon said.

She still couldn't see why this place was so important. Jon guessed she couldn't have known this was the old fairgrounds that E used to rent out all night for Him and the boys. They'd run the whole damned park till the sun came up; E sometimes ridin' the Pippin all night long.

"Amusement parks are for morons and white trash," she said. "Goddamn, I feel sick. Jesus."

Her eyes got real lazy and she stumbled, almost falling to the sidewalk. She caught herself, but one of her high heels came off and Jon walked back to pick it up.

"Here you go," he said, a true gentleman.

"Take me home now, Jon. Or whatever your real name is."

"Why do you say such things, Miss Perfect?" He felt his legs starting to jump and a jolt of electricity shoot into the base of his brain. "You doubt my Christian name?"

She laughed it out before she looked at his face and poked out her lower lip. "Oh, little Johnny, did I make you sad? I'm sorry. You are. You are Jon Burrows. Okay. That's fine by me."

The lines in her face made puzzles in the falling light. Brown dead leaves skittered down the concrete walkway that led over to the Pippin and for some reason Jon felt very sad. He zipped up his leather coat and checked his new boots for any mess.

But she didn't move. He felt for a knife in his pocket and it gave him comfort. His breath comin' real fast through his nose.

She laughed and said, "I'm going to scream now."

"Cops are lookin' for you," he said.

"What?"

"That nigra woman is alive. You didn't even kill her." Jon leaned in close and smelled her neck. "You want another ride, then. Right? If not, I'll take this knife in my pocket and carve up that pretty face."

He pointed out the Zippin Pippin, one of the holy relics of Memphis, standing tall and wooden against the night sky like a dang wonder of the world. "Come on."

Her skin was cold at the base of her spine as the Pippin cranked to the top of its wooden platform ready to shoot down that hill and launch into all them curves and twists and gut-churners.

He remembered comin' to the park when he was a kid and his mamma spendin' every dime she'd made down at the Zippymart so they could stay all day at the park and get treated like somethin' special. She'd buy him hotdogs and cotton candy till his belly would swell and them dark circles under his eyes would seem to disappear in the fun-house mirrors.

The Pippin dipped down low again and he heard Miss Perfect scream loud.

And as they cranked real slow up another hill, waitin' for another drop, he whispered, "I loved you, but Ransom wants you dead."

Perfect's whole body shook and her stomach growled. She tried to run to the dark cove of that bathroom underneath a big oak, but he wouldn't let go of her wrist. He was just a flurry of white sound and booming and swirling black and red light that ran around her brain making it buzz and fry. Goddamn, what had he done to her? What had he given her?

"Fuck you," she said, not sure if the words were coming out or not. "Stay away."

He reached his whole arm around her waist and walked her back to an arcade where every plinking sound and flush of color and noise made her even more sick. She thought about that woman she'd shot and even that family with the dead daughter back in Tunica and she started praying that she'd live. She would not end up a loser and dumped and used like they had been. She would get out of this.

She coughed, heaved, and puked all over herself.

Her lips and face felt disgusting, covered in vomit, her head sunk to her shoulder and she could smell her own odor and it sickened her.

She tried to stand by herself but her feet hung loose and useless like a twisted doll. She tried to be rigid but only slunk more.

"What did you do? What did you do to me?"

"I just gave you a few vitamins, woman," he said.

Her eyes closed again and she felt her stomach keep grumbling and her bladder and bowels fill. She tried to pinch herself and stay tight but the pressure kept on building as her eyes filled with water. Her long legs were loose and exposed through her skirt and her blouse had torn at the shoulder. Dirt on her knees. Puke on her face. Her beautiful blond hair a tangled mess.

She was in a bathroom now, her panties full and soaked and she lay in a corner by a toilet. Little black hairs and smeared dirt and urine were all around her. She felt her skin get tight and the need to puke. She lathered her hands together and rubbed them all over her skirt and looked at her dirty arms and crawled farther into the nasty, horrible corner. She screamed real low and covered her face, tried to curl into a little ball like an animal. She closed her eyes real tight.

She was nasty and useless and no one would ever want her. She screamed again, it was hoarse and low and she could barely hear herself.

She peered up at the wavering figure of Jon. Clean and black-leathered and smiling down at her with his hardened blue eyes and sharpened sideburns. He kicked at her knees trying to bring them back into a more ladylike position. She pulled the material of her skirt over her soiled panties.

"Why are you doing this? Why?"

"Who am I?" he asked.

"Why?"

"Who am I?"

"Jon."

"Who?"

"Jon."

Then she understood and she felt her neck fill with blood and heat and she smelled the horrible smells coming from her armpits. Her head cleared for a moment with her own anger. She gripped the edge of the toilet and wavered to her feet. The bathroom stall had been scrawled on with dirty words and phone numbers. The toilet hadn't been flushed and it looked like the water had been drained from a swamp. She clenched her teeth and stared right into his eyes and wiped her polluted hands on his leather jacket.

"Fuck you!" she screamed. "You are nobody! Nobody."

His lip quivered and he snarled before slapping her hard across the face. "Don't you ever say that. I am more somebody than you'll ever be. *I am somebody!*"

"No, you're not," she said, knowing she was dead anyway. "Do you even know who you are? Are you Elvis? Are you? Are you even Jon? What happened, Jon? Can't you speak? You pathetic little shit."

His eyes squinted and the black circles under his eyes became even more pronounced. Like sharp sickles.

She jabbed his chest with her finger again.

"Where's your mamma, Jon?"

He was crying now and covering his ears as if a high-pitched noise leaked into the room.

"She burned up just like those books you carry with you, didn't she? Did you do it? Did you set fire to her house? What did she do, Jon? Why did you kill your mamma?"

"No!" he screamed. "It's not true. My name is Jesse Garon and I'm from Mississippi and I moved to Memphis to make something of myself. My mamma lives in Hollywood and she's livin'."

Exhausted, he laid his back to the bathroom stall and cried as he pulled a long yellow scarf from his black leather jacket. "This was hers. He gave it to her. She kept it her whole life in her sweet, little pillow. Little sweet girl."

She laughed, tasting the blood from her lip. She laughed and watched him smelling his scarf and covering his face with it as if he could hide.

"Ransom will kill you," she said and stood. "He needs me."

"Ransom tole me make it look all random and such," he said. "They'll find you late tonight. All twisted up and nasty."

"Fuck you, Absalom Roach."

Suddenly, he leaped from the ground and exploded his hands against her chest, slamming her against the metal wall. She choked, not being able to catch her breath. Her eyes filled with tears. Little short breaths of nothing.

Jon briskly twisted the yellow scarf against her neck and cried and babbled to himself, like the cooing of a baby, and then hummed a song that she'd heard before.

"*Wise men say, only fools rush in,*" he sang, almost as if a lullaby.

She heard her voice box crack and she fell to her ass with a squish, the broken, filthy writing on the wall around her bringing no comfort. Her hands felt wet, touching the dead hairs and urine and dirt and she cried looking at a single sentence scratched into the bathroom wall with a key: PRIDE GOETH BEFORE DESTRUCTION, AND AN HAUGHTY SPIRIT BEFORE A FALL. PROVERBS 16:17–19.

The last thing she heard was Jon singing directly and softly into her ear, "*'Cause I can't help, falling in love with you.*"

Chapter 51

THE MEMPHIS MENTAL HEALTH INSTITUTE was everything you could hope for in an insane asylum. The building had to have been designed sometime in the late 'fifties or early 'sixties with its cold white brick and blocked institutional architecture. Very boxy and utilitarian at eight stories. Gave off the same homogenized blandness of those flickering science films that I had to watch in junior high. Everything had that same washed-out feeling. The magnolia trees along the sidewalk seemed dirty and dying. The volleyball nets behind a long row of chain link were wispy and brown, the sidewalks pale and sun-bleached.

I thought about calling Charity Hospital when we got back to U's office. Last night, Loretta's condition had been upgraded to stable. I just wanted to make sure that change continued. I wanted her away from hospitals and soulless dwellings and back home where she belonged.

All around me, I felt like I was being watched. Workers watching my eyes to see if I was coming in to stay. Faceless people who peered from skinny little windows in the building. As U and I walked along a broken sidewalk, the 8:00 A.M. cold made me put my hands in my pockets.

Someone had slapped a flyer for a new rap album on the institute's metal sign. OUT THA FRAME, the words read, blowing in the wind. U started laughing as we passed. I didn't get it. It was cold. It was earlier than I'd been up in ages. I was white.

"What's that?"

"Means you're crazy."

I looked at him.

"You know, not quite thinkin' in the lines."

"Ah-ha," I said and winked at him while shooting a gun made out of my thumb and forefinger. "Got it, G."

"Don't do that. Somebody'll think you're serious."

"Clyde's pretty out tha frame. Isn't he?"

"From what you told me, out the frame, out his mind, out this universe."

"When they were grabbing him back under the bridge, he told one of the handlers that he rode the candy beams of the galaxy highway. But then again, who hasn't?"

"Sometimes I forget who I'm talkin' to, Travers."

Some orderlies took us outside to the volleyball court where we sat at what looked like an old dinette set surrounded by four mismatched plastic chairs. The ground was bumpy and filled with rocks. Grass grew in yellowed splotchy patterns. U and I didn't talk, just yawned and shuffled in our seats feeling the calm that filled the vacant space as sunlight started flooding through the chain-link fence. We were outdoors but I felt like we were in a basement or cavern, the bluish-gray sky simply a painted ceiling.

Within a few minutes, they led Clyde—drawn face and shaky-legged—out to the table situated in the ragged void. We were so exposed and in the open, I felt like we were having a tea party on the fifty-yard line. I smiled up at him, but he didn't seem to notice. Didn't seem to remember the fight, or the day, or who he was. *This was going to be a huge waste of time.*

As I watched him slump into his chair and stare into a far corner of the building where he now lived, I tried to focus on who he'd once been. I tried to think about the Apollo, the sessions at Bluff City, and that brilliant sharp voice on *Dark End*. Those words seeming to come through the wind and my imagination and memories. A phonograph needle catching a man's soul came to mind.

But all I saw was a withered old man. He was just plain beaten. Any brilliance had been stripped away like water eroding the side of a mountain.

He wore a blue gown under a thick bathrobe and paper shoes. His fine hair seemed like feathers blowing against a rock.

"Clyde?" I asked. Just a knock on the door.

His gaze didn't leave the vacant corner where he stared. It wasn't a place you stared. You stared into the sky or a parking lot or at a nice-looking woman. You didn't stare at beams supporting an ugly building or damned old washing machines collected in rusted heaps nearby.

His eyes didn't wander.

"I'm a friend of your sister's," I said. "Loretta. What happened, Clyde? There were men looking for you. What did you get yourself into?"

I felt like I was talking to a second grader.

I put my hand on his back. I wanted to establish some kind of link, but instead felt foolish and manipulative.

His dry lips parted and he moaned. I think it was a moan. Maybe it was the wind sneaking around the buildings and down into the valley where we sat.

The sound again. His lips shifted against each other and finally some more sounds. With a little more effort, that same staring into the blankness of forever, he spoke: "I went to sleep."

"What?" I asked and looked over at U. He nodded and gave me another be-cool gesture. We'd been told he'd been put on some medication that would help with the tantrums. The doctors weren't even sure he'd be able to communicate.

But he did. Sort of.

"After I was born, I went to sleep and woke up other people."

"What do you mean you woke up other people?"

"Some of them was parading, some of them was performing, some of them was doin' movies, stuff like that," he said. "So I woke up with them, and carried on their duty, their performing. For that short period of time, when I was first born."

"Clyde, listen to me," I said. "Tell me about the men."

"They put me to sleep, and I woke up then, woke up in midair, in rain, woke up the rain, the rain was hurting, hurting me, yeah it was hurting me, it was hurting, I could feel it. Snow. Stuff like that. . . . It hurt Mary, too."

"What happened with Mary? Is that why they're after you? I want to help. I want to find out who wants to hurt you."

His eyes suddenly turned to me looking like he wanted to accuse me of coming here and disturbing his delusions. "Hurt?"

"Who?"

"They're dead."

"Who?"

"Eddie and them."

"Mary?"

"She dead."

"What happened?"

"The car is dark at the bottom of a lake. I see them coming but I can't move. My feet stuck down deep."

I folded my hands and covered my mouth and nose. My head pounded from lack of sleep and a bad need for a cup of coffee. I felt blurry.

Then he started. He did it right here. The song. Right in the dead center of a nut-house exercise yard, he started performing. The voice was cracked but clear in its warped, weathered perfection. Almost as if it had been aging for decades for this one moment. The words were sung low and heated and with emotion. But his face was completely impassive. Fucking "Dark End of the Street" in a nut house. The world was upside down and I was excited and nauseated at the same time.

"They're gonna find us," he said. *"They're gonna find us, Lord, some day, you and me, at the dark end of the street."*

I waited for him to trail off into that twirling, dripping line of emotion about *you and me* as if that heartache of not being together in the daylight would last forever. But he didn't. He left it there like the last words of a funky poem. A question mark. A structure too cool to be messed with.

"What happened?" I asked for the twentieth time. I wanted to take in the whole moment and savor it and write about it and let everyone in the world know that I'd heard Clyde James sing "Dark End" one fall morning in Memphis. But I couldn't. I had gone too far from caring about moments and music and poetry and finding beauty in a crazy old man clinging to the one song that made him immortal.

I wanted to find out how he got hooked up with the Dixie Mafia. The sky began to turn purple and black and clouds streaked by in loose, torn colors.

"Who killed them, Clyde?"

He looked at me and smiled. A loose, goofy-old-man smile. His hands outstretched like a circus clown apologizing for dropping the oranges he was juggling. "Don't you see? We all did."

"Bobby Lee Cook?"

His eyes squinted at me and then stared back into the dark space filled with rusted machines that didn't work.

"Let's go," U said. "That night messed him up something terrible."

I didn't move.

"I got a buddy who can get us the case file," U said. "It's all we can do."

I looked at Clyde James as I stood. I cupped my hand around his shoulder, but I didn't want to build a connection anymore. I think I just wanted to pass on some of Loretta's love. I patted his back and gave him a smile that only confused him as he continued to hum his song.

Gooseflesh raised on the back of my neck as we walked away. I heard him speaking, not to me, but to the air. To anything that listened.

"All I am is a voice," he said. "Lost in a dream."

Chapter 52

THE PHRASE *PUBLIC RECORD* is misleading. Most people think it means they have access to all the governmental information they want, anytime they want it. The truth is that the "all" part of the statement varies from state to state—mainly watered down to "some"—and the "anytime" means when they get around to it. Last year, I was helping a fellow tracker look for a death certificate on legendary bluesman Blind Blake in Atlanta and ran into a mighty long clusterfuck. He had the theory that Blake had died somewhere in south Georgia after being hit by a streetcar in the 'twenties and that ole Blake's death would show up somewhere in state records. My written request was never answered. My phone calls were greeted by polite paper sluggers, but no answers were ever given. A trip to Georgia confirmed that no one had even looked for the damned thing.

That's the way it works. Most of the time you have to go to the office yourself. You have to be polite to those paper sluggers and, if you are lucky, they'll crawl down into the cave or depths of hell or wherever those physical records are stored, and bring you back an answer. I've had tons of academics spin these great tales about conspiracies behind public records and how bureaucrats want to keep everything secret. Most of the time that's bullshit. When searching for old files, your biggest enemy is apathy.

As I waited down at Davis Bail Bonds on Poplar, I hoped Ulysses was having luck getting what we needed released. I picked at a paper container of health food he'd bought for me. Some tofu squares in brown rice, broccoli, and cooked carrots. I hunted for a bottle of Crystal. Maybe some pepper. Nothing.

It was about 2:00 P.M. when he finally got back. He slid out of his leather coat, hung it on a mahogany rack, and turned down the jazz playing overhead before plunking down the thick stack of papers he carried under his arm.

I picked it up. About half a phone book.

U made some coffee and returned some phone calls while I took the stack into his lobby and flipped through the pages. He called out from his office: "Be careful with those pictures. I have to return them in the morning. Rest was a copy."

James, Mary/Porter, Eddie

December 17, 1968

The first pages consisted of a detailed report from the Shelby County Medical Examiner. Eddie Porter had multiple injuries. Blunt trauma to the back of the head. Four of his front teeth broken loose. Two found in his stomach. Single gunshot to the base of the skull.

Mary James had died much more cleanly, if there was such a thing. She suffered four knife wounds to her face and a single gunshot that began underneath her jaw and ended up in her brain.

Both died from a .38 caliber bullet.

The crime scene photos, a set of ten, had that same washed-out, grainy-color look of those old Polaroids from the early 'sixties. Grandpa in weird black glasses. Mother with a beehive. Of course, these were larger, eight by tens, with some of the most disturbing images I'd ever seen.

I'd seen men killed. But staring into the warped angle in which pregnant Mary James lay, clutching her belly with eyes open, made me turn my head and flip the page quickly. These were too personal. I shuffled through the rest. The back of James's head. Broken plates on the floor and a plane ticket in a pool of blood.

Two sets of bloody shoe prints. Blood smears in an old kitchen. I swallowed as if my own spit were contaminated.

But I was careful to look thoroughly at each page. Take the time. U brought me some coffee in a mug stamped with logo for his company and I leafed through charts and diagrams of angles that the shooter or shooters used. Everything I saw implied two men.

EVIDENCE LIST:

32 scene photographs

1 brick

1 plane ticket

1 kitchen knife

1 woven rug
2 chairs
1 Formica table
fingerprint samples (doors and windows)
1 wallet
personal papers from James's home

I flipped through the stack quickly looking for copies of what would appear to be letters or notes but only saw more neatly typed pages. What did interest me was the detective log. As with most, they were written by one of a team of two detectives and carried time and place of interviews, what happened, as well as what they personally observed.

1400 hours
December 18, 1968.
Bluff City Records offices, College Street

Interviewed suspect Clyde James at the offices of a local Negro music company. The white owner, Robert Lee Cook, was present as well as a secretery and family of Mr. James. James appeared agitated and shook during the interview. We asked why he wasn't home last night and how he did not discover the bodies. At this point, Mr. Cook interrupted and stated the Mr. James was with him at a party and several witnesses were available to collaborate the story. Mr. James nodded confirmation of his whereabouts. When asked where did he sleep, Mr. James refused to answer. Once again, Mr. Cook tried to intervene, at which point Detective Tyler asked that he and his secretary leave the room. Mr. Cook advised Mr. James not to speak without a lawyer. Mr. James nodded. Upon exiting the offices, Mr. james told us he saw two white males fleeing the home in a green station wagon with wood paneling. We asked when he saw this, Mr. James once again refused to answer. Mr. Cook gave us the name of Bill Hammond, a local attorney. We took the card.

I read on. More interviews. A deposition with Cook where he told a long story about his Christmas party that included sweaty details about the women who attended and intricate facts about appetizers that made me hunger for more than tofu. I thought about Payne's BBQ and looked at my watch before ripping through a few more pages.

Another with Clyde James.

0830
December 20, 1968
433 Rosewood Ave.

Second interview with suspect. We had hoped this meeting would lead to an admission, but it seemed that Mr. James only wanted to further his story about the two white males. We were called by Mr. James earlier in the morning and told that he wished for a confidential talk. We agreed and met Mr. James at his residence. No others were present. Captain Leek was notified. Mr. James elaborated that Mr. Cook was being untruthful on our meeting on Dec. 18. MR. James stated he was at home at the time of the killings and that he fled the home for several hours walking the streets due to the death of his wife and friend. When asked why he did not seek medical attention for them, he stated they were both clearly dead. He continued that he witnessed one male known to him and another he had met on one occasion walk into the home with weapons. He stated he watched the men from the inside of a abandoned car in his yard. He stated he saw the men enter the home and that he heard screams from his wife. Mr. James was asked why he did not intervene and he stated he was unable to, presumably for his own safey. Mr. James stated the second victim, Mr. Edward Porter, entered the home a short time later and then heard two gunshots. The two men fled the home. Mr. James checked on the victim's condition. Seeing they were deceased he began to walk from the home and shortly thereafter became intoxicated with a man unknown to him. Mr. James identified the first male as that of Levi Ransom. He stated Mr. Ransom was an associate of Mr. Cook and was a frequent visitor to the Negro record shop. The second man was described as a juvenile and at another time witnessed to be in the company or Mr. Ransom. Mr.

James only recalled the juvenile as that of Judas. No other details. We left the house at 1030 and discussed Mr. Ransom with Captain Leek. Mr. Ransom is known to have committed several offenses in Shelby County and is believed to have served time at Brushy Mountain.

"Holy shit," I yelled to U.

"Read on, brother," he called back and kept talking to someone on the phone. For the first time, I noticed the slight buzz coming from the big neon sign in his window and the stale smell of his sofa. A funky, rotten smell of recidivist rednecks.

There was an interview with Ransom at a pool hall off Beale Street and the detectives noted that he owned the place. I imagined the pool hall smelling like the sofa and filled with testosterone and nicotine. Ransom denied knowing Cook or Porter or even being in Memphis that day. Ransom said, "I don't hang out with niggers." He was asked about this kid Judas and was described as shaking his head throughout the interview. I could tell the detective didn't give two shits for Ransom by the way he listed a long complicated criminal history after the interview.

My hands were now only filled with a few remaining sheets of paper and I read as fast as I could, searching for more answers. My heart thudded in my chest as I cruised through the interview with the would-be accomplice. It was short. Only two pages. I guessed juveniles weren't part of the public-record thing, because the boy's name and address had been crossed through with a fat black marker.

I took another sip of cold coffee. I wanted a cigarette but instead searched in my coat for a pack of gum. I paced the office for a few minutes.

"So that's it?" I asked, blowing a bubble from the Bazooka.

U shrugged.

"Ransom. . . . What happened to the rest? They never even arrested anyone? Man, this can't be the whole file."

"Look at that first page. Two-twenty-one. Look at your page count at the bottom. They match. I've done this a few more times than you, *pro*fessor."

I put on my coat and tossed him his leather trench.

"Let's go."

"Where?"

"Find that detective."

U shook his head and said, "That mother is probably dead."

"Let's find out."

He tossed me back his coat and walked back into his office and started banging the hell out of his computer keys. I poured some more coffee, downed a little more tofu, and waited.

Chapter 53

U FOUND HIM. He'd found that old bastard, Detective Raymond L. Jenkins, with a computer service called AutoTrack in less than fifteen minutes. I was familiar with the service, my occasional girlfriend had used it in Chicago while we were looking for witnesses to help a blues singer named Ruby Walker get out of prison. Too bad only reporters, cops, and those who worked on the fringes of law enforcement could access it. It would make my life a hell of a lot easier when I was tracking down long-lost singers. But I only asked for favors when I really needed them.

We decided not to call ahead even though there was a possibility that this wasn't even the same man. His age would be about right and U said he found weapons permits that he expected for a retired cop. Besides, he was only a few miles away in the Cooper-Young district in Midtown.

"Strange neighborhood for an old cop," I said, looking at all the meticulously renovated houses, many proudly flying their rainbow flags from porches.

"Not really," U said, taking a turn through a small business district of antique shops, coffee houses, and art galleries. "Probably just holding out for the right buyer." He took a zigzagged pattern through several narrow streets lined with cottages and bungalows painted bright blues and yellows, and wound his way down around a curve to a dead end.

The house didn't really seem to belong with the others. Two-story narrow brick. Seafoam green paint and a cast-iron balcony littered with drying socks and Sansabelt slacks. An upstairs window had been sealed with plywood. The bottom windows had been covered in security bars despite the neighborhood looking like a postcard for the chamber of commerce.

The front door was open and we heard hammering as soon as we got out of U's truck and walked over a reddish dirt lawn.

More hammering. The tinny sounds of a small AM radio. The smell of freshly cut wood.

"Mr. Jenkins?" I called out.

More hammering.

U walked ahead. The walls were mildewed and covered in a splotched gray-green mold. In a narrow hallway, some of the mold had overgrown family photos taken decades ago of a bristle-haired patriarch, his angular, red-haired wife, and three boys. Some unframed shots had been tacked to the wall with toothpicks and seemed like they'd been added by someone other than the person who'd made the family collage. My breath caught in my throat as I saw images of an old woman in a coffin, the same green mold obscuring part of the faded photograph.

I heard U talking to a man down the hall and I followed, the words becoming more distinct and clear as I entered a room that had been stripped of wallpaper and carpet. A half-completed bookshelf stood by a back wall.

Tree branches obscured the view from one dirty window behind Raymond L. Jenkins.

"This is *Detective* Jenkins," U said, nodding to the older man who was looking at U like he'd just been approached by a wandering Bible salesman with a glass eye.

Jenkins was in his seventies, a palish white and just as grizzled as you'd expect. His teeth were stained with nicotine and his later years had made his nose and ears so extremely pronounced they almost gave him a rodent-like appearance. Small pale-blue eyes. He wore boxer shorts with red hearts and a white dress shirt with the sleeves cut out. Navy-blue dress socks and sandals.

The old man took a deep breath, wiped his forehead with an oily rag, and sat down on an overturned bucket. We stood. I could tell U didn't want to soil his four-hundred-dollar jacket. He stepped back a little giving me the go ahead to lead. I knew why. He'd known the subject in about five seconds.

"Detective Jenkins," I said. "I'm looking into an old case of yours. It was a double murder in nineteen sixty-eight. Woman's name was Mary James, she was pregnant at the time, and the man was a musician, name was Eddie Porter. Both were shot in the back of the head."

I felt myself rambling, probably because Jenkins wasn't showing any normal signs of listening. No nodding. No quizzical look. Didn't even seem to be paying attention. He seemed more focused on a hole in the sock of his left foot.

"Do you remember?"

He pulled his foot to his body, examined the sock, and placed his foot back on the floor.

He shook his head, looked over at U, and grinned. He stayed silent. Somewhere down the street someone was mowing the yard. Jenkins's face was covered in white whiskers and he'd spilled grape jelly across the front of his shirt.

"Would you look at the case file if we brought it by?"

"Y'all don't have the right."

"Excuse me?"

He grinned to himself again, full of self-important knowledge that someone still needed him after all these years.

"Y'all don't work for the department. Why do you care?"

"One of the suspects is a friend."

He nodded, then his face crossed with great aggravation with the growing sound of a lawn mower cutting too close to his yard. He stood, cranked open the window, and craned his old head outside. "Damn fudge packers. Taken over this whole street. Suppose to raise property values but all they do is leave little typed notes for me about *my* yard in *my* mailbox. I don't know why those deviants don't go back and hide like they should."

I watched his face heat with anger as he sat back down on the bucket, his eyes flashed once again with a realization of what we were discussing.

He looked at the decaying walls covered in glue and loose bits of wallpaper and the sagging ceiling and sighed. "I'm sorry, don't remember the case."

"Can we bring by that case file? Maybe it'll jar your memory, sir."

"I don't think it needs to be of your concern," he said, and suddenly jumped up and hobbled from the room. "Good day."

U crossed his arms over his chest and said, "Nice man. Think I'll call him Grandpa."

I followed Jenkins into a family room. White sofa. White coffee table. White walls. Even white carpet. But the crispness of the room had long since faded. All the white had become a little more yellowed. The carpet mostly a muddy brown.

Jenkins turned on a 'sixties console television and began watching a Spanish soap opera.

"I need some help, sir," I said. "I can be back in five minutes with that file. Maybe you can just remember a little piece."

About ten seconds later, he turned and looked at me. Full attention now. His rat nose flaring. "Son, I kept every one of my case files. I know every one of 'em like I know my own name. Don't talk to me like I'm some sad old man."

"I need five minutes."

"I need to be left alone."

I didn't move. I watched him slump into a well-worn seat surrounded by opened cans of cheap beer and packs of saltine crackers and Vienna sausages.

He didn't look back. Only spoke: "You playin' with some mighty powerful people, son. And I don't think you've brought enough chips to the game."

I opened my mouth to speak. But he was done. His eyes had glazed back over reflecting with the colorful lights playing on the screen before him and living with the decayed memories of a life he'd known a long time ago.

I planned on coming back with the file. Fuck him, I thought. I could break him down. Shit, probably only needed some decent food and a six-pack. But as U and I walked out the open door, I saw a basket hanging from the wall. A familiar logo stuffed among the bills caught my attention.

A Confederate flag. Three strong stamped letters: SOS.

Chapter 54

HIDDEN PLANS, SECRET AGENDAS. All kinds of things that Jon
didn't care squat about. He'd driven back to Tunica last night, kind of liked
livin' in that penthouse that Mr. Ransom set up. People even brought him
some tinfoil to cover up the windows so he could sleep till noon. He'd prefer to sleep through the day, though. That way the sunlight wouldn't taint
his soul, he thought, stiffenin' the jacket of his denim suit and loosenin' the
yellow scarf around his neck. Dang thing still smelled like magnolias. Ain't
that funny?

He danced a little ole move on the elevator he'd learned from *Elvis:
That's the Way It Is*, and ended the dance in a karate down-block. *"Kiya,"*
he yelled as the door opened to the lobby and he almost near knocked an
ole woman in her snout.

"Sorry, ma'am," he said. He hustled by her, slippin' another Benzedrine
onto his tongue, feelin' the medicine dissolve. He rubbed his hands
together like he was gonna be eatin' a big feast as he stepped into the wide
parking lot lookin' for Ransom's sweet ride.

In the cold, he slipped into the man's truck, adjusted his gold metal
shades, and slunked down into his seat. His legs jumpin' and quiverin' off
the floor. He plunked another stick of gum into his mouth as Ransom
wheeled out onto Highway 61 and headed back to Tunica proper. But
before they hit the little ole brick town, he ducked onto a rutted road into
Nigraville.

Dang. People was livin' out here in some kind of wildness. Houses
slapped together out of rotten wood and old tin. Parts of trailers and
shacks mashed together like somethin' out of his aunt's *National Geo-
graphic* magazines. One house was even built around an old car like that

was some kind of bedroom. Made the place where he'd grown up in Hollywood seem like the Peabody.

All the shacks sank beneath the level of the road in these little gulleys. Smoke and small fires from oil drums kicked up into the cold, ole gray day. Gray and brown. Nothin' else. Streams of smoke seeped out of the back of hot-rodded nigra rides.

Jon nodded. Yeah, he understood. "In the Ghetto." He hummed the song a little bit.

"You all right?" Ransom asked. "Seem a little jumpy."

"Just a mite excited."

"You seen the papers?"

"Don't believe in 'em."

"Said they found Miss Perfect at Libertyland," Ransom said. "That where you left her?"

"Yes, sir."

"That's a public place, kid."

"Said make it random."

Ransom didn't seem too pleased with the words comin' from him, so Jon added a bit. "She was given' me T-R-O-U-B-L-E. Ma' boy. Ma' boy. Was she ever."

"What about leavin' prints?"

"Don't have none," Jon said. "I don't exist."

Ransom didn't say nothin' as they rounded a corner onto a one-lane road and stopped in front a long green shack with a screened-in porch. A skinny black man that Jon had seen with Ransom at the casino was cooking out on a pit made from an oil drum. Guess that's what all these people were doin', livin' off the casinos.

Man gave a toothless smile as they passed.

Jon followed Ransom into the porch where he saw a white man, lookin' young and kind of muscled, in a tan sheriff's outfit. At first Jon thought about boltin' for the front door but eased back a bit when he seen the man give Ransom a real good handshake.

"Jon, this is Sheriff Beckum. Wanted y'all to talk."

Jon took a seat in an old schoolhouse chair. Orange plastic and dirty as hell.

"Everything goin' 'right?" Beckum asked.

"Up twelve points in the polls," he said. "And that's in Nashville."

"I guess ole Tunica was just too small for you," Beckum said. The sheriff sat in an old chair, too. But his was wood and looked like it'd been sittin' around since the beginning of time. He took a cigar from Ransom and lit it with a lot of satisfaction.

Ransom didn't offer Jon nothin'.

Dang sittin' down was about to drive Jon crazy. His leg felt like it was gonna explode. He had so much energy. So much dang vitamins in his system that he wanted to jump through that ole rusted screen and fly to the moon.

"Jon, you listenin'?" Ransom asked.

"Yes, sir."

"Go ahead."

"I said when Travers was up here last, he came with a black fella," Beckum said. "Some bondsman, bounty hunter type named Davis."

The sheriff started laughin' up a mess when he said it. Thought it was funny that a nigra could ever work as such. Jon didn't think that was funny. Black Elvis was one of the finest men he'd ever known.

"Travers will be with him," Ransom said. "Can you do it, Jon?"

Jon smelled the magnolias on his scarf again. He felt a stirring down between his legs.

"That's why I'm here."

"All three this time. The black man, Travers, and the girl."

Jon nodded and kept chewing on his gum, thinkin' about the sweetness of it all.

Ransom laughed and punched Beckum in the shoulder. "He likes 'em sweet and young."

At that, Jon stood and walked back outside. His mind and legs just atinglin' and buzzin'. Memphis was waitin'.

Chapter 55

THE ELECTION SURROUNDED us. Everywhere U and I drove, we saw huge posters, cardboard signs, and billboards for Elias "Honor for Our State" Nix and Jude "Commitment to Our Future" Russell. The election was next week and all the white noise of signs and radio ads and television interviews made my head throb and my eyes feel raw. I kept thinking about the night before and those crazed rednecks at the compound, that rebel flag waving obscenely by Nix's true office, and the men who'd wanted to kill us. I wondered how a man with such a polluted mind could've ever reached such a level. I couldn't even contemplate that he was being seriously considered for such an important office. Then, I remembered Jesse Helms, Strom Thurmond, and Trent Lott.

U turned on Riverside Drive and wound up a twisting hill to the Bluffs overlooking the city. I remembered from my history classes how the early frontiersmen and Indians used the Bluffs for protection against flooding and attacks, even recalling how the French governor of Louisiana had tried to overrun the Chickasaw back in the seventeen hundreds and had his ass handed to him.

As U drove closer to the address we had for Bobby Lee Cook, my stomach twisted and my head pounded more, knowing the only one who could help us hated me beyond words.

"Remind me to stop pissing off people," I said, watching the front of his truck hugging the road, passing million-dollar houses with wrought-iron security gates.

"It's a talent," U said. "You're too good at it."

At the peak of the Bluffs, U pulled in front of a Mediterranean Revival number with lots of stucco and a red barrel-tiled roof. Two vans and

Cook's Cadillac was parked outside. U pulled in, close to the front door, and shut off his engine.

"You want to do this alone?" he asked.

"Could use someone to watch my ass."

U pulled off his shades. "Cool. Didn't want to have to tell Abby and her mean-ass cousin how you got it shot off."

Two girls in sweaty long-sleeve T-shirts and jeans were pulling weeds by a wide marble staircase flanked by squatty palm trees. One was blond, her hair up in a bun, no makeup. The other had red hair pulled into a ponytail and extremely long legs. They were both dirty and grass-stained but I knew from one glance they worked for Cook.

The women were used to spinning on brass poles in air-conditioning, swindling old men into having ten-dollar drinks, and telling tales to customers about dreams they'd never had. I had to laugh. Cook had them doing real work.

We rang the bell and within a minute, the lithe bartender I'd met at the Golden Lotus, the one with short brown hair and a nice stomach, opened the door. She had on an apron and was drying her hands on a towel. I'd really hoped all these women would've been hanging out by his pool in bikinis. Not doing manual labor.

"Cowboy," she said, a tight smile in the corner of her mouth.

"Howdy," I said. "Cook home?"

She looked over at U and then back at me.

"Don't make trouble here. He has people, too, you know."

"No trouble."

"Just a friendly warning," she said, tossing the towel over her shoulder and hooking her thumbs into belt loops along her small waist.

"Appreciated."

She told us to wait in the foyer. We did.

A massive chandelier dripped down from a high ceiling. Big marble statues of naked women eating grapes stood out from the garish red walls. The foyer spread in to an open living room with a sunken pit like the Beatles's pad in *HELP!* Zebra- and Cheetah-printed furniture. Class with a capital K.

U nudged me and I looked by a coat rack near the door. In a glass case for all visitors to see, stood three large trophies celebrating second, third, and fifth place in local bodybuilding championships for men over fifty.

I said, "Always wanted to be Mr. Senior Mid-South."

"Me, too," U said. "What's that say, Airport Holiday Inn?"

"Yeah."

"First class, brother."

Glass walls covered the entire back half of the house as if it had been built in a cutaway to show the interior. Outside, there was a small wooden deck with iron chairs and a table with a Cinzano umbrella. No women. Damn it.

Wind from the Mississippi made knocking sounds against the huge sheet of glass, and outside I could see small, immature pines bending.

A door opened from the southern edge of the house and I heard some awful post-Eagles, Don Henley music blasting from a far room. "All She Wants to Do Is Dance."

Two more young women followed him, both looking tired as hell, as he began pointing to the black granite floor. "Mr. Clean. All over. Watch the carpets. Don't even think about getting them wet."

They nodded but made faces at his back as he passed.

Cook wore tight bicycle shorts, circa nineteen eighty-seven, and this bizarre satin tank top that was just plain disturbing. It really didn't qualify as a shirt since it darted below his nipples and lotion-tanned chest.

He fluffed up the spikes on his gray head and crossed his arms over his chest in order to make his balloon-sized biceps even larger. A massive leather weight belt covered most of his stomach.

"Five minutes," he said.

He walked ahead, back to the weight room, with the bad music blaring, and I looked at U and shrugged. "Maybe he'll give us six. . . . Six would be nice."

He'd filled the room with rows of chrome Nautilus equipment and several racks of free weights. A back wall of windows overlooked the river, but the others were covered in mirrors. A beefy guy in a Golden Lotus T-shirt lay sprawled on a weight bench while being spotted by a guy who, although bald, could've been his twin. The same tanned hide and veined puffy look of a steroid addict.

"Man, this is a hell of a lot better than Saints camp," U said. "Remember?"

"You mean the junkyard? Hell, yes. Had to drive through all those wrecked cars just to get to practice."

"You come here to swap little tales, or to talk?" Cook said, sitting his Spandexed ass on a Nautilus machine and working out his neck in a perpetual nod.

"Don't," U said, waiting for me to drive a truck through his comment. "Fight it."

The beefy man benching re-racked the weight with a clanging thud and grunted as if someone had just stepped on his crotch. I wanted to tell him that 315 pounds didn't really call for a show. But I stayed with U's plan, holding more comments inside.

Then I decided to get right to it. "Why didn't you tell me that you were working with Levi Ransom?"

Cook kept nodding yes, until he gave a big grunt, and cranked out a last rep on the machine.

He wiped off his face with a towel and took a sip from a bottle of Evian.

"We've been through this. Door is back the way you came."

"I saw the police report on Mary James and Eddie Porter. Levi Ransom killed them. You were washing money for the Dixie Mafia. What happened, Cook, needed a favor? You needed to flex a little and prove you were a badass?"

"Fuck you," he said, moving on to a bicep machine for preacher curls. He bent over the bench, almost in a prayerlike pose, and muscled up a bar attached to a pulley system.

"What did Eddie Porter do? Find out about your deal with Ransom?"

He ignored me. I looked around the mirrored room.

U had wandered off. He was talking to the two meatheads. I thought I overheard him giving tips on how to bench more. One of the boys was smiling.

Cook took another sip of water.

"If you'd been straight with me, Loretta wouldn't have been shot."

The intensity in his face broke away. His jaw fell slack.

"No one told you?" I asked. "Didn't figure you to be a true friend of hers anyway."

Then the son of a bitch really snapped.

I could tell he'd been trying to keep it in. Red-faced and breathing deep lungfuls of air. But after I said "true friend," his arms darted out and yanked me into a headlock and began pounding me in the face. He only got off two quick jabs to my cheek and forehead before I pulled my head out and twisted his arm behind his back.

He fell to his knees with a high-pitched scream.

The meatheads ran to him.

But U had drawn a gun and yelled for them to stay. It was the type of command you'd give a dog.

They stayed. Cook buckled with intense pain. I wanted to hold him there forever.

Chapter 56

"COOL IT," I said. I spoke as pleasantly as I could to a man I'd brought to his knees with pain. I twisted his arm an inch higher behind his back.

"You motherfucker," Cook screamed. "Don't you ever say that, you goddamned cocksucker. Come into my house? I'll kill your ass."

I pulled his arm even higher, heard a slight crack, and then let his arm relax about two inches. He grunted; I let him go. He almost fell on his face, but caught himself with the other arm and used the preacher machine to stand.

"They shot her in the chest and left her bleeding on the floor of JoJo's bar. Nice people. Even set fire to the business that JoJo had run for thirty-five years, man. You know what that means? You know what kind of sweat and patience and hard work that takes? She had to lie on the ground of the bar and watch their whole life burn around her while she waited to either bleed to death or catch on fire. Yeah, Cook, you're a great friend to her."

He closed his eyes and stood there for a moment, catching his breath and rotating his arm in its socket.

U walked over and turned off the boombox. He told the men to sit down but one still tried to get to Cook.

"Sit down!" Cook yelled.

We were all quiet for several moments. I think Cook wanted to cry, if he'd had any soul or conscience left. But the only emotion he seemed to possess in grief was shutting his damned mouth.

The wind battered the wall of glass and the sky became dark for a few moments. Then the room became light again, bright yellow beams streaking across the tops of trees lining the Bluffs.

"You come with me," Cook said, pointing outside. "They stay."

I followed him to the deck, hanging stilt-legged off the side of the house.

The view made my stomach jump a little as the wind loosely blew the tops of the trees and my hair. I put my hands in my pockets and stayed silent. Most of the time when you wanted information, it was best to shut up.

Out in the natural light, Cook looked much older than I thought. Small lines had formed above his upper lip and loose folds of skin fell over his eyelids.

"Eddie Porter was a great friend," he said, his hands on the railing as he looked down at the river passing in muddy, swirling circles. "I tried to help him even after I knew."

"Knew what?"

"Eddie Porter stole two hundred and seventy thousand dollars from Bluff City."

I shook my head.

"It's not what you think," he said, his voice more twangy than usual. Less controlled. "It wasn't my money, it was Ransom's. He floated me for the studio and for an Ampex recorder when I got started. He sometimes used us to run through some cash. He never took anything we made, only got back what he'd given. . . . Porter took it all."

"So why did he kill Clyde's wife?"

"Eddie was in love with Mary. Ransom knew it." Cook wouldn't look me in the eye. "Killing him would be too easy. He wanted Eddie to watch Mary hurt for a while."

"Jesus," I said. "So, if Clyde was there, why didn't they kill him, too?"

"Ransom didn't know he was there. Clyde was hiding in some old car outside. Clyde told me about seeing it. I told him to keep quiet, but he'd repeat the story to anyone who'd listen. When Ransom heard about it, he said he was going to go put a bullet in Clyde that night. But I begged him. I begged that hick bastard to leave my friend alone. I told him about Clyde's mind problems and how he was living on the street now. I said he'd be dead in a couple weeks, and I really believed it. I don't think Ransom showed him mercy, I just think he couldn't find him. When Clyde reappeared five years later, everything was buried."

"And Clyde was lost."

"At first, he lived on the street because he wanted to. Didn't want to face nothin'. Then everyone blamed him for Mary's death. Everyone thought he'd killed both of them because of the affair. He was an outcast among musicians who loved Eddie and the whole damned black community in Memphis. Shelters even turned him away 'cause they thought he was a killer. I heard one story about Clyde trying to sleep in a church basement one Christmas and the preacher dragging him out into the cold by his bare feet."

"So why now?" I asked. "Why would Ransom send men to look for Clyde and to mess with Loretta in New Orleans?"

"No, sir," Cook said, as one of his girls came out and handed him a zip-up workout jacket. He slid into it and dabbed his face again with a towel. "Listen, Nick. I don't really give a fuck about you. All right? But Loretta wouldn't want you dead. So go back to New Orleans."

"Will you answer one last question?"

"Your five minutes are long gone."

"Listen to me," I said, getting closer to Cook and smelling his vitamin-fused breath and dried sweat. I watched his eyes flicker with a recognition that the balcony may not have been the best place to take me. His fear made me a little uncomfortable. "I will call up Levi Ransom today and I'll tell him you told me a great story about his life in Memphis music and how you were planning on having lunch with the district attorney next week. I'll tell him what a nice place you have here and how he's just a twisted hick who needs you to run his money. Fair enough? Or you want to keep going?"

He looked back through the glass to the other side, to his television room and his curvy houseworkers and sunken pit complete with stone fireplace. Storm clouds were beginning to gather to the north and sootlike black clouds inched toward a white sun.

"She used to cook for me," Cook said. Sounded as if he was out of breath. Tired.

I sat down and checked my pockets for cigarettes. Old habit.

"Greens. Black-eyed peas and fried chicken that makes my mouth water just thinking about it. Why do you think she did that for me? No one ever treated me like that. I'd been on my own since I was fifteen. This was after she could have left my ass and signed with Stax or Hi or anyone she wanted. Why did she do that?"

"Who was the kid with Ransom? Tell me and I'll leave. You'll never see me again."

"That'd be nice, wouldn't it?" he said and smiled. He gave a short laugh that I could tell was rare. "But that's the question. That's what you've been looking for ever since you came to Memphis, even before you started hassling me."

I rubbed my hands together. My skin was chapped. I wanted to leave Memphis. I was beginning to hate being here. But where would I go now?

"Didn't have to look too hard, Big Chief."

I watched his craggy face. I said: "Kid's name was Judas."

"Yeah, I know his name. Spoiled punk who wanted to piss off his daddy and thought he was gangster at seventeen. Ran errands for Ransom at his pool hall on Beale after he'd been kicked out of some Nashville prep school."

"Still around?"

"Oh, yes," Cook said, smiling. "Might even be our next governor."

I felt a knot form in my throat and a rush of adrenaline heat my blood. My mouth opened a little, feeling dry, and I watched Cook's eyes for a hint that this was a joke.

"Now let me ask you a question, Travers," Cook said. He took off his weathered weight belt, the sun extinguishing on the horizon. "How hard would it be for a U.S. senator to make some nasty crime in the black section of Memphis go away? A U.S. fucking senator. This was 'sixty-eight. Right? Not too many P.C. cops. Most probably swallowed everything that fucker said about segregation."

I was half-listening now. My mind already speeding ahead. I felt like I was barely holding on to the edge of the stilted balcony. I could imagine the wood tearing loose from the house and tumbling down the hill and into the water.

"Two dead blacks," Cook said, now lecturing. "A murder that everyone believed was a domestic thing. Wouldn't take too much to disappear."

I thought about the Sons of the South and Abby's father. An old cop like Raymond L. Jenkins would've been the only one who could've kept an original file, no names blacked out. A blackmail scheme set in motion by a bitter old bastard and only furthered by a misguided Oxford attorney. They could've easily changed the election.

"Russell's been chained to him ever since," Cook said. "Now Ransom is just calling in his chips."

"So Russell flips his stance on gambling?" I asked, looking down at the riverfront and some old tourist paddle wheelers tying up for the storm. "He'll allow it down there?"

Cook watched me and shook his head. "Now why would the Dixie Mafia invest all that money in Tunica if Memphis wasn't that far behind?"

I felt a spot of rain on my cheek. The wind began to blow harder.

I understood why Cook lived on the Bluffs.

Chapter 57

JUDE RUSSELL DIDN'T want him here. He hated every time that son of a bitch ever tried to make contact. The last time he'd seen him was about a week ago when Ole Miss was playing Auburn and Ransom had shown up at a party thrown by the CEO of a company that made kitchen appliances. He stood there and ate fried chicken and drank whiskey with one of his whores like he belonged among them. But Levi Ransom would never belong. He had the stink of gutter trash that seeped from his pores like urine and testosterone. No matter how many millions he stole or killed for, Ransom would always be that yellow-toothed hood that for some twisted reason he'd found so damned appealing when he was a teenager. How stupid could a boy be? He'd alienated everyone who'd tried to help him, thought his daddy was the Antichrist and his mother a babbling drunk. But Levi Ransom, with his greased ducktail and hot-rodded Mustang, was about the coolest thing he'd ever known.

At sixteen, he'd met Ransom at this little pool hall down on Beale. He'd liked the street before it had changed. Blues. Beer. Good dope. Women. Ransom knew every darkened corner of the street. He'd buy him pitchers of beer and let him play pool for free and get women to do things to him that he'd never imagined in the bedroom of his Germantown mansion.

He'd walk over to Russell stretched over the cigarette-burned felt of a pool table and stick two fingers under his nose. He'd point to some teenager, drunk or stoned, leaning against the old brick wall of the bar, and let him know it was his turn. Ransom was like that. He tried to make you think he shared it all.

Russell didn't have too many friends. How could you when you changed boarding schools about every month and most people only wanted to talk about your daddy? Ransom was twenty-five and had a look like he'd been around the world a dozen times and was not too impressed with what he saw. He'd brag about setting fire to a courthouse in south Mississippi when he was fourteen by using a cigarette and pack of matches. He said he'd killed thirteen men, two of them with a buck knife, for not paying their debts.

Most of all, when he was drunk, he'd brag about being part of an organization out of Biloxi. He said he'd gotten in good because his grand-daddy had ties with a man who owned a club down there. Said when he got kicked out of the service, he started running poker and blackjack tables for the man. And pretty soon, Ransom said, he was involved in more complicated games like turning out little girls and using them to bait businessmen. He said a pack of Polaroids could net you a mighty nice return.

He called his pool hall on Beale just a little starter kit. Said it was an office for much bigger things that were happening. But he never did explain what those things were until the night of Russell's seventeenth birthday when they sat loaded up on Falstaff outside a little grocery in south Memphis. Ransom handed him a .45 and told him to go in and get back some change.

Funny how one moment can change your life forever. He should have walked away. He should've understood that Ransom was only using him the way he'd used the little girls he'd turned out. But he didn't. He only thought of a daddy who returned to Memphis from D.C. to talk about the safety of keeping blacks in their place and a mother who had her maid drop off a birthday cake while she drove to Florida with the church deacon.

Russell knew that .45 felt good that night. Felt so good he'd even smacked the head of the fat-ass clerk who'd laughed at him when he asked him to empty the drawer into a paper sack.

Ransom had called that night his baptism. And anytime that he tried to resist the jobs, usually only when he was sober, Ransom would smile at him like he'd been there himself and laugh. "We ain't like other people, you and me. We are takers."

The money didn't mean shit. But the *you and me* part meant everything.

They probably robbed twenty-five stores over the summer of 'sixty-eight while the world fretted over Kennedy and King, men who later became his heroes.

He never knew how much they got. Never really asked. He'd blow almost the whole thing at strip clubs and on whiskey and weed.

He might have stayed in it forever if he hadn't begged Ransom to take him along that night around Christmas. He'd shown up at the pool hall, pissed off at his parents for having some big party that spilled into his bedroom where he'd found some old gray-headed woman looking through his record collection and making fun of the singers' clothes. She said Mick Jagger looked like a girl and dropped the record on the floor like it was infested with bugs.

The woman didn't see him till he called her a withered bag of shit and stole the keys to his mamma's Buick station wagon. He'd found Ransom rolling the pool balls around the table with his fingers and absently looking at his watch.

He could tell that Ransom was awful mad about something as he guided each ball into pockets as if he were their God.

When he saw Russell, he said he didn't have time.

And damn if Russell didn't beg to help. Ransom wasn't even listening to him as he slipped into his coat—that is, until he mentioned stealing his mamma's Buick. At the time, Russell had actually believed Ransom was impressed, not that he didn't want to use his own ride.

Ransom made him drink half a bottle of tequila on the way to that house on Rosewood and handed him a pair of leather gloves. *Shut up. Follow me. Listen to what I say, kid.*

Jesus Christ, Russell thought, his mind a blur of blood and gunshots. Jesus Christ.

Russell broke from the memory and walked along the high log fence around his hunting lodge in Alligator. He heard the hum of a car's motor on the other side and wanted more than anything to keep him out. Especially now.

But just as if he were still seventeen, he pressed the button for the gate to slide open and waited for Ransom to drive through. It was important, Ransom assured him. It was about the election.

The election was two weeks away and he was having nighttime meetings with one of the leaders of the Dixie Mafia. Jesus.

ussell didn't take him inside his hunting lodge. Didn't even offer. He knew Ransom expected to be treated like a guest. Served warm Bourbon on the cold night, maybe a sandwich or dinner prepared. He had to be crazy.

Russell would keep him outside with the rest of the dogs.

Russell had a Browning tucked in the side pocket of his slicker and a flashlight in his hand. They followed a path next to a little creek wrapping the eastern edge of his property as a light, cold rain began to fall.

"I want your word on this, Jude."

Russell kept on walking down the same path he'd been clearing for years. He kicked away some stones from the dirt and looked into the distance where the trees began to gather in a thicket of forest.

Russell stopped, feeling strong on his own land with his own gun. He looked at Ransom's tanned face and bleached teeth. Ransom had animal smarts but didn't know about educated people. He was so stupid, thinking he could still control him after all these years. Russell had left that all behind. He'd gone back to college. Gotten a Masters in business from Vanderbilt, brought his uncle's cotton business into the modern age and doubled their profits, married a fine woman, and raised a good Christian family.

"You listen to me," he said, trying to stop his voice from shaking. "Don't you ever come to my house, walk in my presence, or call me again. Do you understand? I made some mistakes when I was a child. But I am about to be governor of the state of Tennessee. I will have you put in prison if you approach me again. I let you come here only as a warning."

Ransom started cackling and pulled his loose gray hair into a ponytail, knotting the wet mass at the back of his head. His gray hair was receding. His eyes were black.

He smiled at Jude and put his arm around him. Russell felt dirty just smelling the man's rancid breath and pushed him away.

"All right, Jude," he said with that same loose, rotten grin. "That's fair. We'll call it even. You keep those casinos out of Memphis like we agreed and I'll call it square on that couple I killed in Oxford. For you." Ransom spoke a little louder when he said that, like the killings were his present. "I think that's a good old trade. Filled that couple full of holes myself. That fat country boy squirmed on the floor in his own piss talking shit about the South rising again."

"I never asked you."

"No, you never asked. But I'm sure you wanted to be questioned about killing some niggers back in 'sixty-eight. During the election? Didn't you? Would've kind of gotten away from them issues you love so much."

"I didn't even know that lawyer."

"Why'd you send me that file then, like it was a burnin' sack of dogshit left on your porch?"

"That night involved you. Thought you'd want to know."

"Yeah, we are all dirty in this."

Ransom got closer and stuck two fingers under Russell's nose. "We share it all."

The gesture sickened Russell and he felt like he might vomit. The trail grew rockier and suddenly ended in a stretch of high weeds. The wind was cold as hell and made his face feel tight. "How do we know there isn't another copy of that file?"

Ransom shrugged. "We don't."

Russell spit on the ground and kept walking away, back to his house.

"Oh, one more thing," Ransom said. "Seems that someone saw you killin' them niggers that night. Right there in that report. Since you're done with me, I guess I'll leave him."

Russell stopped and turned. "We talked about this. That man is legally insane."

Ransom nodded and stroked his salt-and-pepper beard, taking a wider stance on *his* land. He was wearing all black with crocodile boots. Silver rings and a turquoise bracelet.

"Seems like he's getting better," Ransom said. "And he's gettin' some help from some man named Travers. Guess you know about him already. Don't you? Hard when they come and knock on your door."

"Why is he doing this?"

"Some nigger woman is his friend. Her brother is Clyde James. But don't worry, Jude. We're takin' good care of you, son."

Jude Russell opened his mouth to speak and felt for the gun in his pocket. His fingers couldn't grip it. He couldn't grip the damned gun even though Ransom was right there on his ground. But if he killed him, what would come of that? Shooting any man wouldn't win any votes. And Ransom was just an arm of the Dixie Mafia, others would follow. More powerful men than him in Biloxi.

He pulled his hand from his pocket.

Ransom laughed. "You gonna say something, Jude?"

Chapter 58

SINCE I LEFT New Orleans, I'd been trying to reach JoJo. I'd let the phone ring a million times at his house and then, almost in a masochistic way, I'd listen to Loretta greet me on the bar's voicemail. At home, I'd left him a message with U's number telling him that I was thinking of him. I felt that was all I could do. But that morning, I finally got in touch with Loretta at the hospital. She answered the phone in her room like she owned the whole damned place and didn't have time for small talk.

"You shouldn't be answering the phone."

"Why not?"

"You're sick."

"They got that bullet out, boy."

I asked how she'd been feeling and she told me they got her out of bed last night and that she was finally walking again. She gave me some pretty gruesome particulars on the surgery and how the Lord had kept the bullet away from the important stuff. She said a quarter of an inch either way would've killed her. She told me the story like a testimonial on faith, but it only made me madder and more determined.

"How's JoJo?"

She was quiet for a second. "He ain't happy."

"I'll be back soon," I said. "I'll rebuild that bar with my teeth if I have to."

"Give him a while," she said. "He ain't so sure he wants it back. Insurance made him a decent offer and we thinkin' about headin' up to Clarksdale for a while."

"The farm?" I asked, knowing all about JoJo's dream to clear out land that his family had owned since Reconstruction and renovate the old farmhouse where he grew up. He talked about it all the time. But that's what I always thought he was doing, talking. A few beers always led to discussion about that old farm in Clarksdale. Sometimes I swore he was about to run for the back door with his toolbox.

"You tell me what y'all need," I said.

She paused for a second. Again. "Nick, come home. It's over."

"Not quite."

I told her that I loved her and hung up the pay phone. I sat there for a moment watching a business across the street. Still didn't see what I wanted.

Then I made a call to U. I told him what I'd been doing and asked him to make a few calls. I finished a bottle of Coke and continued to watch the front entrance of a defunct grocery store. A place that Jude Russell had been using for his campaign headquarters.

It was about 11:00 and I hadn't slept since leaving Cook's place last night. Eventually U had turned off the light at his apartment while I watched flickering images from *Support Your Local Sheriff*. Sometime around 2:00 A.M. ole James Garner gave me an idea while Abby slept on a nearby futon.

I had watched the early gray light leak through the curtains and made coffee before driving down Poplar for some hot biscuits from a Krystal. There, at a greasy table, I'd worked out my ideas on a notebook that contained interviews on the life of Guitar Slim.

At the south Memphis grocery, now teeming with Russell supporters, I saw political wrangler Royal Stewart get into an old Audi and drive east.

I smiled.

I had a plan.

By God, I had a plan.

I never gave a shit for country clubs. First off, I hated golf more than cocktail parties of any type, Cajun food served at chain restaurants, the work of Tom Clancy, New Age music, those annoying posters about success and priorities and all that shit (do you really need a poster to remind you?), and men who compete in X-treme sports.

Maybe I was generalizing, but judging from a few fellas I saw grab-assing on a nearby green, I had the feeling that the Memphis Country Club boiled with such high-minded individuals.

The club was pretty much what I expected as I hopped a side fence, watching some security guard, and waded through the Land Rovers and BMWs and other jackass vehicles.

Nearby, Royal Stewart's dirty Audi stood out like a turd on a wedding cake.

Huge oaks and magnolias with wide branches filled the grounds near the main building. I buttoned up my suede coat, stood a little straighter with a manila envelope stuffed with papers, and walked right through the glass doors with purpose. It was about the same way I acted when I walked through the projects; I made myself look like I had somewhere to be.

Inside, the walls were painted green and pink with lots of stained wood. Several glass trophy cases where people stored insignificant awards.

As I rounded a turn, a white-headed woman with impossibly high eyebrows stopped and asked if she could help me. I told her I had plans to meet Mr. Stewart for lunch. With a grunt, she said she didn't recognize the name.

I told her that I guess she couldn't help me after all and kept walking.

Down another turn, I found another woman, this one much more attractive with brownish hair and lots of freckles, standing at a hostess table. I looked around for Stewart.

The room held all women. I noticed most of them wore a hell of a lot of makeup and really uncomfortable, loud outfits. It was as if they were trying to outdo each other on who had worse taste. The far wall was a long plate glass window protecting diners from the eighteenth green.

The women watched me as I looked around. I smiled at a couple. They quickly turned their heads back to their martinis.

The woman asked me if she could help. She looked to be in her early twenties. Tan, with a lot of jewelry.

I told her who I was looking for and she was really nice about it. She walked me down a hall. We were talking about all the wonderful things that the club offered when she abruptly stopped talking and stood at the beginning of a long corridor. It reminded me of those invisible fences that kept barking dogs from me while I jogged Audubon Park.

Down the hall, I saw a bunch of men talking and playing cards in a large paneled room. Cigar smoke trailed out to us.

I looked at her.

"That's as far as you go?"

"House rules. Men only."

"Take one step," I said, looking down at the line where the carpet turned green.

"Might get me fired."

"Really?"

She nodded.

I whistled low, thanked her, and followed the hall. This one was completely lined with glass cases with more insignificant awards in silver and gold. Mostly golf. A few tennis. I looked for Miss Congeniality, but didn't see one.

The room at the end of the walk of fame was more impressive than where the women had been herded. A twenty-foot concave ceiling made the men talking seem more obnoxious, the guffawing in full stereo. Green plaid and long oak tables. The chandeliers were brass.

Paddle fans blew away cigar smoke.

A couple of men turned. Most ignored me and kept drinking beer, absolutely delighted they didn't actually have to work.

A bartender offered me a beer. I declined but asked for some untouched coffee that sat on a nearby burner. He said he'd pour me a cup.

I found Stewart sitting with another man near a large window looking out onto a fairway. Fewer than five miles away were crammed projects, rows of pawnshops, and check-cashing businesses.

"Mr. Stewart," I said.

He looked up at me but resumed talking. He was truly an old gambler, knew by applying any significance upon me that he'd already lost. Apparently, there was some type of fund-raiser later in the evening and he was upset about the P.A. system they planned to use.

I said: "We need to talk."

He continued his conversation. But Stewart's companion, a little fellow who seemed so eager he was actually shaking, was having a hard time listening with me standing there.

The bartender came over with my coffee and I ordered a club sandwich. I loved club sandwiches.

"Does that come with fries?"

"Chips."

"That will do."

Stewart finally turned, looked up at the bartender, and said, "No. That won't do. This man isn't with me and is not a member of the club. Cancel that order."

"Now you've made the bartender uncomfortable, Royal. And this kid, too. You're uncomfortable, aren't you?"

"No," the man said. "I'm fine. Really."

I said: "Well, I am."

Stewart, long gray hair and bleak blue eyes, leaned close to me and said, "You have about twenty seconds to get your ass out of here or I'll have you arrested."

The bartender hadn't moved. The twenty-year-old P.A. master crossed his arms over his Polo shirt.

I smiled and leaned back over the table to Royal. "Has Jude ever told you about 'sixty-eight in Memphis? Sounds like it was a wild ride."

Stewart bit the inside of his cheek and ran his fingers around the brim of a hat that lay by his elbow. He nodded, a man who'd been played out and knew how to walk from the game.

"My apologies," he said in that weathered Memphis accent. "I didn't realize my guest was staying for lunch."

Chapter 59

"I'LL GIVE YOU twenty-four hours," I said, taking a sip of the warm coffee. Felt good to be out of the cold. There was a fireplace near my back and I could feel the heat through my flannel shirt.

"For what?" Stewart asked. The boy had left our discussion group.

"It goes like this. I won't bullshit you or waste your time or play any fucking games. I want Jude Russell out of this election. I have three things. I have a witness, a very credible one," I said, lying, "that puts Jude Russell at the scene of a double homicide in December of 'sixty eight."

He laughed by making absurd breathing noises out of his nose.

"Second, I have another witness that places Russell as a business associate of a known member of the Dixie Mafia. A man named Levi Ransom who I believe has contributed to Jude's campaign fund."

Stewart folded his arms across his chest, perpetually shook his head and swallowed a lot. His blue eyes never left mine. Not for one second would he miss a word I said. He was making mental notes the whole way through.

"You want him to drop from this race? Just because you say you have people who've made up the most outrageous lie I've ever heard?"

"Oh, you mean I would need some hard facts? Shit," I said, scratching my head. "Didn't think about that." I pushed forward a copy of the homicide file U had pulled with a couple pages I'd creatively added. "I guess a police file will have to do. Just mentions his role in the shooting and leaves a lot of unanswered questions about why the investigation wasn't followed. The victims were black. I bet that'll get him tons of votes in south Memphis. You didn't even have to fix up that run-down supermarket down there as a P.R. stunt."

Stewart fiddled with his hands and nodded a few times to himself.

"You're crazy," he said. "Out of your mind nuts."

"No doubt."

The waiter laid down the club sandwich on the table. Toasted white bread. Lots of mayo on the cold cuts. I expected something a little better here, but suddenly knew I shouldn't have.

"I believe you have some phone calls to make," I said, leaving the sandwich and sliding back into my coat. Outside, two men in yellow sweaters watched each other pivoting their hips in a practiced swing.

He said: "It won't work."

"You don't think I'll do it?" I pushed away from the table with my hands and watched his face, his teeth grinding, the blood dripping into his neck. "You don't think I'm clever enough to go to Kinko's and print off about twenty copies of the file, transcribed interviews with contact names and numbers of my sources, and then have a buddy mail them out to every major media outlet in Tennessee and Mississippi? Yeah, I couldn't do that. That would be too much trouble."

His face had been completely drained of color.

I stood. "You have twenty-four hours to find a replacement," I said. "Russell's wife is sick. He has personal issues. His cat died. I don't give a fuck. I'm only giving you this option because the only thing worse than having a killer running this state is having that gun-toting moron and his fools from Jackson win. I don't think we want that. Do we?"

I didn't listen for an answer. I left the copied file and pushed my way through a bar of men with faces flushed with alcohol and sun. They didn't seem to notice me or the conversation. They were too busy talking about themselves. Pushing ahead without ever looking back.

Jon Burrows was tired of circlin' that bail bonds business over on Poplar. He knew the layout real good—hell, you could see most of it through them dang big windows—now he just had to wait till night and sneak into that back door that was unlocked. Make sure all three of 'em were there.

Jon decided to cut on over to Union Avenue while he waited and have a float at Taylor's Café beside the old Memphis Recording Service. He liked the smell of the old Sun Record Studios and the little diner next door where E's founder, Mr. Phillips, used to take coffee in his special booth.

Back then, E would sit at the counter, dreaming about the time when Mr. Phillips would let Him make that big record. 'Course Mr. Phillips always said he didn't discover Elvis, he said that Elvis discovered him.

Jon found a nice spot at the counter, same tin ceiling and checkered floor from E's time, and watched some crazy ole Japanese tourists yammering away about their new T-shirt, or was it one of them Crown Electric grease monkey shirts? Jon couldn't tell, so he turned back to his float. Coca-Cola and vanilla ice cream. Nice ole bubbly sweet mixture.

He thought about Perfect for a while. Thought about that Coca-Cola–bottle shaped body and the sweet taste of her. Then he remembered her lyin' in that filth, or maybe that was just a dream, and then there was no more of her. Kind of like she'd never shared his air.

Jon asked for another float.

The kid workin' the café reminded him of when he first come up to Memphis. Hair greased into a ducktail. Tough long sideburns, longer than even E's, almost down to his chin, and a tattoo on his neck. But he was small in his ways, the way Jon had once been when he'd been Jesse Garon. He never realized how large you could be. Didn't realize all the ways you could grow and be one with E.

But you could tell the kid just liked sharin' the space that the Man once knew. And that made him feel a bond with the fella. Jon pulled out a roll of hunnerds from his pocket and lay down a couple.

"Good luck on your way with E," he said.

"You in a show?" the kid asked.

"I ain't a performer," Jon said.

The kid watched him, making his eyes small. But he scooped up the money like a hungry dog and got to wipin' down the bar.

The bar didn't have a crumb on it, but the kid kept on rubbing it anyway. Kept it smooth and neat. Somethin' about the rag over the wood made Jon think about Ransom.

He thought about Ransom sendin' him up to Memphis for a triple hit with no backup. Just alone.

The kid kept searching for crumbs.

Jon knew he could hit the bond shop and take them all out in two shakes of a lamb's tail. But the dang office was a squirt of piss away from the jail. Them cops would be all over him before he'd hit the door runnin'.

He needed somethin' quieter. He needed somethin' to hush up his gun.

Just as he was thinkin' who in Memphis could handle such a device, the cell phone in the front pocket of Jon's black leather jacket began to ring. He answered it.

It was Ransom.

Ransom said there had been some kind of big change in the plans.

Chapter 60

AT A QUARTER till nine, Jon Burrows, showered, tanned, and shaved in a crisp white dress suit, peered down at the side mirror of the rental car Levi Ransom was driving and watched a beautiful convoy of killers joining them along the highway to Memphis. At first, he'd only noticed the two lunkheads who'd been playing with their Smith & Wessons in the parking lot of the border truck stop where he joined Ransom, but then he saw the pickup holdin' that grizzled fella and the sheriff. Then, an identical rental to the one they were in passed, and two good ole boys in black leather jackets gave a two-fingered wave to ole Levi as they passed and ran ahead for a while.

'Course, Ransom knew who his boy was. He knew that when trouble started comin' down, when they tried to take down Travers, that Jon was his man. That's why he called him back. He didn't want his A-1 rockabilly star locked up in no dang pokey. Jon turned his head and popped a couple more Benzedrine tablets into his mouth.

Felt like he could fly back to Memphis himself. Why wouldn't Ransom speed up? Why was he goin' so dang slow?

Hell, he was ready. Now. Jon looked down at his white double-breasted jacket with matching pants and white zip boots. White shirt. Red tie. Cuff links. He'd borrowed the suit and shoes from the Holy area where they stored His things down in this big warehouse by the airport. He hadn't taken much, just this suit and the black jacket E'd worn on the NBC TV special in 'sixty-eight. He thought it was appropriate 'cause he was thinkin' about all them sweet *Memories* from the last few weeks as he watched the convoy and knawed on his knuckle tryin' to get his leg to quit shakin'. The past sure made you feel kind of funny in the stomach.

"Kid, this is where it all breaks down," Ransom said.

"Yes, sir."

"I've been playin' this game for thirty years and I want it runnin' clean by November. You understand?"

Jon nodded. *Let's go. Let's go. Speed up.*

Ransom smiled to himself as he passed over the Tennessee line, just like a man comin' home from the wilderness to a place he now owned.

M r. Ransom sure didn't take no mess. As soon as they parked by these two ancient, metal bridges, he pulled out a big ole Colt revolver and tucked a handful of bullets into his black coat. It was dark as a black steer's ole butt outside and the bridges looked like somethin' that should've been torn down about a hunnerd years ago. They lay loose and rusted and broken ahead of them, stretchin' over the river all the way to Arkansas. A few of them orange highway lights flashed in the night, warning people not to get too close.

Jon could get close. He had this feelin' buzzin' in his head like he wanted to sprint over to Arkansas and back.

Ransom told the two big dudes with pistols to go back down under one of the old bridges and get ready. Them twin bridges just skippin' over the Mississippi.

The man with withered skin and the sheriff fanned out on the first bridge. The other folks workin' with them were out there somewhere, hidin'.

Ransom walked ahead, past the orange light, and onto the bridge. Jon followed, the old man walkin' way too slow. He had to bite the inside of his cheek just to walk in place.

Jon kept the pace and soon his feet made clankin' sounds on the metal grates. He was just waitin' for the bridge to break loose and for him to tumble out into the night sky where he'd just keep on flyin' back home.

He was kind of twichin' inside when he looked down and saw the big ole river swirlin' and twistin' below. Looked like they was up at least two hunnerd feet in the air.

He took a deep breath and walked along the spaced slats where the railroad cars used to run. He kept followin' Ransom and soon heard him callin' the other boys on a handheld radio.

Come on. Where were they? "Faster."

Ransom looked over at him.

"Nothin'," he said. Gosh dang he wanted to explode inside. His heart felt like it was beatin' like an egg timer.

About twenty feet away, a red balloon twisted in the wind.

Jon ran over to it but Ransom walked.

Jon stared at the red balloon, waitin' for it to pop. Or maybe he was gonna pop.

Finally Ransom strolled on over and ripped a card from its string. Just looked like some Christmas card, but Lord it made Ransom mad. He threw it to the ground and spit over the bridge's railing.

"Come on," he said. "Someone is playin' us."

"Who?"

"Travers's buddy decided he needed a little cash. He's smart. He's runnin' us around to find out how bad we want it."

"How much he gettin'?"

"If we find him?"

Jon nodded.

"Zero."

Jon laughed with him and kept watchin' Ransom's craggy face till he 'bout fell down into the river. His foot hit air where a metal grate used to be. His heart picked up a tick and now beat like it wasn't takin' no pause. Just a tick, tick, tick.

Ransom quickly grabbed his hand, Jon's stomach up in his chest, and helped him onto the railroad line.

"Careful, son," he said. "This bridge was built for the Union Pacific around nineteen-oh-five. Ain't used to people walkin' her."

"How far is that drop?"

Ransom watched his face, the lights of Memphis burning behind them. "Far enough."

Jon looked up and saw the moonlight hitting the unpainted, rusted metal beams and twisting down in purple rays. The light lay in a million crisscrossed patterns that made his head a little dizzy. He felt like he might throw up. His head racin' harder than his body. His body was in a low tremor, maybe Ransom didn't see it.

Ahead, the opening to the bridge on the Tennessee side stood like a big dark mouth. Behind him, Jon couldn't even see where the bridge ended and Arkansas began.

Ransom yelled over to the old man and the sheriff on the twin bridge. They called back that they hadn't found nothin' either.

Jon wondered if E had ever been out here as he tried to keep his body still. He looked at all the old graffiti spellin' out high school classes from the 'fifties and 'sixties and lovers that was probably dead now.

Maybe down on the banks where he'd seen all them bums and street people livin', E may have taken His girl when He was back at Humes High, before the blue storm that had hit the world.

Jon pulled out the yellow scarf from his pocket and wrapped it around his neck as he stepped from the bridge. His whole body shaking harder, like a demon had stepped into his soul and was dancin' like there was a party in hell.

He needed to find Black Elvis. He needed somewhere to get washed out for a few days. He stared down at his hand jumpin' on his thigh like bacon in a skillet.

Jon was about to throw up when he heard a mighty roar.

"Holy shit, get the fuck down!" Ransom yelled, tackling Jon and His holy suit to the ground. Jon reached back for his gun to take Ransom's life, when he saw what Ransom had seen.

And good Lord, his leg started twitchin' and his heart beat a million times a second. He was runnin' another notch higher, runnin' like someone had kicked up the fuel switch on a minibike. "Dang!"

A dozen of them big Army trucks, big as tanks, with bright white K.C. lights on the roofs, came roaring down the dirt road and cut off Ransom's other boys. Must've been fifteen men scrambling down the red clay hill covered in kudzu carrying machine guns and barkin' out orders to each other like it was D Day. They shined lights down on where he lay with Ransom.

Jon searched behind him and he saw a narrow little gutter of dirt that had formed from all the rains last month. If he could scoot back just enough, he could get gone. Run all the way across the bridge. He'd be in Vegas before he slowed down.

As much as he wanted Travers laid up in a pine box, this wasn't his deal.

But as he started to move, he heard bullets raining down from atop of one of them trucks just idling there in the darkness.

"Don't move, kid," Ransom said, inching his gun from beneath his belly and taking aim at three men that were walking toward him.

Ransom was gonna take 'em out.

His boys comin' from the other bridge started firin', all heaven and hell started breakin' loose like that book in the Bible when the dang beast and the four horsemen and all them critters come barkin' out from the center of the earth.

All Jon could do is cover his head and start prayin' to E where he sat with the Lord way up high in a jumpsuit made of gold.

Ulysses Davis laughed hard from the top of the hill where he'd parked the Expedition. As soon as he saw the crew from the Sons of the South wearing night vision goggles and camouflage, he really started laughing his ass off. He smacked the steering wheel looking through his own binoculars and laughed a little more.

"You want to see?"

"Fuck 'em," I said. "Let 'em play it out."

"I tell you, Travers. This was one hell of an idea. What did you tell those boys?"

"Just told their commander that I knew where to find the folks who'd killed one of their finest men in arms, Bill MacDonald. Said those communists would be here in his state for a drug drop with a local gang of Jamaicans."

"Jamaicans?"

"They needed an additional incentive."

U shook his head and put down the binoculars. He took a big swig of water and watched the battle, sparks flashing from the muzzles of the automatic weapons. "Wasn't that fancy with Beckum? Just told him that I'd sell your old tired ass out for a quarter."

"How much, really?"

"I'm not sayin'. Let's just say you were on special."

We both laughed for a while and then he cranked the car and we started to pull away. For some reason, though, I decided to glance down the hill and maybe catch a bit of that fucker Ransom getting sliced in half.

I wanted it. I did. But part of me also felt disgusted for following through on my fantasies. I'd killed those bastards, just as if I'd stalked them and knifed them in the gut.

We could only pray that the Sons of the South would take a hard hit for wiping them out. U planned on calling the police as soon as we got back on Poplar.

I couldn't see much. As U turned the car and started to drive away, I saw more camouflage dudes running through a war that they thought they'd never fight. The chance for an actual mission had to have been irresistible.

One image did catch me, though. A person that sure as hell didn't belong in the battle. A young girl was walking through the men—as if she was supernatural and impervious to bullets—head up and hands at her sides. *Abby.*

Chapter 61

U TOLD ME HE'D meet me at the base of the bridge after I grabbed Abby; so I bolted from his truck searching. I tried to keep my footing on the steep weedy hill with my boots while I watched about half of the Humvees load up with soldiers and peel out, high beams scattered under the bridges and over the darkened dirt road. But several others remained, waiting to be loaded with wounded men. Among them, I found Abby again, she was walking, but kind of stumbling, over the broken ground near the place where I'd found Clyde James. A million years ago.

I ran after her, my Glock tight in my hand. Safety off. Seventeen shots ready to go.

I called her name.

She seemed deafened by all the gunfire from a few minutes ago. She stared straight ahead, still wearing my tattered blue jean jacket, looking stubborn and unwavering past a bunch of bodies. One of the dead men raised his head.

It was Jesse Garon in a white suit with an older man with a beard. The man yelled off something, fired at two of the SOS soldiers, and dropped them both to the ground. The crack of his gun sounded like a breaking whip. After the shots, Garon and the man got to their feet, saw me pointing my gun at them, then looked to the north at a cliff and then south at four more SOS soldiers racing toward them.

They launched into a run back onto the bridge; Abby didn't even break stride as I yelled for her.

She reached down to one of the dead soldiers, grabbed his handgun, and began chasing the man and Garon onto the darkened bridge.

After waiting for a break in the firing, I ran onto the old bridge. My feet thumping and nearly tripping over the old wooden slats. Brown water swirled several hundred feet below. Cars passed on the new bridge to the south. I could hear their engines buzz and the whoosh of water under me.

Minutes later, I found Abby.

Running from behind, I grabbed a good chunk of the jean jacket like it was a quarterback's jersey and pulled her into me. She was so determined to track Garon and the man she hadn't even heard me follow. Her breath was loose and ragged.

She grunted and fought, but I twisted her close, trying to catch my breath, and at the same time hug her. She continued to wriggle and hit and finally I had to pin her arms to her sides and said, "Slow. We got 'em. Slow."

She slowed the wriggling, didn't hit me again, and her eyes began to register a little less wild light through her scattered blond hair. To the north, the humpbacks of the Hernando-Desoto Bridge burned in broken patterns of small white lights.

As her breathing slowed, I tried to take the gun from her hand.

But she fought back.

She stepped away and pointed the barrel at me. I raised my hands.

Over her shoulder, I saw lights moving closer to us from the Arkansas side. I thought it might be a train, but the rotted planks underneath my feet made me change my mind.

It was a truck. U's truck.

I recognized the familiar pattern of the Expedition's headlights and the solid familiar clack of his door closing. He was walking to us.

I could make out his hulking shape moving close and felt a bit of relief.

Then I heard a groan and rumble and my heart dropped into the pit of my stomach as I saw that big truck drop from sight. A horrible groan of metal and the snapping of brittle wood. The truck was swallowed up in a huge black hole.

A mammoth splash of water erupted from under us.

Then it was silent for several seconds. A biting wind gnawed at my fingers resting on the rusted metal of the bridge. Wind whipped off the river and made a howling house as it flew through the crevices of metal.

I saw the cab of the truck, floating like a huge bubble, drift past and then dip, roll, and disappear into the bottom of the river.

I couldn't speak. I couldn't see anything. Dust had kicked up from the broken bridge.

But then I saw U walking toward us, through the moonlight and dust, a look on his face that was pissed off as hell. A look, for once, I was glad to see.

"Goddamn it!" he yelled to me.

"You see them?" I shouted back.

"Must've dropped over the side before they got over water."

Abby aimed the gun at U.

"Abby," I said, reaching around her body to hold her arms down. "It's fine. It's U."

"I heard him on the phone," she said, holding on to the gun. "He made a deal with Ransom."

U swaggered to a stop ahead of us. She looked up at him, eyes determined as hell, as I tried to pull the gun away.

"It was planned, Abby. We're playing Ransom."

She looked at me.

Then back at U.

Her body grew slack, the gun dropped to her side, and I slowly let my arms go from around her body. She looked up at the crooked rusted supports of the bridge.

"C'mon, Abby," U said. "Let's go home."

"Where, U?" she said, not moving. Abby looked like she wanted to hit something.

Toward the Arkansas line, I saw a shapeless form emerge from the darkness that had swallowed U's truck.

"Stay here," I said. I gripped her arms pretty damned tight to get her attention. "Stay put."

She nodded.

U branched off on the south edge and I took the north. More shapes were moving.

As soon as I walked to the big hole in the bridge, the shape had disappeared. I aimed my gun at one of the steel supports. I knew I'd seen a person moving but I thought maybe he'd fallen back through the hole. Made me uneasy as hell even being close to its rough form and the shadowed, black water moving below.

I walked backward and saw Jesse Garon scaling up one of the supports, trying to hide. *Son of a bitch.*

I ran over to follow him but then I heard a scream from Abby.

I couldn't see her as I ran back to where we'd parted. The light was much better facing the Tennessee entrance and I knew she had to be hidden behind one of the beams.

I slowed my walk, trying to recall where I'd heard the scream.

I kept my eyes focused for any slight movement behind each rusted cove.

I walked. Slow. I pointed my gun and nearly fired at some birds nesting in some rafters above. They flew away in a peppered pattern in the dull glow of Memphis lights.

Then I heard the click of a gun.

Abby had the bearded man in a headlock. She had her pistol pointed at his head. She'd been screaming out of anger as she held his head tight into the crook of her elbow.

I lowered my gun.

She screwed the muzzle tighter into his ear. He was an older man, rough skin and black eyes. He wore an intensity on his face like this was a moment he'd relived a thousand times and would escape once again.

"Abby, I got him."

"It's him," she said. "It's Ransom."

U jogged from across the bridge. He slowed when he saw Abby. I wanted so badly for her to shoot Ransom. I wanted it to happen but the words coming out of my mouth pleaded for her to be calm.

"Let U have him." I wasn't making sense to myself.

She kept pushing him back to the Tennessee side of the bridge until Ransom tripped over a railroad tie. The light and shadows broke about every few feet over my face until we found her half covered in darkness, a foot on Ransom's throat.

She had the gun pointed at his head.

Ransom laughed and tried to move out from underneath her. "Your daddy just laid there, beggin' while we shot him. Genetics is a funny thing. You ain't got it in you either."

"Abby, leave him," I said.

He pulled free, stood, and dusted his coat. More a gesture of power than trying to get clean. He didn't even look in our direction, trying to make himself believe we'd follow Abby's lead.

He said: "Y'all take care."

I was getting ready to pull the trigger when the gun fired in Abby's hand and Ransom stumbled back, finally falling to his knees.

As he felt for the blood rushing from his heart, he wore an expression of someone caught in another's nightmare.

He seemed to be thinking as he lay in shock, *This wasn't the way it was supposed to turn out.*

The shot didn't even faze U, who broke apart from us and ran back to where his truck had disappeared.

We jogged together, almost as if training camp were last summer, and I heard him talking shit the same as he'd done back then. But this time it wasn't about his coaches or his first wife. He was mad at me. "Who is gonna pay for that, Travers? And, damn, you know I can't take your car. It's more of a piece of shit than it's ever been."

He stopped, winded, and looked up into the slatted high beams. About thirty feet up, we saw Garon holding on to a crosswalk. He smiled down to us and waved.

U said: "Had a CD changer in the back."

I gripped the steel beams and found a foothold in crisscrossed slats held in place by rusted rivets. The wind cut into my ear canals and made sharp, whistling sounds.

"Don't even," U said.

I found another foothold.

And another.

"Crazy motherfucker," was the last thing I heard before I got higher into the bridge's supports and about ten feet away from Garon.

He kept smiling down at me the whole time. Each step I made, each foothold, I got more angry. I couldn't stop seeing Loretta lying there. I couldn't stop thinking about JoJo's bar and my life and suddenly I felt like I was at the edge of this cliff. Jon was there. Standing. Looking down at me.

I gripped tight onto the crossbeam where he stood.

My stomach swayed when I stupidly glanced down at the swirling water below us, hundreds of feet. Freezing wind clawing at my fingers, making it tough to get a grip.

Garon didn't move. Didn't try to knock me off the ridge.

He stood on a crosswalk fashioned from three beams. Enough to walk.

Keep your balance without tumbling off. As I walked toward him, he aimed a gun at my chest.

I couldn't breathe and the wind cutting into my ears made me feel like I was bleeding.

He pulled the trigger.

Click.

Again.

Click.

"I'm not going to kill you," I said. I was out of breath. I wanted to kill him. "Why'd you come back? After everything in New Orleans. Why'd you come back for me?"

He mumbled something.

"What?" I yelled.

"You killed me."

He wore an ill-fitting white suit with a yellow scarf around his neck. His face was reddened and chafed and his sideburns were bushy and uneven. He had a face pockmarked with acne scars and his eyes showed the distracted glassy look of someone truly mentally ill. It was the same with Clyde.

"Stay there," I said.

He shook, his whole body convulsing like an electric current was shooting through him. His eyes rolled into the back of his head. "Evil and lives," he said.

"What?"

"Evil and lives," he said, laughing. "It never really ends. We're all just on a train bound for Tulsa."

All of sudden, he rushed me and I dropped to my knees, getting a firm grip on the walk. Size wasn't a factor up here.

As I hung on, he kept going.

He didn't want to kill me at all.

I watched him sail over the edge of the bridge, his arms outstretched like he was in flight with his legs pinned together, until he disappeared hundreds of feet below into the Mississippi.

Chapter 62

IT WAS THANKSGIVING, one of those worn, gray days when all you wanted to do was lie inside and eat and watch parades and footballs games. Maybe nap a little bit. Abby hated that feeling. She hated being sluggish and full and lazy, so she begged Maggie to take her down Old Taylor Road to the stables and get their horses out for a run. Abby brought Hank along for the ride in Maggie's beat-up Rabbit and soon they had the horses saddled up and began beating a fine path beside a nameless creek, dodging tree branches and jostling along until the horses' breath made foggy patterns in the dark mist.

The air smelled of barbecue fires and moldy leaves as she kicked her horse in the side for a good run in an open clearing of high, yellow grass that had once been a cotton field. Abby's horse jumped ahead of Maggie and she laughed and yelled as they got closer and closer back to another clearing up on a hill dotted with rolls of hay leading to an old house and then back to the stables.

She hadn't told Maggie yet about buying the land, the stables, and the horses. She wasn't sure how her cousin would take it. She'd think it was charity, giving her a job and a business to run. But since Abby had sold her parents' house and planned on traveling awhile, she got a little scared. She needed a place of her own.

They both slowed to a gallop, Abby tucking her beaten suede boots tight into the stirrups and ducking beneath the hardened fingers of a bare oak and the long, dying strands of a willow.

Hank ran ahead of them and quickly disappeared after sniffing out a rabbit. The path widened for a moment, by a pool of stagnant green water littered with cypress stumps and a few dead birds. Abby reigned in her horse and jostled down the other way, passing the ruins of an old house some said belonged to a Confederate captain. Her father always used to say that the Yankees burned down the house and killed the man's family. Said when the man walked back from Georgia, he found everything he'd built destroyed.

There was only a stone floor and a chimney, a base really, but Abby had always thought it would be fine place to build a house someday.

"What do you think?" she asked Maggie.

"Fine," she said. "I don't know if the Johnsons would ever sell it, though."

"They would," Abby said, looking down the last bit of path into the clearing and the stables. Her last day in Oxford before driving up to Memphis for her flight. "I mean, they did."

Maggie shook her head and steadied her horse's feet. "That wasn't necessary."

"Will you take care of it?" she asked, taking off her straw cowboy hat and fingering away her loose hair.

Maggie nodded that she would. And that was it. No fight. No more talking. Not even an explanation of how it would all work out. They'd been friends since Abby was born and it wasn't necessary.

"You heard from Nick?" Maggie asked. Her sharp green eyes looking exotic and bright against her dark skin and hair.

"Only took you two hours to ask today."

"Well?"

"He's back in New Orleans. Called me yesterday."

"And?"

"Said he was going to finish some book he'd been working on about a blues singer. Said it helped having something to keep his mind off things."

"He can keep his mind on me."

Abby laughed.

"He'll come around," Maggie said, smiling and putting a hand on her very round denimed hip. "They always do."

Abby trotted her horse into the stable. The wood there was ancient, been there since the turn of the century, and had the same coloring of driftwood. She unbuckled the saddle and, despite the cold, removed a sweaty blanket from the animal's back.

After Abby finished putting away the saddle and rig, Maggie tossed her a pitchfork.

"Nothin's changed," Maggie said.

Abby smiled and said, "Nothin'."

She worked for a while cleaning out the stable, until the sky grew darker and they both knew that the families back at Maggie's house would wonder where they went. Nothing had changed. Maggie was sixteen and Abby was ten.

"You gonna be all right out there, wherever you're going?"

"Firenze."

"Which is a fancy word for . . . ?"

"Italy."

"And you'll be fine?"

From the base of the road and rumbling up a dirt path, Abby watched a massive Chevy Silverado pickup, black with tons of extra chrome, pass the sagging cattle gate and drive to the barns where they worked. The windows had been tinted and Maggie squinted through the darkening light to watch for the driver.

"Did I say I was going alone?"

Maggie narrowed her eyes.

The door opened and Raven, all lanky and James Dean in his deep indigo jeans and pressed snap-button shirt, got out. He'd slicked back his long black hair and even shaved. The leather on his pointed black boots shined in the glow of his headlights.

"Too late for supper?" he asked.

Maggie grinned, it was one of those true Maggie expressions where you could tell she was overflowing with skepticism but kept her teeth clamped tight. Still, she managed to keep smiling and speak. "Yeah. Plenty left. Follow us to the house and pull up a chair."

Abby smiled, and for a moment looked back through the narrow back gate of the stables where, framed in purple gray light, sat the old house. Come spring that strange relic would be a fine place to begin.

He was a strange, lone figure walking along Elvis Presley Boulevard that Thanksgiving Day. A skinny black man in a white jumpsuit studded in rhinestones. Black wig with sideburns, oversized metal glasses. He followed the curving rock wall that hugged the holy estate scrawled with words and prayers for the Man. They always changed. Prayers of thanks during the winter became prayers of sorrow in the fall. He'd seen the words in Japanese and German. Nasty letters from women still hot for Him after all these years. Tourists who often wrote the date they'd arrived as if carving their immortality on a religious relic.

But for the truly devout, it was a place of contact. Leaving personal messages that only a few would understand. The last time Black Elvis had come through Memphis as he dipped down to Florida for more tribute acts, he'd received word on the forty-third stone from the gates that one of the True Believers needed some guidance. A young man from Mississippi who held more faith than any man he'd ever met.

When they broke company a while back, the young man said he'd soon leave word in the same place if everything worked out as planned. Good wishes. Maybe a prayer. Or, again, the need for help.

As a couple Hondas raced by Black Elvis on the holy boulevard, the shops sitting dark across the street, he stood high in his patent-leather boots and checked the rock.

No wish. No prayers.

Just a simple message dated three days ago.

JESSE GARON LIVES!

The words were signed by the loopy signature of a man named Lucky Jackson who listed his home as Las Vegas, Nevada.

Black Elvis smiled.

He'd look him up when he got there.

Epilogue

ALL THAT REMAINED of JoJo's Blues Bar was a blackened shell of stucco and brick with charred beams running overhead where a mess of crows had decided to roost. I scanned the ruins and noticed the skeletal remnants of chairs and tables, even crushed red, blue, and green ceramic Christmas lights in the soot and rubble. The old jukebox that once shined in chrome and neon sat in a deflated lump next to a black brick wall where the Sheetrock had been eaten to the bone by flames. Warped and fried old Chess and V.J. 45s littered out of the side of the machine like discarded pie plates.

As awful as things turned out, I was still glad to be back in New Orleans and out of Memphis.

My plan with U had worked, for the most part, the way we'd hoped. Neither of us had fired a shot and Abby had used one of the Sons of the South's guns to kill Ransom before throwing it into the river. U was a little worried about the cops finding his truck and that nice little dent he left in the bridge, so he'd concocted a story about chasing a bounty on one of Ransom's henchmen. That was about it.

The shitstorm landed on the Sons of the South. They'd really left themselves swinging in the wind, leaving bullet casings and cartridges, tire tracks and rappelling equipment near the bridge. They even abandoned one of their damned Hummers and pretended like some black kids had broken in to their compound and taken it for a spin. Several were arrested. Several were dead. Besides Ransom, their names didn't mean anything to me.

Elias Nix was mentioned in the *Commercial-Appeal* for his loose association. But by the time the arrests took place, Nix was old news. When Jude Russell bowed out just days before the election due to an "undisclosed medical problem," a former U.S. senator and state favorite on the lecture circuit decided to take one last ride for the party.

His win over Nix was so big that the ten o'clock newscasts declared him the winner barring a massive natural disaster.

There was no satisfaction in my role. I wished none of it had ever happened. I wished I could close my eyes and open them again, watching the lights brightening inside the bar and hearing JoJo's keys jangling on his hip as he opened up.

I heard a shuffle behind me.

The crows flew off in a flock, their black feathers almost blue in the afternoon sun, as JoJo peeked through an opening where those big Creole doors had stood. He reached down and found the handle and lock in a pile of ash, his keys in his other hand.

"You want to help me lock up?"

"JoJo," I said, resting on my haunches and finding a half-eaten framed picture of a blues man named Earl Snooks. We called him Henry. I showed it to JoJo as he peered over my shoulder. "Jesus."

"Jesus? He can't help us now," he said. Across the street, I noticed his Cadillac chugging exhaust into the cold air.

"You goin' somewhere?" I asked.

"Headed back up Highway 61 for a while," he said. "Not hidin'. Just searchin'."

I squinted into his deep black face framed by the bright white light. "You mind if I stop by sometime?"

"Listen, Nick," he said, his hands shaking on the meat of my back arm. I never knew that man's hands to shake ever. He was the definition of steady. "Why didn't you tell me about what you was doin' for Loretta?"

"Didn't think it was necessary at the time."

He took the photograph of Snooks from my hand and studied his old friend's face. "You want it?" he asked, handing it back.

"No, I remember him."

I walked with him back to the Cadillac and talked to him over the long car door where he'd rested his elbows.

"What you gonna do?" he asked.

"Not far behind you," I said, smiling. "A woman I met in Oxford invited me up to take riding lessons."

"That what they callin' it now?" he said and laughed. It was a JoJo laugh, deep and weathered and came from deep within him. It made me